D1130429

MAY 1 7 2004

By_____

DEAD HEAT

Nick Oldham

This first world edition published in Great Britain 2004 by
SEVERN HOUSE PUBLISHERS LTD of
9–15 High Street, Sutton, Surrey SM1 1DF.
This first world edition published in the USA 2004 by
SEVERN HOUSE PUBLISHERS INC of
595 Madison Avenue, New York, N.Y. 10022.

British Library Cataloguing in Publication Data

Oldham, Nick, 1956-
    Dead heat
    1.   Christie, Henry (Fictitious character) - Fiction
    2.   Police - England - Blackpool - Fiction
    3.   Corruption investigation - England - Fiction
    4.   Detective and mystery stories
    I.   Title
    823.9'14 [F]

    ISBN 0-7278-5979-X

Typeset by Palimpsest Book Production Ltd.,
Polmont, Stirlingshire, Scotland.
Printed and bound in Great Britain by
MPG Books Ltd., Bodmin, Cornwall.

This is for the two men in my life –
my father, Edward Vincent Oldham,
and my son, Philip Joseph Oldham

Prologue

He had just rolled the body into the shallow grave when the headlights hit him. The main beam sliced through the trees like a strobe, catching him in their glare, then moved on. Initially he froze, spade in hand. Then as the lights passed him he dropped quickly into the grave on top of the body.

He knelt on the dead man's stomach, keeping low and peering over the edge of the grave. The body hissed, groaned and twisted underneath the weight of his knees and something glugged obscenely out of its mouth. But this did not affect Verner. After all, he had killed the man in the first place and brought him to this deserted spot, where his intention was to quicklime and bury the body.

Yet now it transpired that it was not such a deserted spot after all.

Verner cursed, keeping his head down, annoyed with himself for not having heard the vehicle approach in the first place. But, to be fair, he had been digging hard – concentrating, sweating, his heart and ears pounding with the physical exertion of that – having just dragged the body of a fully grown man twenty metres through the trees before depositing it into the newly prepared resting place. His mind had been fixed on the task in hand, so it was not impossible for a car to sneak up without him knowing until the last moment. It was something he would have to think about for the future. It had never happened before and he was damned if it would ever happen again.

The vehicle, which had a quiet engine, was on the hard-packed track which curved through the forest. It was being driven some fifty metres into the trees beyond where Verner was hiding on top of the corpse. It moved slowly and Verner caught the occasional glimpse of its bodywork reflecting light from the half-moon hanging up in the clear night sky. The headlights were doused and the car slowed to a halt, then the engine was killed. Silence returned to the forest. Nothing seemed to be moving.

At first, when the headlights surprised him, Verner assumed that the appearance of the car was just a rotten coincidence. Someone else was up in the woods, up to something. That was all. A courting couple, maybe. Possibly poachers.

But as the car stayed parked there on the track, Verner began to feel differently about it. He blinked and wiped the sweat from his forehead. Instinct was now telling him he had been followed, or perhaps the man on whose corpse he was now balanced had been followed. Whoever was in the car was either looking for him, or the dead man, or both.

Car doors opened, were closed quietly. Voices shushed and whispered to each other. A torch beam came on, went off.

Two men, Verner worked out. His hand gripped the spade tighter. He slightly adjusted his position on the body, causing wind to be passed. Verner screwed up his nose and wafted the smell away with distaste. Then he regained control of his breathing and heart rate.

At least whoever it was had not spotted him in the headlights, that much was obvious. They did not know where he was and that gave him the advantage. Then he remembered his own car parked deep amongst the trees to his left, about a hundred metres away from where the intruding car and its occupants had stopped. Verner knew that a quick search would easily reveal the spot where he had driven off the track, then the car would soon be discovered. They would see the blood mess inside it, where much of the dead man's brains were still splodged on the passenger door and window. It would be an easy further step to find the drag marks made by the dead man's heels all the way to the grave. If they had anything about them, Verner knew they would soon be here.

His mind whizzed as it weighed up the options.

He could slide off into the woods and get away. That would be an easy enough thing to do, but it was not something he could realistically think of doing. His job had only been half-completed. There were too many forensic links left behind in the vehicle. His fingerprints were all over it. No doubt there was some DNA lurking in there too. Very messy and unprofessional. Not Verner's scene at all. He was paid good money to get jobs done – to kill people and dispose of them without them ever being found again – and, just as importantly, without him ever being connected to the disappearance.

Shit. This was not a good situation to be in.

Suddenly he was feeling quite vulnerable.

One of the men called out, 'Let's wander this way.'

Verner expected a male response – but it was a woman's voice which replied.

'OK.'

So – not two men after all. Verner had been wrong. Perhaps it was a courting couple after all and all they wanted was somewhere to consummate their relationship. Verner did not allow himself to relax, though.

He fidgeted on the dead man's stomach, causing the corpse to burp quite loudly into the night. Verner touched a finger to the man's lips, shushing him gently.

Torch beams played down the track as the two people walked along it. Occasionally their lights flashed into the trees. They were now almost at where Verner had driven his 4x4 offroad into the trees.

He held his breath.

They stopped, drew close to each other and whispered. Verner could not hear what was being said, but their words seemed to be urgent, rushed. Verner's eyebrows knitted together. One of the two people broke away and jogged back to their car, opened it, reached in and then returned to their companion down the track.

Verner heard the next words as clear as a bell.

It was the woman speaking. 'DC Coniston to Control . . . DC Coniston to Control . . . receiving?' There was a pause whilst a reply was awaited. Then she said the words once more. 'DC Coniston to Control . . .' Still nothing came back. 'Shit, the bloody things are still not working properly,' she said, 'or this must be a real blackspot here.'

Only then did Verner exhale as he said to himself, You'd better believe it, babe. This is a real blackspot for you.

So they were cops. And they could not radio for assistance. Aah, poor little mites. How very sad. All alone in the spooky dark forest with a big bad wolf watching them hungrily.

Verner watched their torches progress down the track, then they stopped again. He knew they had found the point where he had driven off, where the grass had been flattened and his tyre tracks disappeared into the woods. This, he thought, is where things will turn interesting. But he knew that whatever happened from this moment on, the two cops could not be allowed to live.

Earlier that same day . . .

The surveillance had not gone well that evening. It was one of those jobs when it seemed that if anything could go wrong, it did.

The team came on duty at 4 p.m., less than a day after another surveillance operation which had lasted four solid days and taken them from one end of the country and back again. So they were all, if not exhausted, pretty well worn out and in need of a longer break . . . which was not a good start in itself.

Not one of the team moaned or complained though. They all loved the job they did. It was exciting and rewarding at its best, though more often than not they were faced with hours or even days of tedium when nothing was happening, when targets were not moving. But even during these periods, it was fun because they made it so.

They assembled at the small, discreet office they used as their base on a business park in Prestwich, Greater Manchester. Each grabbed their personal-issue body radio and that was when the first problem of the tour manifested itself. As they tested the radios, they crackled with static and sometimes just stayed plain dead. There were a few frowns within the team, but no one really thought anything of it. They assumed that when they got out on the road, the radio signal would probably be OK.

There were six police officers making up the team. Five were dressed in casual-to-scruffy clothing, not one of them remotely resembling a cop. Even the ones who looked like cops when they first joined the unit no longer looked anything like. They had grown and developed into their roles, become cool, laid back, able to melt into any background.

The sixth member of the team was in his motorcycle leathers.

Detective Constable Jo Coniston was the newest member of the surveillance unit, two months into the job following many weeks of extensive training. She sat at the table in the briefing room, mug of black coffee in hand, a tiny smirk of satisfaction playing on her lips.

She was ecstatically happy.

She had been a police officer for just over four years, all that time spent as a uniformed bobby on the beat. It had been a tough, exciting time at the sharpest end of policing imaginable, working the cauldron that was Moss Side, Manchester. The posting had opened Jo's eyes to a world she had only ever imagined existed in horror nightmares. A world in which a shooting occurred almost daily, where drugs, violence and intimidation ruled a frightened community and where the police could only hope to keep a lid on things – on a good day.

She had been first on the scene of four murders, two of which had been innocent bystanders caught in the crossfire of a drive-by shooting. She had administered first aid at six other shootings and stabbings and had made one arrest for murder during which the suspect assaulted her remorselessly with a hammer in his attempt to escape. But she held on tight until assistance came. She received a Chief Constable's Commendation for that effort, plus four days in hospital suffering from concussion and a broken wrist.

Four solid years of it made her crave for a change of scene. When she got wind that the Surveillance Branch were looking for female applicants, she put in a report and, following a tough initial test, she was accepted as a member.

Jo sat quietly at the table, listening to the quiet banter of her teammates, content in her choice of career move. A couple of years following villains around the country would do her very nicely, thank you, she thought. Then she would apply for a job on CID after she had taken her Sergeant's promotion examination. Professionally, the next few years were pretty much mapped out in her mind. It had been a good decision to join the police and she was forever thankful that her mother had dragged her to a careers convention where her imagination had been fired up by a detective on the police stand. His lurid tales of life as a cop had totally won her over.

In personal terms, though, she was not as clear. A slight frown came on her face as she thought about her most recently ditched boyfriend. Then she shrugged it off and the smile returned to her pretty face. She looked up from her brew as the team leader, Sergeant Al Major breezed into the room, a set of brown files under his arm and a big smile on his face.

'Hi, people,' he said as brightly as his personality. 'Everyone well?'

The small talk had ceased on Major's arrival. The team focused on him and the job in hand.

'You may be surprised to learn,' Major announced, 'that today we are back on the trail of our old friend and foe, Andy Turner.'

A groan chorused from the team.

'I know, I know,' Major said, holding his hands up in defeat, 'but one day we're gonna get this bastard bang-to-rights, if you young-uns will pardon the rather traditional turn of phrase.' Major began to pass out the folders, one to each team member. Jo took hers eagerly and opened it. Yes! she thought. She had been itching to get involved in an operation which targeted Andy Turner, a man who boasted that the law would never touch him as long as he lived.

As ever, Al Major's briefing was precise and detailed. It took half an hour, gave some of the past history of their target, Andy Turner, and brought the team up to date with the latest intelligence available on him.

Turner was only a young man, twenty-five years old, yet he had established himself in certain parts of Manchester and Lancashire as a ruthless operator, very wild and unpredictable in his approach; a man with no conscience whatsoever. He was no master criminal in that he was not discreet with his actions or lifestyle, nor was he particularly wary of the law.

6

Cops did not frighten him. Courts did not even make him think twice. He had tried to mow down one policeman who tried to arrest him a few years earlier, had gone on the run and been arrested in Spain when he tried the same with a Spanish cop. On his subsequent extradition he had been jailed for two years and let it be known at his trial that he would gladly kill any cop who got in his way. On his release from prison, the Crown Court judge who had sentenced him had been killed in a hit-and-run car accident. It was never proved, though it was strongly suspected, that Turner had murdered him.

He had laid low for some time following this and intelligence reports had him dotted around Europe, particularly in Spain and Portugal, establishing contacts and dealing drugs and guns. He disappeared from that scene after a German drug dealer was found dead with two bullets in his brain. Again, Turner was suspected, but there was no actual evidence to link him to the crime.

And now he was back on home turf, beginning to expand a drug-dealing network in north Manchester and into Lancashire.

His methods were brutal, but such was his cold-blooded reputation, that no one would ever challenge or testify against him and very few would risk informing on him to the cops.

The police wanted to nail him – badly.

He was very surveillance-conscious though. All previous operations had been binned, but now they were going for him again with the intention of building up a conspiracy case against him.

'OK, guys 'n' gals,' Al Major said as his briefing drew to a close, 'that's about the long and short of it. Let me reiterate: this man is very, very dangerous. He could well be carrying a firearm. At the very least he'll have a flick-knife on him and if something goes wrong and you're unfortunate enough to come face to face to face with him and he makes you as a cop, he'll have a go at you. Be wary,' he finished.

Jo Coniston went into the admin office and picked up a set of keys for the battered Nissan she and her partner would be using that evening.

'Hey – got there before me,' a voice exclaimed behind her. It was her partner, Dale O'Brien, another newish member of

7

the Surveillance Branch. Jo liked him well enough, but she did not really believe he had what it took to be a good surveillance officer. He seemed to have very little patience, did not enjoy 'sitting' on things, always wanted to be on the move, delving and probing. Jo gave him another couple of months before he decided to transfer into something more appropriate, such as pro-active CID work.

'Yeah,' she said, teasing him by dangling them, then whisking the keys out of the flexing grasp of his long fingers. 'I'll drive – at least for the first few hours.' She almost said, 'The first half of the tour of duty,' but checked herself because these days a normal tour of duty was not eight, ten or even twelve hours. Fourteen was the usual length and there was no way she wanted to drive for seven solid hours.

O'Brien shrugged happily. 'OK.' He spun out of the office, nearly colliding with Al Major, who was on his way in. 'Oops, sorry, Sarge,' he said, twisting away and curling out through the door.

Major watched him go with a paternal shake of the head. Then he looked at Jo.

She coughed and made to leave behind her partner. Major's hand shot across in front of her. His fingers gripped the doorjamb tightly, preventing her from leaving. His face, usually bright and open, darkened like a hurricane. His mouth tightened.

Jo's heart rate upped dramatically at the same time as her stomach sank. She had wanted to avoid this.

'Let me out, please,' she said quietly, her voice quavering.

'Bitch,' he hissed. He checked over his shoulder. No one was close by. 'You shouldn't have done it.'

'I don't want to talk about it anymore, Alan, please.'

Major said nothing, but stared dangerously at her. For a moment she thought he was going to hit her. She knew that if they had been anywhere else than on police premises, he would have done.

'Excuse me, boss.' Dale O'Brien had returned unexpectedly. He ducked under Major's arm-barrier. 'Forgot my notepad.' He came into the office and Major's face returned to it's normal, affable self.

'. . . So,' Major said, as though he and Jo were having a work-related conversation, 'any problems on that point, let's chat.' He winked at her in a friendly way and made his way down the corridor to the supervisor's office.

Jo exhaled a lungful of air.

'You ready yet?' O'Brien demanded of her.

'Yeah, yeah.' She pulled herself together. 'Here.' She tossed him the car keys, which he caught against his chest. 'You drive. I've changed my mind.'

'Oh brill,' he said with a wide grin.

One of the reasons why people were terrified of Andrew Turner was that he believed in sorting things out himself. He described the drug barons or top-class criminals who hired goons to do their dirty work for them as 'shitless wonders', holding such people in contempt. They had no real bottle or courage. Not like him. Turner had the 'real shit' to do things himself, to get his hands bloodied and, where necessary, put his own forefinger around a trigger and pull the thing backwards and make a big bang. That was why he believed he stood apart from all the others, all the so-called hardmen.

Andy Turner had the 'shit'.

And that evening he was on his way to show someone just how powerful his shit was.

Turner had recently moved out of Manchester to docklands in Preston. He owned an apartment overlooking King George Dock, now a marina full of yachts, pleasure boats and retail outlets. The move out to the sticks was not through any personal fear on his behalf, because Turner was afraid of no one, but just through a bit of common sense. Cop-wise the innards of the city of Manchester were becoming a little too hot for him. He needed somewhere cool where he could chill, and Preston suited him fine. He could be on the motorway within minutes and in Manchester in just over half an hour, so he now commuted as and when required. Quite often he did not go into the city for days on end, doing much of his wheeling and dealing over mobile phones and arranging his meetings at pubs, restaurants and hotels outside the environs of Manchester. He tried to keep his visits to the city to a minimum because he knew that if the cops sighted him, he would either be harassed or surveilled.

Today, though, he needed to get into the heart of the city and cause some grief before having a very important meeting.

The night before he had been out on the town in Preston, cruising around the pubs and clubs, revelling in the anonymity, even though one or two wise-looking guys eyeballed him. He easily picked up a woman, aged about thirty-five, on the prowl for a good fuck, and took her back to his apartment. They had a long bout of very drunken sex followed by almost twelve hours of alcohol-induced sleep. On waking, Turner screwed her again before literally forcing her out of the door with a £50 note crumpled in her mitt by way of compensation.

'Will I see you again?' she pleaded.

Turner laughed. 'Fuck off,' he said and slammed the door in her face.

Without any further thought for her, he got ready. A four-mile run on the treadmill, twenty minutes on the weights, then a shower before dressing in jeans and T-shirt. He packed a zip-up jacket, shirt, chinos and a pair of loafers into a sports bag, then made his way to the secured underground car park.

As ever he took time checking his car carefully for any tracking devices, but found nothing. He knew the cops were capable of anything.

A minute later, the wide tyres squealing dramatically, he exited the car park through the security barrier. As he did a left, he had to slam his brakes on.

The woman he had so unceremoniously ejected from the flat was standing in front of the car, bedraggled and forlorn.

Turner wound his window down, stuck his head out and before she could utter a word, he shouted, 'Do us all a favour, sweetheart – just fuck off and count yer blessings. Otherwise they'll be draggin' yer body out of the docks. Get me?'

Before she replied, Turner pressed down hard on the accelerator and his big Mercedes surged powerfully away. He shook his head in disbelief, curled his lips with disdain. He had no time for women. As far as he was concerned they were good for two things only: sex with him and sex with people he wanted to do business with. As regards the latter, Turner was convinced that a good blowjob or arse-fuck was usually a dead-cert deal clincher. The old ways were always the best. He did not even bother to glance in his rear-view mirror to look at her, just drove down to Strand Road and purred out towards the motorway.

He was looking forward to Manchester.

Dale O'Brien, Jo's partner for the day, did a quick check of the car before setting out: water, oil, lights and tyres and found everything to be working OK. It was an old, battered Nissan, with a nodding dog, fluffy dice and a shabby exterior, belying the fact that underneath it was a police car maintained to a high standard. He swung into the driver's seat next to Jo, who, sat in the passenger seat, was ostensibly reading her briefing pack. Her mind was not on it, particularly. Al Major had thrown her well off balance.

The rest of the surveillance team were going through much the same sort of pre-road rigmarole, including the motorcyclist, who was often a vital part of the mechanism of keeping targets pin-pointed as they moved around the country. He had just checked his big machine, mounted it and fired up. The bike sounded lovely, purring away like a pussycat, then roaring like a tiger as he twisted the throttle back. He slotted down his visor, engaged first and crept slowly out of the garage.

Jo and O'Brien gave him a wave.

He reached the gates of the secure compound and waited for them to swing open. He turned his machine into the road, leaned into the turn and gunned the bike away.

But his rear tyre had a very tiny patch of oil on it which he had not noticed. It could have come from anywhere. The garage floor. The bike's engine. The road, maybe. No one would ever know. Not that it mattered where it came from, it's the effect it had that mattered.

As the biker angled into the turn out of the gates, the oil patch made the back wheel slide sideways uncontrollably, even though it was only travelling at a slow speed. The rider could not keep it upright and though he tried, it slithered away and crashed to the ground before he could leap off, trapping his left leg underneath.

Jo and O'Brien saw it happen.

It was not a spectacular accident by any means. In fact as accidents go, it was rather pathetic.

'Shit!' O'Brien gasped. He leapt out of the Nissan and ran towards the stricken, trapped motorcyclist. Jo was right behind him as were the other members of the surveillance team.

The biker may not have fallen far and it may only have been his machine that dropped on him, but it was plainly obvious from the shape of his left shin that it had snapped like a twiglet. The team eased the bike off him and he screamed in a very animal-like way when one of them accidentally kicked his left foot.

Al Major jogged up and saw the damage. 'Someone call an ambulance.' One of the team responded and dashed back into the unit.

Jo gently removed her colleague's helmet and placed her thigh under his head for him to rest on.

'This doesn't half cock things up,' the biker said with a wan smile. Beads of pain-induced sweat cascaded down his forehead. 'Bugger,' he added, then passed out.

Turner kept to the speed limit on the motorway, just cruising, enjoying the ride, letting everyone pass him, not wanting to draw attention to himself. He peeled off the M61 and picked up the road into Salford, taking extra care to keep his speed down again on a stretch of road populated by speed cameras. Once in Salford, on the edge of the city, he worked his way to an area behind the police station on the Crescent to a block of small industrial units. He drove the Mercedes into one of the units, a one-man car maintenance business owned by one of his friends, a guy called McNally.

'Mac,' Turner greeted the owner of the garage as he climbed out of the Merc.

Dressed in oily overalls, McNally wiped his hands on rag, emerged from underneath a car on the ramp and sauntered towards Turner. Something in McNally's manner did not sit quite right with Turner, who was always switched on to body language. His intuition had saved his skin a number of times. McNally seemed edgy, nervous, his smile sheepish and obviously forced.

'Andy, how goes it?'

'Mmm, good,' Turner responded cautiously. His inner warning bells sounding caution. 'Gonna leave the motor here as usual,' Turner said, thumbing towards the Merc.

'No probs.'

The two men were standing close to each other. Turner's face changed, became serious and hard. 'Anything you'd like to tell me, Mac?'

McNally was taken aback – and it showed. 'Eh? No, no . . . what do you mean?'

'I mean I'm good at reading people. That's why I'm still alive, Mac, and I can see you're not one hundred per cent.'

'Oh, yeah, suppose not.' McNally relaxed and breathed out a sigh. 'Just struggling really. Been chasing some bad debts all day, some real hard bastards. Just pissed off that's all.'

'I'm pretty good at bringing debts in,' Turner said with a nasty smile which was chilled by McNally's explanation. Turner was easily spooked by other people's behaviour, even if it was rooted in innocence. He trusted no one and was always searching for signs of betrayal.

'No, it's all right,' McNally said. 'I'll sort 'em. It's a legit debt, if you know what I mean?'

Turner shrugged. 'Just ask if you need any help.'

'I'm obliged – thanks, Andy.'

Turner did a quick check of his watch. 'I'll be back to pick this up as and when,' he said, referring to the Merc. 'See how the day pans out.'

'Got your keys for this place?' McNally asked. 'I won't be here after six.'

Turner nodded. He pulled his change of clothing from the boot of the Merc.

A dull-grey Peugeot 405 drew up outside the unit. Turner gave McNally a wave, strode out to it and slid into the passenger seat. He rarely took the Mercedes into the city when he did business. It turned too many heads, was too recognizable and telegraphed to people that he was about.

Today he wanted to keep a low profile and parading about in a 'big fuck-off Merc' as he called it, was no way of doing that. Even the hot-headed Turner knew that much. Today was a day for discretion. Eventually.

It took almost forty minutes for the ambulance to arrive on the scene of the accident. During that time the injured biker drifted – worryingly – in and out of consciousness. Jo Coniston stayed with him throughout, comforting and reassuring him, until two very apologetic paramedics eventually carried him into the ambulance. He was rushed to hospital, accompanied by one of the other team members, thereby further reducing the numbers for the surveillance job on Andy Turner.

Jo's knee joints had almost seized up by remaining folded in one cramped position for such a long length of time. She stood up stiffly, hopping painfully as blood surged back into her lower legs.

Al Major moved in and assisted her to keep balanced.

'Thanks,' she said begrudgingly, easing her elbow out of his fingers.

'You were very good there,' he told her. 'Showing you care for someone – but you haven't shown you care about *me*, have you?' His voice was tinged with anger.

'Don't start Al, just DO NOT START,' she warned him.

'You ready to roll now?' Dale O'Brien piped up from the garage door.

'Coming,' she chirped and walked away from Major.

Major hissed two words into her ear as she passed. 'Selfish bitch.'

Stern-faced, she ignored him and made her way back to the car, in which O'Brien waited, engine idling. She dropped into the passenger seat and slammed the door. 'Let's friggin' go,' she growled. 'And you can run that bastard down if you want.'

They drove out. Major stepped aside and, bowing like a matador, waved them through. Jo stared dead ahead, but she could feel Al's piercing eyes burning into her temple. Only when they had turned out of the compound did she realize she was holding her breath. She exhaled with relief, turned brightly to O'Brien with a wide smile, happy to be out on the road, tracking a crim.

'I don't know about you, Dale, but I could murder a brew.'

For Andrew Turner that evening was about matters of credibility. So that there would be a record of events, the driver who picked him up from McNally's garage was equipped with a digital camera to keep a contemporaneous record. At the end of the day, once credentials had been established, the camera and its contents would be destroyed completely.

Turner was driven from Salford, edging around the city centre, out to Crumpsall, to the area around North Manchester General Hospital – a building, Turner thought with an evil smirk, which might just come in useful. Especially the A & E unit.

Sitting there in the passenger seat, he started to get twitchy with anticipation.

'Got me a "whacker" then?' Turner asked the driver, whose name was Newman.

'Under the seat.'

Turner reached down between his legs. His fingers alighted on a wooden baseball bat, which he drew out and tested for weight and balance by smacking it firmly into the palm of his hand. It felt good.

'Nice,' he commented.

'It's got a lead core,' Newman said.

Turner slid it back, then reclined the seat, closing his eyes for a few moments. His mind slipped back to the night before, thinking about the woman he had picked up at Tokyo Joe's nightclub. She had been a good fuck – twice – but what a silly, pathetic bitch! Hanging around outside the apartment like a love-struck teenager. Immature, that's what she was. Why did it have to be anything other than a good shag?

His eyelids clicked open. His inner warning bells – an instinct he had grown to trust – clanged a few times.

The prospect of her hanging around after he had gone made him feel slightly wary. Maybe he should have picked her up

15

and dumped her in town . . . got her away from his pad . . . too late to worry now.

'Is Goldy likely to be at home? We're not going to end up chasing round like a pair of blue-arsed flies, are we?'

'He'll be there,' Newman assured him. 'He's expecting a delivery from his supplier, so I'm told, so he'll be geared up for it. Won't be going out.'

'Looks like he's going to get more than he expected,' Turner laughed cruelly. He put his seat upright. 'You OK with that digital camera?'

'Yeah. Been practising on Lesley.'

'Is she a good subject?'

'Depends how pissed she gets.'

'Well, this is gonna be fast and hard, so you'd better be ready to click away. I won't be hanging around: in and out. Forty whacks, then I'm gone straight after the lecture. You'd better be right behind me.'

Newman shrugged. 'I'll be there.' He slowed and turned into a leafy side road of old, well-constructed terraced houses, most now bed-sits or flats. Newman drove down the road, maintaining the same speed. 'It's that one – number eight,' he said without pointing or looking. 'Goldman lives on the first floor. The door to his flat is the first one you come to on the landing. He keeps it well locked. We won't be able to boot it down. It's made of toughened steel but painted to look like wood. He only lets in people he knows. Got a good peep-hole and there's plenty of locks behind it . . . not easy to get through.' Newman pulled in a hundred metres down the road. 'That means we have to get him to open it for us.'

'Does he operate alone? Will anyone else be in the flat?'

'He's alone,' Newman confirmed.

'Mmm,' Turner ruminated. 'Shit.'

'Don't worry though. I know somebody he knows.' Newman grinned, showing cigarette-stained teeth. 'Someone who'll get the door open for a ton.'

'A ton?' blurted Turner.

'Worth every penny . . . have you got it?'

'Yeah, yeah . . . so where is this guy?'

'It's a bird, actually.' Newman looked across the road.

16

Leaning on the gable end of a house was a scrawny-looking young woman, early twenties. She wore a T-shirt which showed her tummy and the ring pierced through her navel, and a pair of jeans. She was smoking nervously, flicking back scraggy unwashed hair from her drug-ravaged young face. 'There.' He wound his window down and beckoned. 'Denise, luv, c'm'ere.'

She continued to glance anxiously around as though she had not seen or heard him. Maybe she hadn't. Maybe she was trapped in her own world. Then she set off across the road, tossed the cigarette away, and folded her arms underneath her small breasts. Newman reached over his seat and unlocked the back door for her. Her thin body entered the car. She looked defiantly at the two men in the front seats, her eyes wild at first, as though she blamed them solely for her predicament. Then they glazed over to become lifeless. Turner saw the scars on the inside of her spindly arms, more visible evidence of heavy drug abuse and self harm. She looked like she attempted suicide on a regular basis. Turner knew the type. People like her were the epitome of his usual customer.

'OK, sweetie?'

She nodded reluctantly.

'You up for this?' Newman went on.

She shrugged. 'Yeah, whatever.'

'This is Andy.' Newman indicated Turner. Denise gave him a crooked smile. From somewhere on her person she produced a hand-rolled cigarette, lit it and blew grey smoke into the car.

'Hundred quid. No negotiation,' she said as a lungful of acrid smoke left her nostrils and mouth.

'Fine,' Turner said. 'You do the job, you get the dosh.'

'Up front.'

Newman and Turner exchanged glances. Turner shrugged and dug into a pocket, pulling out a wodge of twenties. He peeled five off and held them out to her. Her eyes suddenly became alive again, focusing on them hungrily. She did not try to take it. Too many people had teased her with money, only to play snatchey-snatchey with her.

'You get the door open, get out of the way. That's all

you have to do,' Turner said. 'Dead simple. Money for old rope.'

'I know.'

He tossed the money on to her lap. She took it and eased it into the back pocket of her jeans.

'What you gonna do?'

'That,' Turner said, 'you don't need to know.'

She shrugged. She did not give a shit, even though she had enough imagination to guess. The pairs of disposable latex gloves each man was easing on to his hands were a bit of a giveaway.

'What is it with you and Al?' Dale O'Brien asked Jo innocently enough, but she could see he was burning with curiosity.

They were sitting in a Little Chef, not far away from Manchester Prison, more famously known as Strangeways, drinking exorbitantly priced cups of tea – which would be claimed back on expenses at the end of the month.

Jo took a sip of hers, savouring its expense. 'Just crap,' she said.

'You been having an affair?' O'Brien asked directly.

Jo spluttered on the tea, placed the cup down and wiped her mouth. 'Bit to the bloody point, that, Dale!'

'Sorry.'

'Well, anyway, yeah . . . you could say that. We were an item.' She tweaked her fingers on the word 'item'. She sounded wistful. 'But it didn't work out.' She finished her tea and said, 'Let's move.'

'Once she's in, give her half a minute,' Newman said, looking into his rear-view mirror. He watched the girl walk towards the front door of the flats, and press a button on the intercom. She leaned on the wall and talked into the speaker, then stood upright for a moment before pushing the door open.

'She's in,' Turner said. He was contorted round in his seat, also observing Denise's progress. He spun around and picked up the baseball bat, which he concealed underneath his jacket when he got out of the car.

He and Newman crossed the road and walked side by side down the pavement to the door.

'What a good girl,' Turner said. As promised, Denise had wedged the door open with one of her trainers. Turner muscled his way in, followed by Newman. They stopped at the foot of the stairs leading up to the first-floor landing. Turner motioned Newman to complete silence by touching his lips with a finger and withdrew the baseball bat from its place of concealment. He positioned a foot on the first step.

The sound of the girl's voice filtered down to them.

'Yeah, I know I'm early, Goldy, but I'm fuckin' desperate. I need it now and I've got the cash . . . look.' It was obvious she was talking through the steel door to the dealer, who was all nice and snug and safe in his little fortress.

There was a muffled response from Goldman which could not be made out down at ground level.

'Yeah, thank fuck for that, Goldy,' Denise said.

What could be heard on the ground floor was the unmistakable sound of bolts being drawn back and a key in the lock.

'Come on,' Turner whispered, dashing quickly up the stairs, bounding on to the landing and dropping into a crouch in a corner. Newman came up behind him, digital camera at the ready. Denise was down the narrow corridor, standing outside the first door. She did not even glance in their direction, but stepped back a yard (with the trainer missing from her left foot) from the door. She dropped her lighted cigarette and stooped to pick it up, overbalancing slightly, making more room for Turner and Newman to move in.

Drug dealers have a very finely honed sense of self-preservation. If they don't have, they don't stay in business for long.

When Goldman peered with one eye through his spy hole in response to the persistent knocking on his door and saw the distorted figure of Denise through the fish-eye lens, his brow creased with puzzlement. She was one of his regulars, a good payer either in cash or blowjobs, but usually he dealt with her in another location, out in the streets. She had been to his flat occasionally, but it was only yesterday he had supplied her with a quarter gram of heroin. He did not expect to see her so soon – and certainly not at his abode.

His hands hesitated on the numerous locks and bolts which secured his steel-backed door. Something did not feel quite right. 'I only saw you yesterday, girl. Our next meet is tomorrow. You know that. I don't deal from here.'

'I know man, I know,' she'd pleaded convincingly. 'I'm desperate, had a really bad night, really withdrawing, shaking like mad.'

Goldman knew what that was like, for he, too, was an addict. Aches, tremors, sweating and freezing, sneezing and yawning. Any combination of these effects. He felt for her.

'You got cash?'

'Yeah.'

'Show me,' he insisted through the door.

'Oh, fuckin' hell, Goldy,' she whined.

'Look, you're a day early and I'm a nervous guy.'

'Yeah, I know I'm early Goldy, but I'm fuckin' desperate. I need it now and I've got the cash . . . look.'

Goldy saw her wave a handful of notes up to the spy hole.

'OK, OK, hang on.'

'Yeah, thank fuck for that, Goldy,' she said and stepped away from the door as he unlocked it.

The heavy door swung open, its hinges well oiled and maintained. Goldman appeared on the threshold and looked down at Denise as she wobbled and reached for the burning cigarette on the worn floor. He immediately noticed her missing trainer.

She caught his eye as she glanced up and in that split second Goldman knew he had been set up by one of his best customers.

He was already moving backwards into his flat when Turner leapt up from his crouch and swung the baseball bat in a wide arc at Goldman's head.

It connected with a hollow smack, right across the bridge of his nose, which crumbled instantly, sending him staggering backwards down the short hallway, into the living room, pursued by the vengeful forms of Turner and Newman, coming after him like a pair of devils.

Goldman's nose had broken marvellously, blood gushing everywhere down the front of his T-shirt, which originally had been white.

As Turner roared from the hallway into the living room, he wielded the bat again, this time whacking it sideways across Goldman's temple, knocking him to the ground, senseless. Behind Turner, Newman ducked and weaved to get the best angles he could in order to record the terrible assault on camera. He got one great shot of Goldman as he pitched floorwards, then another, as on the way down, Turner managed to get another blow in on the back of the drug dealer's skull.

Goldman lay between his furniture, writhing slowly and moaning piteously face down in the pool of blood spreading underneath his face, bubbles foaming as he laboured to breathe.

Turner's chest rose and fell from his short burst of exertion. There was a large smile on his face, one of victory.

'Here – get one of this,' he instructed Newman. Turner bestrode Goldman's prostrate form, rested the tip of the bat in the middle of the injured man's back, between the shoulder blades, and placed his hands one on top of the other on the tip of the bat, as though he was a great white hunter astride a kill.

Newman fired away.

'Now this.' Turner reached down and grabbed Goldman's ponytail. He heaved his head up and held his blood-drenched face to the camera. 'Get this,' he told Newman.

'Got it!'

Turner dropped Goldman's face back on to the carpet. It smashed into the puddle with a squelch. Now he was not moving at all.

'Think he's dead?' Newman asked.

'No, he's still breathing . . . I think.'

More often than not, surveillance operations are very specific in that the location of the target is usually known and he or she is picked up from that point and followed by the team until the operation is either called off or the cops move in and make an arrest. The surveillance team is never used for this latter purpose. Occasionally some ops are run on an ad hoc basis by putting a team into an area which the target is known to frequent, hoping there is a sighting from which the team would then pick up the target and slot themselves into place.

As was the case that afternoon and evening.

But this type of op can be frustrating, especially when the target does not put in an appearance.

The team had gravitated to the Rusholme area of Manchester, a location well known for the high number of Asian restaurants along the main street. Andy Turner was known to do quite a lot of his business in this part of the city. He was suspected of trading with Asians, who made up a large proportion of the local community in Rusholme. Much of the heroin which found its way on to these streets originated in Pakistan, coming in from the north-west frontier, through Turkey and some of the former Soviet republics and across Europe.

Jo Coniston and Dale O'Brien were sitting in their car on a side street, facing towards the main road through Rusholme, becoming very bored with the way the afternoon was progressing into evening. They had exhausted 'I spy' and medleys of Beatles songs and were sitting in glum silence, listening to sporadic radio transmissions between other team members, aware that the radios were still not working properly. They had a tendency to pack up half-way through a conversation. Very annoying.

'I'm going for a stroll,' O'Brien announced.

Jo sank down in her seat and reclined it. 'Don't blame you,' she said. 'This is just so bloody wishy-washy . . . needle-in-a-haystack job. He's never gonna turn up, y'know.'

'I know.' O'Brien climbed out and walked down to the main road, turned out of sight. She closed her eyes after locking the car doors, this being the sort of area where anything could happen, especially to a lone woman in a car. She exhaled a long, fed-up sigh.

Goldman was not dead, but he was not well. Blood continued to cascade out of his nose, indicating that his heart was still beating, and the blows to his head had knocked him unconscious for a few seconds. He came round with massive brain pain.

Newman hoisted him up off the floor, avoiding getting any blood on his own clothes, whilst Turner scoured the flat. He returned from the kitchen, shaking his head in wonderment.

'A right little drug dealer's set-up,' he said. In the kitchen he had found an array of mobile phones and pagers, neatly piled up bank statements, coded lists of contacts; wraps, bags, weighing scales, crushed paracetamol tablets, bicarbonate of soda and four microwave ovens. 'Ready for a delivery, I'd say. Isn't that right Goldy, you Jewish twat?'

He tapped Goldman on the crown of his head with his bat. The dealer, now seated on a chair, swooned and dropped his bloodied face into his blood-covered hands. He did not respond to Turner's question, nor his derogatory racial remark.

'I asked you a question.'

Goldman mumbled something and held his head, which felt as though it had been smashed like an egg.

Turner positioned himself on the arm of a chair. 'Now then, you little shit, a little budgie's told me that you've been dealing on my patch without my say so. Very rude thing to do, that. Don't like it.'

Goldman slavered out a gobful of blood down between his legs.

'It's got to stop. Where do you keep your cash, boyo?'

'What cash?' he managed to reply.

'Don't mess – any cash you have in this house, I want it. So where is it? Pay up and stop dealing on my streets and I'll call it quits.'

'Fuck off.'

'Wrong answer.'

Turner slid what could have been a friendly arm around Goldman's shoulders and gave him a hug. He beamed at Newman. 'Photo opportunity.'

Newman caught the tender moment on the digital camera.

Turner punched Goldie hard on the side of his head, twice, so hard he hurt his knuckles.

Goldman's brain felt like it had been dislodged. He dragged himself slowly up from the floor, clinging to the furniture.

'You know who I am, don't you?' Turner said.

Goldman gasped a yes.

23

'Then you know I have a reputation to maintain, don't you?' It was not a question, it was an explanation. 'So you have a choice about this, don't you?' Once again, it was not a question. This time it was a statement of facts. 'Accept you made a mistake, hold your hands up, say sorry, pay up – and live! Then I might even think about letting you deal for me.'

'Fuck off.' Goldman spat out a mouthful of blood at Turner which splattered obscenely across his T-shirt.

Turner looked down at the mess and said, 'Oh,' with disappointment.

They took five steady minutes over the beating which followed, taking Goldy to within a whisper of his life.

'That's enough,' Turner said, holding Newman back. Both men stepped away. Goldman was curled up in a foetal ball in a corner of the room, his face mashed to an unrecognizable pulp, his jaw twisted and broken; his hands had been hammered by Turner's baseball bat, the bones smashed and broken. Both assailants had jumped on his chest, stomping down on his ribs, breaking many of them and almost killing him in the process.

Turner knew when to back off. He had beaten many people senseless in his time and prided himself on his judgement. He did not want Goldman dead because he actually might be of some use once he had recovered. It looked like he had a pretty good set-up here and Turner thought he might be able to take advantage of it.

'Let's find the dosh now,' Turner said. He was breathing heavily with exertion, sweating profusely, as was Newman.

They turned Goldman's drum upside down. Carpets were ripped up, cupboards emptied, as they searched hard for the money which they knew must be somewhere in the flat. They went to all the well-known hiding places and the ones which were not so well known. Eventually they found it by taking off the plastic cover protecting the electrical shower in the bathroom. The money was in a waterproof plastic wallet. Four thousand pounds, all in twenties.

Turner counted it and peeled off two hundred for Newman. 'On account,' he said.

In the living room, Goldman had somehow managed to get

himself into a sitting position, jammed into the corner of the room to prevent himself from falling over. He could only open one eye – and that one only just. The other, his right, had already swollen to the size of a cricket ball and was much the same colour. His wheezed as he breathed, his chest sounding like metal scraping over sandstone. As he inhaled and exhaled, he moaned painfully.

'Found it,' Turner said gleefully, wafting the money in front of Goldman's face. Just for spite, he placed his foot on Goldman's shoulder and pushed him back down on to the floor. Goldman could not stop himself from sliding, his useless broken hands unable to hold him. Turner stood on Goldman's outstretched left palm and pirouetted on the heel of his trainer, making Goldman scream in agony. He left the drug dealer still shrieking as he and Newman left, slamming the reinforced outer door behind him, ensuring the screams became muffled and inconsequential.

At 9 p.m., Newman dropped Turner off at the Star of India restaurant in Rusholme. Turner had changed, having disposed of his blood-splattered gear from the assault on Goldman. The clothing had been left with Newman to dispose of by fire.

On alighting from the car, Turner kept his head bowed down and walked swiftly across the pavement to the restaurant.

Inside it was fairly quiet. Just a few customers eating their curries, mainly white people.

Turner stood by the till as a little Pakistani waiter greeted him and took him to a table at the far end of the dining room where he could sit with his back against the wall and face the door, with the option of a quick getaway through a side door should the need arise.

'Not seen you recently, sir,' the Pakistani said.

'Busy guy, Ali, busy guy.' Turner sat down and was offered the menu. He shook his head. 'Usual.'

'OK, sir.

'And be quick.'

'Yessir.'

Turner settled back, feeling buoyant. The Goldman incident had made him feel fresh and alive. Hurting others gave him a great deal of satisfaction, that and making a living out of other people's misery. He loved preying on the weaknesses of others. It was very, very pleasurable. He also believed that the 'Goldman incident', as he liked to now call it, would be a very good indication of his management skills to someone he would be meeting later, someone very influential.

A waiter deposited a pint of very cold lager on Turner's table. He took a long, slow swig of it, feeling it flow all the way down his neck and into his empty stomach.

A few minutes later his Chicken Vindaloo arrived. He tucked into it with relish. Beating the living shit out of people gave him a healthy appetite.

It was a long sigh, followed by a deep stretch, brought about by boredom and several hours spent in a car, watching and waiting. Jo Coniston eyeballed her partner.

O'Brien's chin dropped on to his chest, then jerked up quickly as he fought sleep. 'Christ,' he mumbled, 'nearly went there.'

'Nearly?' she quipped, 'you've been snoring for ten minutes.'

'Haven't!'

'This is just shit,' Jo griped. 'Needle in a bloody haystack. Why?' she demanded. 'Why, why, why?'

O'Brien yawned. 'Could be worse. Could have to work for a living.'

'I'm going for a walk.'

She hoisted herself out of the car, feeling her bones starting to ache. Her senses told her that tonight was going to be one horrendous waste of time. The mixed and exciting aroma of Indian cooking reached her fine nostrils as she sniffed in the Rusholme night air. Suddenly she was ravenously hungry.

Beads of sweat from eating a hot curry as opposed to sweat from beating a man senseless dribbled down Andy Turner's forehead. He wiped himself with a napkin and took a draught from the new pint of lager which had just arrived at the table.

It was 9.30 p.m., about time someone showed up.

26

As if on cue, the door of the restaurant opened and a figure entered the establishment. It was not the person he was expecting, unless the person happened to be a woman, which he did not think would be the case. Turner watched her as he sipped his beer. A waiter showed her to a table near the window and left her with a menu.

Turner liked the look of her. Very pretty, short dark hair, a little snub nose and nice wide lips which he immediately imagined working on him.

The waiter returned to her with a bottle of water and took her order. She sat drinking the fizzy water, glancing shyly around the restaurant, checking out the other customers. She seemed to look at him for a fraction longer than anyone else and Turner allowed himself a grin, but she seemed not to notice. Her eyes dropped and she stared at the table cloth, then looked out of the window at the busy street beyond.

The smells had been just too much for Jo Coniston. She had not eaten since coming on duty and she was famished. She turned into a decent-ish-looking restaurant – there were several on the strip which looked highly suspicious and should be avoided at all costs – with the intention of having a quick drink and a starter. Maybe a mixed kebab, she had thought, just to fill the gap. Maybe spend ten to fifteen minutes inside, then head back to the car.

The waiter was all over her, his eyes spending too much time hovering in the vicinity of her boobs. But at least he was attentive. He brought her a drink, took her order and promised speedy service.

Only as she took a sip of her mineral water and let her own eyes do a bit of roving, did her heart nearly stop.

Because there he was, large as life and twice as menacing. Andy Bloody Turner. Sitting not twenty feet away from her at the back of the restaurant.

Stay calm, she instructed herself as her blood coursed through her veins like fire. She hoped her face did not register surprise, but thought it might have done. She realized her gaze had stayed on him for more than a split second, a contact often long enough to alert a switched-on villain. But had he seen that? She prayed not.

How had they missed him coming into the restaurant? Her team was crawling round the area like lice and somehow their target had walked straight through them, sat down, ordered a fucking meal.

Christ. What to do? Having herself ordered food, she had trapped herself. If she got up and left before it came, would it draw attention to her?

She turned to the window, pretending to look out. She pressed the flesh-coloured transmit button affixed to the palm of her hand, tilted her head slightly to move her mouth a little closer to the button-shaped mike on her collar. Trying desperately not to move her lips – why were there no miming sessions in the surveillance training programme? – she said, 'Anyone hearing me? I have an eyeball . . . repeat, I have an eyeball . . . Star of India.'

Outside a big four-wheel-drive monstrosity pulled up and double parked. Jo noticed that the steering wheel was on the left-hand side and the man who was driving was able to get out straight on to the pavement.

No one replied to her transmission. She spoke again, urgently. 'Dale? Ronnie? Ken? Anyone hearing me? I have an eyeball . . . repeat, eyeball.'

The driver of the 4x4 entered the restaurant. He looked at her as he walked past. A very bad feeling, something akin to the pain she had endured when her appendix had to come out, creased the pit of her stomach. Somehow she knew this guy had come to meet Turner. And pick him up – otherwise why leave the car outside in such a ridiculous position? She fumbled in her pocket, pulled out her mobile phone and started to dial frantically.

'Andrew Turner?'

Turner had watched him come into the restaurant. He did not recognize him, but knew he had come from the Spaniard. Turner nodded and appraised him. He looked hard and mean and ready to move. It did not faze Turner, who said, 'Yeah, that's me.'

'My orders are to pick you up and convey you to Mr Lopez.'

Turner quaffed the last of his pint and wiped his lips. He stood up and was glad to see that he was bigger and wider than the man who had come for him. But yet the man's eyes screamed danger and even Turner felt something almost tangible emanating from him.

'You carrying?'

'Nope.'

'Let me check. Mr Lopez does not like to be surprised.'

'I said I wasn't.'

'I don't give a damn what you said. I got a job to do and if you do not comply, then I walk out of here. If you don't let me check, you don't have a meet.'

Turner rolled his jaw ruminatively, peering down his nose at a man who was, after all, only a driver, weighing up whether the issue was worth pushing. He decided to back down.

'OK.' For the sake of business he relented and lifted his arms.

The driver skimmed him quickly, lightly, effectively quartering his body within a few seconds. Turner knew he had been searched well. This guy knew his trade.

'What about you?' Turner sneered.

The man considered Turner and his face broke into a crooked grin. He spun on his heels and Turner followed him out to the car. As he passed the attractive woman seated alone at the table near the door, who was talking on her mobile, Turner blew her a kiss. He heard her say, 'Hiya, sweetie.'

There was some kind of a meet on. That much was obvious from what Jo had seen happen, having watched the interaction between the two men by means of the reflection in the window. The quick chat. The search. The exit. Turner was on his way to see someone very important.

Her phone connected at the very moment Turner came alongside her at the table and blew her a kiss. As O'Brien answered, she found herself saying, 'Hiya sweetie,' and almost choking on her words.

29

'Hello to you, too,' O'Brien responded in a deep, suggestive voice. 'I didn't know we had something going.'

'We don't. My radio's down,' Jo babbled quickly. 'I've eyeballed the target and he's just getting into a big four-wheel-drive parked outside the Star of India.'

'Jesus.'

'Where are you?'

'I'm out of the car, about five minutes from it, down in the Frog.' O'Brien was referring to a pub about a quarter of a mile away, on the way to the city centre. 'I got bored too.'

'Shit . . . well . . .' Jo braved herself to openly watch the big vehicle muscle its way into the evening traffic towards the city, causing other traffic to brake hard with a cacophony of angry horns. The driver stuck up a middle finger and accelerated away. 'He's headed your way, Dale . . . get out of the pub and watch out for a big Yank-style four-by-four. I'm gonna leg it to the car.'

Jo rose from the table, surprising the waiter who was on his way to her with the much anticipated mixed kebab. His Indian accent failed him as he immediately – and rightly – believed she was going to do a runner, although most people did that after they had eaten.

'Oi! Where the fuck do you think you're going?' he shouted at Jo's retreating back.

'Sorry pal, got to rush,' she yelled as she exited, did a cartoon-like skid and hared towards the car. She dodged around numerous people now out for a night on the pavements of Rusholme, then veered into the street where the car was parked unattended – and locked. The realization that she could not drive the car away only hit her as she saw the vehicle. She slowed to a trot, then a walk, and when she got to the car, she kicked it in frustration. Dale had the keys.

Her mobile chirped: O'Brien.

'Jo – the four-wheel-drive,' he panted, 'just gone past me then U-turned again, heading back to Rusholme. Obviously surveillance-conscious.'

'Yeah, good – but I can't get in the car. You've got the bloody keys.'

'I'm running now,' O'Brien said, his phone going dead.

30

Jo went back to the main road and stood on the corner of the street to watch, hopefully, for Turner's reappearance. She decided to use the time constructively and keyed the number of one of her other team members into the phone. She was going to alert them one by one.

'Hey – you!'

Jo twirled. It was the Indian waiter.

'Hey, you – you order food, we cook it – you fuckin' pay for it,' he said.

'Shit!' Her eyes rolled heavenwards. 'Look – just fuck off, will you? I haven't time to explain, okay?'

'I'll call the cops.'

The 4x4 containing Turner and his unknown chauffeur crawled past in the traffic, which was heavy now.

'I am the cops,' Jo blasted him, keeping one eye on the traffic and the other on the irate little waiter. She extracted her warrant card with a flourish and shoved it into his face. The 4x4 was disappearing in traffic now.

'Don't give you a right to do what you did,' chuntered the waiter.

'Look, just fuck off, will you? I'll make it right, but just now I'm a bit busy.'

'Jo!' screamed Dale O'Brien, appearing on the scene at a run. He went straight for the car, clicking the remote as he got to it, diving into the driving seat.

'We'll settle up with you, honest,' Jo assured the waiter. She backed away from him, hands palm forwards, placating him. 'Honest.' She jumped into the car next to O'Brien. 'What a bleedin' cock-up,' she said. 'Go left – he went thataway.'

She sat back and took a deep breath.

Next to her, O'Brien was breathing frantically and his hands and feet were dithering on the controls. He edged the car into the evening traffic, poking its nose out hopefully. No one was for letting him out.

'Come on for God's sake,' he muttered under his breath. 'C'mon you impolite bastards, let me out.' He thumped the steering wheel.

'We're gonna lose him,' Jo stated, feet tapping. 'What a cock-up.'

'I can't believe this traffic.'

There was a gap a millisecond wide and O'Brien went for it, his tyres skidding and the car lurching across the line of cars, only to find there was no gap at all to get into on the opposite carriageway, thereby finding himself stuck at an angle halfway across the road, completely halting traffic in one direction. No one was feeling patient and horns began to sound, but then someone did slow for him and wave him in. He gave a relieved wave and shot into the line and started to crawl along – only to pass Turner in the 4x4 going back in the opposite direction towards the city. He had spun round again.

'This is a bloody farce,' Jo simpered, keeping her face firmly forward-facing.

'Where's everybody else?' O'Brien demanded.

Jo spoke into her radio again. It was dead. So was O'Brien's.

She reverted to her mobile phone again, not having completed the call she had started earlier to one of her other colleagues. She saw that her battery charge indicator was low.

'Right, right, right, if he can do it, so can I.' stated O'Brien. This time he was ruthless. He swung the car into a gap that wasn't there and completed a spectacular U-turn so he was now heading in the same direction as their target. 'If I see the bastard going back the other way again, I'll bloody cry.'

'Can't get through,' Jo said, pulling the mobile away from her ear. She pressed redial.

O'Brien squeezed in a double overtake, not recommended in such busy circumstances, but he pulled it off without damage or injury and stood on the accelerator, tail-gating the car ahead.

'Nothing!' Jo spat contemptuously at her phone. 'Aaargh!' she screamed angrily, then screamed again, this time in fear, as O'Brien executed another daring overtake followed by a wicked swerve into a space which he alone created.

'How the hell did you get in here?'

'I'm good at getting big things into tight places,' he boasted.

Jo chuckled, the tension released for a moment. Then she shook her phone, still unable to get through. She tried the number of another team member. This time she connected. 'Ken . . . it's Jo . . . we've eyeballed the target . . . he's headed towards . . .' Click. Whirr. The line went dead as the signal broke. 'Shit. I do not effin' believe this. Technology, I've shit it.' She watched the signal-strength bars reappear on the mobile-phone display. She redialled again.

As they hit a set of traffic lights on red, they found themselves stuck in a long queue of traffic.

'Can you see him, or have we lost him?' Jo asked.

O'Brien opened his window and stuck his head out, craning to see. 'Dunno.'

With the mobile to her ear, Jo opened the door and, holding the door pillar, swung herself up to get an elevated view across the roofs of the cars in front of her.

O'Brien heard her slam a hand down on the roof. He ducked instinctively. She dropped back into her seat. 'About eight cars ahead,' she said, her phone still stuck to her ear. She pulled it away and glared crossly at it. 'Blooming thing,' she said and threw it down in the footwell. 'Gimme yours,' she demanded of O'Brien and held out her hand.

The traffic began moving slowly.

'You're very cautious,' Andy Turner commented, following the numerous U-turns.

The man in the driving seat said nothing, concentrated on driving and checking his mirrors.

'I like that,' Turner said.

'Don't get to like anything about me,' the man warned.

The cars moved so slowly that by the time they reached the traffic lights, they were turning back to red, Turner's vehicle having gone through towards the city. Jo looked aghast as the amber light appeared. O'Brien swore, then took a chance.

He pulled out and accelerated past the car in front and shot the red light. He made it over the junction before the cross-traffic began to move.

'Well done,' Jo breathed.

O'Brien held on tight to the wheel, but made no reply.

'I just hope he hasn't seen us carrying out death manoeuvres and basically doing everything we can to draw attention to ourselves, y'know? Us being undercover, highly trained surveillance operatives and all? So far we've done everything we shouldn't have.'

'What's new? It's usually a wing and a prayer at the best of times. At least we're still in touch with him.'

'But not with the rest of the team,' Jo said miserably. She tried to call Ken on O'Brien's mobile, but could not make a connection despite there being a charge in his battery and a strong signal. 'Somebody up there doesn't like us tonight,' she said. She tried another team member and this time got through.

The 4x4 weaved through the centre of Manchester, emerging on the other side of the city on the A56, which led out past Manchester Prison, towards Prestwich and Bury.

O'Brien hung in behind him, keeping as far back as he dared without actually losing sight. It was not ideal. A one-car follow was always tough, but it was all he had. There was no doubt that, just at that moment, the team was in disarray and there seemed little hope of pulling it back together. Jo had contacted some of the others and they were doing their best to play catch-up, but she was beginning to despair a little because the battery on O'Brien's mobile was losing strength and the radios still did not work, even with a change of channel. She used the phone sparingly, but knew it would not last for long and she also knew that the further Turner travelled, the more stretched and ineffective the team would be.

Not a comforting scenario.

The only good side of it was that the 4x4 was such a big vehicle it was fairly easy to keep tabs on, particularly with its cluster of high-level brakes across the rear window, which shone like Blackpool illuminations every time the brake pedal got pressed.

Turner and his driver took them past the entrance to Sedgley Park, Greater Manchester Police's training school, then into Prestwich, staying on the main road all the way.

Jo speculated where they could be headed.

'Motorway junction's up ahead,' she mumbled. 'Straight across to Bury, or left on to the M60 ring road towards south Manchester, or east out towards Rochdale, or beyond to Leeds.

34

If he goes on to the motorway either direction and puts his foot down, I think we're snookered.'

'Let's not give up yet,' said O'Brien grimly.

They followed through Prestwich and approached the motorway junction. On the left, just before the roundabout was a petrol station which the 4x4 drew into. O'Brien sailed past on to the roundabout. This gave Jo the opportunity to scribble down the registered number of the car and to have a glimpse of the driver again as he climbed out and went to a pump. She saw he was looking around warily and that he actually watched her drive past.

O'Brien went on to the roundabout, circled it twice, covered by fairly heavy traffic. Turner's vehicle rolled off the forecourt and accelerated straight down on to the M60 southbound as O'Brien was three-quarters of the way through his third circle.

'Motorway,' Jo said unnecessarily. She quickly relayed the message to another team member who was still trying to get through heavy theatre traffic on Deansgate in Manchester City centre, which was a long way away now. They might as well be on the moon. She and O'Brien were effectively on their own.

O'Brien tore down the motorway slip road and hit the main carriageway at 70mph, cutting ruthlessly into the first lane, out into the middle, then into the fast. He was expecting not to come into close contact with the 4x4, but suddenly there it was ahead of them in the middle lane, travelling sedately. Another tactic for the surveillance-conscious criminal – and O'Brien almost fell for it. Instinctively he took his foot off the gas and drifted into the centre lane, dropping about half a dozen cars behind the target.

'That was a bit close for comfort. I hope he hasn't made us,' said Jo. If they had passed the 4x4 she knew they would definitely have been blown out of the water and that would have been the end of the night's operation. As it was, they were clinging to the remnants.

Then, just to make matters worse, the big car lurched out into the fast lane and surged forwards.

'Bugger!' O'Brien cursed.

They were lucky to see the back end of the 4x4 leaving the motorway on the exit which looped round on to the M61. They were only just able to cut sharply across the traffic themselves and throw up road dust as their car angled across the chevron markings on the exit. By the time they reached the point where the M60 joined the M61, and there was also the choice of going onto the A666 towards Bolton, the 4x4 had beaten them. It was nowhere to be seen.

Al Major was not amused.

'You incompetent idiot,' he sneered down the phone. At her end, Jo Coniston could see his face in her mind's eye. She bit her tongue and thought better than to point out what an ill-judged and purely hopeful operation it had been from the word go . . . and that she had done well to even come across Turner in the first place . . . and, and, and . . . but she didn't. She kept her mouth firmly closed.

'What do you want us to do?' She was standing at a pay phone at Bolton West Motorway Services on the M61, formerly known as Anderton Services. Dale O'Brien was standing behind her, hopping from foot to foot as she got their bollocking.

There was silence at the other end of the phone whilst Major thought about his response. Jo handed O'Brien a slip of paper on which she had written the result of the PNC check on the 4x4 registered number – it had come back with no current keeper.

'Call it a day,' Major decided. 'I'll debrief when you get back.'

Jo knew what that meant – a real roasting, probably with his anger directed mostly at her for no other reason than she had dumped him.

'OK.' She hung up, turned to her hyperactive partner. 'Back to base for a court martial . . . except I don't feel like rushing back – let's have a coffee here first.'

Andy Turner shifted uncomfortably. He felt like he was being interviewed for a job – although he had to use his imagination somewhat because he had never actually worked in his life other than in a criminal capacity and interviews for such positions were fairly unstructured at best. He looked across the table at the Spaniard, feeling himself bubbling with frustration.

The Spaniard was a very important man. He was a scout on the lookout for business opportunities for his boss, a very big underworld figure based in Barcelona. Turner knew he was lucky to get to talk to him, to pitch his business. If he could get this guy's nod, he would be going sky high.

It was not easy. The guy was cagey and inquisitive. Questions, questions, questions – and he had done his homework on Turner, something which Turner found disquieting.

Turner realized he had to keep his cool. Don't get riled. Go with the flow. Answer the questions. Tell the truth where necessary, otherwise bullshit . . . but above all, do not lose it.

'Tell me about your organization,' the Spaniard said. He was sitting with his back to the wall, sipping from a glass of chilled mineral water with lemon. He was casually dressed and came across as confident and knowledgeable, but Turner did not like the man's mouth at all. It reminded him of something . . . then he remembered and became fascinated by the lips because he knew exactly what they looked like. Turner had once visited the Sea-Life Centre at Blackpool, just to see the sharks, but the stingrays had also caught his attention. The way they moved, the way they could actually rise out of the water and stay upright, showing their mouths and the white undersides of their bodies. They had pink, anaemic-looking lips, just like this Spaniard. Obscene, somehow.

'What do you want to know?' Turner asked, masking the revulsion of the thought: this man had lips like a stingray.

The pink lips turned down. He shrugged his shoulders a little. He was becoming irritated by Turner, who he thought was merely a small-fry time-waster on the make. He wondered how he had been duped into this meeting. He knew his boss would not be overly impressed with this one.

'Your structure. How does it work? Do you have firewalls in place?'

'What the fuck's a firewall?'

'A firewall is a layer, or layers, of protection. It prevents leakage. It's a safety mechanism ensuring that the people who need to be shielded are shielded, so that mistakes at a low level do not have repercussions further up.'

'Uh, right,' said Turner numbly, failing to inspire confidence.

'So . . . your organization?' the Spaniard prompted.

Turner blew out his cheeks, stumped a little. 'Fluid,' he said. 'Nothing formal . . . very loose, yet safe.'

'OK,' said the Spaniard, 'describe how you would get a consignment on to the streets. How would the consumer be dealt with? What's your process from receipt to consumption?'

'Pretty simple, really. I've got several little labs dotted around the city. The goods would go into them for processing and packaging. They then get sold on to the dealers for street distribution. I got about twenty people doing the dirty for me around the north of the city. Some areas are well sewn up and I'm moving into others, expanding bit by bit.'

'A small operation then,' the Spaniard observed. 'Not as large as we were led to believe.'

Turner felt his feathers ruffle. 'I've been in this business over ten years. I've worked across Europe and the north of England. I'm a hands-on guy. I like to keep control, keep my finger on the pulse. I need to expand now . . . yeah, it's a small operation, but it's fucking profitable and I do very well, thank you.'

'Do you have any respect for the law?'

The question threw Turner. 'Eh? Do I fuck! Cops and courts mean nothing to me. I ran a cop down once. I shit on cops.'

'Interesting,' the ray-lipped man remarked.

'Cops are frightened of me. People are frightened of me. I scare the shite out of people. No one gives evidence against me. I see to that personally.'

'How?'

'Midnight visits. Phone calls. Beatings . . . I don't mess around and I don't get anyone else to do my dirty work for me. No one frightens me.'

'Hm,' murmured the Spaniard, unimpressed. Turner did not pick up on the less than wonderful reception to the news of the ways in which he dealt with people. 'I believe you were responsible for the death of Wolfgang Meyer in Germany, about a year ago.'

'If you think I'm going to say I did that, then you're wrong, pal. How do I know you're not wired up?'

'You don't . . . but I'm not, and you did, didn't you?'

A dangerous smile fractured on Turner's face. He nodded and pointed to the Spaniard with his forefinger. He clicked his thumb, as though cocking a revolver. 'Bang, bang,' he whispered.

'So you deal harshly and effectively with wrongdoers?'

'He was causing problems . . . in fact,' Turner began boastfully, 'I've sorted a problem just today.' His hands slid under his jacket and emerged with a set of photographs which he passed across. 'This man was operating on my area without permission. Now he ain't,' he said proudly.

The Spaniard fanned out the photographs on the table. He winced at the blood-soaked tableaux depicted in the digital images.

'Personal service,' Turner gloated.

The Spaniard stacked the photographs as though they were a pack of playing cards. He handed them back. 'We cannot do business, Mr Turner.'

'I beg your fuckin' pardon, spik?'

The Spaniard looked impassively at Turner and licked his pale pink lips. 'Your organization is not sophisticated enough. There are too many holes and you are far too unbalanced. You do not have respect for law enforcement . . . No, let me finish,' he indicated to an agitated Turner. 'Whilst our business is illegal, we treat day-to-day law enforcement with dignity, because we do not wish to fall foul of it through stupidity.'

'Stupidity, you stupid bastard! Are you calling me stupid?'

'Hot-headed, reckless.'

'You are just another shitless wonder,' Turner blasted and shot angrily to his feet, towering over the Spaniard, who did not flinch. 'I've shat people like you.'

Suddenly, standing behind him, was the man who had driven him to this meeting. Turner saw him and snarled. He spun to the Spaniard. 'You do business with me, or I'll waste you, you cunt.' He held his fist underneath his nose, so close that the hairs on the back of his hand were clearly individually visible. Again, the Spaniard did not move. His eyes rose slowly and met Turner's.

'You are a loose cannon. You are unstable and unpredictable. My boss is not interested in you. Just be pleased I met and listened to you today. Not many people have that privilege. This meeting is now over.'

'Privilege, you twat!' Turner's fist shook angrily. Other people in the establishment were beginning to take an interest in proceedings. 'Privilege? I'm gonna fuck you and your boss up good and proper, mate, you shitless wonders.'

The driver stepped up close behind Turner. 'That's enough. Behave yourself.'

There was a doom-laden pause during which Turner could have gone either way. Eventually he stood upright again, still glaring with ferocity. 'You've made a mistake here, mister big-shot. I will screw your operation up, big style. You will regret this.'

The Spaniard pursed his lips pensively. 'Mr Verner will take you back. *Adiós.*' He nodded at the driver, who nodded back with understanding.

They were in no rush to return. In fact Jo Coniston did not want to go back – ever. She did not want to have any form of interaction with Al Major, particularly after this evening's very unsuccessful operation against Andy Turner, which, she was certain, would be put down to her. She would be Major's scapegoat.

After the coffee at the motorway services, she and O'Brien drove east along the M61 into Lancashire. They came off at Chorley. Instead of looping back on to the motorway as they should have done, Jo – who was now driving – went towards Chorley down the A6.

As they circuited the town centre, she suddenly turned left and headed towards Rivington.

'Fancy a little drive through the country?' she said.

'Seems I have no choice in the matter,' smiled O'Brien. 'Just so long as you don't pretend to run out of petrol in the middle of nowhere and expect to have your wicked way with me.'

The withering glance from female to male told him there would be zero chance of that happening.

Verner knew what he had to do and did not dawdle. Turner stormed out of the restaurant ahead of him, his fuming rage apparent with every footfall. Verner followed as Turner went out and stalked toward the 4x4, amused by the antics.

'Come on, get the car open,' Turner demanded.

Verner pointed the remote and the doors unlocked with a squelching noise. Turner swung in and dropped on to the front passenger seat.

'Who the fuck does he think he is?' he insisted.

As he slid the key into the ignition, Verner said, 'A very powerful man – and you should not have spoken to him like that.'

'When I say he'll regret it – he'll regret it,' Turner said dangerously.

Verner was fiddling with the ignition – apparently. Trying to get the key turned.

In reality, he was reaching to the small shelf under the dash on which loose change might normally be stored, though in this case a small revolver was resting on it. Verner's hand slid over it, his fingers slotting into place around it.

He moved silkily, almost without speed it seemed, yet he was lightning quick. He sat upright, twisted towards Turner slightly and raised the weapon. It had a stubby barrel and was loaded with bullets designed to enter the heads of victims, ping around like a bagatelle causing massive brain damage and hopefully not exit outside the other side of the head. Turner did not see it coming. He was facing away from Verner, staring moodily out of the door window.

Verner put the muzzle against the back quarter of Turner's head, just above the ear. As soon as he touched, he pulled the trigger – twice. The sound was dreadful in the confines of the vehicle, but no so bad as the damage caused to the inside of Turner's cranium.

Verner's wrist recoiled slightly with the power of the shots and he ducked quickly in an effort to dodge the inevitable back-spray of brain tissue and juice as Turner's head twisted grotesquely and smashed against the window.

After a series of brutal jerks of his body's nervous system, Turner's whole being relaxed as he died.

Verner pulled him upright and drew the seat belt across his chest, then pushed him up against the door jamb and wedged him there at an angle. His head lolled down, chin on chest.

Verner set off with his dead passenger.

The roads around Rivington were dark and winding, often unlit by street lamps. Jo decided she needed a razz to get something fundamental out of her pent-up system. She floored the accelerator pedal and told O'Brien to hold on for the ride of a lifetime.

He did as instructed.

Jo threw the car around the unlit country roads, going for broke around blind corners and long straight stretches, braking hard, changing up and down, fast and accurately, pushing the car to its screaming limits.

She was thoroughly enjoying herself, though her companion had a look of abject dread on his countenance. Even without being able to see him properly, Jo knew O'Brien's complexion had gone sickly grey. However, he remained silent, probably numbed by the experience he was having.

'Yee-hah!' she yelled as she roared down a forest road.

'Jesus Christ – look out!' screamed O'Brien, breaking his silence.

Ahead, just in the extremity of the main beam, was a big, black shape with eyes that were red rubies in the headlights.

A deer.

Jo wrestled with the wheel, cursing, slamming on the brakes. But she could not do anything to avoid hitting the stationary beast, which remained facing them, defiant in the centre of the road.

'Oh no,' uttered O'Brien.

Jo braced herself for the impact. O'Brien cowered and covered his eyes, instinctively bringing his knees up for protection, and waited for the deer to come crashing through the windscreen.

But with a mighty, unbelievably muscular and giant leap, the deer was gone into the pitch-black woods. It was as though it had never been there in the first place.

The car swerved to a halt, slewed at an angle to the road. The engine stalled with a judder. The new silence was almost tangible.

Jo sat there, hands gripping the wheel, knuckles white, breathing unsteady, feeling very ill. She stared at the road, unsure if there ever had been a deer there in the first place, whether it had just been a mirage.

Slowly she turned her head and looked at O'Brien. He was shaking visibly.

'I need a fag,' he said.

'Me too.'

'You don't smoke.'

'Do now.'

They climbed out of the car and leaned against it. O'Brien lit up and offered one to Jo, but she refused. Alcohol was what she needed really.

'Sorry 'bout that,' she said meekly.

'Got it out of your system then?'

She nodded.

'Let's go back, nice 'n' easy and we might just be able to get to the pub for a drinkie-pooh if we're lucky.' He ground out his quarter-smoked cig.

'Good speech.'

'And I'll drive,' he said, rushing to the driver's seat before she could argue the toss. Dragging her feet, she got in next to him. He set off more sedately. He drove past Rivington Barn in the direction of Horwich, a small town west of Bolton. He intended to cut back down on to the M61 and get back into Manchester that way.

The 4x4 passed them going in the opposite direction as they reached the motorway junction.

The dead man was annoying Verner intensely. He would not stay sitting upright, kept lolling about as though he was . . . dead.

'Sit the fuck up,' Verner said angrily, pushing the drooping figure back into the corner of the seat, trying to wedge him by the stanchion. Turner was being uncooperative, even though it was not really his fault. Verner did not stop driving, but tried to keep Turner in place with his outstretched left arm, doing all the driving with his right.

He knew where he was going. Earlier that afternoon, during daylight hours, he had combed the area around the reservoir at Rivington. It was not as though he knew for definite that he would have to kill Turner, but the omens were not good, and he liked to be prepared. He had been informed of the plans for the evening and knew he might need somewhere suitable to dispose of a body. He found what he thought would be the ideal location.

He knew that the meeting would be taking place between Turner and the Spaniard at a restaurant just off the M61 near to Horwich. So he had spent his time driving around the area, checking out locations. He thought the thickly wooded environs of Rivington were a fairly good place. There were lots of tracks running off the road into the forest, which was dark, quiet and, he assumed, would be somewhere he would be unlikely to be interrupted late in the evening. He even picked the forest track and the place he would dig. If it came to it.

It did – and that was where he was headed.

Jo and O'Brien hit the motorway junction fast. O'Brien tore around the roundabout, tyres screeching as he held on tight to the steering wheel, looping round and back in the direction of the 4x4. By the time he reached the next roundabout – right towards Bolton, left towards Horwich – there was no sign of it.

'Bugger!' he said. 'Which way?' He turned to Jo for some inspiration.

She shrugged helplessly. 'Eeni-meeni-minie-mo,' she began, index finger flicking from left to right as she applied the scientific approach to solving the problem. 'That way,' she declared, pointing left.

'Back to where we came from?'

'Well, go that fucking way, then,' she growled.

'No, no, no,' O'Brien said. There was a queue of cars behind them, all becoming annoyed. 'We'll go your way,' he said, resigned, 'but I'll bet it's the wrong way.'

'If you keep this up it won't matter which way he's gone, will it?'

Shaking his head, O'Brien pointed the car back towards Horwich. He just knew they were travelling in the wrong direction.

It was not particularly late, but Bill Gordon, who had been drinking heavily, was now rat-arsed. As he staggered out of the pub door and lurched to his car on the pub car park, the cool night air hit him slap-bang in the face and almost floored him. Nevertheless he regained his composure, pulled himself upright as only a drunk can, and slewed to his car.

If anyone had asked him, Bill Gordon would have said that he was pretty much okay. Yesh, okay. Maybe he'd been drinking steadily since noon, but that was the key – steady. And that is how after more than ten pints of bitter and several wee chasers, and four packets of crisps to soak it all up, he knew he was more than capable of driving safely home.

The door key slid in, no problem. So did the ignition key. He even fitted his seat belt. And home was less than a mile away. If he had been over the limit, he would have walked. He belched loudly and edged the car lumpily towards the car-park exit.

O'Brien sped along the A673 to Horwich. It was a narrow road through a built-up area, but he took no notice of the speed limits because he knew he would soon be doing an about-turn to Bolton. As he reached a set of traffic lights, they changed to red and he slowed reluctantly.

He cursed.

'I think that's him,' cried Jo.

Beyond the junction, several cars were heading towards the centre of Horwich.

'How can you be sure?'

'I can't, but it looks like it.' She pointed excitedly.

The lights changed to green.

*   *   *

Bill Gordon – drunk, middle aged, no convictions, in full employment all his adult life, a man who had successfully negotiated his way home in his car whilst drunk literally hundreds of times – waited patiently at the car-park exit for traffic to clear. His judgement was sound as a pound.

He hummed a happy tune as he revved the engine of his Vauxhall Vectra, whilst holding the car stationary on the clutch.

At court later, he strenuously denied he was to blame for the accident.

The fact he was holding the steering wheel, was sitting in the driver's seat, in control of the car, did not in any way make him feel inclined to plead guilty to the charges laid before him.

This stance did not prevent him being convicted. He lost his licence for five years, was fined over a thousand pounds and was sent to prison for three months.

No, he felt he was not to blame for his foot slipping off the clutch and the car hurtling into the stream of traffic passing from left to right in front of him.

He did not hit Verner's four-wheel-drive monster, but slammed into the car behind it, smashing into the passenger side and forcing the vehicle into the path of a Transit van coming the opposite way.

Verner saw the accident in his rear-view mirror. Obviously he did not stop as a witness, kept going.

At first it was all confusion, chaos and cars in front. O'Brien came to a sudden halt and stopped only inches away from the car in front.

'Been a bump ahead,' Jo said, craning her neck.

'Shit.' O'Brien punched the wheel.

Jo jumped out and sprinted towards the scene of the accident. It looked a bad one. Three vehicles, two head-on by the looks. No one in any of them appeared to be moving. She was torn momentarily between her duty to save life and to find out what Andy Turner was up to.

'Job for the traffic department,' she decided and jogged past the carnage.

About 200 metres down the road, she saw the 4x4 in the

46

outside lane of the road, signalling to turn right towards Rivington. Then it turned.

She doubled back, passing the scene of the accident again, feeling bad about it, but not bad enough to stop and offer assistance.

'He's gone towards Rivington,' she gasped to O'Brien. 'Do you know a way round?'

'No,' he admitted.

'In that case go on the pavement.'

He eyed her in amazement. She shrugged. 'It's your decision, but we'll lose him if we don't do something.'

'OK,' he said meekly. He reversed away from the car in front, stopping just a hair's thickness short of the one behind, yanked the wheel down and mounted the kerb.

'Not good,' he decided as they bounced along.

Jo hung on to the hand rail above the door. 'You're the guy at the wheel. No one's held a gun to your head. If you kill a pedestrian, it'll be down to you, not me.'

'Thanks a bunch,' he responded, misery in his voice. 'Shit.' Ahead, a group of people had already gathered to gawk at the accident. O'Brien flashed his lights and pipped his horn. A look of startled disbelief filled the faces of several people. They stepped or jumped out of the way and O'Brien drove through the gap. He kept his eyes fixed firmly on the route ahead, not daring to look at anyone. He emerged on the far side without having added to the mayhem too much.

'I don't believe what I just did,' he said.

'You better had – now put your foot down.'

'He's done a disappearing trick,' O'Brien said with disappointment. He sniffed. 'Eeh, smell that engine.'

They were almost back in Chorley town centre after hurtling through the country roads around Rivington, then combing and re-combing them without success. He had floored the accelerator and spent most of the chase in first or second gear, screwing the car to its limits to catch the 4x4, which seemed to have vanished off the face of the earth. Hence the reek of the engine.

'He must've gone like shit off a shovel,' O'Brien moaned

and the bitter engine fumes wafted into the cab. 'We shoulda caught him. I drove like a maniac.'

White-faced, dithery and clinging to the door handle, Jo had to agree. She swallowed, feeling slightly poorly. O'Brien had flung the car around the roads like a rally driver, but unlike her, seemed to be in total control of the machine. Even so, she had hoped they did not meet up with another – or the same – suicidal deer.

Now, it seemed, they had lost Turner for good. Their last chance gone. Or maybe not, she thought. 'Let's head back the way we came,' she suggested. 'Nice 'n' slow and have a look up some of those foresty-type tracks. Maybe he turned off for some reason.'

'Why? Why would he have done that?'

'How do I know? It's just a thought. Take it or leave it.'

It was close to midnight as O'Brien turned off the road and on to one of the tracks that cut through the forest.

'Last one, this,' he said, 'then we go home.'

'I'll have that,' Jo conceded. She was tired and coming to the conclusion that Turner was definitely gone now. 'Drive up this one, turn round and we'll call it quits.'

O'Brien nodded. The thrill of the chase had worn off. He wanted to get home, via a late-night hostelry, and get some shut-eye.

Jo peered through the headlights as the car crunched slowly up the track. She, too, had had enough. Just intended to concentrate for a few more minutes.

O'Brien yawned, wide and loud and shook his head.

'I thought I saw something,' Jo said quickly, leaning forward, almost pushing her nose up to the windscreen.

'If only.'

'No, I did. A glint of something in the trees. Stop. Kill the lights.'

'Now what?'

'Let's have a look.' Jo reached for the torch under her seat, a powerful dragon-lite. She got out, switching the torch on, then off. O'Brien climbed out too, a less powerful torch in his hand.

'Let's wander this way,' he said.

'OK.' They started to walk along the track, torches on. Jo halted suddenly. 'Look – there,' her voice rasped hoarsely. She directed the torch beam on to the edge of the track, where, clearly, there were indents made in the verge where a vehicle had been driven off into the trees. She flashed her torch into the trees, picking out the shape of the 4x4 in there.

Quickly she shut off the torch. As did O'Brien. He sidled up beside her.

'What're we going to do?' O'Brien asked.

'Well, put it this way, there's a good chance we've been spotted now, so I think we might as well go and investigate, don't you? I'm bloody curious to know what's going on, aren't you? The surveillance is cocked up, so we might as well show our hand and see what's happening.'

'OK, but I don't like this,' he admitted.

'Me neither. Just stay here, I'll go back and get a radio and see if we can get through.' Jo ran back to their car, then jogged back to O'Brien. She tried to call in, but there was no response. 'Shit, the bloody things are still not working properly, or this must be a real blackspot here.'

'Let's have a look,' O'Brien whispered. Their torches came on simultaneously and they both stepped off the track into the undergrowth. They were at the 4x4 within seconds.

'No one with it,' O'Brien observed as he approached, shining his torch. He walked up to the driver's door and shone it in. 'Shit,' he gasped.

Jo was behind him. She shone her more powerful beam into the vehicle.

'Wooo,' she said, pursing her lips.

There was blood swathed across the inside of the passenger door, pools of it on the seat.

'Not good,' said O'Brien nervously edging his way carefully around the 4x4. He stood by the passenger window, which was pasted in blood. He shone his torch around his feet and saw the drag marks along the forest floor. Jo joined him, saw what he was looking at.

She looked at him, worried. 'Bloody hell – I think our Mr Turner is a dead un.'

'Let's follow them, now that we're here.'

Jo nodded. 'Keep to one side of the marks.'

They found the unattended grave, and the body of Andy Turner. Their torch beams played over him.

Verner was behind them, just feet away. They had not seen or heard him, had no idea he was so close.

He rose out of the undergrowth, his spade held high over his head.

He went for the man first.

TWO YEARS LATER

One

Henry Christie wondered what sort of reception would be waiting for him on his return to work. There would certainly be no celebrations. It would, he guessed, be a muted affair at best. The banners and the bunting would not be out. There would be no party poppers or streamers and no champagne would be opened. More likely there would be cautious, sideways glances; one or two nods and maybe, if he was lucky, the Chief Superintendent would say hello. The main thing would be that he would have a tattered reputation to repair and to do so would be an uphill struggle of massive proportions. After all, who wanted to work for a supervisor whose judgement had been deemed very, very suspect?

He parked his car on the secure police-rented level of the multi-storey car park adjacent to Blackpool Central Police Station and climbed out, ensuring he locked it. He walked to the door which opened out on to the public mezzanine which stretched between the front of Blackpool Magistrates' Court and the front entrance of the police station. Once through the door, he paused for a moment to savour the ever present chilled sea breeze. He looked upwards at the monstrosity that was the cop shop. Eight floors of concrete ugliness. He had spent many years of his police service here and was returning after an enforced absence – a suspension from duty, actually – having lost his temporary rank of Detective Chief Inspector, back to Detective Inspector – and also his coveted role as a Senior Investigating Officer based at Headquarters in the team responsible for investigating murders and other serious crimes. It had been his ideal job.

To his left he glanced at the steps leading up to the court. A few early arrivals for the day's proceedings had gathered in a motley group, smoking roll-ups, hunched miserably together. They peered up from their huddle and scowled at Henry, who recognized each and every one of the little toerags.

He waved and smiled at them.

They did not respond. Not one of them was brave enough to give him a middle finger or even a lazy 'V'.

'Shitbags,' Henry mumbled to himself. 'Nice to see the faces haven't changed.' He walked to the police station, feeling eight sets of eyes burning into his back.

A few very depressed and grey-looking people were waiting at the enquiry desk.

Henry slid his swipe card through the scanner, half expecting it not to work. But it did. He pushed open the door which led into the innards of the station. With a certain degree of trepidation, he stepped across the threshold and let the door click shut behind him.

It was the first time he had set foot in a police station in four months. It gave him a strange, queasy feeling. He had been to Headquarters on several occasions recently, the last time being for the full hearing into his disciplinary case when he was cleared of any wrongdoing. But other than on those closely supervised visits when he had been treated like a terrorist, he had not been allowed on police property.

But now he was back with a warrant card, swipe card and full police powers.

He allowed himself the faintest flicker of a smile. Then the enormity of the situation hit him like a sock full of pennies. He blew out his cheeks and, avoiding the elevator because he wasn't going to risk getting trapped in a confined space with possibly someone he did not want to be with, began to climb the stairs . . .

'. . . Daddy, Daddy!' The harsh shrieking voice cut sharply into Henry Christie's daydream. He had been well immersed in his thoughts, so deep he had totally lost track of everything in his pipe dream of returning to work totally exonerated by the disciplinary panel. He shook his head and twisted in the direction of his youngest daughter, Leanne. She was standing at the conservatory door, her body language expressing complete impatience with him.

'Oh, OK, love . . . are you ready to make tracks?'

'Dad, I have been so ready for an age. I couldn't find you.'

'I've been sitting here, reading the papers like I do every Sunday, while I wait for you to get ready.'

'Dad,' Leanne said pointedly, 'you weren't reading the papers, you were in a trance . . . and now it's time to go or we'll be late.'

'OK.' He pushed himself out of the low cane sofa and looked at Leanne. She was growing up very quickly now, blossoming out of childhood into a beautiful young woman. As ever, Henry's ticker jarred a little at the thought of his little babykins and at how much he had missed her development over the years because of his misguided dedication to being a cop. His other, eldest, daughter, Jenny, was now in her late teens and he had seen virtually nothing of her growth, other than remembering being surprised and stunned from time to time at her progress.

Not good. Even if he did get back to work, in future the job would come well down on the list from now on. First and foremost was his family.

Leanne was dressed for her new hobby. Tight jodhpurs, riding boots and a sleeveless fleecy top, finished off with a short riding crop, thin leather gloves and a hard hat. She was now into riding horses each Sunday morning. Since Henry's suspension from duty he had been able, and willingly volunteered, to take her to the riding school and pick her up. It was one of those fatherly type of duties he had never been able to carry out. It had always been Kate who had taken the girls to Brownies or to swimming lessons, or to birthday parties. Henry was trying to make up for lost time . . . and whereas most other parents he met whinged and bleated about the dreary tasks, he found he loved every minute of it, could not get enough.

'So what were you thinking about?' Leanne asked as they went out to the car.

'Going back to work,' he admitted. 'If it ever happens.'

'Oh,' she said, knowing how delicate a subject it all was. She knew he was nowhere near going back yet; that the date for the discipline hearing had not been set and that the court proceedings surrounding it all had not even been listed. 'Anyway,' she said, changing the subject with the subtlety of a sledge hammer, 'I hope I get to ride Silver today.' She sighed longingly. 'He's a wonderful horse . . . so responsive . . . I've heard he might be up for sale.' She looked slyly at her father, who was reversing the car out of the drive.

'Not a chance,' he said without even glancing at her, keeping his chin firmly on his right shoulder as he manoeuvred into the road.

'I didn't mean we should buy him,' Leanne lied.

Henry rammed the car into first. 'Yeah, right.'

'But if we did, I'd look after him, Dad, honest.'

It was Henry's turn to sigh. It was a short, irritated sigh, accompanied by the word, 'Nope.'

Leanne folded her arms and stared directly forward, jaw rotating crossly.

'Maybe I'll get you a hamster,' Henry offered.

The jaw ceased its rotation.

'How about a pet rat?'

'Dad – shut it,' she told him, but a smile flickered on her lovely lips and suddenly her cross mood changed. 'I hope Kelly's there and Charlotte . . . if they are, can we go for a McDonald's after?'

'We'll have to see.'

'Oh good,' she beamed and clapped her hands at the thought.

It was about four miles to the riding stables, which were situated in the countryside in the Marton area of Blackpool. As Henry slowed down at the stables, Leanne leapt out of the car almost before it had stopped because she had spotted Kelly already. Henry drew to a halt on the rough area of hard ground they called the car park and chuckled to himself as he watched Leanne run off. She was totally happy. Doing well at school. Brilliant at home and great company to be with. Kate had told Henry that both girls were more content than they had ever been for years. Henry knew that implicit in that remark was that their happiness was directly related to his regular presence at home.

A big Mercedes coupé pulled in alongside Henry's Mondeo.

It was driven by the mother of Charlotte, one of the girls mentioned by Leanne, whom she had met through riding.

Charlotte was in the front passenger seat next to her mother. Henry saw that the youngster was looking pretty morose. She got out and sauntered towards the stables, dragging her feet, watched by her mother from the car.

Henry smiled at Charlotte's mother as he got out of the car. She gave him an eyes-to-heaven look.

With a couple of sections of the *Sunday Times* under his arm which he'd brought from home, Henry went to the indoor riding school. It had become his practice to watch Leanne begin her hour-long session, then mosey out to the portacabin-cum-café near to the main stable block where he would consume copious amounts of cheap coffee and a sausage sandwich and read the paper until Leanne showed up, usually red faced, exhausted and exhilarated after the lesson.

There was a small seating area down one side of the school with two tiers of benches. He sat himself down, shivering in the chill, blowing out his breath in spurts, trying to make smoke rings.

Riding was not for him. Horses did nothing for him. Not since the time when, as a young, headstrong police constable, he'd thought that life in the Mounted Branch looked glamorous, controlling football crowds and attracting young ladies who swooned over huge sweaty beasts – and horses too. He had managed to get a place on the coveted sixteen-week equitation course, where he then discovered it was not as pleasant as it seemed from the outside. The course was held in deep mid-winter and stables are harsh, unforgiving places to be when the temperature drops below zero. He found he detested the hard work involved, nor – and more fundamentally – did he particularly like horses either. But he stuck it until the eighth week, when he came a cropper. During a lesson on a particularly stroppy horse, it bucked and threw him. He broke his right wrist and bruised his lower spine. And that was the last he ever saw of the Mounted Branch. He had learned enough about riding to see him through the occasional holiday escapade when the girls wanted an hour's cross-country, but that was all. No regrets about not becoming a mounted officer.

Leanne's class came into the indoor arena and began to work out.

His daughter was proficient on the back of a horse. She had been riding about six months – longer than any other interest she had ever had – and worked hard to progress her ability. She seemed good at the basics and her balance was near perfect.

Not that Henry knew much about things like balance and the seat, but she seemed to be a natural.

He watched the lesson for a while, then decided it was time for food and drink. He edged his way across the bench, past Charlotte's mother, who was perched at the end. She moved her knees for him. He said thanks and smiled again. He did not ever remember her staying to watch her daughter ride in the past.

The portacabin café was a haven of heat. He settled down at a Formica-topped table in one corner with a chipped mug of coffee, toasted sausage sandwich and newspaper spread out in front of him.

There were a few people in the cabin, mostly young girls giggling in huddles, discussing boys, pop stars and horses, in that order.

Again, Henry was slightly surprised to see Charlotte's mother buying herself a coffee at the counter. He had never seen her in the cabin before today. He thought nothing of it and began to read the headlines about the police in London discovering deadly poisons in the hands of Middle Eastern terrorists. It was an ongoing story, one he had been following with relish and not a little envy.

He was, he had to admit, beginning to miss being a cop. He felt like he was in limbo, trapped and unable to do anything. If only he had a crystal ball and could forecast his future – one way or the other – he would be a whole lot happier.

As he read the story he became aware of someone standing in front of him. When he looked up, for some reason it was not unexpected that it was Charlotte's mother.

'Hello,' he said.

'Mind if I join you?'

He shuffled uncomfortably in the plastic chair. 'Er, not at all,' he frowned.

She sat opposite, cradling her mug of steaming coffee in her hands. She placed a plastic lunch box down by her feet. She blew on the hot liquid. 'I'm Charlotte's mum,' she said. Henry nodded. 'And you are Leanne's dad.' He nodded again. He closed his newspaper. He had moved on to a story about Blackpool and its planned regeneration as the Las Vegas and gambling capital of Europe, which he doubted would ever happen. He folded the paper to one side and gave his attention to the lady sitting opposite, who, he noticed for the first time at such close range, was extremely attractive.

She had well-cared-for, shiny, bobbed blonde hair, wide blue eyes, a slightly flat, elf-like nose and a full mouth which looked very biteable. Her chin was the feature that, if anything, let her down. It was slightly square and jutting, giving her face a hard edge that, as Henry appraised her more, took away the first impression, but only to a few degrees. She was dressed sloppily in loose sweatshirt and jeans.

It was the first time he had ever been so close to her. He had been aware of her dropping Charlotte off in the past and picking her up again an hour later, but he had only seen glimpses of her in one of several classy motors. He got the impression she was good looking (and knew it) and was obviously loaded, but had thought no more about her. In his newly adopted role in life of being a devoted husband and loving father – as opposed to his former mantle of adulterer and absent parent – he had surgically cut out registering the presence and possibilities of other women. All he wanted now was a simple life without complex entanglements and he never thought about other women any more. At least that had been the case for the last four months and it was his intention for it to be so for the rest of his life.

He assumed that, for whatever reason, Charlotte's mum was having to stay on site to wait for her daughter today instead of dumping her and collecting later, and all she wanted was to pass the time by chatting with someone caught in the same situation.

'Your daughter's riding is coming along well.'

'Thanks,' said Henry. 'She's really keen.'

'Charlotte's been riding for some years now and wasn't

getting any better. That's why we decided to bring her here so she could see how other girls were getting along, maybe help her get better.'

'Oh,' said Henry, uncomprehending.

'Since meeting Leanne she has improved.'

'Good,' said Henry, still puzzled about what was going on here. 'She was at another riding school, then?' he probed.

'No, we gave her lessons at home.'

'In the living room?'

'No,' she laughed. 'We have stables and a small indoor arena.'

'Oh, right, of course you do.'

'You're confused . . .' The woman held out her hand. Henry shook it. It was hot from holding the coffee. 'My name's Tara . . . Tara Wickson.'

'Pleased to meet you. I'm Henry Christie.'

She had shrugged when she said her name, in a gesture which seemed to suggest Henry should know who she was.

He did not and knew she would have to reveal more if anything further was likely to dawn on him. 'Wow . . . you've got your own stables,' he said for something to say, trying to sound impressed.

'Yes, we have a couple of race horses and some jumpers.'

Henry's face showed shock and distaste. He could no longer hold back his feelings.

'You don't like horses,' Tara said with a lop-sided smile.

'Can't think of one horse on my Christmas card list. I suppose they're a necessary evil, especially if you're learning to ride.'

Tara Wickson's nice smile continued unabated. She looked into his eyes. He gulped and glanced quickly down at his hands and coughed uncomfortably. He checked the time. Twenty minutes to go. Then he thought that maybe he was being stupid and arrogant. Just because a woman looked directly at him did not mean she was gagging to go to bed with him. You arrogant bastard, he thought about himself and raised his eyes. She was far too young for him anyway.

She was sipping her coffee, her eyes still on him over the rim of her mug. Nice eyes.

'You're a policeman, aren't you? Charlotte said Leanne had told her. A detective? Am I right?'

'Sort of.' He suddenly felt quite awkward. What else had Leanne told Charlotte?

'Are you on special leave, or something?'

Henry guffawed. 'Or something,' he confirmed coldly.

'Oh sorry, I'm treading on thin ice here, aren't I?'

Henry opened his mouth to say something, thought better of it, shut it and grinned.

'Leanne hasn't actually said very much, in case you're worrying and planning to beat her soundly later.'

'Kids talk,' he said philosophically. 'I wouldn't want to gag her.' Then he made a snap decision and didn't know why. He said, 'Yes, I am a policeman. I am a detective, but it's not special leave. I'm suspended from duty. I'm being investigated, you might say.'

Tara leaned back and eyed him thoughtfully. 'For dishonesty?' she asked bluntly.

He shook his head. 'Stupidity . . . lack of judgement . . . disobeying a lawful order.' Then he quickly clammed up. Why was he telling her this crap?

'To be honest, I already know,' she said.

'Oh.' He put his mug to his mouth and swigged from what was an empty receptacle. 'Mm,' he murmured, glaring into the mug.

'You're very prickly about it. I can understand that. It can't be an easy time for you.'

'No, but I've had lots of holidays out of it.'

'So Leanne said.'

'I will beat her soundly after all,' Henry decided.

'Are you bored?'

'What? Here and now? Or with the situation I'm in?'

'Bored by the amount of time you now have to kill.'

'It is getting to me. Good at first, all that time to loll about, then it begins to pall somewhat. A bit like retirement, I would think.'

'How do you fill your time?'

Henry looked at her square on. His expression told her that enough was enough. Even he wasn't sure how they had got here, but he felt it was time to call a halt to the conversation. He had said enough to someone who was just a stranger. 'How do you fill yours?' he asked.

She blinked and said openly, 'Shopping. Dining out. Sex. The usual, you know? When you're rich, that is. Oh, horses, too.'

'You're rich then? You wanna tell me?'

'Not really.' Her voice was suddenly as tight as a closed drawbridge.

'Shall we talk about the kids?' Henry suggested, picking up on her vibes.

'No,' she snapped, then relaxed. 'Look . . . time to come clean, Mr Christie. I'm actually not just here for personal chit-chat, as pleasant as that may be. I'll tell you my problem and I wonder if you could help me.'

'Tell you what, let's do it over a new cup of coffee each. I'm old-fashioned like that.' He picked up the mugs and bought two new brews.

'Thanks.' She curled her fingers around the mug again like it was a comfort blanket. Henry noticed her nails were beautifully manicured and wondered if caring for her body was in her list of activities. She looked exceptionally well groomed. 'I'll be honest, I have asked around a bit about you before coming to see you. You come highly recommended.'

'By who?'

She tapped her nose. 'Can't say . . . but what it is, we have a few problems up at the stables and I wondered if you'd investigate them for me.'

'I'm a cop on suspension. Stripped of all powers. I don't investigate things any more . . . and if it's something the police should be looking at, why don't you call in the local bobbies?'

'They have been in but they're not interested. Things to do with horses are obviously not on their priority lists, or whatever they call them. The first time I called the police, they took three days to come.'

'Doesn't surprise me,' he said, having heard far worse stories, 'But I take it it's a fairly minor matter then? Why not employ a private investigator?'

'Could do, I suppose – but here you are, a cop without portfolio and you've got time on your hands. I'd really appreciate it.'

'It would be remiss of me, at this point, if I didn't ask what the problem is,' he said, trying to show some interest. Whatever it was, warning bells were ringing in his ears, because it would cause further complications in his already over-complicated life, particularly if what she was asking him to do conflicted with him being suspended from duty.

Tara leaned down by her side and reached for the small sandwich box she had earlier put on the floor. She placed it on the table between them and prised the lid off. Inside was something wrapped in tin foil. She opened whatever it was whilst it was still in situ in the box, folding back the corners of the foil to reveal its contents.

Henry did not know what he was looking at. Even so, his guts churned and a shiver shot through him. It looked like a piece of minute steak, but with hairs on it and was triangular in shape, and deep brown, almost black in colour.

'What the hell's that?' he recoiled.

'A horse's ear.'

It was a long time since Henry had felt queasy at the sight of anything. The job of being a cop had seen to the complete desensitization of his psyche, but a severed horse's ear had certainly hit the mark.

The offending item was back in its tin foil, back in the sandwich box and out of sight. He and Tara Wickson were outside in the fresh air, walking back to the stable blocks. The lesson was due to finish shortly and the girls would soon be reappearing.

'Do you carry that with you all the time? It's certainly an effective calling card.'

'No, I don't.'

They walked on in silence until they reached a corner of a stable block where they paused. Tara leaned against the wall, drawing up one foot.

'It belongs to Charlotte's favourite horse, Chopin. A big, bay gelding. Soft as the day is long. When she went to see him this morning, first thing, she found him with his ear cut off and knife slashes across his rump and his tail chopped to pieces. There was blood everywhere. Poor animal, he was terrified.'

'Bloody hell,' said Henry.

'Yeah, he was in a real state – and so was Charlotte.'

'I can imagine . . . yet she came riding?'

'I thought it best. She enjoys it and it stops her dwelling on it for a while.'

'She did look unhappy,' Henry recalled.

'She was – is – but I know the other girls will drag her out of it.' Tara pulled a packet of cigarettes out of her pocket and offered one to Henry, who shook his head. Smoking was one of the few bad habits he did not have. She lit one and took a deep drag, exhaling the lungful of smoke with obvious relief. Henry watched her smoke. 'It's the third horse we've had mutilated.'

'All in the stables overnight?'

'Yes.'

'What's your security like?'

'Good. At least I thought so.'

'Do you have staff at the stables?'

'Yeah – but not on site.'

Henry suggested, 'Have you upset anyone recently?'

'Not that I know of.' She shrugged and smoked some more. 'I'll pay you if you come and investigate for us. A grand up front, even if all you do is come along and ask a few pertinent questions of different people. Then, if you stay longer charge me whatever you want to charge. I need to get this sorted and the local cops or our own security people don't seem interested or capable.'

'Your own security people?'

'Mmm . . . tossers.'

'What do you mean, your own security people?'

'My husband's businesses need security on the sites he owns. We use them for the stables, too.'

'What does your husband do?'

'Mainly he's a building contractor. Has other interests, too.' She looked unimpressed as she spoke. 'Haulage, import and export, all sorts of boring crap, building-site clearance. It's the building sites that need security to stop pilfering.'

'Who is your husband?'

'John Lloyd Wickson.'

Now things made more sense to Henry. Pieces were slotting into place. He did not know Tara Wickson, but knew of John Lloyd Wickson, certainly by reputation.

Suddenly, interrupting his thoughts, came a burst of laughter as the three girls, Kelly, Charlotte and Leanne, appeared from the stables. They were red-faced, breathless and happy.

Quickly, Tara said, 'If you come along and take a look at things, the payment will be discreet. Nothing official. Cash in hand. A grand, minimum.'

'Dad! Dad!' Leanne shouted, running towards him. 'What about McDonald's . . . please, please, pleeeease!' The other two girls were right behind her.

'What about it, Mum?' Charlotte said to Tara.

'I don't mind, but where's Kelly's mum or dad? I'll take you all, then drop you all back off at home – if you don't mind, Henry, and if Kelly's parents don't have a problem.'

'Sure,' said Henry. 'No probs.'

'Here's my mum,' Kelly exclaimed and ran off towards her. Charlotte and Leanne drifted away, chattering excitedly. Leaving Henry and Tara.

'So . . . will you do it?' Her eyes pleaded with him and he went weak. Women did that to him: one look and he was hooked. He was a tart.

'I really don't think I can promise anything,' he said with a new-found inner strength, which immediately wilted under Tara's saddened gaze. 'OK, OK, I'll come and have a look round, but as much as I'd like a thousand pounds in my back pocket, I'll have to forego any payment, thanks very much. It could make things a bit . . . difficult,' he said, screwing up his face. 'These things are apt to get out.'

'You are too honest for your own good,' Tara smiled. She handed him a card with her phone numbers on it. 'Mobile and home,' she said, her eyes holding his again. She also described exactly where she lived and how to get to the house. 'Maybe I could pay you in kind,' she said mischievously.

So Henry was right after all. She did want to go to bed with him.

Two

'**S**urprise visitors!'

Kate Christie sat up sharply and looked out of the front window. She and Henry were sat with trays on their laps, eating Sunday tea whilst watching the natural history segment on BBC2. This had become a ritual over the last couple of months. Just the two of them, no daughters. They always seemed to be out at friends. Henry had grown to appreciate this time with Kate – preparing the meal together, drinking wine as they did, then sitting side by side on the settee, usually in silence as they ate and watched nature in the raw. It was something he had never done before on a regular basis, chilling out with her, and he found himself to be slightly annoyed to be interrupted by the unexpected guests, whoever they were. He and Kate were actually divorced, but were back together and had been for some time. Things were going pretty well. One day soon, he would be asking her to re-marry him. He tore his eyes away from a pride of lions feasting on an unfortunate antelope.

From where Kate was sitting, she had the view out of the window to the drive at the front of the house. Henry had to crane his neck to see who had landed.

There was a massive four-wheel-drive monster in the driveway behind the family Mondeo.

Henry relaxed and smiled.

'I wonder what they're doing here,' he said, rising and rushing with his tray into the kitchen, depositing it on a work surface, then striding down the hall to the front door, opening it just before the bell rang.

Two kids raced towards him, toddlers, and grabbed his legs affectionately, but with a force that nearly toppled him over. 'Hey, hey,' he warned, 'steady on.'

Behind the children were the parents, the Donaldsons.

'Well this is a turn-up for the books,' Henry beamed.

'In the area, just passing, thought we'd call in and say hi,' said the big American, Karl Donaldson. He extended his huge paw, grabbed Henry's tiny one, shook it, dragged Henry to him and encircled him with a bear hug. Henry had no choice but to succumb until, ribs almost broken, he was freed. Henry turned to Karen. They embraced with less pressure and kissed.

'You look really well, all of you,' Henry said, appraising them, bending down to kiddie level and rubbing the heads of both little boys.

'Henry! Invite them in,' Kate's voice ordered behind him.

'Kate!' shrieked Karen, shouldering Henry aside and hurtling towards her.

Henry shrugged at Donaldson. 'Maybe we should swap partners,' he suggested. 'You and me together and those two together. Life would be much simpler.'

'I don't really want to sleep with you,' Donaldson admitted.

'Oh, OK,' Henry said, feigning disappointment. 'You'd better come in then.'

How the two men managed to pull it off, neither was sure, but after rustling up some grub for the uninvited foursome, Henry and Donaldson were allowed out to the pub.

They were given one hour maximum.

The pub was on the outer edge of the housing estate on which Henry lived. It was a modern, soulless sort of place which made big-bucks from serving up food that Henry described as 'pre-packaged crap'. In truth, the food was not that bad and he and Kate and the girls had had occasional meals there. It was called the Tram and Tower, references to two of Blackpool's many delights. It was divided into two sections, restaurant and bar. Without exception the bar was always quiet, even when the restaurant was heaving.

Henry and Donaldson sat opposite the entrance, giving themselves a good wide-angled view of the happenings in and around the bar. Henry glanced at Donaldson as he gazed around the room, then he himself looked around to see that each woman in the place was getting an eyeful, either slyly or obviously, of the big, bronzed, good-looking bastard sat next to him. Henry had often contemplated, in a very sexist way, that he could have had a fantastic life for himself just feasting off Donaldson's cast-offs. Henry believed that the American was one of the few men who, truly, could have the choice of any woman he wanted. Henry hated him deeply because of this.

However, Henry also knew that Donaldson was deep into fidelity and worshipped Karen. Henry wished that he was as angelic as his friend because, all too often, his tarnished halo had slipped.

'It's good to see you, you ugly swine.'

'And you, pal.'

They had been friends for half a dozen years now. Donaldson worked for the FBI's legal attaché in London. The two men had met when Donaldson had been investigating American mob activity in the north-west of England. They had since worked together on a number of investigations and had become good friends. Donaldson had met and subsequently married Karen, who had been a serving police officer in the Lancashire Constabulary at the time. She had since transferred to the Metropolitan Police and they lived within commuting distance of the capital. Donaldson travelled in daily to his office in the American Embassy on Grosvenor Square and Karen drove to the Police Staff College at Bramshill, where she was seconded as a lecturer on the Strategic Command Course. Their life seemed settled and idyllic.

'How ya doing?' Donaldson asked. 'You look a whole lot better than when I last saw you.' Which was a week after Henry had been suspended.

Henry shrugged. 'Learning to take it as it comes.'

Donaldson was concerned, though. He knew Henry of old and had seen him crack before. 'You sure you're coping?'

'Yeah. It's helped that me and Kate are really together now. She's been a rock.'

'Good . . . when's the full inquest?'

'Not sure yet. Don't even know when the trial is. Don't even know when my internal hearing is . . . but I have a sneaking feeling they might go for me before the court trial.'

'Why?'

'To get rid. To cover their backs. To make them look good. They need a scapegoat and I'm going to be it, I reckon.'

'You did nothing wrong, Henry.' Donaldson sipped his Stella Artois. 'There's no way they'll nail you.'

'Karl . . . a cop got shot and wounded, a vital witness almost died and then two baddies ended up dead . . . they might have a case, y'know. The more I dwell on it . . .' Henry stared into space, his mouth distorted glumly. 'Sometimes I think I might give up without a fight . . . see if I can get out with my pension intact.'

'Don't you ever fucking dare,' Donaldson warned him. 'Now you really are worrying me.'

'They've closed ranks, Karl, and they've got all the ammo.'

Both men drank their lagers in silence. Eventually Henry inhaled a deep breath. 'So what drags you up here – really?'

'A combination. An opportunity to mix family business and business business. We've visited the in-laws and Karen's going to stay on for the week with the terrible duo. I'm working up here tomorrow, going back to London for the rest of the week, then coming back on Saturday to pick up Karen et al.'

'I suppose you're doing what I think you're doing?'

'Yeah, Zeke,' Donaldson said. A look of severe anguish crossed his face. He took a long draught of Stella.

Mm, Zeke, thought Henry, experiencing a sudden flashback to the scene of a double murder under the shadow of a motorway bridge. Two men lying there, one across the other, both with their heads blown apart. One of them was Zeke. Or to be more correct, his real name was Carlos Hiero and he was an undercover FBI agent working deep down in a gang controlled by a Spaniard called Mendoza who had links with American Mafia families. Zeke was his code name and he had been unfortunate enough to have been discovered. The other man was called Marty Cragg, a local hoodlum who owed Mendoza money he was unable to repay. Both had been ruthlessly assassinated on Mendoza's orders.

Henry knew that Zeke's undercover status had been rumbled by the indiscretions of Karl Donaldson's boss down at the Legat; Phillipa Bottram had been weak and foolish enough to let her bisexual appetite get her drawn into divulging confidential information to a woman with connections to Mendoza's criminal gang. It had been Donaldson's courage to have Bottram put under surveillance that netted her wrongdoing.

'How is the investigation going?'

'As regards Zeke, the murder investigation is getting nowhere. We're no closer to Mendoza yet, though our intelligence suggests he did order the hit and may well have been present when it happened. Your investigation is, quite rightly, concentrating on tracking down the hit man. We – the FBI – are going for Mendoza, but he's wrapped in cotton wool . . . although,' Donaldson said mysteriously, 'I might just be getting somewhere on that front. Dunno. Can't say more yet.'

'A source?' asked Henry.

'As I said – can't say.'

Henry understood. Informants were fickle things. Getting them was like playing a trout on the fly. More often than not, they swam away never to be lured again. 'What about Phillipa Bottram?'

Donaldson snorted, disgusted. 'That bitch –' he almost spat the word – 'as good as pulled the trigger on Zeke herself, and what happened? Ill-health pension.'

Henry snorted too. 'The FBI sounds just like our lot.'

'No cojones. She's back home in the States, free as a bird. No blemish on her character. Not what you know, but who you know. She's well in with the top political brass, I figure . . . or is that me being cynical, but if I'd done what she'd done, my testicles would be stuck down my throat by now.' Donaldson's face mirrored his feelings.

'Outrageous.'

'We're pretty sure the hit man's killed at least two more people for Mendoza since. One in France, one in Andorra.'

'Any leads?'

Donaldson shook his head. 'It's the weapon that links them, same as the one used for Zeke and Cragg. Your – Lancashire's, that is – investigation is widening. Lots of trips to exotic locations for your boys. Barcelona and Paris, France, to name but two.'

70

'Could've been me jetting off,' Henry said wistfully. 'Not to be, though.' He rolled his eyes as he thought about what he was missing. Not just the 'jollys', as they called them, but the cut and thrust of high-profile inquiries. 'But, I have been asked to do a bit of investigating work on the side for the mother of a friend of Leanne's.'

'Oh?'

'Yeah and whilst it's hardly international stuff, it might be a bit of something to do, have some fun.' He drained his pint and did a time check. He looked at his and his companion's empty glass. 'At least two more, I reckon.' He gathered them up. 'Same again?'

Deep in the undergrowth, Verner smiled to himself as he looked through the night sights. He was enjoying himself because this was just a bit different from the usual stuff he was paid to do. It was fun and easy and for once, although this did not make any difference to him in the least, no one was going to get hurt. Only animals. Only horses. The people would just get a scare.

It was 9 p.m. He watched the security guard saunter boredly around the stables some 200 metres away from his position.

From where he was, on a hill to the south of the stables, he had a good view across the main yard, which was open at one side, but with stable blocks on the other three sides. Each stable door was now locked and bolted, the hired stable-lad having carried out this task an hour earlier, then left for home. Each horse was now locked up and safe for the night.

He watched the security guard walk from door to door, trying each lock. Then he spun his view around to the main house, again a good 200 metres away to his left. Lights blazed at most windows, the family at home. Not a problem, thought Verner.

The sound of the engine starting up made him arc the night sights back to the stables. It was the security guard driving away in his van, the 'Wickson Security' logo on the side of it. He watched the van drive past the front of the main house, then down the long driveway to the main road.

Now the yard was still. The fluorescent yellow lights shone brightly.

Verner relaxed and thought about the hours to come.

His orders were to up the stakes tonight. So far, things had been pretty mild. 'Put the fear of God into them,' he had been instructed.

He thought about the horses he had hurt previously. And smiled. He enjoyed hurting. He enjoyed killing, too. But hurting was like a sport, a pastime, whereas killing was a profession.

Hurting had been fun. He had wondered what it would be like to hurt a horse, wondered if he would actually have disliked doing it, hurting a poor, dumb, defenceless creature. But it had been excellent because they were not actually dumb enough not to show terror in their eyes. As he'd slashed them, their expressions had been glorious to behold.

Tonight, though, he had been told to go one step further.

The pair made it back with about thirty seconds to spare – just at the point where the ladies were getting a little agitated and the children, because it was late and they were tired, fractious.

Kate and Henry stood at the door and waved Karl and his family off. As the 4x4 turned out of sight, Henry slid his arm around Kate's slim waist and planted a kiss on the side of her face.

She pulled away from him slightly.

'Drink equals friskiness with you, doesn't it?'

'Not necessarily,' he said, mocking offence. Then, 'OK – yes it does.'

They closed the front door and melted into each other's arms. 'It's a good job I've had half a bottle of Blossom Hill red then, isn't it?' Her face tilted up. He kissed her slowly, gently, deliberately.

'Think we've got time to . . . y'know? Before the girls get back?'

'Is it going to be a slowie or a quickie?'

'Long and slow . . . I've had a drink, remember?'

She gulped. 'Even if they come back, they wouldn't interrupt us, would they?'

'Wouldn't dare.' Henry took her hand and led her upstairs, feeling very frisky indeed.

The chill of the night did not bother Verner. He had been in far colder, more uncomfortable places.

It was an hour since the security patrol had left. At the main house, some lights had been turned off, leaving only the main lounge and one bedroom light on. The time was slowly approaching. His watch said 10.17.

There was some movement in the stable yard. Quickly he put the night sights to his eyes.

It was a teenage girl, dressed in jeans and a sweatshirt top. She was edging her way around the yard, keeping to the shadows. What the hell was she up to? And who the hell was she? He could not quite get a sharp focus on her face, but he kept the glasses held firmly to his eyes, watching her movements. It was obvious she was trying to keep unseen. She dashed quickly across the yard, then back into the darkness of the stables. Verner could clearly see her at the door of one of the loose boxes. She was messing with the lock. Suddenly the door opened and she went inside, closing it behind her.

'Shit,' Verner breathed to himself. A delay, maybe a complication. What was she up to? He breathed out, relaxed, waited.

Ten minutes later she emerged, locking the stable door behind her. She paused, rushed across the yard and disappeared behind the building that was the tack room. Verner next picked her up in his sights as she ran towards the main house.

Twenty minutes after that, the security patrol car re-entered the grounds and parked in the middle of the stable yard. The driver got out and checked each stable door carefully, then left.

Security sure is tight, Verner thought.

Henry's promise to Kate came true. Their lovemaking was long and sensual, not always slow, sometimes fast and furious and with abandon, but always – always – with love and respect. It was as though he and Kate had just invented sex. It reminded him of the times all the years before when they were courting

73

and then newly wed when they went for it at every opportunity – and they were determined to enjoy it to the full today.

When their daughters arrived home together, Henry slowed down to a stop, remaining deep inside Kate, who, with mischief, used her internal muscles to drive him wild, making Henry gasp with pleasure.

'Oi,' he warned her.

'What?' she said innocently.

Jenny shouted, 'Good night you two – we know what you're doing!' The girls giggled naughtily, then went to their respective bedrooms.

Henry and Kate laughed quietly. Sex had never been so much fun for them.

'Now then,' he said, 'time to get my own back.'

When it was over, they lay embracing face to face, locked tight in each other's limbs.

'That was lovely,' Kate sighed, her face nuzzling one of Henry's nipples.

He breathed out contentedly and closed his eyes.

Sometime later as they lay dozing, Henry said, 'I got propositioned today.'

Doing the horse had been a lot of fun. It was a power thing. Slashing cuts across the buttocks with a cut-throat razor, then going for one of the eyes, driving the stiletto into the eyeball, causing it to burst with a fantastic 'pop' and a spray of clear liquid. Then slicing off its mane and shearing the tail.

All good fun and very necessary to prove a point.

Kate did not like the idea at all. It showed in her whole demeanour and tone of voice. At least Henry was not surprised and he was ready for it with his argument, which, admittedly, he knew was pretty thin.

'You could get into trouble,' Kate informed him.

'It's just gonna be me bummin' around, asking a few questions, that's all. I know four people in the area with convictions for mutilating horses. It'll probably be one of them. They're easy people to deal with for someone like me. Just very weird.'

'I didn't mean that,' Kate said coldly. 'I meant with work.' She sighed through her nose, a sure sign she was pissed off. She was sat up in bed, knees drawn up with her arms folded around them. Still naked. 'You've got enough problems without having more by doing some unofficial investigating.'

'I'm not going to get paid for it. It'll just be helping a friend of my daughter.'

'Hm,' sniffed Kate. She shook her head. Did not like it one bit.

Henry lay next to her, also naked. Both of them were well tanned from frequent forays to the sun during his time of suspension. Both were trim and fit-looking. Henry ran a hand up the underside of her thigh, stopping at her buttocks. He allowed a finger to touch her sex. She shivered involuntarily and closed her eyes.

'Don't,' she said weakly. 'That won't change my mind. I don't think you should get involved in anything, whatever it is, love. You need to keep focused on clearing your name, nothing else. Clearing your name and getting back to work.'

'I know, I know.' He rolled on to his back, slid his hands behind his head. 'Just sounded like . . . summat to do.'

'The front room needs redecorating.'

'You know what I mean.'

'Yeah, yeah, I know.' He shut his eyes and curled his lips sardonically. Suddenly Kate planted a kiss on his mouth, hard, then let it dissolve into a wet mush of tongue, saliva and teeth, gums and the insides of each other's mouths. She reached down and grabbed hold of him, forcing a grunt to escape from his throat. She eased a leg over him, slid him inside her and moved over him, rotating her hips slowly. She was very good at this.

Henry did not admit it to her, but he would not change his mind either. He had stubbornly decided to himself that he would be taking a look into Tara Wickson's mutilated horses, no matter how much sex he had on a plate.

Verner unlocked the tack room by jemmying the hasp off, and was inside quickly. The aroma of cleaned leather greeted him. Down one wall were complete tack sets for eight horses

– saddles, bridles, blankets, everything required to kit out a horse. They smelled lovely, he thought. What a shame.

He started at the far corner of the room, splashing out the petrol on the floor and as high up the wooden walls as possible, and on the equipment. The smell of accelerant soon replaced that of leather. He breathed it in and it sent him slightly dizzy.

He tossed a lighted match into the room. The fumes caught it immediately with a hissing boom as air got sucked into the flames. The man smiled and stepped smartly out of the tack room, leaving the door ajar to help with airflow.

The wooden structure was ablaze within seconds.

Henry Christie waited in the corridor. Which corridor it was, he could not be certain, but he was waiting his turn, elbows on knees, hands interlocked, fingers twiddling. His stomach churned. He felt sick. He was waiting to go into the hearing, to be called into the internal discipline proceedings which would seal his fate.

Someone drifted by in front of him. He looked up. A woman's face sneered at him.

'No chance, Henry . . . you're going . . . going . . .' Then she was gone.

Henry suddenly noticed he was not wearing any socks or shoes. He was barefoot and his feet were in sand. He wriggled his toes. The sand was warm.

A bell began to ring.

Henry knew it was his summons to the beginning of the end of his career.

The bell continued to ring.

Henry shook his head. Kate dug him in the side. 'Answer the phone,' she muttered groggily.

The ringing continued and somewhere between sleep, dreams and wakefulness, Henry reached out to the bedside phone, fumbling in the dark, almost knocking the lamp off the cabinet.

'Hello,' he said. His tongue was stuck to the roof of his mouth and the word was more a snorted breath than a properly formed sound.

'Is that Henry Christie?' a female voice asked, sounding worried.

Henry propped himself on to an elbow and squinted at the red figures of the digital alarm clock. 03:40. God, it was just like being in the cops and being on call, he thought fleetingly.

'Yep.'

'I'm really sorry to disturb you. This is Tara Wickson, we spoke yesterday at the riding school?'

Henry recognized the voice and thought, Twenty to bloody four in the morning! It was the first time for a long time that he'd been woken at this time, other than because of his state of mind. This better be good.

'Yeah, it's OK.' He found his voice. He switched the bedside light on. 'What is it? Something happened?'

'You could say that. Someone's tried to burn down the stables. Could you please come? I'm really sorry it's such a crap time and even though the police are here, I'd really like you to come and have a look and help.' She sounded desperate, close to tears and hysteria, just keeping a lid on it. 'One of the horses has been mutilated, too, others have . . .' There was a sob in her voice as she failed to complete the sentence. 'Oh God, it's awful.'

Henry glanced at Kate. She was awake now, listening and glaring.

'No,' her lips formed silently. 'NO WAY.'

Henry dithered. He was stuck between the strong desire to poke his nose into other people's business and his wish to appease Kate. Both had their pros and cons, but what swung it for him was the arrogant belief that he could talk his way round Kate and make it OK. After all, he had done it so many times before.

He turned away from her and spoke into the phone.

'Give me half an hour.'

'Thanks, thanks,' Tara gushed.

He hung up and swivelled very, very gingerly to Kate. 'Sorry,' he said pathetically. She slumped back angrily, defeated, and pulled the duvet over her head.

'I despair,' she said.

77

'I knew you'd understand.' He reached for his underpants, a glimmer of a smile on his lips.

His excitement was almost uncontrollable. Adrenalin rinsed through his veins as he drove out towards the Wickson household just as a reluctant dawn was beginning to crack the night sky open. That same old feeling of trepidation and anticipation came back: approaching the unknown, wondering where it would all lead, who he would meet, who he would have conflict with, what would it show him about human nature and – most of all – what it would reveal about himself. It was fantastic, nothing could ever touch it.

The Wickson place was on the outskirts of Poulton-le-Fylde, one of Blackpool's more salubrious neighbouring towns.

As the sky grew a slightly lighter shade of pale, he could see smoke rising in the distance.

Henry's throat was parched, mainly because of the beer he had drunk in the pub before bed. He should have thrown some coffee down before setting off, but he had been eager to get going. To get, for the first time in months, to the scene of a crime.

Three

The old feeling stayed with him as he drove down the long driveway towards the house, which was dead ahead of him, and the stables, which were to his right.

Looking across he could see a lot of chaotic activity. Two fire engines, two marked police cars and an ambulance, as well as other vehicles. Blue lights rotated a-plenty. Dozens of people, it seemed, scurried about and the reflective jackets of the uniformed services glistened against the blue lights, head-lights and the approaching daylight.

Henry parked outside the house, not wishing to add to the confusion of vehicles and bodies down at the scene. This was an old habit of his. Whenever and wherever possible he liked to approach any crime scene from a distance. 'I like to come from downwind, with the sun at my back,' he was fond of saying. He always felt it gave him an advantage . . . somehow. It allowed him to make assessments and start shuffling the pack of cards in his head that was his combination of experience, skills and abilities of being a detective.

Not that he was a detective at present, just a cop on suspension.

So what the hell was he doing here?

The question hit him hard as he pulled up and parked on the gravel at the front of the Wickson house. He sat with his hands resting at the ten to two position on the steering wheel and thought seriously about withdrawing.

Curiosity got the better of him.

He looked at the house in front of him, a big, double-fronted, extensively extended and modernized former farmhouse. All the lights were on, the front door open. It was a house that oozed wealth. To the left side of it he could now make out a tennis court and beyond that a helicopter landing pad. He thought it would be safe to assume there would be a swimming pool out back somewhere.

All in all, very nice. The domicile of a rich and successful person, as Henry knew John Lloyd Wickson was. Henry, an avid reader of the county magazine *Lancashire Life* – mainly to gawp enviously at the property pages – had seen Wickson several times in the social pages. He was always attending charity events, race meetings and had been profiled on a couple of occasions by the magazine's money section. Henry thought he should re-read one of the profiles sometime. But he did remember enough to recall that Wickson's wealth was estimated somewhere in the region of about fifty million. Not bad for somebody who began his working life as a bricklayer, or so the story went.

As he got out of the car, he glanced at the other cars parked on the gravel. One was the Mercedes Tara Wickson had been driving, another was a huge Bentley, a lovely car which Henry estimated would cost over a hundred and twenty grand. He was surrounded by big bucks, that much was obvious.

He turned away from the Bentley, then stopped dead in his tracks. There were another three cars on the gravel. One was a Ford Focus with a blue light clamped to the roof. Henry thought it probably belonged to the senior Fire Officer on scene, another, he guessed, was a plain cop car, but it was the third one which he instantly recognized and made him think, Oh bollocks! It was Jane Roscoe's car.

The sight of it almost made him jump back into his car and tear-arse away immediately. But, valiantly, he braced himself and trudged onwards.

The stables, some 200 metres to the right of the house, were accessed by means of a narrow lane just wide enough to allow passage for one vehicle, with drainage channels and fields on either side. Henry stepped aside to let the ambulance drive away. It did not seem to be in much of a hurry, so he guessed there were no patients on board. Perhaps it had been called as a precautionary measure. He walked on into the stable yard, the ever brightening dawn allowing him to get his bearings and make sense of the geography of the area. It was with a surprised jolt that he realized that the banks of the River Wyre were perhaps only a hundred metres away to his left as he walked to the stables.

It was very apparent where the seat of the fire had been.

There was a huddle of people scrummed down near the bonnet of one of the police cars: cops, fire fighters and Tara Wickson. Tara was gesticulating wildly. One of the cops was trying to keep her calm, using soothing hand movements. Henry recognized one of the uniformed cops, and another of the plain-clothed variety.

He held back a second, made up his mind, and approached the conflab.

Tara Wickson saw him coming and the frustration and exasperation in her body language seemed to wither and die. Her shoulders drooped. She broke away from the group of officials and made toward him. She stopped in front of him, her face a brave mask, which immediately crumbled. She bowed her head and started to sob in big, raking breaths which rattled her small frame.

'Get hold of me, Henry,' she pleaded. 'Squeeze me.'

Making sure there was no possible sexual connotation to this act, he put his arms around her and did as she wanted, though for the life of him he did not know why he did it. Instinct? He patted her back and almost said, 'There, there.'

The detective Henry had recognized came and stood behind Tara, a disgusted expression on her face. She grimaced at him over Tara.

'Henry, what the hell are you doing here?' She surveyed him, head tilted back, eyes looking down her nose.

Henry managed a shrug. 'Hello, Jane.' Tara stepped back and wiped her hands down her tear-stained face.

DI Jane Roscoe shook her head in disbelief.

This, Henry thought sardonically, was always going to be the problem: the distinct possibility of doing some unofficial digging on behalf of someone and bumping into the real cops who would get very shirty at any encroachment on to their patch. And in this case, to make matters worse, a real cop with whom he had recently been 'involved' and who was also a witness in the internal discipline proceedings being brought against him.

With a bit of soft prodding and cooing words, Henry managed to steer Tara Wickson back to the house, where in the kitchen he made a pot of tea for her and left her in the capable hands of a policewoman who looked pretty bloody annoyed to be doing such womanly work. 'Does it have to be a woman looking after her?' she whispered hoarsely. 'This is so sexist.' She folded her arms underneath her ample bosom.

'It's called caring for victims,' Henry told her in reaction to the expression on her face.

The policewoman almost sneered at him.

'Someone's got to do it,' he added. Political correctness interfering with the practicalities of policing often irked him intensely. To Tara, he said, 'I'll be back to have a chat once I've had a word with the detective inspector, OK?' The proximity of the policewoman made him aver from adding the word 'love' at the end of his sentence. She would probably have thought it sexist and patronizing.

Jane Roscoe was still in discussion with the Fire Service when Henry got back to the scene. She was deep into it and Henry did not interrupt.

He took the opportunity to have a closer look at the seat of the fire – in a row of loose boxes now completely flattened, charred and blackened. There were a couple of fire fighters still damping down and ensuring the fire would not reignite, spraying copious amounts of brown water on the debris from hoses they had run all the way down to the River Wyre. They were pretty much destroying any chance of recovering any useful evidence. Henry did not comment. Not his problem.

It was a mess. Out of a block of six stables, three had been completely destroyed, one partially burned down, the two remaining seeming relatively untouched. A building adjacent to the block had also been razed to the ground. Henry stood back and let his eyes wander around the devastation. He sniffed the air. In the smoke there was the unmistakable reek which Henry recognized straight away. One of those smells that, once inhaled, is never forgotten: the smell of burned flesh.

In this case, he assumed, horse flesh.

He gagged a little at the combination of the smell and the thought. The memory of the severed ear came back vividly to him.

Jane Roscoe was nodding at the Chief Fire Officer in such a way as to indicate their conversation was concluding. She shook his hand, broke away and walked to Henry. He watched her and, under his scrutiny, she dropped her gaze and looked away until she reached him. She stood a couple of feet away from him, raised her face and stared challengingly at him.

'Hello, Henry.'

'Jane.' He nearly bowed.

'Nasty business,' she observed.

He was not completely certain what she meant. There could easily have been a double meaning in her words because of their past history.

'This, you mean?' He jerked his head towards the remnants of the stables.

'What else would I be referring to?' she said flatly. 'Of course I mean the bloody fire.'

'Fair dos,' he said, backing off. 'What happened?'

'The stables have burned down.'

Mmm, he thought weakly. This was plainly not going to be easy. It was blindingly obvious Jane was still very prickly about the way things had ended between them and she wasn't going to give him an easy ride.

'I'll have that. But why have they burned down?'

'Because they've been set on fire?'

'Stop it, Jane.'

'OK,' she said. 'What's it got to do with you anyway?'

'Mrs Wickson has asked me to do a bit of poking around for her.'

Jane snorted. 'Poking around for her? Or poking around in her?'

'Stop it,' he warned her again.

'OK, OK, OK, I've stopped. Honest.'

'Apparently some of the horses have been mutilated in the past and the police haven't been very, let's say, result-orientated. She asked if I'd do a bit of snooping for her, see

83

if I could turn anything up . . . then this happens even before I come and do an initial inquiry.'

'You being a detective on suspension with no powers and no backup and plenty of time on your hands?' Jane interrupted.

'Something like that,' Henry said. His voice was beginning to betray his growing annoyance, which seemed to please Jane by the look on her face. He guessed she might just enjoy some sadistic pleasure in winding him up.

'Is that such a good idea?' she wanted to know.

'Probably not, but I'm doing it as a favour for her and I'm not getting paid for it in any way, shape or form,' he said pointedly, 'and because the local plods haven't really done anything much to help in the past, is there anything to suggest things are going to be different just because there's been a fire here? I can't see I'll be treading on anybody's toes, because it's more than likely there won't be any cops walking around here, doing their jobs, will there?' He sounded like Mr Moaner from Whinge Crescent, Cops 'r' Crapsville – and he quite liked his little tirade from the other side of the fence.

A smoke-filled silence descended between them, broken when Jane said, 'I miss you, Henry.'

'And I miss you, too, Jane, but we need to move on.' It sounded hard and the words did not come easily out of his mouth.

'You bastard.'

'Maybe . . . but can we get on with this? If you're going to help me, fine. If not I'll just dig around for info by myself. Actually, we might be of benefit to each other. I'll let you know what I find out, if you do the same for me.'

'I'll see,' she relented.

'I take it you're the night cover DI?'

'For my sins – and they are plenty.' She gave Henry a long, appraising look, swallowed and nodded, as if accepting the icy situation between them. It was obviously over and out.

'Is this an accident?' Henry asked about the fire. He sniffed up, smelling the petrol fumes.

'The Fire Brigade don't think so. They reckon accelerant has been used. The seat of the fire was in this building which used to store the tack. It burned down a treat and caught the adjoining stables. Have a look at this.' Jane moved to the first of the stables, now a dirty, ashy-grey, muddy mess. She pointed to the floor. Henry followed the line of her finger and, initially, could not make out what she was pointing at.

Then he made sense of what he was seeing.

There was a dark, black shape amongst the debris on the floor. The shape of a horse which had been burned to a frazzle.

Henry stepped back, shocked, but said nothing. He turned away and caught a gulp of fresh air amongst the rising smoke. His head slowly revolved back. He eyed Jane, who stood there impassively.

'There's another dead horse in the next stable,' she said, matter of fact.

Henry checked himself to get a grip. He had seen numerous dead bodies during the course of his career, but they had been human beings – exclusively – with the exception of a few dog accidents he'd reported during his time as a probationer PC in uniform, over twenty-five years earlier. He had seen bodies dismembered, blown to bits, drowned, shot, knifed, you name it, he'd dealt with it. But the sight and stench of a roasted horse was actually making him queasy. What was it about horses? he thought. He did not even like the beasts.

'I'll take your word for it.'

'They got the other horses out in time, released them into a field.'

'Anyone, any person hurt?'

'No.'

'Arson, then?'

'Very perceptive.'

'I'm sharp like that. Used to be a detective.'

'The best,' Jane said under her breath.

Henry did not quite catch it. 'Eh?'

'Nothing,' she said quickly, covering her tracks. 'Anyway,' she coughed, 'the burned-down buildings and the horse steaks are not everything. Come here.'

She took him across the stable yard, treading carefully over the hosepipes.

It was truly morning now. The sun was squinting in the sky. Things could be seen very clearly now with the fresh, raw light of that time of day. Henry surveyed the devastation the fire had wrought. His upper lips curled in distaste. He was beginning to feel that anger which had often driven him in the past. The anger born of the belief that no one should be allowed to get away with such crimes. It was an emotion that had often spurred him on when he had been a 'real' detective. Now that his status had changed, it did not mean that the anger and drive was any less within him.

Jane Roscoe was a few feet ahead of him. She was dressed in a very practical trouser suit that did little for her. Henry experienced a sudden pang of something in the pit of his tummy he could not quite explain. All he knew was that it was linked to the affair he and Jane had been conducting.

She went to a stable door, stopped and faced Henry. 'I could see you were affected by the dead horse.' He did not deny it. 'There's a mutilated horse in here,' she declared.

'Someone seems to have a downer on the Wicksons,' he said.

She nodded. 'It's not nice. You don't have to see it if you don't want.'

'Let's do it,' he said bravely.

Seconds later he wished he hadn't been so bold.

A truck from the local knacker's yard was reversing into the stables when Henry and Jane reappeared from the loose box. They watched as the two thick-set men in blood-stained overalls ran chunky chains around the corpse of the horse in the burned-out stable next to the tack room.

'How much of an interest will the police be taking in the plight of the Wickson's now?' he asked.

She yawned. 'Some, I suppose.'

'I take it this isn't the first job you've been to tonight?'

'No – a serious wounding in Blackpool, an iffy suicide in Lytham and another bad assault in Fleetwood.'

'Busy night.'

'Normal night.'

'I'm envious.'

'Don't be – it's generally shite I get turned out to. Thick, poor people, hurting other thick, poor people. Or, as in this case, hurting thick, rich people.'

'You've become a cynic.'

'You made me into one, Henry.' She turned to him, sorrow in her eyes. 'I thought love could see anyone through anything.'

He was stumped.

'I was wrong, wasn't I?' she said simply and walked away.

Behind him, the stable door opened and Charlotte Wickson, Tara's daughter, emerged, together with the vet who had been treating the horse. Charlotte was tearful and deeply upset because it was her horse, Chopin, her own, her very own. And someone had violated him again. He had already had an ear severed. Now this torture.

'He'll be all right, won't he?' she said to the vet.

'Yes, he will, but he's going to need a lot of care and attention from now on. The wounds will heal. He'll never see again through that eye – but he'll be able to get used to that, eventually, though I would not recommend jumping any more. It's the psychological damage that'll take time to heal. Do you think you can give him all the love and attention he needs?'

Charlotte nodded bravely.

'I'll be back later in the day to remove that eye under anaesthetic. I'll call in to see your mother before I go,' the vet said, nodded sharply at Henry and ambled across the yard.

Henry heard Charlotte emit a long, stuttering sigh.

'How you doing?' he asked her.

'Shit,' she said, startling him. 'He's a mess, isn't he?'

'Yep.' Henry could not actually shake the vivid image of the injured horse from out of his mind. The slashes, the cuts, the fear in the eyes. 'So what's this all about?' he asked Charlotte.

The young girl shrugged, her eyes slitting momentarily in a gesture Henry had seen on hundreds of people in the past. It made him become alert, because he had not expected it from her. It meant she knew something, or had some idea.

'Who do you think did this?'

'How would I know?' Her voice contained a trace of irritation. 'There's hundreds of suspects out there,' she said with a sneer. 'Fucking hundreds – including me.' She pushed her way past Henry and hurried towards the house. Henry was tempted to give chase, but refrained. She could wait till later.

Jane Roscoe was standing on the other side of the yard, observing the interaction with interest. Henry mooched across to her, hands thrust deep in his jeans pockets.

'How much time are the police going to dedicate to these particular crimes?' Henry persisted.

'How much time would you, Henry? Some wooden buildings have been burned down, a couple of dumb horses have been killed, another one cut to ribbons. No one's been hurt. I have a desk full of unsolved crimes which are performance indicators and this one isn't. I'll refer it to the Arson Team and let them get on with it.'

'It'll get a good half hour, then?'

'If they're lucky.'

'In that case, it won't hurt very much if I do some snooping around on behalf of the family.'

'You are very misguided, Henry. If I were you, I'd leave it be. The Wickson family are a pretty sad bunch—'

'How do you know?' Now she had alerted his senses.

Her eyes went very snake-like. 'I just do,' she said in a tone that left Henry in no doubt: Don't push it, is what she was saying.

'I haven't seen John Wickson, husband and father,' Henry said. 'Is he knocking about?'

'Away on business, but on his way back now, I believe.'

Henry and Jane regarded each other. His nostrils were filled with the smell of burnt wood and flesh. Neither spoke even though both of them knew there was a great deal of unfinished business between them. Despite Henry's urge to delve into her feelings, he held back, not wanting to go down there and re-light the flames he had well and truly doused months before.

'Any news on the inquest? Trial? My discipline hearing?' he asked instead, hoping to steer the conversation away from anything connected with their emotional entanglement to a subject which he knew was equally controversial. He should not have been surprised when she said, 'You know I can't talk to you about that. I've been warned not to.'

'Seems like we have little common ground, then.'

'None at all, I'd say.' She raised her eyebrows. 'But if you're in any way curious, I'm well over you, Henry. I might miss you, but that's all, and that's receding nicely. It would be silly to rake over old coals.' She sniffed and glanced at the remnants of the stables and tack room. She looked back at Henry. 'Ironic, eh, that we should meet again and be talking over something that's been destroyed?'

'Highly.' Henry was suddenly distracted. He cocked his head to one side and listened intently, his face screwed up as he concentrated.

'What is it?'

'Approaching helicopter.' He lifted up a finger for hush. The noise, faint at first, increased steadily. He looked east towards the rising sun, squinting and shielding his eyes. The noise grew to a throb.

A helicopter appeared over the horizon, the sun behind it.

At first Henry thought it was the Force helicopter, but it wasn't. It was too small.

It buzzed overhead and in one flash of sunlight across the fuselage he made out the words 'Wickson Industries'.

'John Lloyd Wickson,' Jane shouted over the sound of the rotor blades.

'Daddy's come home . . . that's nice.'

The helicopter swooped and dropped gently to the heli-pad on the other side of the main house. It hovered, then came to rest. Two figures climbed out, heads low, running towards the house.

'I'm going to go and meet him,' Jane said, adding, begrudgingly, 'Come if you want.'

'How kind.'

They set off together.

'Oh, got some news for you, Henry.'

'What would that be?'

'We're getting a new Chief Constable. Have you heard?'

'No.'

As they walked, Henry could actually feel a rift between them which seemed insurmountable. It was a mistake for him to have turned out, he realized, but then again, how could he have known he would be bumping into Jane Roscoe, someone he hadn't seen or spoken to for such a long time? If it had been any other detective inspector, there might have been fewer problems.

Henry – unknowingly – grunted in frustration.

'What?' Jane asked.

He gave her a look of query. 'I didn't say anything.'

'You did.'

'Nothing, it was nothing.' As he looked at her, something caught his eye in the distance behind her – on the hillside, maybe a quarter of a mile away. He thought nothing of it. Just his eyes playing tricks or just the early dawn sun catching something. Then it was there again. He stopped, stared, thought better of it and caught up with Jane, who had not paused.

'I think we're being spied on.'

'Paranoid as ever.'

'No – someone's watching us from up there.' Jane started to turn. Henry snapped, 'Keep going, don't look.'

When he reached the house he said, 'I'm going to have a look. I'm curious.'

Jane shook her head sadly. 'It'll be nothing. Just hens.'

'Hens?' The reply puzzled him, then he shook it off. 'Maybe it is hens, or maybe it's the person who set fire to the place, noseying about what's going on . . . returning to the scene of the crime. One of life's true clichés, I know, but one that's served me well in the past. People come back to gloat. Human nature.'

'Lecture over? And, anyway, what would you know about human nature?' she said harshly.

Without a further word he walked off to his car, giving a little wave, and saying, 'Hens?' under his breath. Jane watched him, wanting to tell him to be careful, but could not bring herself to say the words which would betray her true feelings for the man who had dumped her, the man she yearned for.

She stood rooted to the spot, seeing Henry drive all the way off the property, only turning to the house when his car went out of the gates. She went to the open front door. From inside she could hear the sound of raised voices. Before knocking, she glanced over her shoulder and her stomach churned as her eyes also caught something bright on the hillside. Not a hen, she thought stupidly, not unless it's wearing shiny jewellery.

Henry was glad of any excuse to get away from Jane, happy to retreat from an interaction that was starting to confuse and worry him. He thought that he was over her, but seeing her again had rekindled the feelings and jumbled up his mind, and he did not like it at all. He was trying not to do emotion anymore.

He drove down a country lane and pulled in close by a roadside hedge, about a mile and a half away from the house. He calculated that if he walked back to the Wickson house across the countryside and fields from where he was, he should, somewhere along the line, pass the point where he saw the glint of reflected light. That was his theory, anyway.

The sun was creeping nicely up the sky. It would be a crisp, clear day. There was a nippy chill in the air and his breath was clearly visible. He locked the car and trotted down the road a hundred metres or so. He was about to hop over a five-barred gate, when he saw a car parked just off the road, in some bushes opposite. It was a strange place for a vehicle at any time. He walked over to it and gave it a once over. Then he returned to the gate and clambered over it. On landing, his trainers sank with a squelch into the ground. He muttered a curse, eased his feet out of the muddy patch and picked his way carefully across the grass. Cows grazed in the field, or just stood there doing whatever cows did with the cud. Henry steered clear of them. He was wary of their herd instinct. He had once dealt with the death of a man who had been trampled by cows which had chased him and his dog and cornered them. It had been a gruesome, muddy death. Ever since then Henry had gladly applied his stereotype to all big, four-legged creatures: don't trust the bastards.

The cows watched him with suspicion, all of them. But none made a move towards him. Much to his relief he made it unscathed to the opposite side of the field, where he mounted a stile which deposited him in the next field, this time populated by sheep. He had more time for sheep, never having had to deal

91

with a murder by a gang of them. They saw him and ran away bleating with fear, all gathering together in a corner, staring accusingly at him. He liked to have that sort of power over animals.

'Mint sauce,' he said under his breath and made it to the opposite side of the field, where there was no stile to be found, just a drainage channel and a barbed-wire fence separating the field from a wooded copse. Henry's feet were soaking wet, as were his legs up as far as his knees. Even though he had managed to avoid deep mud, the ground was soft and the going hard.

The channel in front of him was at least six feet wide, the fence beyond about four feet high. The channel was not doing a particularly good job as it was filled with water. The folly of what he was doing now struck him and he thought about retracing his steps. But it should not now be too far from where he had seen the reflection. Through the trees, out the other side, up the hill and down the other side should put him there. He hoped.

'Bugger.' He decided to take a run at the channel. He went back a few steps, accelerated and launched himself across the ditch. He lost his footing on the mushy grass as he pushed off, slipped and only just managed to reach the other side, where he totally lost grip. In an effort which required a great degree of physical exertion, he grabbed for a fence post. He missed. Went slap-down into the ground and slithered into the channel.

He lay face down for a few, very pissed-off moments, before struggling to his feet and dragging himself up to the fence with a slurp. He held on and looked down at himself with a sneer of annoyance. He was now wet through from waist to foot, covered in slime and mud and probably now carrying that infectious disease that rats passed in their urine which was fatal to humans. He clambered over the fence, catching his jeans on a barb and ripping them. His best – and only – pair of Levis.

He would have liked to laugh at the situation, but somehow the humour of the moment did not permeate through to him. He just felt stupid. And wet. And muddy. And wished he had stayed in bed.

After resting a moment to get his breath back, he began to trudge through the copse where every branch and twig seemed to snatch and grab at him, trying to hold him back. He found himself becoming increasingly angry and this made him less thoughtful about what he was doing. Instead of being sneaky and careful, he was thumping and crashing his way through the undergrowth like an elephant. He was more concerned with fighting trees than tiptoeing up behind a felon.

He burst through the other side of the copse into the light. He was breathing hard, so he stopped to let his lungs relax a little, then he ploughed on up the hillside on the other side of which, he guessed, would be the spy on the camp.

The going was easier up the slope, even though the hill was quite steep. On reaching the summit he crouched low, went down on to his knees, aware of the possible folly of revealing himself against the sky. Now he was being more cautious about his approach. He edged to the top of the hill, keeping down, but not quite on his stomach because he did not want to get any dirtier and wetter than he already was.

He raised his face gradually and peered over the crest of the hill, down towards a small scrubby area. Beyond that he had a good view of the stables, the house and the road connecting the two. Well beyond the house he could see the river. He knew he was about right in his positioning and that somewhere below him on the down slope was the point where he had seen the light.

There was still a lot of activity at the stables. The fire service were there, continuing their damping down. He made out a number of people emerging from the main house, one of which was Jane Roscoe. She stopped and, he imagined, looked across in his direction. He almost gave her a wave.

A small white van appeared in the driveway leading up to the house bearing the Lancashire Constabulary crest on the doors and the words 'Scientific Support' in black on the sides. The crime scene investigators had arrived, making Henry feel a little more reassured about the way Jane was intending to investigate the offence.

Henry looked beyond the house to some fairly dilapidated

93

farm buildings. They seemed incongruous against the refurbished luxury of the farmhouse that was the Wickson family home. A couple of old, articulated fuel tankers stood in the yard formed by these buildings. Henry squinted thoughtfully at the scenario. He tried to recall something which was lurking at the back of his cranium. Old farm buildings, old fuel tankers . . . what did that mean?

Suddenly he was not thinking about old buildings and trucks.

A movement had cut into the periphery of his vision, making his head jerk away from what he was surveying.

He stretched his neck, a feeling of high tension shooting through his body, certain he had seen something below. In the bushes, just to the right of his position. Something . . . someone . . . had definitely moved. But even as he stared and focused, he could see nothing.

He remained motionless, alert, did not move another muscle.

Only then did he realize just how dry his mouth had become and how remorselessly his heart was ramming against his rib cage. His eyes were sharp and his brain was now digesting the pros and cons of the stupidity of his current position.

Supposing there was somebody down there? Supposing it was the person who had set fire to the stables and maimed a horse? Would that person be a pleasant companion for a morning stroll back into the arms of the real police? What would happen if that person did not want to cooperate and was twice as big, wide and nasty as Henry? Henry had been stripped of his powers and could not legally do half of the things he had been doing without a second thought for the past twenty-odd years. Whoever it was down there would be well likely to be a mad, raving lunatic with instability problems of epic proportions. So what would Henry do if he came face to face with this deranged individual?

He could not radio for help. The personal radio, the bane of many a cop's life, the piece of equipment that Henry had only ever used when it suited him, was no longer in his tool kit. And now he missed it like mad. He felt naked and vulnerable.

Nor did he have any handcuffs.

Nor an extending baton.

Nor CS spray.

He realized with a lead-like thump that he was very much on his own out here. The resources of law and order were no longer at his beck and call.

Though he did have his mobile phone.

Staring down the slope in front of him, he hoped that what he had seen was a sheep doing a bit of lurking, as opposed to an arsonist and horse-molester. He could handle a sheep, however violent it became.

But it was not a sheep.

It was someone who was very good at not being seen. It was a man dressed in army-type combat camouflage clothing, edging on his stomach along the line of the field. Henry's mouth opened with a pop as he registered the fact that this man was more than good. He was almost invisible and it took a lot of blinking and re-focusing on Henry's part to keep him in sight.

Henry watched, fascinated. He found it tempting to stand up and begin waving his arms about to attract someone's attention down at the stables, but at such a distance he guessed it would be a fairly useless gesture – and it would warn the man they were on to him.

The figure crawled into a cluster of trees.

Henry's eyes kept with him.

Maybe the guy was innocent. He could just be a perv or maybe a white supremacist out on manoeuvres . . . one and the same, Henry thought.

However, innocent, guilty or just plain perverted, Henry knew the guy had to be collared and spoken to.

Henry watched as the man lay out on his stomach, twisted round and settled in the trees.

Henry was puzzled. He glanced towards the Wickson house. Three people, including Jane Roscoe, were still at the front of the house. He looked back at the prostrate figure and an ice-cold sensation shot through Henry's lower abdomen. There was something familiar about the position the man had adopted.

Henry began to move.

Fast.

After setting fire to the stables, Verner had retreated to his position on the hillside to watch the fun and games. They were gratifyingly splendid. The stable block lit up the night sky, flames rising high with the occasional crack as something inside exploded sending showers of sparks up into the atmosphere.

All extremely satisfying.

Watching the lights come on in the house. People dashing about like headless chickens. Panic setting in. The more fortunate horses being rescued from loose boxes and being turned out into an adjoining field. Then, almost twenty-five minutes later, the arrival of the fire brigade and the cops, by which time the tack room and some stables had been destroyed.

Verner did not move from his position for hours whilst he watched all the activity, using his night sights and then, as the night ebbed, his binoculars.

Other cops arrived. An ambulance turned up.

All this from just a little match and a splash of petrol.

He found himself giggling quite a lot.

Then the helicopter belonging to John Lloyd Wickson landed on the pad.

Now Verner was going to have more fun than ever. He came out of his hiding place and crawled along to another position where he had set up the rifle. He squirmed into the prostrate firing position and sighted down the barrel of the gun, picking out the figure of Wickson, who was standing at the front of his house, together with two other people. Wickson started to strut towards the stables.

He was an easy target.

Henry pushed himself over the brow of the hill, whilst at the same time using his mobile phone and trying to tab to Jane Roscoe's number which he still had stored in his phone. He hoped her number had not changed and even as he rose, a flash of thought went through his mind: Why did I keep her number?

He found it, pressed the call button and stumbled down the hill to where the man was lying in what Henry had recognized as the prone firing position.

He held the phone to his ear. He was about a hundred metres from the man as the phone rang out.

Jane Roscoe was not the sort of person to make snap judgements about people, but in the case of John Lloyd Wickson, she made an exception.

He was a dislikeable, arrogant shit-head, even if he was rich.

He immediately started by throwing his weight around, taking little notice of what she had to say and genuinely seemed surprised that, in this day and age, a woman could be a detective inspector.

She became increasingly angry with him as he flounced around his home, barking orders at people, shouting at his wife and snarling at his daughter. He had no hint of compassion about him, seemed purely self-centred.

Jane was very close to grabbing him and slapping his vermin-like features.

Eventually he relented somewhat and after a flurry of tirades at his family, he turned to Jane and said, 'I'm going down to look at the stables now – talk to me on the way.'

Then he was gone, hurrying through the house accompanied by the man who had arrived with him in the helicopter. Jane learned this was Wickson's head of security, a man she vaguely and uncomfortably recognized, but could not quite place. He was called Jake Coulton.

The three of them left the house and Wickson paused for a few moments at the front door to speak in hushed tones to Coulton, then set off for the stables. Jane scurried behind, trying to keep to the pace. As they got on to the track to the stables, her phone went.

'It's me, Henry,' came the breathless voice.

Instinctively Jane looked across to the distant hillside where she saw a tiny figure running down the hill.

'What is it?' she asked impatiently.

'Guy . . . up here . . . with a gun . . .' Henry panted.

And with that, the ping of the first bullet zipped by and dust flew up on the track just feet ahead of Wickson, followed a millisecond later by the crack of the shot.

'Get the fuck down!' Jane screamed. She dived for Wickson who had stopped in his tracks, incomprehension on his face. His security man had walked on, unaware that anything had happened. Jane rugby-tackled Wickson, smashed him to the ground and rolled him to the edge of the track, into the deep, wet ditch parallel to it. 'Somebody's shooting at you.'

The message got through to the security guy as another bullet lifted the track surface by his feet.

Henry had no way of being sure that his message had got through to Jane. As his run down the slope gathered momentum, his heels jarring, he yelled into his phone hoping that Roscoe understood what he was trying to say.

Whilst speaking, he heard the first shot crack in the morning air, like Indiana Jones's whip hitting its target.

Even pounding down the hill, getting faster and faster, Henry knew he should have veered away and gone to ground, to protect himself.

But his desire to protect life, ingrained deeply over the course of his career, made him – stupidly, some might say – carry on. The mobile phone dropped out of his hand and disappeared in the wet grass.

Verner heard Henry's thundering approach.

He fired another shot across the bows of John Lloyd Wickson, the noise whipping the air again, then twisted round to face Henry, trying to point the rifle at him. It snagged in the low branches of the tree and before he could bring the barrel round and aim and fire, Henry leapt wildly at him.

But Verner was quick.

He recovered and was able to use the rifle as a baton. He caught Henry a hard, well-aimed blow to the side of the head just before Henry could actually grab him. The impact twisted Henry's neck and sent him rolling across the grass.

Henry's mind was jarred for one black moment, but as he

hit the grass, clarity returned and he rolled up into a kneeling position, facing Verner who was still trying to pull the gun round and get it pointed at him. Henry pounced again, like an athlete leaving starting blocks.

He palmed the barrel of the gun away and went for the man holding it.

Henry would be the first to admit that he wasn't really a fighter. Although he had been through many scrapes in his time, often coming off poorly, he did not have the technique of a trained attacker. He had been taught many defensive tactics, but few which went the other way and he knew that his best strengths lay in his ability to overpower, rather than beat into submission.

When faced with someone who really knew what he was doing, Henry knew there would be a good chance of coming off second best.

Although Henry clearly had the advantage of position and the fact that the man on the ground had relinquished the rifle, Henry did not see the blow coming. It was just a blur as the man's left fist connected. Suddenly Henry's jaw jarred, his head jerked upwards and then it was him on the floor, the man having now recovered his position.

A glint of steel. In Verner's right hand there was now a knife. It sliced through the air towards Henry's abdomen. His eyes shot open and he reacted by twisting to one side, but not quite far enough and quick enough. He felt the blade slice through his clothing and along the edge of his ribs. His skin split with an exquisite sort of pain. He gasped, continued twisting away, and the knife rose again, this time plunging back down towards his chest.

Henry's hands grasped Verner's wrist, just preventing the point of the blade from piercing his ribs, halting it less than an inch above his chest.

Henry and Verner stared into each other's eyes.

Verner laughed.

It was the moment Henry needed. Just that one moment which was a lack of concentration on Verner's part.

He kicked out, connecting with Verner's left hip.

This time Verner went sprawling and the knife flipped out

of his grasp, spinning away and embedding itself in the soft ground.

Henry was up, going for him.

But Verner had also recovered, was up on his feet, powering towards Henry. They met like a couple of trucks in a head-on collision, then grappled with each other like wrestlers. They teetered over and rolled down the slope, hitting, kicking and trying to head-butt each other, both frenzied, fighting their own separate agendas.

They fought with the ferocity of bears.

When they stopped rolling, Henry found himself trapped underneath Verner. Verner's right hand was around his wind-pipe, squeezing hard and forcing Henry's head back, his knees pinning Henry's arms to the ground.

Henry gurgled, fought, writhed and desperately tried to break free.

Jane Roscoe raised her head to where she had last seen Henry Christie on the hillside. Now she could not see anyone.

'Keep your head down,' she warned Wickson. He complied, crouching deep in the drainage channel, his face now like a frightened mouse. It was an expression that warmed the cockles of Jane's heart, even though she, too, was terrified. It showed Wickson for what he was. She spoke into her mobile. 'Henry, Henry, what's going on?'

The connection was still open, but she could hear nothing.

She opened her shoulder bag and pulled out her personal radio. Her message to control room was quick and succinct.

Henry could feel that the back of his head was in water, a puddle or something, and that the man on him was trying to strangle him and push his head under the water. Centimetre by centimetre, Henry knew he was going under. The water was touching his ears now.

He managed to release one arm from under Verner's knee.

Without hesitation, Henry clouted him across the head, his hand bunched into a fist with his thumb forming a hard pointed 'v' which he drove into Verner's temple.

The blow knocked him sideways.

Both men rose to their feet and faced each other, circling now. Suddenly Verner was holding a spray canister of something in his hand.

Henry did not want to get a face full of whatever was in it. Could have been anything from CS to acid.

He stepped back and held up his hands. But it did not make any difference to Verner, who sprayed it at Henry.

Verner turned and ran.

'Henry?' Jane heard Henry's voice calling through the mobile.

'Yeah,' he croaked. 'I let him get away . . . Ahh, Jesus.'

'What is it? You sound awful.'

'I am.' He coughed and spluttered. 'He just CSed me.' He coughed and made a choking noise. 'Christ! And my windpipe's crushed, and I've been fucking stabbed . . . I'm tired, wet, beaten up . . . but other than that –' he coughed again –'feelin' fine.'

'Stop whining . . . where is he now?'

'He can't be too far way . . . obviously I can't see a bloody thing either at the moment. My eyes are streaming. How about turning the helicopter out for a start, then get a dog and some ARVs up and around here.'

'Already on their way,' she said crisply.

'The guy's dangerous,' Henry warned.

'I gathered that.'

'Everyone down there OK?'

'Well, nice of you to ask . . . yes . . . shaken and stirred.' Jane looked at Wickson and his security man, deep in conversation with each other again. Wickson was as pale as white paint, but the security guy, Coulton, looked cool and composed. 'Do you need an ambulance?' she asked Henry.

He was sitting on a rock, holding his face into the breeze, desperately trying to keep his eyes wide open to get the CS blown out. His nose was running uncontrollably and his eyes burned like fire. He managed to look down at the cut on his side by pulling up his shirt. It was not as bad as he had thought, though the sight of it made him feel a bit woozy. It was just a slash across the skin. 'I could do with looking at, I think, but I'm not ambulance material . . . at least I don't think so,' he said vaguely. Then: 'I'm gonna make it back to my car, somehow. I'll be all right. It might be an idea to get a few checkpoints set up. This guy'll have transport of some sort. There was a car parked off the road not far away from mine, could be his.'

'I've arranged some checkpoints to be manned.'

'In that case, you're well ahead of me.'

He pressed the end-call button on his mobile and stood up shakily. The exertion of the encounter had left him feeling weak kneed. He was in need of food and drink, as well as TLC. He did not feel he had the energy to make it back to his car, but there was no way he could have got the helicopter to air lift him out of there.

His mobile rang again. It was Roscoe. 'Henry . . . description of the guy, please.'

The cut on his side opened wider as he made his way back across the fields to his car and was starting to really hurt. By the time he reached his car, it was bleeding quite badly, causing him to reappraise the severity of the wound. He was glad to see his car and the thought of sitting in the driver's seat and resting was very nice.

He fished out his car keys and pointed the remote lock at the Mondeo. As he opened the door, Verner stepped out from behind the car.

Henry swore and thought, Shit really does happen, doesn't it?

There was a pistol in his hand, pointed at Henry's guts.

'Keys please.' Verner extended his left hand, wiggling his fingers, indicating they should be given to him.

Henry shook his head and uttered a snort, furious for not thinking of this possibility. He held the keys out on the palm of his right hand.

'Throw them to me,' Verner instructed. 'Nothing stupid, or you're dead on the spot.'

Henry heaved them gently underhand. They handed with a clatter at Verner's feet.

'Good guy,' Verner nodded appreciatively. Henry saw that he was not even breathing heavily, as opposed to himself. He was still close to needing a ventilator and though he thought himself pretty fit these days, he realized that gently jogging a few miles every day did not prepare you for a cross-country hike, a life-or-death struggle with a deranged gunman and arsonist, and another hike back with a slashed side and CS in your face. Verner bent down and picked up the keys with his free hand, never once allowing the gun to waver away from Henry's body mass, nor his eyes to leave Henry. 'Now I want you to turn round and close your eyes.'

Henry had been intrigued about what the next step would be. Presumably the man did not intend to kill him. He could have done that already. Henry guessed that what was going to happen was that he was now going to be whacked from behind with the pistol butt. If aimed correctly and with the required force, he would be driven into unconsciousness and hopefully the blow would not kill him or, worse, cause irreparable brain damage.

He tensed himself, then almost jumped out of his skin when the muzzle of the firearm was poked into the back of his neck, just below his right ear.

'You're a pretty resourceful guy,' Verner complimented Henry. 'Thanks for letting the tyres down on my car.'

'Pleasure.'

Verner's mouth was very close to Henry's ear. He could feel the hot breath on it. 'How did you know where to look?'

'Reflected light.'

'Ahh . . . mistake number one . . . sunlight on binocular lenses . . . it's a good job you're not a martial arts expert, otherwise I'd have been right up the shitter.'

'You are up the shitter,' Henry said through clenched teeth. The muzzle, still pressed hard into his neck, was terrifyingly unsettling. He was finding it impossible to breathe properly. The thought of a bullet tearing itself through his brain cortex was sending him close to the edge.

'How do you work that one out?'

'There's cops everywhere looking for you. You'll never get away.' Despite the fear he was experiencing, Henry was trying to sound utterly convincing. He knew the reality of the situation was that they'd be lucky to rustle up half a dozen officers. 'There's cops and cop-dogs everywhere.'

'British bobbies. I shit 'em for breakfast.'

Suddenly both men were overpowered by a massive, buffeting sound which rocked them on their feet.

'And of course the force helicopter!' Henry yelled as, on cue, there was the beast itself hovering less than a hundred feet above them in the morning sky. The sound of its approach had been effectively muted by the surrounding trees.

'Stay exactly where you are and drop your weapon,' a God-like voice boomed down through the 750-watt skyshout PA system attached to the underside of the helicopter. Also, under the nose of the helicopter, was a video camera pointed directly at the two men.

'As if,' Verner said.

The helicopter adjusted its position above them and both men swayed with the immense downdraught from the rotor blades.

'Change of plan,' Verner shouted above the noise. 'You can drive me out of this.'

Henry shook his head bravely and said, 'No.'

Verner spun him round roughly and held the gun to his head, forcing it into the bridge of his nose, between his eyes.

'Or you can die now, if you like.'

Henry looked down either side of the pistol into Verner's eyes. He was not kidding and it showed in his pupils. Henry said nothing.

'I'll take that as a yes,' Verner said.

Four

With the very dangerous-looking pistol pointed unwaveringly at Henry's abdomen, Verner backed away and gestured for Henry to get into the car behind the wheel whilst he slid into the passenger seat alongside his hostage. He tossed the keys back to Henry and said, 'Get driving.'

Henry started the engine after his dithering hand had only just managed to slot the ignition key in.

'This isn't going to happen,' he insisted. 'Now the helicopter's here, you'll never get away.'

'In that case, you'll die and I'll go to prison,' Verner responded with indifference. 'Now drive the car.' He raised the pistol and levelled it at Henry's head, 'or I'll splatter your nice grey brains all over it.'

'Can't argue with that,' Henry said, selecting first with a crunch.

As soon as the vigilant crew – known as the Air Support Unit – of Lancashire Constabulary's Eurocopter EC135 located Henry Christie's car and the incident taking place next to it, the observer began a radio commentary. At the same time, video footage was being transmitted by way of the microwave downlink to the comms room at Blackpool and at the force control room at police headquarters, near Preston.

It so happened that this was the first day at work for the newly appointed Chief Constable, who, instead of going into his office, had decided to start the day as he meant to go on: by scaring the staff shitless by turning up early and unexpectedly – which was why he wandered unannounced into the control room, just to see what was going on and to put the wind up people.

The Force Incident Manager – the FIM – the duty inspector in charge of the control room that morning, nearly had heart failure when the new Chief appeared. But he pulled himself together very quickly and briefed him on the events of the morning.

The Chief peered at the downloaded pictures from the hovering helicopter which were as clear as a bell on the FIM's monitor at his desk. He gasped with the sound a tomato makes when squashed as he saw the figures on the screen.

The FIM stared quizzically at the new boss of the force, whose head was tilted sideways as he looked at the monitor. 'Surely not,' the FIM thought he heard the Chief whisper with complete disbelief. 'Surely not – not on my first day?'

'Pardon, sir?'

The Chief shook his head. 'I said, "surely fucking not"!' He was not known to mince his words.

Jane Roscoe, isolated from events back at the Wickson household, could only listen to what was happening over her personal radio. There was a feeling of utter, empty dread inside her as the ASU observer described in detail the armed man getting into the car with his weapon pointed at Henry.

As Henry's car moved off with Henry at the wheel, Jane listened intently, her heart thumping loudly, breath short.

The management of the incident in terms of what was now happening on the road was the responsibility of the FIM. It was down to him to take charge, deploy personnel, get tactical firearms advice from the on-call adviser, and also to keep the people informed who needed to be informed. This included the on-call superintendent who took overall strategic command of the incident and the ACC (Operations), who was required to quality-assure the whole thing as it panned out.

Jane felt powerless. All she could do was tell the helicopter crew that the man being held at gunpoint was a colleague, albeit one on suspension, and that he was most definitely acting under duress. She could only then sit back and let it unfold.

But there was something she could do, she thought firmly: pin John Lloyd Wickson down and demand he tell her what all this was about.

The radio crackled busily as ARVs, a dog patrol and other

uniformed officers converged on the scene as they were deployed by the FIM, who, despite having the new Chief hovering over his shoulder like an old woman, was keeping very cool and laid back about the whole thing.

Also trying to keep cool and laid back about the whole thing, but actually fighting back sheer panic which rose up in him like bile, was the man who had been taken hostage, Henry Christie.

'Where do you want to go?' Henry asked. His sweating and very slippy hands were having major problems gripping the steering wheel.

'Head for the motorway,' said Verner, who definitely was cool and laid back.

Henry shook his head. 'Bad move.'

'I'll be the judge of that,' Verner retorted, impressing and frightening Henry with his attitude. This was a guy who was actually enjoying himself.

Henry worked his way along the country lanes surrounding Poulton-le-Fylde before emerging on to the A585 and picking up the signs for the M55. It was an area he knew well, as he did most of Lancashire. He drove carefully but quickly and the pace seemed to be keeping the kidnapper happy. Overhead they could hear the beating sound of the helicopter, but it remained out of their line of sight, just tailing them.

As Henry motored towards the motorway, the first police car appeared in his rear-view mirror. It was a liveried Ford Galaxy with smoked windows. Henry recognized it immediately as an Armed Response Unit. Two constables would be on board, both, he guessed, having had permission from the FIM for covert arming at the very least.

It slotted in behind, keeping its distance, as Henry expected it would as there were now many tight rules and procedures governing police pursuits and firearms incidents which would be rigorously enforced by the FIM.

The gunman saw the car and grunted. 'Company.'

'You should have laid low in the fields,' Henry told him.

'Maybe . . . anyway, shut your fucking face.' He rammed the gun into Henry's jaw – hard. Henry emitted a cry of pain when he felt the squidgy inside of his mouth split on a molar and tasted blood. 'You a cop?'

'In a manner of speaking.'

'What does that mean?'

'Suspended.'

'A bent cop . . . my favourite type.' Verner twisted round and saw that another police car had joined the chase. 'We got a convoy,' he smirked. His attention reverted to Henry. 'What were you doing at the stables?'

'It's a long story and I doubt you've got time to listen to it. I also doubt you'll have time to listen to very much, actually.'

Up ahead was a set of traffic lights controlling a junction at which five roads converged on the main road. It was known, unsurprisingly, as Five Lane Ends. The lights were on red. Traffic was starting to build up.

'Should I stop?' Henry asked hopefully. He saw Verner's lips twist.

'What do you think?'

Henry approached the short queue of traffic up to the lights. He positioned the Mondeo on the outside and put his foot down, whizzing past the stationary line. Oncoming vehicles swerved away, anger and not a little shock on the drivers' faces. Henry gunned the car towards the lights.

At the junction, a large milk tanker emerged from the side road to Henry's left, startling him. 'Shit!' He spun the wheel, only just managing to keep hold of it with his damp hands. The tanker driver did not see him until the last moment and anchored on, but in so doing sent the rear end of the huge truck jack knifing sideways. Henry veered around the front end of the tanker, certain he was about to be crushed to death. He closed his eyes. They missed connecting by less than the width of a blade of grass and Henry pulled away, eyes now open, with the sound of the tanker's horn blaring in his ears.

Throughout the manoeuvre, Verner stayed calmly seated, his left hand holding on to the handle in the roof of the car, just above his door, his right hand laid out down his lap, holding the gun.

Once through the hazard he bounced round on his seat. 'Fucking brilliant,' he chirped.

The two following police cars had been left behind, their way blocked by the tanker at least for the moment. Obviously the helicopter remained overhead, unshakeable.

'There's another set of lights ahead. We need to turn right at them to get to the motorway,' Henry informed Verner.

'Do what you have to do to get through them without stopping,' he was instructed.

They were at the next lights within seconds. Once again they were on red. Henry sped past the line of cars waiting there, going down the wrong side of the road, forcing oncoming cars to get out of his way. He almost lost the Mondeo as he yanked down the wheel and skidded right. The back end snaked as the tyres lost their grip and the wheel spun out of his hands. But then he was back in control, amazed he had made it, relieved to still be in one piece. Now it was a straight, if fairly narrow, road to the motorway which he would join at junction 3.

'Nice again,' commented Verner. 'Keep going fast – I'm a speed merchant and I like it.'

Henry accelerated.

'So what are they going to do?' Verner pointed to the car roof, indicating he was talking about the helicopter and the police. 'Force us off the road?'

'No. Follow us, maybe try to deflate the tyres with a stinger, but keep following, mainly.'

'Have you got a police radio?'

'I'm suspended, remember?' He concentrated on an overtake in some hatch markings in the middle of the road. They were about two miles from the motorway junction. He swerved in before a head-on with oncoming traffic. 'They don't give radios to bent cops.'

'Give me your mobile phone.'

'Why?'

'What's your name?'

'Henry Christie – what's yours?'

'Well, Henry Christie, just do as I tell you and don't answer back. My name you don't need to know – now gimme the phone.'

Henry tasted the blood on his tongue and for the first time since the journey to hell – or wherever it was going – began,

109

he felt the pain of the knife slash on his side. He glanced down and saw a lot of blood on his tee shirt. He did not like the sight. On other people he did not mind blood, on himself he was not terribly keen.

He eased the phone out of his pocket.

'I want to contact them,' Verner said.

'Dial 999.'

'Don't be funny.'

'I'm not. I don't know the direct number of the control rooms, but you'll get through on treble-nine.'

Verner was looking at the display on the phone. 'Battery's going,' he murmured. He tabbed through the menu.

'Who's Jane R?'

'The detective back at the stables,' said Henry, instantly regretting it.

'She'll do.' Verner called her up.

Jane was entering John Wickson's house when her phone rang, scaring the jitters out of her when she saw Henry's name on the display.

'Henry? Are you all right?' She heard a hollow laugh in response to the question.

'He's all right – at the moment,' Verner's voice said.

'Who is this?' she demanded.

'I think you know who I am . . . now listen . . . get them to call off the helicopter and all pursuing vehicles, otherwise Henry is going to suffer a fate called death.'

'Wha— ?'

'I'll kill him if you don't pull off all these nasty cops – understand? Have a chat with Henry. I'm sure he'll confirm everything.'

Verner gave Henry the phone. He held it to his left ear with his left hand whilst driving with his right. He cursed the newer mobile phones, which were now so small it was impossible to wedge them on your shoulder any more, making it more dangerous than ever to use a phone whilst driving, especially travelling at 80mph on a country road.

'Henry, are you all right?'

'One hundred per cent.'

'Does he mean it?'

Henry eyed his captor. 'Yeah, he means it.'

'Shall I call the hounds off?'

'It would suit me . . . so far he hasn't actually killed anybody, but if he gets pressured, that'll change, and it'll be me. I'd rather it wasn't.'

'I'll see what I can do.'

'Thanks.'

'And Henry—'

Verner snatched the phone out of Henry's hand and shouted down it into Jane's ear. 'Call the bastards off and he'll live . . . that's your choice.' He ended the phone call and tossed the mobile into the footwell.

The signpost ahead of them told them they were approaching the roundabout at junction 3.

Suddenly a strange sensation came over Henry.

This had all happened so quickly that he hadn't had time to think about it. He'd been forced into his car, forced to drive – and he had done. He'd stayed cool and kept alive, remained calm and intrepid, at least on the outside, despite having a knife gash down his side (beginning to become a problem) and a gun rammed into his face (blood in mouth tasting horrible).

Now he was getting angry and the last thing he wanted was for this guy to get away. A man who had mutilated horses, caused thousands of pounds worth of damage and taken pot-shots at people. The prospect of him driving the man to some spot where he felt safe enough to escape, where he would probably ditch Henry and bugger off with the Mondeo – if, indeed, he did plan on letting Henry live – did not sit right with Henry at all. All his instincts as a cop, honed over the last quarter of a century, screamed that this man should not be allowed to get away.

Henry wanted to see this guy behind bars. The 'how' this was going to be achieved was what eluded him.

He knew it would have to be something drastic, something done whilst other cops were in the vicinity.

But what?

*   *   *

111

Jane's hands were shaking, as was her voice, when she spoke into her radio and interrupted a transmission from HQ control room to the helicopter.

'Are you still in contact?' the FIM asked her when she had finished.

'No.'

The FIM sat back in his swivel chair. He had a desk on a raised dais, giving him a commanding view across the control room and the banks of TV monitors relaying pictures from the numerous motorway cameras positioned around Lancashire's main arteries. He looked at the monitor on his desk which had the downloaded link from the helicopter on it.

The new Chief Constable was standing behind the FIM. He had been joined by the ACC (Operations) and they were in deep discussion.

The FIM leaned forward and spoke into his radio mike.

'All patrols, including Oscar November 99, to withdraw from the pursuit. I repeat, all patrols, including the helicopter, to withdraw from the pursuit.'

If the Chief wanted to overrule him on that, then he was quite happy. There was no way he wanted blood on his hands.

He looked over his shoulder at the Chief and the ACC, and shrugged.

It was the only decision he could have made in the circumstances. Keeping people alive was his job.

Henry had to slow right down when he hit the motorway junction. There was a lot of early morning traffic on it, none of which knew that a Ford Mondeo, travelling at excessive speed, was coming in their direction, driven by a man with a gun pointed at him. Two police cars were parked ready on the roundabout.

Henry sped down the slip road in the direction of Preston, joining the main carriageway at 70mph. His mind was in turmoil as he grappled with the decision about a course of action.

The mobile phone in the footwell rang. Henry winced slightly at his chosen ring tone, about which he'd had a severe ribbing from his daughters because they said it showed his advancing age: the riff from Jumpin' Jack Flash.

'Stones' fan, eh?' said Verner.

For the first time he didn't give Henry his full attention.

He reached down between his legs to pick up the phone, which was just beyond his fingertips, making him stretch a little further.

Henry saw his chance.

Verner took his eyes off Henry, who gritted his teeth and, with his left hand, rammed Verner's head against the glove compartment, finding all the strength he had and drawing it into his left arm. He knew he would have no second chances and everything he had went into the assault.

At the same time he slammed the brakes on and swerved on to the hard shoulder at an acute angle, smoke pouring from the screeching tyres as they left a black skid trail behind them.

Whilst the car was still in motion, Henry released the steering wheel and with his right hand, went for Verner's gun.

Henry was totally concentrated on winning. The fact that his foot had come off the brake pedal and the car was lurching towards the side of the road, had no meaning for him. The danger for him was inside the car. All he was focused on doing was hammering Verner's head on the dash to knock him senseless or unconscious or dead, and disarming him.

But Verner was good.

Henry did not manage to pound his head into the dash as intended. Somehow his grip slipped. Verner squared round to Henry, who did manage to keep hold of Verner's gun hand and keep the pistol pointed down.

The car hit the grass verge with a thud.

Henry punched Verner in the face.

Verner pulled the trigger and a deafening bullet was discharged, burying itself somewhere near the accelerator pedal, miraculously missing Henry's legs.

The car bounced upwards on the grass and Henry fell back against his door which burst open. He found himself spinning out of the hole where the door once was, then hitting the ground hard and rolling over and over across the tarmac towards the first lane of the motorway. Everything was confused, as if he was in a vortex. He cracked his head, but then rolled up on to his knees, looking back at the car wondering what the fuck had just happened.

Stuck up on the grass verge, it's nose pointed skywards, it's front end was crushed and it's front wheels were stuck out at an ugly angle.

Verner was running away. He had vaulted the fence by the roadside and was running across farmland. He seemed unhurt.

Henry had stood up without realizing it. He staggered backwards a few steps, knew this was a bad thing, so stumbled across the hard shoulder, hopefully reducing the chance of being flattened by an HGV.

He watched Verner running towards woodland.

Henry did not have the energy to give chase, but he did not need to bother. The helicopter was back overhead and four police cars pulled in behind him, uniformed officers alighting. One was a dog man, whom Henry recognized. His name was Tim and his dog was called Lancon Griff – officially. Unofficially the German Shepherd was known as Fang for obvious reasons, which, Henry prayed, would soon become apparent to the man who had just put him through a mini-version of hell.

The hard shoulder of the M55 east-bound became the temporary home of the police search operation to capture the runaway. There were now eight police vehicles of varying types parked on the red tarmac area, all with blue lights flashing.

There had been a drugs raid in Blackpool that morning, maintaining the Constabulary's policy of 'a raid a day' and the Support Unit officers who had carried it out had been redeployed to the motorway to assist with the manhunt. About fifteen officers under the command of an inspector were being briefed at the top of the grass verge.

They were being told that the man had run across several fields and had gone to ground in Medlar Woods, less than a mile from the motorway. The helicopter had lost him in the trees and was maintaining a holding position over the area. They were pretty sure he was still in there.

The plan was to form a loose cordon around the perimeter of the woods, consisting of armed and unarmed personnel, then

114

to enter the woods with two unleashed dogs, their handlers and armed back-up, to quarter the woods systematically and flush the bastard out. (The word 'bastard' was used in the briefing.)

Henry was sitting in the back of a Support Unit personnel carrier amidst their equipment of plastic riot shields and door-opening equipment. He was clutching his side whilst sipping a cup of hot tea, thoughtfully provided by one of the officers. They had called an ambulance for him which seemed to be taking forever to arrive.

He had called home to apprise Kate of the horrible mess he'd got himself into. Whilst concerned and distressed, she was also seething with him. Henry could see all his good work at home crumbling away. He would have a lot of rebuilding to do, he thought. Not good. It was a thought almost as painful as his cut.

He lay back across a bench seat and closed his eyes, wishing he had stayed firmly in bed, wrapped in Kate's arms. He groaned with a mixture of pain and stupidity. He had got everything he deserved.

The officers moved down into the fields beyond the motorway, then spread out as they approached Medlar Woods. It took another fifteen minutes for them to encircle the woods. Then the dogs were set loose.

Verner was deep undercover, watching the approach of the officers from the motorway. He wore a smile on his face as he thought of the way in which his captive, Henry Christie, had managed to get the better of him. The motherfucker, he thought, picturing Henry. I gave him half a chance and he took it. Verner uttered a cynical laugh.

He had not dropped the pistol, but apart from that, a knife and one other weapon, he had no other means of attack or defence.

There were armed cops coming towards him. Lots of them. Each armed with a pistol – a Glock – and an MP5 machine pistol. And there were two dogs, which frightened Verner more than the armed cops. And at least a dozen normal cops dressed in overalls.

He was outgunned and out manoeuvred, particularly with the damned helicopter hovering up there.

But he wasn't beaten yet.

The ambulance arrived eventually and, because they were facing east down the motorway, they took Henry to Preston Royal Infirmary. After the triage nurse told him he was nowhere near the top of the treatment list and applied a tatty dressing to the wound with instructions to keep it held on tight, he was then directed to the waiting room. He saw, and nearly cried with frustration, that the digital display in the waiting room said it would be at least three hours before he would be seen by a doctor. He sauntered to the newsagent shop and bought himself a bottle of water, a Mars bar and a newspaper, heading back to the waiting room to bed in for a long, mind-numbing wait on a plastic, bottom-numbing chair. He called Kate from the payphone – the battery on his mobile had given up – and spent some time reassuring her he would be OK. She was frantic and wanted to come to him, but he fended her off, saying he could cope . . . although he wasn't too sure how he would be getting home. Just as he'd set off in the ambulance, a recovery truck had arrived on scene to rescue the very sorry-looking Ford Mondeo from the grass verge. He hadn't had the heart to tell Kate what a mess the car was in. He told her he would ring later, when he knew more. Then she could come and collect him, but in the meantime he would be fine by himself.

In the waiting room a shroud of weariness engulfed him. His aches and pains were ebbing, thanks to the paracetamols doled out in triage, but the feeling of stupidity was like a tide coming in.

He unfolded the newspaper and flipped to the back page.

The dogs were eager. Lancon Griff and Lancon Bart were both highly experienced tracker dogs who knew their business well. They moved into the trees, controlled by their handlers, each dog alert, ready and sensing the possibility of flesh and bone. Juicy.

Their handlers were kitted out with ballistic armour, as were the firearms officers accompanying them.

They were as tense as the dogs.

But not quite as tense as the man hidden deep in the undergrowth, watching their relentless approach. He was being hunted, a change of perspective from what was his usual state of affairs. He was normally the hunter. He was the one who normally scared people. But he knew he was trapped in here. The crew of the helicopter had seen him enter the woods. They knew he was in there somewhere and they had all day to find him.

Verner knew he had to take a risk if he wanted to escape. Slowly he raised himself on to one knee, dug his toe into the soft ground and launched himself upwards and began running through the trees.

The dogs spotted him, howling with delight, whilst behind them their handlers shouted instructions which the dogs probably never heard.

Fang locked on to his target with all the speed, accuracy and tenacity of a Patriot missile. Bart was twenty metres behind him. Fang's head went down, ears back, as sleek as that missile, instinctively veering round objects such as tree trunks, flying over underbrush, his eyes wide with blood-scented anticipation.

Verner ran.

Fang closed in.

Suddenly Verner stopped dead in his tracks, spun on his heels and pointed the pistol at the onrushing canine.

Fang did not hesitate. A gun meant nothing to him.

Verner dropped the gun and presented the dog with his left forearm, which Fang gratefully took as he leapt like the Hound of the Baskervilles at his quarry, leaving the ground with all four feet and seizing the arm within jaws that could crush bone like biscuit. He forced Verner over.

Verner screamed as those powerful hinges bit into him.

'Griff – down! Griff – down! Now!' screamed the handler.

Griff – Fang – held on a few moments longer than he should have, and in that brief period of time looked Verner straight in the eyes. Verner could have sworn he saw sheer disappointment in the wolf-like eyes. Slowly the big dog opened his jaws and released a nicely punctured arm.

117

Fang stepped back to reveal three armed cops half-circled around Verner, MP5s aimed at him.

'Armed police!' one of them shouted. 'Keep still and do as you are told and you will not be harmed.'

Verner cradled his injured arm. 'I want to be taken to hospital, now,' he demanded, getting the request in straight away. 'That dog bit me and me leg is also injured from the accident.'

'I don't give a fuck what you want,' the armed cop responded. 'You do as I say.'

Jane Roscoe rushed into the waiting room, desperate to see Henry. He was engrossed in the newspaper and did not see her arrive. He only looked up when he became aware of someone standing in front of him.

'Jane – what are you doing here?'

Her face was white with worry, her hair a mess, clothes in disarray. 'I was concerned about you,' she admitted. Somehow everything then seemed to drain out of her, energy palpably leaving her. Henry saw it go, like a spirit. He reached out and steered her to the empty chair beside him. 'Sorry,' she said, 'just tired. Been a bit of a busy night.'

'I'll get you a tea, with sugar in it for energy.'

He left her and extracted two cups of sweet tea from the rather obstinate machine in the waiting room.

'Ta,' she said, taking a sip, sighing as it went down, and regaining her composure. 'Sorry, Henry. How are you?'

Before he could answer, she was called up on her radio, which was in her shoulder bag.

'Receiving,' she said.

'Just for your information – suspect arrested.'

Jane glanced at Henry. 'Any further details?'

'Not yet, except he is en route to PRI, apparently having been "dogged".'

'Is he being escorted by armed units?

'Affirmative.'

'Received, thanks.' To Henry, she said, 'He's coming here.'

'I'll bet the bastard gets treated before I do,' he moaned miserably.

Five

Henry checked his watch. It was almost 9 a.m. He was surprised it was not later. He felt as though he had been up for a day at least, not just a matter of hours. He and Jane Roscoe were standing outside the casualty department with plastic cups of tea in their hands, getting some warmth out of the sun which was still rising slowly in an ice-blue sky. Sitting in the waiting room had become stifling, particularly as it got busier and busier with more sick and lame people hanging about looking sorry for themselves. Henry had suggested they stand outside and Jane, now a little recovered from her energy-sap, agreed quickly.

They leaned on each other as they walked out of the door, but separated once outside by the ambulance bay.

'Can I ask you a question?'

'Go ahead.'

'Do you have any idea what the hell is going on up at the Wickson's?' Henry probed. He watched her face, sure he would be able to tell if she lied. She looked away before answering and he knew he'd got her. She was about to fib.

'No idea, but as you said, somebody's obviously got it in for them, though.'

Henry accepted the untruth. He could tell she knew more than she was letting on, but in some respects he did not blame her for not telling him. After all, he wasn't a cop any more. Not at the moment, anyway.

'That's an understatement. They must have some very nasty enemies.'

'Mm,' she agreed and looked him straight in the eye. 'Very nasty.'

Henry chuckled, realizing he would get no further with

119

her. 'The guy they're bringing in here is a very dangerous individual. A bit mad, I'd say, but very dangerous. Now why would someone as dangerous as him, whoever he is, be connected to John Lloyd Wickson, local multi-millionaire and celeb?' It wasn't a question he expected to be answered. The expression on Jane's face told him he was right.

'What exactly went on up the hill and in the car?' she asked.

Henry's side twinged. He winced, gasped and then creased over as pain shot through him.

'Henry . . . ?'

'I'm OK.' His voice was a croaky whisper.

'Maybe we should sit back down?'

'Yeah, maybe.'

Before they could move, a police convoy drove into the hospital grounds, one armed-response unit on either end of an ambulance. The ambulance cut dramatically into the bay outside Casualty whilst the two police units stopped and disgorged their armed occupants, MP5s draped across their chests, ready for deployment.

Henry and Jane stepped out of the way, but remained in a position from which they could see into the ambulance when the doors opened.

Inside, it was pretty busy. Two armed cops, one paramedic and the casualty on a stretcher.

The hospital had been informed of the arrival previously and a small team of nurses, a doctor and a porter turned out to the back of the ambulance.

'I didn't get that treatment,' Henry said. Jane smiled.

The casualty was handcuffed and strapped on to the stretcher. He was expertly removed from the back of the ambulance and slid on to the wheeled gurney brought by the porter. The paramedic was explaining to the doctor what had happened. Henry caught a few words, 'Car accident . . . been unconscious . . . some sort of leg injury . . . bitten by a police dog,' as the stretcher was wheeled swiftly past.

The man on the stretcher did not look particularly unwell, but Henry knew why he had been brought to hospital rather than taken straight into a custody office. His injuries would have meant that he would have had to come to hospital at some stage, so by bringing him in first and getting him sorted meant that his medical condition would be gotten out of the way and the custody sergeant would be booking someone in who would be fit to detain. It was always a royal pain in the bum taking prisoners back and forth to hospital. Best to get it done and dusted before they actually came in if at all possible.

Henry glanced briefly at a fancy Lexus with smoked-glass windows being driven on to the hospital car park, then followed the procession back into the hospital. He needed to sit down.

Jane said, 'I'll go and sort this out.' She hurried ahead, leaving him to hobble along unassisted. When she got a few yards ahead of him, she stopped and turned back. 'Henry . . . I just want you to know it's great to see you again, even if you did bin me . . . and though I was really worried about you in the car and all, I really am over you. Honest.' She came back and patted his shoulder patronizingly, then legged it.

Henry shuffled on. The painkillers were wearing off already.

He had gone only a matter of feet further when he heard a voice calling him that made his blood freeze.

'Henry Christie,' it boomed.

Henry felt the colour drain from his face.

'Henry! Come here, you shit.'

Slowly, he eased himself round.

It was the new Chief Constable of Lancashire Constabulary calling him. His name was Robert Fanshaw-Bayley, often referred to as 'FB' by those who loved and loathed him.

'Fuckin' bastard,' Henry breathed.

The hospital staff wheeled the injured prisoner into an emergency treatment room, well away from any public view. It was tight in there with two armed cops, two nurses, a doctor and the patient himself, all crammed in behind the drawn curtains of the ETR.

The doctor was making an initial assessment.

'These'll have to come off,' said the harassed and overworked young man, indicating the rigid handcuffs. 'I can't treat anyone who is shackled.' He shone a torch into Verner's left eye. Neither of the cops made a move. The doctor's head swivelled and his tired eyes locked on one of the officers. 'These handcuffs come off.' There was no room for argument in his voice.

Henry found a chair in one corner of the waiting room from which he could view the comings and goings. Within minutes of the prisoner arriving the place was swarming with cops. At the head of all this activity and loving every moment of it was the strutting figure of Fanshaw-Bayley.

Henry knew FB well. Over the years Henry had worked for him in a number of different roles as FB had risen through the ranks of the Constabulary as a detective. He had last been in the force as an ACC in charge of Operations but had left to take up a job in Her Majesty's Inspector of Constabulary. Since Henry had been on suspension, FB had applied for and been successfully selected as the new Chief Constable when the old one moved down to the Metropolitan Police as a Commissioner.

And now he was back.

Henry's nemesis.

His experience of FB had, more often than not, been negative, although Henry secretly believed that FB quite liked him. A bit. It was just that FB tended to use Henry and his skills without consideration of the damage it might do to him. Henry had suffered under FB, but in some respects had also thrived.

When FB left the force for the HMIC, his leaving present to Henry had been to transfer him on to the SIO team. But it was whilst he was a member of that team that Henry had been suspended from duty.

The reappearance of FB on the scene did not make Henry feel any more confident about his future.

FB took no prisoners. He was ruthless and vicious.

Henry watched him coming towards him. He did not stand up.

FB beckoned him out of his seat.

Despite himself, Henry stood up grudgingly and reopened the cut on his side again.

'What's up with you?'

'Nothing . . . I'm sure it'll heal.'

'Walk with me, Henry.' FB twisted on his heels and headed towards the exit. Henry tried to keep pace, then thought better of it. It hurt too much.

'You'd better walk at my speed. I'm crippled.'

Henry could have sworn he heard the new Chief Constable 'tut'. Even so, he slowed down a gear.

'I'm told you are suspended. I didn't know,' FB said. 'The question to be asked, therefore, is – why are you involved at the Wicksons'?'

'Just doing a favour for a friend.'

FB's lips curled. 'Keep away, Henry. If you know what's good for you. I don't want you being compromised. In your position it would look pretty bad. Know what I mean?'

Henry said nothing.

'Just make your statement, keep out of Jane Roscoe's knickers, and get yourself sorted – one way or the other.'

'What's going on up there?'

'Fucked if I know and fucked if you're going to get to know,' FB stated categorically. 'Now leave it be.'

Jane Roscoe had no choice but to comply with the doctor's orders. The cuffs came off. She watched as one of the firearms officers released them, whilst another officer with his MP5 in the firing position, stood back and made sure that the prisoner did not do anything stupid.

Verner rubbed his wrists, then presented his left arm for the doctor to inspect. There were four puncture wounds in it. Very deep.

The doctor moved in as the firearms officer stepped back.

'You say you blacked out after the accident?'

'That's right.'

'You banged your head?'

'No – a cop was smashing my head against the dashboard of the car – that's where these injuries came from.' He pointed to his face. 'That's why we had the accident. I think I cracked my head on the windscreen, too. I don't remember much. Next thing I was being savaged by a police dog. I have a screaming headache. Feels very bad.'

123

'I'll have a nurse dress the bites. You'll need a tetanus injection, then we'll get you down to X-ray.' The doctor spoke to Jane. 'He'll have to be here at least twenty-four hours for observation.'

She nodded. 'And he'll be under guard for every second of that time.'

'Whatever,' the doctor shrugged.

Jane looked at Verner. 'What's your name?'

He lay back and closed his eyes, making no response, but making it plainly obvious she would get nowhere with him.

'Suit yourself.'

Verner opened one eye, surveyed her, then closed it.

'Henry Christie!'

He looked up. Amazingly a nurse was calling his name. He managed to raise his hand and she led him to a treatment room, where she sat him down and left him. 'Someone will be here to see you soon,' she promised him with a smile and swished out of the cubicle.

Henry eased himself into the chair and settled himself down for what he imagined would be another protracted wait.

They took the prisoner down to X-ray in a wheelchair. He was making the most of it, playing very poorly and not responding to any questions from the cops. Jane let him go, accompanied by the two armed officers and his handcuffs now replaced.

'Watch him,' she hissed to one of the officers. He nodded.

Verner was wheeled into the waiting room of the X-ray department, where a nurse took his newly created record from one of the cops. She went into the little office and began tapping the sparse details into her computer.

'I have the right to make a phone call,' Verner said.

The officers did not respond, but stared impassively at him.

'If you deny me my rights, I'll sue you both, take you to court. I'll name both of you in the petition.'

'Do I look like a guy who gives a shit,' one of the officers commented.

'Look, I know I've been a bad boy, but I need to make a

call, OK? To my solicitor. He needs to know I'm here. He'll have me back on the streets in no time and you two will lose your jobs because you denied me my rights.'

The officers glanced at each other and shrugged. They were not for budging and neither was going to be drawn into any conversation with this man.

'It's not as though you have to release me from the cuffs,' he said, getting to his feet. The officers backed off. Their hands touched their weapons. 'Hey, I'm not about to do anything. I'm not stupid. Look, my mobile phone is still tucked down the back of my pants. You lot missed it when you searched me. You found the knife but not the phone.'

They remained wary.

'Look, guys,' Verner said reasonably, 'I honestly won't do anything stupid. If I turn round, one of you gets the phone from down the back. I'll tell you the number I'm going to dial and you can listen to my end of the conversation. If you don't like what you're hearing, just grab the phone off me.' He turned round. 'Come on, guys, be reasonable.' The officers, tense, did not move. Verner held up his cuffed wrists. 'I can't do anything, can I? These cuffs make sure of that.'

'I don't know,' said the officer who had spoken to him before.

Verner gripped the back of the wheelchair. 'I'll keep my hands here, out of your way, OK? The phone's down the back of my pants. How you missed it when you searched me, I don't know. You've got to take it off me sometime – why not now and why not let me make my phone call?'

They eyed each other uncertainly, then gave a slight nod. One slid his MP5 off and placed it by the door, well out of reach. The other had his weapon at the ready, aimed at the prisoner, covering his partner.

The phone was hooked down Verner's combat trousers. It was easily missed, but should not have been, and the officer wasn't too surprised when he found it. No doubt it would have been discovered once the guy had been taken to a police station, but the quick search in the open had failed to find it. The officer stepped back and had a quick look at the phone.

Verner turned round.

'Anything other than a straightforward conversation, and I grab it off you – OK?'

'Sure, anything.'

He handed the phone to Verner, who began thumbing the keypad.

'This is the number I'm going to call,' he said.

Henry was being treated at last: the knife slash down his ribcage, having been cleaned, was now being pulled together with strips of plaster. It was not a deep cut and did not require stitches. Henry was assured it would heal easily and scar less, which was nice to hear. His body was a mess of lines and impact marks anyway. He did not want to add another to his history of collateral damage.

'Your man's down in X-ray,' Jane Roscoe said to him. She had appeared as the last piece of plaster was being applied to Henry's abdomen.

'I wish I'd smashed his head harder,' Henry admitted wistfully. 'Then maybe he'd be in a mortuary.'

'Then you'd be in trouble, wouldn't you?' Jane yawned and stretched, fighting off the tiredness of the long night shift. 'Once he's been taken to a ward, I'm off.' She rolled her neck. She only lived around the corner from the hospital, in Fulwood.

The nurse who had been treating Henry withdrew, her job finished.

'Have you told hubby you're busy?' Henry teased.

'Yes,' she said stiffly. 'Have you told wifey?'

Henry nodded.

A silence fell as they regarded each other, a deep longing there, a big sense of unfinished business.

'I'm sorry,' Henry said.

'Don't be. We all have to make decisions. You decided to be with Kate. I had to stay with hubby, as you call him . . . so, no, that's actually wrong, I didn't make a decision, Henry. You made it for me, didn't you? Anyway,' she tried to sound bright and upbeat, 'it's all history now. Onwards and upwards, eh?' She was close to tears. 'Trouble is, I still want to hold you . . .'

Henry gritted his teeth. Get me out of here, he thought in panic. And again: I should not have gone to the Wicksons'. With my reputation, there was no way it could have gone smoothly.

'FB back in force, eh?' he said: quick subject change.

'Your big friend, isn't he?'

'Hardly,' Henry snorted. 'But I think we understand one another. Sorry, that should be: we hate one another. I'm just useful to him on occasions, when it suits him. Otherwise, I'm just disposable.'

Once again an uncomfortable silence hit them.

They looked longingly at each other, but before either of them could say anything they would regret, a uniformed constable literally skidded into the cubicle. In the corridor behind him a rush of cops hurtled past, together with some nursing staff.

'What is it?' Jane demanded.

The look on his face said everything. Henry knew it was bad and even before the young lad had a chance to respond, Henry was pulling on his blood-stained T-shirt.

'Dunno . . . sounds like shots've been heard down in X-ray.'

'Shit.' Jane glanced quickly at Henry, who was already moving fast and with purpose.

'Come on.' He dropped off the bed and followed the officer out of the treatment room, twisted left down towards X-ray, which, Henry knew from previous experience, was a long way from Casualty.

All three began to pick up speed.

'I hope this isn't what I think it is,' Jane pleaded.

From then on they raced silently, following the signs over-head and the arrows underfoot.

Two minutes later they were on the corridor. Ahead, a group of people were gathered around the door to the X-ray department. A cop was pushing them back, out of the way.

Jane fished out her warrant card in case she wasn't immediately recognized. She slowed down and elbowed her way through the onlookers. 'Excuse me, excuse me.' Henry settled in her slipstream. She flashed her card at the officer on the door.

'DI Roscoe. Blackpool CID,' she announced. She thumbed Henry and said, 'He's with me.'

The officer stepped aside.

In the X-ray waiting room it was carnage. Three bodies were splayed out on the tiled floor, the two armed officers and the reception nurse. All had head wounds, all three were face down in their own pools of black-red blood and brain fragments. Blood splashes were all over the walls and furniture.

A doctor was kneeling beside the nurse, his fingers at her neck checking for vital signs. He stood up, his face a terrible mask, and shook his head. 'All three dead,' he announced quietly.

Jane said nothing, but she could feel her feet becoming leaden, the pit of her stomach burn.

Henry looked at the scene.

This was not his murder, and he knew he could go no further into the room for fear of destroying evidence.

Two police officers had been gunned down and one nurse.

And the prisoner had escaped.

Henry wondered if he had an accomplice.

For a very quick moment Henry actually felt relief that he was on suspension. Not my problem, he told himself, trying to make himself believe it. Not my job. Well maybe it wasn't in theory, but he knew damn well that if it had been he knew exactly where his next port of call would be once the practicalities of scene preservation and search for the escapee had been taken care of.

If it was his job, he would be muscling very heavily into John Lloyd Wickson's personal space because he was certain that he had a bloody good story to tell and Henry would have wrung it out of him with his hands around Wickson's neck if necessary.

Henry had seen enough. With very mixed emotions churning around inside him, he drew back to let the real cops get on with the business. He would have loved to be involved in it, despite the fact that two colleagues had been gunned down, plus the nurse. The other side of him still said it was nothing to do with him, that he had enough problems of his own, so fuck the lot of them. His experience and expertise would be invaluable, but fuck the lot of them.

He wandered back to the waiting room.

Just before his treatment he had phoned Kate and arranged for her to come down to the hospital in her car with a change of clothing for him. He expected her in about an hour and was going to kill time with fresh air, coffee and painkillers.

The coffee came first. Once that was in hand he left the hospital and walked to the car park, next to which was a grassed area from which he could view all arrivals. He sat down and stuffed two more paracetamols into his mouth, washing them down with the coffee.

Police activity increased.

Uniforms and detectives and scientists arrived. The helicopter appeared again.

He watched it all with an air of detachment.

Two van loads of Support Unit officers landed; two dog vans screeched in.

He knew there would be an extensive search of the hospital and its grounds and the surrounding streets. He would have laid odds there and then that there was no way on this earth that the prisoner would be found.

There would be no chance of him now being dressed in his combat gear. It would not surprise Henry if he had tied up some poor unfortunate and stolen his clothes, wallet and any other belongings which were of use and dumped him dead in some out-of-the-way broom cupboard in the hospital. He would have hot-wired a car and be well on his way down the motorway by now.

The fresh air was reviving him. The coffee was hitting the mark. The drugs were doing their work.

He was watching traffic travelling along Sharoe Green Lane outside the hospital. It was a busy road. He could see as far as the traffic lights at the junction with the A6. He frowned as a big American Jeep turned off the A6 and came in his direction. His bottom lip drooped stupidly. It was the sort of car he would recognize anywhere. And the bulk of the driver confirmed the recognition. It was Karl Donaldson.

What the hell was the Yank doing here? Had Kate asked

129

him to come to pick Henry up for her? Henry knew Karl was working on the murder case they had briefly discussed in the pub last night. He had said he was spending the day up north before returning to London. But why was he here?

Henry stood up, his side pinching painfully.

Donaldson signalled to turn right and entered the hospital grounds, easily spotting Henry on the grass, pulling in nearby. Henry hobbled down to him. The American lowered his window and from that moment, Henry knew that Donaldson had not come to see him.

'What the hell're you doin' here, Henry?'

'I could ask you the same thing.'

Donaldson's eyes narrowed. 'Anything in connection with John Lloyd Wickson?'

'Could be,' Henry said mysteriously.

Donaldson's eyes narrowed even further as he surveyed his limey friend. 'Yes or no,' he demanded.

Henry relented. 'Remember I mentioned the little investigation job last night?'

'At the Wicksons?' Donaldson said in disbelief.

'H-hm. I sorta caught a guy who was taking potshots at Wickson earlier this morning,' said Henry, recalling that he had not mentioned the name Wickson to Donaldson whilst they were in the pub.

'You're the one who caught him!'

'More or less.'

'I didn't get told that.'

'And now he's escaped – after killing two police officers and a nurse.'

'Jesus. I wasn't told that either.'

'Only just happened.' Henry looked at all the police cars which had been abandoned outside Casualty. 'Hence all the cop cars. Er . . . what were you told?' Henry smiled. 'Why are you here? Has this something to do with Zeke?' Donaldson's face changed. 'It bloody has, hasn't it?'

Donaldson avoided the question and said, 'We need to talk – later.' He squinted at Henry again and tilted his head. 'You've been hurt, haven't you?'

'Just stabbed in the chest, that's all. I'll recover.' He opened his jacket to reveal his shirt. 'He only plunged a knife into my heart, nothing serious.'

'Stay put, pal . . . I'll see you later.' Donaldson jabbed his foot down and swung the Jeep away, parking it on double yellow lines, half on the footpath. He jumped out and trotted into the hospital.

Henry sat back down, intrigued about what was going on.

Verner had done as Henry had guessed. Once he had dealt with his captors and made the terrified nurse find a handcuff key on one of the dead cops, then killed her, he had walked calmly out of X-ray in the opposite direction to Casualty. He looked at and weighed up each male he passed in the corridors.

One, he estimated, was about right.

Within a minute the man was naked, trussed up with wire from a kettle and dumped in an empty room. Verner put the man's clothes on and strolled out through the back of the hospital, where he stumbled into a staff car park.

Seconds later he was driving a Ford Focus out of the hospital, along Sharoe Green Lane, on to the A6 and down to Broughton, where he joined the M6 south. Fifteen minutes after escaping he was on the M61 heading towards Manchester.

An hour down the line and Kate had still not shown. Henry could imagine what she was going through, so he called her on the pay phone in the waiting room. She sounded flustered and out of breath.

'I'm in the middle of Preston. I'm following hospital signs, but I keep looping back into the town centre.'

Henry was aware she was not familiar with the newly crowned city of Preston. She had only been there a handful of times in her life, being very much a Blackpool girl. He calmed her down, ascertained exactly where she was and directed her from that point to the hospital, which was nowhere near the centre of the city.

'See you in a few minutes.'

'OK, love,' she said, sounding more relieved.

'And I'll make sure I meet you outside the hospital.'

He hung up.

131

Since Donaldson had arrived, Henry had not spoken to anyone about what was going on. He watched with more interest now, but decided to stay away from the action in spite of his inner urges to do otherwise. Something told him that his involvement with this was not over yet, anyway, so he would wait and see what came his way.

Having said that, he thought he should tell Jane that he was about to be picked up and driven home.

He made his way back into the Casualty waiting room. There was no sign of anyone he needed to speak to. He made his way down to X-ray.

It was still a mass of confusion. Henry hoped Jane had taken firm control of the scene. As he approached the police cordon tape stretched across the corridor, his progress was halted by a constable with a clipboard.

'You can't go any further. Sorry, mate.'

'I could do with talking to DI Roscoe.'

'I'm afraid she's very busy.'

'Just a moment of her time, please.'

The cop shook his head. 'I'll take your name and a number and get her to call you, if you like.' Then he had a thought. 'Unless you're a witness.'

'I was first at the scene with the DI, actually.'

The officer shrugged, now not interested. 'I've been told to let no one through.'

'OK,' said Henry. He fished out his phone and saw the battery was actually showing some charge now. He thought mobile-phone batteries were the strangest of things. Sometimes they go on forever with little or no charge showing, other times they just seemed to die on a whim. He keyed in Jane's number. It rang, but was not answered. When the answer phone clicked in, Henry ended the call.

With leaden feet he began walking out of the hospital to wait for Kate, who should not be too far away now. It hit him hard, like a kick in the testicles, that he was not wanted or needed. They could do very well without him and the realization hurt him. Hurt him hard.

Once again he experienced great regret about ever turning out to help Tara Wickson. He had been a fool. If he had not

132

got out of bed, none of this would have happened – but then something else struck him. If he had not got out of bed it was possible that John Wickson might be dead now. Or, worse still, Jane Roscoe. Yes. Actually he had done some good. He had saved lives. That realization gave him a speck of comfort.

Kate arrived the moment Henry set foot outside.

She jumped out of the car and ran to him.

'Henry, I've been so worried.'

He gave her a very cautious hug and kissed her forehead. He had never been so happy to see her and could not wait to get home.

Six

Henry Christie's daily life had developed some kind of routine. These days he was always up and about before the rest of the family surfaced and no matter what the weather, he would don a T-shirt, shorts and trainers, and push himself out for a three-mile run.

At the beginning of his suspension it had been run-walk, run-walk and had taken him in excess of thirty minutes to complete his route. Now, four months down the line, he had trimmed the time to twenty minutes, a pace which made him sweat, his heart beat and lungs expand. He had no great desire to go much faster, but he was tempted to increase the distance.

The running had helped him to lose weight, as had his move on to a diet on which he ate just as much as ever, but ate the right things. Fruit and veg instead of chips and pies, the staple diet of many a detective.

Towards the end of his run, the route took him past a newsagent's, into which he popped each day to collect a paper.

He usually got home about 7.15 a.m., slid into the shower, got dressed and then dragged everyone else out of their pits. As the three females who made up Henry's household fought over bathrooms, showers and toiletries, Henry started getting breakfasts ready.

Kate rarely ate more than one piece of toast. Often Henry had to force that down her. She was not a morning person. Leanne, the youngest daughter, started her day with cereal and several slices of banana on toast; Jenny, the eldest, varied from nothing to a fat-boy's fry-up, so Henry left her to her own devices.

Himself, he had black filtered coffee, the All Day roast from Booths, the local supermarket, and wholemeal toast spread with Tiptree Shredless marmalade. He then retreated to the conservatory with that and his newspaper.

He usually ran the girls to school and college before returning home and mapping out his day. This involved a mixture of gardening, decorating, shopping, studying for an OU degree (something he had always promised himself), preparing the evening meal and, three times a week, a trip to the YMCA for a workout on the rowing machines.

Suspension, he often said, had made him a new man. He was only sorry that suspension had been the catalyst. He was doing things now he should have been doing for years.

He had become content with the way things were going, though he was increasingly missing work, hence his decision to fill time by acceding to Tara Wickson's request.

His discipline hearing, the inquests he was involved in, and the court cases, were very much on his mind all the time. He was desperate to clear his name, but he knew that would come when it came. He was determined not to let bleak thoughts destroy him, like when he had been talking to Donaldson in the pub. That state of mind was a rarity and he intended to keep it that way, hard though it was.

Now his routine had been disrupted.

He had become involved in something which had taken him artificially back to police work and it had opened up a trapdoor in his mind he had been trying to keep closed.

The Wickson thing had set his mind churning. It made him realize just how much he missed being a cop.

On returning home with Kate that Monday morning, he had spent the rest of the day recovering by chilling out, dozing and generally doing nothing. Kate took the day off work and pandered to his every need whilst also taking every opportunity to get digs into him about how foolhardy he had been. She did not let it rest, was relentless.

When he heard nothing more from the police or Karl Donaldson that day, Henry decided his life should return to the 'normality' it had assumed during his suspension.

So the next day, Tuesday, even though he was stiff, sore, and patched up, he dragged himself out of bed and went for his morning constitutional, a run that was a limp as much as

135

anything. He did not push himself hard, just took it easy and arrived at the newsagent's five minutes later than usual, buying a copy of the *Mail*. He leafed through the pages as he walked out of the shop, trying to find some coverage of yesterday's incidents.

Page 6. Two cops and a nurse dead. Page bloody 6, he thought. It only made page 6. It had been all over the early evening TV news the night before, but by the time the later bulletins came on, it had been superseded by more pressing matters concerning the adoption or not debate surrounding the euro.

He stood outside the shop, holding the newspaper up whilst he glanced quickly through the item which told him little more than he already knew. A massive manhunt was under way and that was about it. He closed the paper, his thoughts with the families of the two dead cops, and folded it tight. He was about to resume jogging when a car drew in alongside him.

It was a big Lexus with smoked windows and a personalized number plate.

Henry had seen the car at the hospital yesterday and knew who it belongd to.

The driver's window opened smoothly.

'Henry – get in – need to talk.' It was FB.

He stopped running, the car slowed with him and halted.

'About what?'

'I think you know.'

'No, I don't.'

'Get the fuck in,' FB insisted.

The rear door opened, revealing the presence of Donaldson in the back seat, a big smile on his wide-jawed face. Henry bent down and looked past FB. In the front passenger seat was Jane Roscoe. In contrast to Donaldson's face, hers was stern and glacial. 'Hello, Henry,' she said.

'Come on, pal,' Donaldson said, shuffling across the grey leather seat to make room.

Henry's resistance crumbled. His shoulders fell and a sigh went out of him. He climbed in, a sense of foreboding surrounding him, but nevertheless he climbed in.

Because he was excited.

*   *   *

136

It was impossible for Henry to avoid Kate's razor cut of a stare as he rushed round the house to get ready – shower, shave and dress – whilst Donaldson, Jane and FB sat outside in the Lexus waiting patiently for him.

'You mean you haven't actually asked them what it's all about?' she demanded of him while he hopped around the bedroom, trying to get his underpants on and over-balancing.

'No.'

'Why not?'

'They said they'd tell me over breakfast.'

'Is it something to do with this Wickson business?'

'I don't know, but I assume so.'

'Don't let them railroad you into doing something stupid.'

'I won't,' he lied.

'Surely,' she said, opening her arms, 'surely they can't want you to get involved? You've made a statement, you've done your duty and now you're back to being suspended. They can't want you to get involved, can they?'

'Love, I just don't know.' He fastened his jeans and slipped a T-shirt over his head. 'Let me go and find out, eh?'

'I don't trust them,' she said, her pretty mouth turning down at the corners. 'Especially that FB. He's used you before. Don't let him do it again. And Karl! I thought he was trustworthy, now I'm not so sure. And Jane Roscoe . . .' Her voice trailed off.

'Look, love,' Henry said, this time more soothingly. He sat next to her on the bed and draped an arm across her shoulders. 'It'll be OK. I'll watch my back. They probably just want to pick my brain, that's all.'

'Henry, all I want is for you to clear your name and get back to work.' She looked really sad, very close to tears. 'I don't want things to get complicated . . . and that Jane Roscoe's there too.' She looked at Henry. His guts catapulted, even though he was certain Kate knew nothing about his brief affair with Roscoe . . . but he also knew that wives just know things.

'What do you mean?' he asked innocently.

Kate shook her head. 'Doesn't matter.'

FB hooted impatiently on his horn, a sound which seemed to reflect the affluence of the Lexus.

'Better get going.' Henry gave Kate a quick hug and kissed her cheek, then set off downstairs, already questioning his own reasons for accepting the invitation. Was it because he saw the chance to get back into doing some detective work? Did he see it as a chance to get back into the firm's good books? Or was it because Jane Roscoe was involved? Or a combination of all those factors?

Kate was close behind him on the stairs and at the front door. She made a point of embracing and kissing him goodbye, then glaring into Jane Roscoe's eyes as Henry walked to FB's car. When Henry turned to wave, Kate's expression morphed from dagger into flower and she gave him a loving smile.

Roscoe turned away from her and folded her arms defensively.

Henry slid into the back seat next to Donaldson, behind Jane.

'A very touching display,' FB said sarcastically, knocking the gear stick into 'D' and smoothly moving away.

Jane muttered something under her breath. Henry leaned forwards. 'What did you say?' he asked angrily.

'Nothing,' she said, deliberately not looking round.

'Yes, you did,' he persisted.

'No, I didn't,' she said.

Henry was about to say something he would clearly have regretted, but a hand on his shoulder – a big, American hand – gently eased him back into the seat. Henry bit his lip.

'I know where we'll go for brekkie,' FB announced.

Known as the White Café, it was situated on south promenade, amongst the sand dunes, on the seafront at St Anne's. It was in a fabulous position and even had free parking for patrons. Business was always brisk.

Henry had been many times over the years, but had never taken anyone there other than Kate and the girls and, though this was a working breakfast, it felt peculiar to be sitting opposite Jane Roscoe, bearing in mind their recent history.

'I'll buy,' FB announced grandly, stunning Henry. FB was

legendary for his tightness, but it all slotted into place when he boasted, 'seeing as I now earn more that a hundred grand a year and get a huge car allowance. I reckon it's my treat.' Henry's stun turned to repugnance, reminding him why he disliked the small man's character so much.

'I never got a chance to congratulate you on your new job,' Henry said, picking up a menu. Against his better judgement and present diet, and because FB was paying, he decided that he was going to order the most expensive, greasy breakfast there was. He was going to get his money's worth out of the new Chief Constable whilst he could.

'That's very nice of you, Henry.'

They all fell silent and chose their food. None of the freeloaders chose cheap options. When FB came back from the counter after ordering, he was as white as the bill in his hand.

'Bloody nearly cleaned me out,' he moaned, sliding a tray of drinks and cutlery on to the table. Henry wondered how long FB would keep to-ing and fro-ing for other people. Not long, he suspected.

FB sat down. 'To business,' he declared. His face turned granite. 'I want to know exactly why you are involved with John Lloyd Wickson and his family and what you were doing up at his house and stables. No bull allowed.'

Satisfying FB took a long time. He put Henry through the wringer. If it had not been for the fact that breakfast hadn't arrived, Henry would have made his excuses and left. As it was, he was hungry.

'It's simply this, and this is my final word on the subject: I was bored shitless. I got asked to do something that sounded half-interesting to pass some time and I ended up getting involved in something I didn't know existed.' He looked at Donaldson. 'And I suspect your presence here means there's something big to this.'

Donaldson's face could not be read.

FB glanced at the American. It was only the sliver of a look, but Henry caught it – just. FB had known Donaldson as long as Henry, all having met on the occasion when Donaldson was investigating American mob activity in the north-west of England. Donaldson had never shown much respect for FB, and their relationship was, to say the least, icy. From the look FB, just gave him, Henry guessed this was still the case.

'I just want to know, Henry,' FB said, 'if you are involved in any way with the Wickson family. That's what this is about.'

'As I said, only in as much as my daughter knows their daughter from riding lessons and that is all.' Henry held up his hands in defeat.

'OK, I'll accept that,' said FB magnanimously.

A waiter appeared from the kitchen bearing a tray with several meals on. 'Order six,' he called.

'That's us,' FB hollered.

The food was duly delivered. Once the waiter had gone, FB said to Donaldson, 'Over to you, Yank.'

All eyes alighted on him.

Henry felt someone's foot touch him under the table. He knew it was Jane's, but he did not flinch.

'It's complex.'

'Keep it simple, then,' FB suggested.

Donaldson took a ruminative second and Henry thought that his fried egg – sunny side up – might just have found its way on to FB's lap, but his friend's resilience was grade 'A'.

'As you know, the investigation into the death of Zeke, my undercover agent, and Marty Cragg is ongoing . . . both men killed by the same guy, the hits ordered by a Spanish criminal called Mendoza.'

Henry knew this. Mendoza was a very big operator in Europe. He had a finger in many pies: drugs, prostitution, blackmail, illegal immigrants . . . just to highlight a few of his speciality areas. Mendoza had strong links with Italian Mafia families and also, by default, to American ones. It was for this reason that Zeke had infiltrated Mendoza's organization. Unfortunately, like the previous u/c agent before him, his cover had been blown and then his head had been blown off. Both agents had been murdered by the same hit man, using the same weapon.

Yes, Henry knew all this. Even so, he listened with interest, waiting for the Wickson connection.

'Obviously I've been unwilling to put another undercover agent into Mendoza's set-up. He's been bitten twice already and I would only be putting a third guy into danger, so it's a no-go. Instead we've spent time on intelligence, human sources and surveillance. It's a slow process, as you know.'

Henry nodded.

'Mendoza is surveillance-conscious, very, very careful and is not a man of habit.'

Henry nodded again, slightly impatiently. Jane's foot brushed against his again. He drew his legs underneath his chair, out of reach, he hoped. Or maybe it was touch by accident and his arrogance – believing that she was still in love with him – was once again surfacing.

'John Lloyd Wickson is a multi-millionaire,' said Donaldson. 'Self-made, ruthless, always operating on the edge of what he does—'

'And he's not got a red cent,' FB interrupted. Henry had seen that the head of Lancashire's finest had been itching to butt in.

'Exactly,' Donaldson confirmed, 'he's completely broke.'

'Ahh,' said Henry. 'Interesting. How do you explain the helicopter, farmhouse, cars and all the trappings?'

'Window dressing,' Donaldson said.

'All on the drip,' Jane said.

FB turned and gave her a disgusted stare as if to say, 'Shut it, love.' Jane shifted awkwardly on her seat, her gaze falling to her hands.

'He's stretched to his limit,' Donaldson said. 'We've been into his bank accounts, at least the ones we can find, and they tell a pretty rotten story. Bad management, bad forecasting . . . bad everything.'

'And now he's in debt to the Mafia?' Henry ventured.

'Let him finish before you start drawing conclusions like that,' FB admonished him.

Henry tapped the table with the end of his fork, wondering if he should plunge it into FB's heart. If he had one. He speared a sausage instead and kept quiet.

141

'He's got a lot of businesses,' Donaldson continued. 'One involving the importation of stone-crushers, which he then assembles, and then sells them or further exports them to Europe. The goods involved originate from a company in the States. We have intelligence to suggest that Wickson has been importing these crushers from the States and is being paid handsomely by the Mafia to provide cover for the importation of drugs into the UK.'

'Has he any previous criminal history?' Henry asked.

FB shook his head. 'Just one assault in his late teens.'

'So how have the Mafia got their hooks into him?'

'We're not altogether sure,' Donaldson admitted. 'But it is a well-known fact that la Cosa Nostra, the Mafia to you, are continually on the lookout for business opportunities . . . and I say the word "business" loosely. They have people working for them in every conceivable industry or service, feeding information to them. Most of it is never used, but some is.'

'You believe someone in an American engineering company which makes these crushers has tipped them off about Wickson's dire financial plight and they've muscled in on him?' Henry worked out.

'Could be, could be,' said Donaldson.

'Where does yesterday's gunman episode fit into all this?'

'Not absolutely sure about that one,' Donaldson admitted.

'And Mendoza?'

Donaldson's face creased into a very pained expression. He did not know exactly what to say to Henry.

'Tell me.'

Donaldson, Jane and FB interchanged looks. FB nodded.

'OK. Your guys recovered the weaponry belonging to the shooter on the hillside. All very interesting. Two things in particular. Firstly the pistol he used when he kidnapped you . . . a STAR make, originating from Spain. Model 30PK, nine millimetre, holds fifteen rounds. The STAR is one of the few decent firearms made in Spain, actually, in an industry that has a pretty bad reputation.'

FB stifled a yawn at all this technical stuff, then inserted a fried tomato into the hole that was his mouth. Donaldson pretended not to notice, going on to say, 'I'm telling you this because we know what type of weapon was used to kill Zeke and Marty Cragg. A nine millimetre. I fast-tracked the gun through our ballistics department because we couldn't jump the backlog of yours in Huntingdon. Early tests and comparisons show it is more than likely to be the same weapon used to kill Zeke and Cragg.'

'You mean I've been fighting a professional hit man?'

Donaldson nodded seriously. FB smirked. Jane looked very worried. Henry sat back, not remotely hungry any more. He pushed his plate away, the breakfast only half-eaten.

'Not want that?' FB asked in disbelief.

Henry shook his head numbly. 'Lost my appetite.'

FB helped himself to the last sausage and dipped it in the egg yolk on Henry's plate before scoffing it.

'He killed Marty Cragg and I had the bastard . . . we had the bastard . . . and he got away . . . ?'

'And don't forget he nailed two good cops before he scarpered,' FB said through his food. 'And on my first day as Chief Constable. How do you think that makes me look?' he demanded. 'I had to tell their families yesterday. It wasn't nice. I've got the media and the police authority on my back now, pushing for a quick result. It's shit I could have done without, thank you.'

Henry wondered how FB had broken the news to the grieving families, but then he knew: FB would have done it well. As well as it could have been done. As brusque, unpleasant and politically incorrect as he was when he knew he could get away with it, he could be the caring, professional cop when he had to be. He was a master at playing the game to his advantage, otherwise he would never have made it to Chief. Henry knew FB was no fool.

'Anything on the weapon that killed the officers?' Henry asked. He knew it had been quickly established that their own weapons had not been used against them.

'.22 calibre bullets, nothing more yet,' Jane said.

'I do have a thought about that – and that's the second thing,' Donaldson said. He pondered for a moment. 'I might be wrong, but I think I know how he might have let your lads keep a gun on him.'

143

Henry picked up on this immediately. 'Something that was a gun, but didn't look like one?'

'Right! I'll bet they thought he had a mobile phone on him.'

'You're kidding,' FB exclaimed, stopping just short of his mouth with a forkful of food.

'It'll be something like that,' Donaldson said. 'French cops seized two mobile phones earlier this year, except they weren't, they were guns capable of firing four bullets. The digital touch pads are used as triggers. They look pretty much identical to normal cell phones on the outside, but they come apart in the middle to reveal a four-chamber secret compartment for .22 calibre bullets which are shot out of the end. Lethal up to about ten metres. They were found during a raid on a gangster's house in Rouen, a gangster who, incidentally, is connected to Mendoza. They're made in Eastern Europe and actually surfaced in Belgium in 2001.'

The information did not stop FB from eating.

'But it's only a theory,' Donaldson said. 'We may never know.'

Silence descended on the table whilst FB digested his breakfast and the other two digested the news.

Henry exhaled. His coffee cup was empty. 'Are you buying more drinks, boss?'

'Jane – refills,' FB ordered the DI. 'There's a love.'

Henry saw her reaction. Red spread from her neck upwards. She visibly bristled. Henry waited to see if she would say anything. He knew she would. She leaned on the table to FB. 'Don't ever call me "love" again – sir – or you might regret it.' She pushed herself up. 'Coffees all round?' she enquired pleasantly.

Henry closed his eyes momentarily and thought about the complexity of the relationships around the table. Him and FB; FB and Donaldson; Jane and FB; him and Donaldson; him and Jane. It made him weary. Maybe he could do without this, wherever 'this' was going. Maybe he would just go home and be suspended. Accept whatever came his way, then coast up to retirement in some backwater job, like Best Value or something.

But that wasn't him at all. He might think it, but he couldn't do it.

'Where do I come into this?' he found himself asking.

Jane returned with four mugs of milky coffee. Henry scraped the skin off his with the handle of his fork, then took a sip. It was hot and slightly sweet, reminding him of the coffee he used to drink as a youngster. This café was the only place he knew could recreate it and for a moment he was back with his mother in their little house in a hilltop village in East Lancashire where he had been born and bred and brought up until he was ten. His mother was now dead, had been for about eight years. Suddenly and unexpectedly, he missed her. Milky coffee had been her speciality.

He shook himself out of that fast, wondering where it had come from. He had not thought about his mother for a long time and felt guilty.

'You OK, Henry?' Donaldson said, noticing his friend's momentarily spaced-out behaviour.

'Yeah, sorta déjà-vu for a split second.'

FB sat back, replete, and slapped his tummy. He had certainly put on weight since gravitating into the highest echelons of the police service. Too much money, too much good living. He reminded Henry of a Pot-bellied Pig. 'Where do you come into this?' he echoed Henry's question. 'Let me lay this on the line, Henry. I actually don't want you involved in this in any way. You're suspended and it makes things very complicated if you get involved in anything to do with police work. There is no precedent for it.'

'What am I doing here, then?'

FB's eyes narrowed to slits. He looked sideways and distastefully at Donaldson. 'We are under some pressure to solve the Marty Cragg murder. It's been going on for too long and yes, that is a criticism of the SIO team. In my books they should have got it bottomed by now.'

Easier said than done, Henry thought, especially given the complexity of the job. People like Mendoza and professional hit men are not easy people to bring to justice.

'The investigation is under strain,' FB reiterated, 'and the Home Office and the Police Authority have revealed their disquiet.'

145

'And my bosses want progress too,' Donaldson said. 'Mendoza has killed two of our guys now. We want him, as you might say quaintly, "fettling". We are keen to pursue any line we can. The Wickson connection has only just come to light and by pure chance you're already involved in the family for another reason.

'We would like you to stay in there, purely from the point of view of information and intelligence-gathering, nothing else. Mrs Wickson invited you in to dig around on some horse mutilation that's been going on at the stables – which could be connected – so we want you to carry on with that, get as close into the family as you can and see what dirt lies under the rock that hides the Wicksons – and get a direct line to Mendoza, if poss.'

'But I'm suspended. I have no police powers,' Henry persisted.

'Like I said, there's no precedent for this,' FB said. 'So yes, you would be acting purely as a civilian, nothing more.'

'No back-up? No resources?'

'Nowt.'

Henry shot a hard glance at Jane, then Karl Donaldson. 'Do you support this, Karl?'

'It was his fucking idea,' FB blurted, almost choking. 'He seems to think you might do a good job. And, may I remind you, you might be suspended from duty, but you are on full pay.'

'And you think that obliges me to do this for you?'

FB nodded. Yes, he did.

Henry's mind clicked and whirred. He did want to get involved, but it had to be on his terms with his own safeguards in place.

'What's in it for me?' he said and held eye contact with FB.

'Do you know, I couldn't fucking believe my eyes.' FB and Henry were on the beach close to the White Café. The other two were sat on a picnic bench outside the café whilst Henry and the Chief strolled side by side in the sand. 'On my first day I decide to start off in the control room and the first thing I see is the helicopter download of you being bloody hijacked.'

'Sorry.'

'I didn't know about your suspension then. Can't say I'm

surprised though. You sail close to the wind . . . but this lack of judgement thing . . . ? Disobeying a lawful order?' FB shook his head in disbelief as though he could not get his thoughts round it. 'A witness shot and severely injured, a cop shot too?'

'Neither have died.'

'Hardly the point, Henry.'

'True, but I'm not to blame for it happening. I went through the correct procedure to get a firearms operation authorized and it got kicked out . . . I still had a vulnerable witness on my hands who needed moving urgently.'

'I reviewed the case last night.' FB stopped, picked up a flat pebble and skimmed it across the surface of a large rock pool. 'You never went through the correct procedure at all, just went ahead off your own bat and it went pear-shaped. You're a loose cannon, always have been, Henry, and now you're about to get your comeuppance.'

'My request for a firearms operation was turned down.'

'It says in the report that you never made the request.'

'That's bollocks.'

'I'm just telling you what it says, what, in fact, a highly respected detective chief superintendent says.'

'In that case I'm completely fucked, because I know you'll believe him and not me. That's how it works, isn't it? The organization looks after its chiefs and the Indians can just go and screw themselves?'

'The discipline hearing is in two weeks' time.'

'I didn't know that.'

'You could be getting your P45.'

Henry said nothing for a few moments, then: 'In that case I'm not interested in this Wickson business. I don't feel inclined to do anything for the Constabulary.' He sounded sad, broken. 'Shit,' he murmured, picked up a palm-sized pebble and lobbed it across the beach. A tear formed on his lower eyelid.

'I can understand that, except for one thing . . . I actually believe your story. I mean, you are a loose cannon, no doubt. You fly by the seat of your pants, but you've got great instinct and you've always come through for the organization in spite of the way it's treated you.

'The Wickson thing is very big, Henry. I knew about it before I came back to the force and I'm keen to get something done about it, especially now that two officers are down and that nurse. I want to catch that killer and I believe that Wickson could well lead us to him and Mendoza, maybe, and some bigger sharks. You could help. You might not discover anything, but so what? At least you'd have helped. You asked me what's in it for you?'

Henry nodded. 'Don't try to blackmail me emotionally about the greater good and all that,' Henry warned him.

'I won't, but what I will do is closely review the discipline case immediately.'

'Is that it?'

'Henry, I believe what you're telling me. I'll get to the truth of the matter, trust me. I scare the shit out of people, as you know.' There was a glint of steel in his eyes. 'But don't misunderstand me . . . if you don't take on the Wickson job, I won't help you at all. Even if you do take it on, you're on your own. Like you said, no resources, no back-up. You'll be operating totally independently and if anyone asks me, I'll deny these conversations. I cannot officially condone you getting involved in this and that's the public line I'll take. The only thing I will offer is for DI Roscoe to be an unofficial point of contact for you. You two can work that as you see fit. She's pretty busy because I've put her in charge of the inquiry into the deaths at the hospital, which will link into the Cragg inquiry, so you'll have to balance it out somehow. That's the deal.'

'Does Jane know about this yet?'

'No.'

Henry guffawed and wazzed another large pebble, speechless at the way FB operated. If anyone was the loose cannon, it was he. Compared to him, Henry was a boring, by-the-book, regulation poodle.

'What's your answer?'

'What if Mrs Wickson doesn't want me back?'

'Then we're back to scenario one: you're suspended and about to lose your job and most of a big, fat pension.'

'How very persuasive you are in your arguments, FB,' Henry shrugged. 'OK, I'll do it.'

Seven

Henry needed another shot of caffeine. He could have done with something stronger but it was too early and he had made it a point to steer clear of the bottle throughout the stressor of suspension and wasn't going to start now, even though his stress levels were pretty high on the Richter scale. He felt he had somehow backed himself into a trap, accidentally maybe, but here he was, as his favourite rock band the Rolling Stones put it, 'Between a Rock and a Hard Place.'

He was alone in the White Café now. He had declined the offer of a lift from FB. He needed some time to get his thoughts together and though it was a good six-mile journey home, he told them he would find his own way there.

This time he ordered a black coffee, strong and filtered. He'd had enough of the milky stuff. It had taken him to a place he did not want to go to. He leaned his elbows on the glass-topped table, his hands supporting his chin as he looked out across the sand dunes to the distant sea.

He breathed in deep. Exhaled slowly.

Trapped by accident, he thought. Not my fault. Wrong time, wrong place. But he was under no illusions that he did not have any choice in the matter now. FB was a totally ruthless operator and Henry knew that without him on his side he would be completely stuffed at the discipline hearing. FB could make or break him and if he, Henry, did not help out, he would be snapped like a twig in a forest, a twig that no one would hear breaking.

What niggled him was that Karl Donaldson had put the idea into FB's noggin. FB had obviously tweaked it and then used it for his own ends. Karl would not have seen that side of things. It was something that Henry felt he would have to

149

address with his American friend. Henry gave a short, inner laugh. Despite Donaldson's undoubted ability as an FBI field agent and crime-fighter, he was a little naïve in the ways of the world sometimes. Maybe that was a trait of all Americans.

In the meantime, Henry had to work out how to get back into the Wickson family home fairly unobtrusively at the same time as a massive policing operation was intruding on them in a big way. One thing Henry knew for sure was that he did not want to know where the cops were up to with their inquiries. His experience as an undercover cop was that it was imperative not to know, then it was impossible to trip yourself up by revealing a snippet of information which you had no right to know, one which might alert a switched-on subject. He had to distance himself from the police, otherwise his credibility with the Wicksons could be jeopardized.

He speculated about how best to go about his assignment. The thoughts made him wonder what it would be like to be a private investigator, acting alone all the time. Henry was used to having an organization of 5,000 people behind him. A Human Resources Department (or 'Human Remains' as cops often referred to it), an intelligence unit, cops with guns, dogs and lots of equipment, a Training Centre, numerous support departments – a bloody big, complex piece of human machinery to back him up, or to roll on without him. It worked both ways.

Here he would be alone, with the exception of contact with Jane Roscoe, whatever use that would be, and his own resourcefulness.

He felt like he had been stripped.

And it was not comfortable.

His coffee gave him an extra kick. He looked around the café, the people inside it. He took in their faces and returned to one, that of a woman who kept staring at him.

He caught her gaze. She frowned and looked away. Henry was sure he did not know her, but got the impression she thought she knew him. But a lot of people knew him. It came with the territory of being a cop, or, he laughed to himself, a private eye. Henry Christie PI. It had a certain, discordant ring to it.

The woman was staring at him again, transfixed. Henry looked out to sea and sank some more coffee.

Firstly he would give Tara Wickson a ring. Check out how she was feeling. See if she wanted anything more from him . . .

'You don't know me, do you?'

Henry's head swivelled. He was not surprised to see the woman from the nearby table standing next to him. Henry put her about his age, but she seemed older for some reason. There was a great sadness around her eyes which immediately touched Henry. He had seen it before. It was the look of loss.

'No, I don't,' he admitted.

'I don't actually know your name, but I know you, I recognize you.' Her eyes were watery, almost tearful. 'I'm sorry, but could I have some of your time?'

'Uh – sure.' She took a seat without further invitation. 'What can I do for you?' His brow was deeply furrowed.

'Six years ago, it was, maybe a little longer, I'm not sure . . . yes, it would be a little longer. Time has lost its meaning for me. I'm just floating around now, treading water until I die.'

Henry's warning signals blared out. Oh-oh, nutter. 'Oh,' he said.

'I know what you're thinking.' The woman smiled a sad smile. Henry relaxed. He knew his first assessment had been correct: loss, bereavement, but not mad. She shook her head. 'Sometimes I think I am going bonkers, but I'm not. Going mad would be a release from the hell I'm in.'

'What can I do for you?' he asked again.

'Six years ago you were on a stand at a careers convention at the University of Central Lancashire.'

'Yes, I was.' Henry recalled it vividly. Two days of sheer hell, inundated with hundreds of rude students asking him about life as a plod. It was not something he had volunteered for, but FB – then a chief superintendent – had volunteered him. Two torrid days of smiling and pleasantries at students who were mostly shits, with the occasional one showing real interest.

'You changed my daughter's life,' the woman said.

Henry began to feel uneasy.

'She'd been drifting, really. Not a clue what she wanted to do. She was due to get her degree and she simply had no idea what to do with her life, so she went to the careers convention and dragged me along with her. The woman scratched her chin and gazed over Henry's shoulder, seeing something. 'You changed her life and I don't even know your name.'

Henry told her.

'I think you were a detective sergeant then. I remember that, too.'

There had been representatives from all walks of Constabulary life: uniform foot patrol, dogs, horses, support staff and many others including himself, the only detective on the stand, the only one foolish enough to get snared into it. Even in plain clothes he could find nowhere to hide.

'My daughter was called Jo Coniston.'

Henry blinked. He knew no names from the convention, could hardly even recall any of the faces, was just glad to get away at the end of it.

'She spoke to every one of the people on the police stand, and you know what? It just captured her imagination. You were the last one she spoke to and you told her all about being a detective, told her all about your career . . .'

He continued to wrack his brains. One of the things he prided himself on was his memory. Names, faces, cars, houses . . . usually related to crims.

The woman opened her handbag and took out a photograph. She showed it to Henry.

Then he recognized her. Tall and gawky, just on the verge of turning into a lovely young woman. Long brown hair constantly falling into her eyes, which were wide, blue, innocent, yet knowing. Yes, there had been something special about her.

'I remember the face now,' he said, frowning. He asked the next question with a sense of dread. 'You said she was called Jo Coniston. What do you mean by that?'

The woman seemed not to hear him. 'She joined the police six months later . . . GMP . . . always talking about the conversation she had with you.' She fished out another photograph. It was one of Jo in uniform, probably on the day of her

152

passing-out parade at Bruche, the police training centre down in Warrington. Hair now short, figure slightly fuller, a look of no-nonsense on her face but coupled with a wonderful smile filled with sunshine.

'What happened?' Henry asked.

'I don't know, I just don't know what happened to my beautiful daughter.' She caught back a sob, inhaled deeply to control herself and slid the photos back into her bag. 'She got a job on the surveillance branch eventually. Loved it, just loved the job. One night she and another officer simply disappeared,' she said flatly.

'Disappeared?'

'Disappeared.'

'No bodies were found, were they?' Henry said. It was really a statement rather than a question because now he remembered the job. It was one which made the news across the north quite extensively for a while. 'About two years ago. Lots of speculation about it, even that she ran off with her partner, if I recall right.'

The woman snorted. 'If she had done that, she would have told me. We spoke on the phone every day. I saw her twice a week. I would have known if something like that had been going on.'

'Parents often say that,' Henry said gently. 'Often they're wrong.'

'Not with me and Jo,' she said stubbornly.

'Er . . . sorry . . . I don't know your name.'

'Brenda Coniston.'

Henry nodded. 'OK, Brenda . . .' He shrugged, then squinted at her. 'We've bumped into each other . . . coincidences happen . . . I'm really sorry about Jo, but I can only assume that everything was done at the time to trace her. The police just don't let their staff disappear. They try to find them. Cops are actually very good at finding folk – unless your daughter didn't want to be found. Could that be the case?' It sounded highly unlikely, but he asked anyway.

Brenda did not look remotely convinced. 'I've been thinking about this for the last two years, Mr Christie, and it's been tearing me apart. If she had decided to elope with this guy,

I know, I just know that sooner or later, she would have made contact with me . . . at least in a little way. We were so close.'

Henry kept silent.

'I'm sure she's dead. The police think she's dead. All right, there's no bodies been found.' Her lips began to tremble. 'She's been murdered, hasn't she, Mr Christie?'

'You're my contact, you come and pick me up,' Henry whined down the phone to Jane Roscoe.

'I'm not your anything, officially, and besides which I'm running a triple murder, so I don't have time to kow-tow to your every whim.'

'But I'm one of your leading operatives.'

'No, you're not – not officially, so bog off and either walk home or get a taxi. FB offered you a lift and you declined, so tough!'

'But I came out without any money,' he lied.

'Shanks' pony, then, innit?' said stiffly, ending the call abruptly.

Henry stared at his dead mobile and sighed.

Mrs Coniston had gone; accompanied by the woman friend she was with, leaving Henry feeling as though he had kicked off a chain of events, which had subsequently led to her daughter's disappearance. That was all he needed, a guilt trip on top of all his other woes. That had been the reason he had phoned Jane to cadge a lift home. Guilt. Guilt about dumping her. He wanted to know how she was really getting on.

He stood up, feeling that he had imbibed too much caffeine now. His hands were shaking, as though with DTs.

All of a sudden he felt he could not win at anything.

He decided to clear his head by walking into St Anne's town centre and hopping into a taxi from there.

The staff in the café waved him off, glad to see him go.

Outside, he trotted down the steps as Jane Roscoe drew up in her car. She lowered her window and forced a reluctant smile on to her lips. 'Get in.'

*   *   *

154

'I'll make this perfectly clear to you, Henry. I am not going back down the road of our relationship. It's over. Zip. Kaput. Done. OK? No post-mortems, no recriminations, no further involvement. Got that?'

Henry nodded numbly.

'You did what you did and I got over you and let's leave it at that. I miss you, OK, but that gets less each day.'

'Fine,' he said thinly.

They rode in silence.

'Why come and pick me up then?'

'Because FB has put me in charge of the investigation into the deaths of two police officers and a nurse. The trail leads firmly back to John Lloyd Wickson and if we – the police, that is – can't open his can of worms, then I'm hoping that you – not the real police, that is – might at least prise the lid off. It's a purely selfish thing. I've got a job to do, I need your help and you won't help by sitting in a café all day drinking milky coffee. Although you couldn't have paid for it because you didn't come out with any money.'

'I fibbed.'

'I know.'

'So what's you plan, unofficial boss?'

'I'm going to drop you off at home, I'm going to go and see John Lloyd Wickson, then you're going to see Mrs Wickson and hopefully keep your dick out of her gob, and get her to spill some beans.'

'Oooh, good plan.'

'Got a better one?'

'Yes, but it involved me, you and sex.'

Jane's head remained dead straight. Henry saw redness creep up her neck. She was easily embarrassed and driven to anger. She did not respond, but gripped the steering wheel tighter. Henry was very sorry he had said it. Once again he knew his forefinger was hovering over the self-destruct button. He apologized – and meant it.

She relaxed, allowing her shoulders to droop.

'Y'know,' she said wistfully, 'the sex was the best ever . . . but it's never going to happen again.'

Henry knew she meant it. 'By the way,' he said, changing

155

the subject, 'by the way, I haven't got a car to use, as mine is in dock. How can I be expected to get out and about on all this unofficial business without one? Hm?'

'I'll see what I can arrange.'

It was approaching midday when Jane dropped him off at home. He watched her drive away, but she did not look back to see him all forlorn. Once her car had gone, Henry let himself into the house, which was quiet and empty. It was good to be alone.

He sat down by the phone in the lounge with his Filofax. It was a dog-eared specimen, almost ten years old, which he updated regularly, unable to grasp any of the benefits of having a palm-sized computerized personal organizer. He preferred the substance of pen and paper, could trust it more. He opened the leather-bound book and rooted out the card Tara Wickson had given him. He dialled her home number: engaged. Then her mobile: no response. He hung up and riffled through the Filofax to find another number he wished to call, that of a Detective Inspector in Greater Manchester Police called Brindle. He knew this would be a long shot, because cops work numbers change with the wind. He was not disappointed. It came back unobtainable. It was a number the guy had given him six years before.

This made him move to the number of another officer in GMP with whom he'd had dealings recently. This was a successful connection and he gave Henry the new number of the DI, who, he was told, was now a DCI.

Before phoning, he tried the Wickson numbers again. They were as before.

Then he tried the DCI's number, which, he had been told, was a direct line to his desk.

It was answered on the first ring. 'DCI Brindle, can I help?'

'Hi, John, it's Henry Christie from Lancs Constab.' Henry determined it was more appropriate, if slightly deceitful, to let the man think Henry was still officially a cop, even though doing so made Henry feel nervous. 'Didn't know you'd moved up a rank. Congratulations.'

'Thanks, Henry.'

They exchanged the usual pleasantries before the DCI asked what he could do for Henry. He explained about bumping into Jo Coniston's mother and what she had said.

'Obviously I don't know anything about it, so I was just curious and felt a bit of an obligation to ask a few questions. Quite clearly Mrs Coniston believes that not enough was done at the time.'

'Hm. I wasn't involved in any way, but it was a strange one. A MIR was set up and ran for a few months, but nothing came of it. There was no actual evidence of foul play, but yeah, it was an odd one. No bodies, nothing really. I don't know if there's anywhere you can go with it, to be honest.'

Henry asked, 'Is there any way of looking at the file papers?' He did not want to push things, knew he really had no right to ask, whether he was a real cop or not. 'Fresh pair of eyes?'

'Are you offering your services?'

'I am an SIO and whilst my workload is crippling –' here Henry winced – 'I wouldn't mind having the chance to have a glance through the stuff if at all possible. Just as a favour to this woman.'

The DCI considered the request. 'I'll get back to you.'

Henry gave him his mobile number and thanked him. When he hung up he found he was sweating and his hands were still shaking a little. The result of lying. And lots of coffee.

He was unsure what to do next, having retried the Wickson number and still getting no response.

So having found himself with some time on his hands and being such a good new man, he did some cleaning up, got the washer working (with washing in it, even) and after a short wrestling match with the recalcitrant ironing board, did some ironing too.

It was one of the most therapeutic activities he had ever done. He could quite easily have bragged that he had never ironed clothing very much during his life, other than when he had no choice in the matter. Now he loved it. Smoothing clothes down with a hot, steaming iron, putting razor-sharp creases into things, transforming crumpled items into nice, presentable, lovingly pressed clothing: from knickers to shirts. He was amazed at what he had been missing all his life.

He was half-way through the pile of clothing, lost in thoughts, when his mobile rang. It was the DCI from GMP.

'Henry, done a few minutes digging on Jo Coniston. It's still an open murder/missing person's file. Her team leader at the time, a sergeant called Al Major on the surveillance branch, might be worth having a chat with. I'm sure he'd be able to give you some initial background. I don't really know more than that.'

'Is he still on surveillance, based in Prestwich?'

'Yeah . . . I've had a word with the SIO who ran the initial investigation and he'd be more than happy for you to take a look at it.'

'Thanks, that's good. But it is unofficial, though if I do find anything, things could change.'

'Understood . . . Bye, Henry . . . Speak again soon.'

And let's just pray that you or the SIO don't phone Lancashire and ask to speak to me, or I'm goosed, Henry thought. He plugged his mobile phone into the charger and resumed ironing, wondering if he could make some sort of living by taking in other folks' washing. It could supplement his meagre income from the private eye business.

Half an hour later, ironing done, he put his feet up.

The house phone rang. It was Jane Roscoe.

'Got off your lardy fat arse yet?' was her opening salvo.

'I'm doing telephone enquiries in between washing, ironing and general household duties,' he came back haughtily.

'I've seen Wickson.'

'And?'

'Nothing. He claims all innocence. No idea why anyone would want to take a pop at him or burn his stables down. No one has any grudges against him. He's as white as a white person can be.'

'And a liar.'

'A big fat one,' Jane confirmed. 'But he's made it perfectly clear that he doesn't want any police rooting around him or his business.' Jane snorted. 'No chance of that. Do you think you'll be able to get into Tara?'

'I'll try . . . I've been trying . . . no reply on the phone. Where did you speak to Wickson?

'A huge building site is being cleared off Bloomfield Road, near to the footy ground. He's got a site office there, got a few machines on it, crushing the stone and tidying the place up.'

'You wouldn't know if missus was at home then?'

'Nope.'

'OK, I'll try her again, but only if I can claim the cost of my calls back.'

'Henry – just fucking do it. You still get paid an inspector's wage, don't you?'

'You sound like FB—'

He was left holding a dead phone, which he placed back in its cradle, then lifted back to his ear. It was only then he heard the peculiar tone that indicated a message had been left on the answerphone service. He had been called whilst on the line to Jane. He dialled 1471 first.

It had once been a huge factory which had fallen into disuse and over the years had become an eyesore. John Lloyd Wickson had seen its development potential years earlier and had kept close tabs on the progress of the building, which had gone through several hands before coming on to the open market earlier in the year. He had bought it for a snip because the owners were desperate to get rid of a useless piece of land.

Wickson knew he could develop it and make money at every stage of the process, from demolition to disposal of the hardcore, to eventually building on it as per his vision: a site combining a housing estate, some retail outlets, a hotel, a small business park and, as far as the council was concerned, the icing on the cake: Wickson's promise to build a new primary school for free.

At the very least, Wickson would make £5 million personally. If it all went to plan.

Wickson stood in the site office, a portacabin which overlooked Bloomfield Road. A few hundred metres up the road was the football club which, one day, he promised himself, he would own. Just for the fun. He looked across the site, now more or less flattened after demolition. His massive crushers

159

and screeners had moved in, turning the bricks and rubble into saleable hardcore, from which he would make a small fortune.

There was money to be made from everything.

Then his face fell as he locked on to the woman detective inspector who had just been to see him. She was parked in her car on Bloomfield Road, mobile phone to her ear. He watched her, a sneer on his face.

Behind him in the portacabin, Jake Coulton, his head of security, was just getting to the end of a phone call at the desk. He hung up and came to stand behind Wickson, seeing his point of view.

'Bad news,' Coulton said, mirroring his boss's thoughts.

'Indeed,' Wickson said. 'We need to keep the police at arms' length. They mustn't be allowed to start sniffing around . . . Any thoughts?'

'Money buys things, people,' Coulton said.

'Meaning?'

'If we get the stables cleared, like now, don't hang about, I could be doing some ducking 'n' diving with the Fire Brigade. If we destroy all evidence of arson and the chief fire officer says it wasn't arson, who could argue with those findings? That would be one less reason for the cops to be nosing around.'

Wickson turned and appraised his employee. 'The reek of petrol was a bit of a giveaway.'

'I'm sure that could be explained away,' Coulton smiled. 'But what's a smell? You can't bottle it and take it to court. If the price was right . . . I mean, electrical faults cause so many fires, sadly.'

'Don't they just.' Wickson bit his lip. 'Fix it.'

'Will do.'

'But what about the guy with the gun? There'll be a lot of pressure from that angle. That could be very uncomfortable. The "why" he was here, shooting at you. Now he's killed two cops they aren't going to let it go so easy.'

'You know why he was here.'

'I do, but the cops don't. Thing is, he'll be back if we don't sort something,' he warned.

Wickson nodded, nostrils flaring. 'Could we sort it?'

'Let me think about it.'

Their eyes moved to Jane Roscoe, still sat in her car.

'Bitch,' Coulton said.

Wickson sighed. 'Let's move a crusher and an excavator up to the stables, start getting the place tidied up.'

The call was from an unknown number. 'You were called at 2.05 p.m. today. The caller withheld their number.'

Henry went on to 1571, the answerphone.

He had never gone so cold in his life. He recognized the voice immediately.

'Henry, hi, how are you?' the recorded message began. 'You're the only person who has ever got the better of me. I respect that. It also annoys me intensely. So remember one thing, Henry Christie, I've got your number and I'll be calling again – in person.'

Eight

Jane Roscoe turned up at Henry's house next morning at eight. She had brought a pool car for him to use, a Vauxhall Astra with three wheel trims missing and several dents in the bodywork. A very weary-looking vehicle, past its heyday. She knocked on the front door, which was answered by a very frosty Kate Christie.

'Hello, Kate.'

Kate nodded. 'What can I do for you?'

'Brought a car for Henry to use.' She dangled the ignition key in front of Kate's nose. 'But I need him to give me a lift back to the nick.'

Henry, unaware it was Jane at the door, trotted downstairs and stepped into the hallway. He was taken aback to see her. 'Jane, hello.'

'Said I'd sort something for you,' she said through Kate, as though she wasn't there. She held up the key.

'Oh, thanks.'

Kate glared at Henry. 'But she needs a lift back in it.'

'Ahh, right.'

The three of them stood there for an incredibly awkward moment. Kate made the first move, shoving her way past Henry, muttering, 'You'd better take her.' She retreated into the kitchen and closed the door – loudly.

Henry shot Jane a look that said it all and followed it up by getting close in to her, almost nose to nose, then finding himself unable to say anything.

'She doesn't know about us, does she?' Jane asked, a glimmer of a devilish smile on her face. 'You haven't spilled the beans?'

'No, I haven't,' he whispered hoarsely, then shook his head. 'Stay there.'

162

He went into the kitchen, where he found Kate holding tightly to the edge of the kitchen sink, staring out of the window, her bottom lip pulled up over her top one, trying not to crack.

'What's up, love?' He touched her shoulder.

He was now absolutely certain she knew about him and Jane. He had not told her, nor had anyone else to his knowledge, but somehow she knew. Kate shrugged his hand off her.

'You fool, Henry . . . Why are you doing this . . . getting involved? Can't you see they're using you?'

The relief in Henry's body was almost visible. She didn't know!

He could have danced a jig.

'Honey, it'll be all right . . . FB's sanctioned it. It's all above board,'

'Then why don't they reinstate you properly?'

'Because what they want me to do wouldn't work if they did.'

'They could reinstate you and not tell anyone.'

And that was a good point.

'Gizza hug.' He held out his arms and she turned into them just as the kitchen door opened and the Tasmanian devil-like Leanne burst in, all energy. Jane had a clear view of Henry with Kate held close to his chest. 'I still have to go through a discipline hearing, whatever,' he said weakly. 'And I'm still a cop, getting paid a cop's wages.'

'I know . . . but be careful, Henry. That Fanshaw-Bayley has taken advantage of you in the past and her . . .' Kate looked daggers at Jane. Her voice dropped a semitone. 'There's something about her . . . I don't know . . . I wouldn't touch her with a bargepole.'

'OK, you two,' said Leanne, who had been observing this little scene with a mixture of misunderstanding, puzzlement and cynicism. She'd waited long enough. 'What's for breakfast?'

Henry pecked Kate's cheek. Out of the corner of his eye, he saw Jane wheel away in disgust. 'I'll speak soon, let you know what's happening.' He gave Leanne a hug and kiss, grabbed his fleece and followed Jane up the driveway. At the rather bedraggled car, she tossed the key to Henry, who caught it double-handed.

'You drive.' She got in and Henry slid into the driver's seat, starting an engine which blew out a cloud of black smoke of atom bomb proportions from the exhaust. The engine sounded rough and out of sync, such was the fate of Constabulary vehicles close to the scrap heap.

'You must have called in some big favours to get me this one,' he said sarcastically.

'Someone found it rotting in the police garage at Accrington, so don't look a gift horse in the mouth. At least it's not local and won't be recognized.'

Henry looked round the inside of it. There was a gaping hole in the dash where the force radio set had once fitted. There was a pull-ring dangling from the roof by the door which had once connected to the now-missing police stop sign on the back parcel shelf. The sign might have been missing, but the hinges which held it in place were still there. If he had inspected the outside of the car he would have seen where the word 'POLICE' had once been stuck on the doors. It would not require anyone of any great intellect to put two and two together.

'There's no spare tyre, by the way.'

'Nice,' he said, driving away.

Jane sniffed and murmured something he did not make out.

'You seem to have the bit between your teeth,' he commented.

'Henry – I am a scorned woman. I'm over you, but I'm still going to get some enjoyment out of it.'

He raised his eyebrows.

'So you're not over me?'

'Oh, yes, I am,' she said forcefully. 'But I didn't expect to be bumping into you so soon and it's thrown me a bit, OK?'

'Sorry.'

Jane expelled all the air from her lungs and started again. 'I know you want to give it your best with Kate, so don't worry. I won't do or say anything to jeopardize that – unless you really piss me off.'

164

'Thanks. I won't.'

'Want to know how the investigation's going?'

'No.'

'Didn't think you would.'

'I have good reason not to,' he explained. 'If I know too much, I might give something away, then my position's up the creek.'

The rest of the journey continued in a strained silence. Henry considered whether or not to tell Jane about the phone call from Verner, but decided not to. It probably wouldn't achieve much and would make Jane worry.

Jane was the first to break silence, when Henry stopped on Hornby Road, about a quarter of a mile from the station.

'What's this?'

'Where you get out.'

'Here? Why?'

'I don't really want to be seen with any active cops if I can help it. Wouldn't do my image any good, would it?'

'It'll take me bloody ages to walk in.'

Henry closed and opened his eyes very slowly in a way that said he would not be swayed.

'I'm going to go home, have some breakfast. Then I might just have a trip into Manchester.'

'Why? What're you going to do?'

'Shopping,' he lied, just to wind her up, although he knew it wasn't a good idea. 'Day out with Kate. Pre-planned. Trafford Centre.'

Jane shot out of the car and slammed the door closed. She stomped off towards the cop shop without a backwards glance, something Henry was getting used to. He manoeuvred into traffic and sailed past her. Neither gave the other a second glance.

Henry had worked as an undercover police officer in the past. He was one of the sixty or so fully trained u/c detectives in the country. As such he had some fairly close links with surveillance branches in forces across the north-west, and knew where each one of them was based.

He used this knowledge to make his way to Greater

Manchester's surveillance branch located discreetly on a business estate in Prestwich on the west side of the city.

It had changed little since he was last there. He drove past the entrance of the high-walled compound and pulled in around the corner, wondering how best to handle the situation.

He dialled Al Major's mobile.

'Hullo.' These people were very tight with greetings because they could never be one hundred per cent sure who was calling them. Criminals spend lots of money trying to track down locations of surveillance units as well as the phone numbers and addresses of surveillance cops.

Henry introduced himself and kept his reason for calling brief. He said that he'd had authorization from DCI Brindle, his friend he had called the day before. He did not let on that he was suspended or that this was a purely personal enquiry, because it might not have gone down well. He also knew that people like Al Major were very canny people – it came with the territory – so Henry encouraged him to call Brindle just to double-check. He asked him to do it now.

Reluctantly, Major agreed.

Literally, whilst he waited for the return call, if there was going to be one, Henry sat and twiddled his thumbs, made a cat's cradle, did a bit of nose picking and let him mind do some stream-of-consciousness rambling.

He began to think about coincidences. He truly believed that coincidence was the catalyst to fate. Life was all about coincidences and they, in turn, led to consequences. Such as the reason for him being here today because he had bumped into a missing girl's mother, a girl he had influenced into joining the cops, setting her off on a journey that may well have resulted in her death. If it had been another officer on the stand at that careers convention, she might still be alive.

How spooky that was, he thought. Then: not so spooky, actually. He had met people in the strangest circumstances in the past, sometimes without any great consequence. At a Rolling Stones concert in 1982 he had met an old friend he had not seen since junior school in a crowd of 80,000 people. Once on holiday in Portugal, many years before, he had been with Kate in their pre-child days when they were accosted by a bar tout, trying to drum up business for some back-street dive or other in Albufeira. Now that had been a coincidence with consequences, because Henry recognized the lad as being wanted for murder in Blackburn. Henry did not know him personally, but had seen his photo circulated. Much to Kate's annoyance Henry had let the guy lead them into a bar for cut-price drinks; he then engaged him in conversation and the lad was northern buffoon enough to tell them he came from Blackburn and people called him Norky, two facts that confirmed Henry's belief. The Portuguese cops visited him two days later. Coincidence to consequence to fate, fate being life imprisonment in this case.

Yeah, life was just a series of coincidences, some of which had greater ramifications than others.

His phone rang.

'Hi, Al.'

'You can come round and see me. Want to make an appointment?'

'How about in two minutes?'

'Er, well . . . er,' Major stalled, stunned.

'I'm in the vicinity. Strike while the iron's hot?'

'You know where I work?'

'I do. Be there in two shakes of a lamb's tail,' he said brightly and ended the call.

He parked outside the perimeter wall, walked to the gate and pressed the intercom buzzer.

'Hello?'

'I have an appointment to see Al Major. DI Henry Christie from Lancashire.'

'Someone'll be with you in a mo.'

Henry saw a young guy saunter out of the building.

'Can I help you?'

Tricky. No badge, no warrant card, no ID. 'I'm here to see Al Major. DI Christie from Lancs. It's a while since I was last here,' he went on quickly, going for the friendly bullshit approach. 'Last time was when I was working on the Jacky Lee job.' Henry dropped a name he knew everyone would react to. Lee had been a gangster, a big one, but had met his end gruesomely in Henry's presence a few years before.

'I was u/c on that,' he said, knowing he was pushing it because undercover cops never tell anyone about their work, especially people they've never met before. This officer looked young and impressionable. Maybe he could get away with it.

His eyes lit up.

'Come in then.' He opened the side gate and let Henry step through. It was pretty much procedure these days that all non-uniformed staff wore their ID cards visible all the time whilst on police premises. He knew he would have to keep this officer's attention away from the fact that he wasn't wearing his.

'I was there when he got killed,' Henry boasted uncomfortably. Even when he was showing off for a purpose, it did not sit easily with him.

'Wow.'

'Nasty. Russian Mafia.'

'Big stuff.'

They reached the door of the main building as another man appeared. Henry's eyes focused quickly on his displayed warrant card. It was Al Major. Sergeant Al Major. Sergeant Major. Henry's hand shot out. 'Al – Henry Christie.'

Major's damp flaccid hand shook Henry's firm dry one with no enthusiasm.

'Thanks for taking the time to see me. I know it was short notice.'

'That's OK.' The other officer excused himself and went into the building. 'Come in, my office is down here.' Major took him down a short corridor and turned into the supervisor's office, which, apart from furniture, computers and mounds of paperwork, was empty. 'Coffee?' Henry said yes. Major directed him to a seat, then came back from the filter machine with a mug of steaming black coffee. Major sat at a desk. 'What can I do for you?'

Henry explained his meeting with Jo Coniston's mother, his own very tenuous link to Jo and that he felt a certain obligation to review the job and that he had permission from the GMP hierarchy to do so.

'I don't think you'll find much to help you. It was a real strange do, but we put a lot of resources into it and she just vanished, as did Dale O'Brien, her partner. Couldn't say if they were murdered or not, but it seems a good possibility.'

'Two cops go missing and there's no trace? Wow? What about their vehicle?'

'No trace either – never found.'

'Any leads at all?'

Major shook his head. Henry angled his head back slightly and looked quizzically at Major, trying to weigh him up. For some reason Henry was not getting good vibes. The hairs on the back of his neck crinkled up as a very old feeling crept through him. That of deep suspicion. But why?

'Was there any suggestion of a liaison, shall we say, between them?'

Major shrugged. He glanced at the wall clock in a very obvious way, saying non-verbally to Henry that time was short.

'What was the job that night?'

'Er . . . one of those hit and miss ones. Surveillance on a guy called Andy Turner. Every heard of him?'

Oh yes, Henry knew Turner. He nodded.

'It was one of those "Let's see if we can find him cold, then follow him" jobs.'

'Did you find him?'

'Jo spotted him in Rusholme, then we lost contact, basically. They followed him towards Bury, and then lost him on the motorway.'

'And you never see the officers again?'

'That's about the long and short of it.'

'And their car never turned up?'

'No.'

'And their personal vehicles – were they left parked here?'

'Yeah – returned to their families.'

'How long did the inquiry run?'

'Three, four months.'

'Were you involved in it?'

'What? The inquiry?'

'Yes.'

'Yeah – they were my officers.'

'What's your take on it, Al?'

'We did all we could, nothing turned up, end of story.'

169

'What about Andy Turner?'

'Hasn't been seen since, either.'

'Could he have killed them and done a runner?'

'Could have.'

'But what's your personal take on it? Your hypothesis?' Henry pushed him.

'I haven't got one, sir.'

'You're a cop. All cops have gut feelings about jobs, about mysteries. And this is a mystery, isn't it? And you knew them both. You supervised them, I'm told.'

'Look, I don't know where you're going with this, but I was questioned extensively when this all happened. I played a big part in the investigation and it all came to nothing. I don't have a clue about it. Yeah, it's a mystery and we did everything we could to solve it, but we didn't and I've tried to lay it to rest. They were my staff. They disappeared. How do you think that makes me feel? Not good, I can tell you. I want to lay those ghosts to rest, sir. You coming digging at the behest of a grieving relative won't change a thing other than to resurrect the past.'

Henry's eyes became cold and unforgiving. 'You seem a bit too blasé about it, Al . . . I'm not getting nice signals from you.'

Major stood up. 'I have things to do.'

Henry drank the remainder of his coffee and got to his feet. He and Major were of similar build and height, though Major was probably ten years younger. 'Personal question,' Henry said. 'No doubt you've been asked it, but I'll ask again.' Major waited. 'What was your relationship with Jo Coniston?'

Major snorted at the stupidity of the question, but Henry saw him shift slightly. He had hit a nerve.

'Purely professional.' He eyed Henry, daring a challenge.

'Yeah, right.'

'But she was a slag, I'll tell you that for nothing,' he said with venom. 'Now, as I said, I've got work to do, DI Christie. Next time come through the proper channels if you wish to interview me. Don't just cold-call me.'

*   *   *

170

Henry descended on to the M60, slotted into the heavy line of traffic in the first lane, weaved out into the middle and put his foot down. He was swearing to himself, feeling frustrated at not having a warrant card and the powers that came with it. If he had, his next move would have been to get the file on the two missing cops and spend some quality time going through it. He banged the steering wheel of the beat-up Astra, swerved into the first lane and exited the motorway, joining the M61 Preston-bound. He kept his foot down and took the car up to a very unsteady 85mph, not caring if cops with speed guns were anywhere about.

Al Major bugged him. A supervisor should have been devastated that two officers under his control had disappeared without trace. Major did not seem to be bothered.

Five minutes down the M61, across to Henry's right was Rivington Pike. Henry looked at the huge hill, with the TV masts beyond, somewhere he and Kate often walked. A place of good memories for him.

He wondered how to get his hands on the file. Although officially still classed as open, he knew it would be gathering dust at GMP headquarters now; given an occasional review, then put away again when no further evidence came to light. Such was the way of the world. There was little chance of him worming his way into GMP Headquarters in his unofficial capacity. They definitely would want to see his ID before he got any further than the front door. The only source of background he could think of which was available to him was from the newspapers of the time, probably the *Manchester Evening News* being the best bet. He would have to find a library with it on micro-fiche and that would mean a trip back to Manchester. He doubted whether a library local to him would have it in the archives.

He sighed. Maybe he had done all he could. He had no obligation to the girl and her family . . . but yet he hated to let anything like this go without wringing its neck first. Maybe he did have an obligation to Jo Coniston, even if he found her alive and well, living a riotous life of debauchery in Rio. He doubted that would be the case.

From what he knew so far, he guessed that she was dead

and so was her partner. Could very well be that Andy Turner might well have the answer. That was a line of enquiry that appealed to him. Find Turner and that would give him some answers. Henry knew where to go to mainline on that one.

He looked at the display on his ringing mobile and groaned. Mobiles were the curse of the modern day. He hated them with a passion.

'Hello, Jane,' he said.

'It's not Jane. It's your fucking Chief Constable using her phone.'

'Oh.'

'You might well say "oh", Henry,' FB stormed loudly. 'Why the fuck have you gone to Manchester? You should be sniffing round the Wicksons, not the bleedin' Trafford Centre. What the fuck has that got to do with the Wicksons?'

'Nowt.'

'Well, get your sorry arse back to Blackpool and get doing what you're paid to do, not gallivanting around the north-west using up county petrol.'

A typical burst of FB, Henry thought, as the Chief ended the call as abruptly as he'd started it. Henry whizzed up the M6, then did a left on to the M55. Soon Blackpool Tower was in sight.

He turned off at junction 3, glancing across to the other side of the motorway where his abduction experience had ended on the hard shoulder. He was going to retrace the route back down the A585 to Poulton-le-Fylde and drive to the Wickson house. It was eerie driving back along the road, one he knew very well, knowing that not very long before, his life had been in terrible danger driving along the same.

He thought about the possibility of dying as he drove along. When he'd been a young cop, the thought had never bothered him because he thought he was immortal, but as age dragged him on, he became more worried than ever about it. He was concerned that he would miss his daughters growing older, seeing them develop into young women and begin their own lives. He did not want to miss any of that because he had

172

completely missed them growing up. The job had always taken precedence. Now, he had determined, it was family that would take first place. This was despite his strong, lingering feelings for Jane Roscoe. He knew he would never seriously consider rekindling their relationship now, even though he seemed incapable of stopping himself from flirting with her, going all doe-eyed and gooey. There was no future in it.

He arrived at the entrance to the Wicksons' and turned up the driveway. Across to the right were the stables. A JCB excavator was shovelling up the remains of the burned-down stables into a tidy stack from which the charred pieces of wood were then scooped up into the back of a massive truck. Work had already started on stable-block rebuild. Parked on the site was also a crusher for the stones and rubble shovelled up by the excavator. It was not in use at that moment.

So busy was he looking at this, he only just stopped in time and pulled in tight to allow what he at first thought was a milk tanker to come down the drive in the opposite direction. As the vehicle squeezed past him, he realized it was not a milk tanker. And why should it have been? This was not a working farm. It was an old articulated fuel tanker. He looked up at the driver and was surprised to see a cigarette in the guy's mouth. Then it manoeuvred past him and was gone.

Henry shook his head, wondering why such a huge tanker was here. Probably delivering oil for the central heating. But it was a very big tanker and he knew that, usually, small rigid tankers brought oil to houses. Then he recalled seeing the dilapidated farm buildings at the rear of the house from the time he was on the hillside. There had been two articulated fuel tankers in the yard then.

His mouth turned down at the corners, his mind actively ingesting these snippets of information. He pressed on and drove to the gravelled parking area at the front of the house. The Bentley and Mercedes were parked there, and a couple of other less grand cars. He drew the Astra in next to the Bentley, relishing the juxtaposition of machines. He got out and rang the front door bell, waiting and whistling. No reply. He looked to the stables again, watching the land-clearing activity. Turning round, he saw a figure riding up the driveway on a horse.

It was Tara.

No . . . he was wrong . . . as the horse and rider got nearer, he saw it was Charlotte, not Tara, in the saddle. From a distance it was an easy mistake to make.

She walked the horse towards the house. Henry approached her.

'Good morning, Charlotte.'

'Hi,' she said cautiously.

'Nice horse.'

'He'll do.'

'How's Chopin?'

'Poorly.' She brought the horse to a halt in front of Henry. He took a wary step back. 'What're you doing here?'

'Your mum asked me, remember?'

'Oh yeah.' She dismounted.

'Is she in?'

'Dunno. Don't care, really.' She hooked the reins over the horse's head. 'Have to walk him in from here. The machines,' she explained. 'Don't want to ride him in case he gets spooked. He can be a handful.' She slapped the horse's neck.

'What's he called?'

'Phoenix.'

'Hello, Phoenix,' Henry said to the beast. Its ears pricked forwards at the mention of its name. Charlotte started to lead him towards the stables. Henry walked along with her. 'No school today?'

'No,' she said shortly, offering no explanation. She did not seem to be in any mood to chat.

'Any progress on the fire?' he asked.

'What do you mean?'

'Are the police getting anywhere with their enquiries?'

'Apparently it was caused by an electrical fault, so there's nothing for them to do.'

This revelation jolted Henry. He thought it better to say nothing. He watched Charlotte slyly out of the corner of his eye as she walked the horse past the excavator and crusher. She was Leanne's age, but looked older. She was very thin and had dark rings around her eyes which accentuated her high, fashion-model cheekbones. She was close to being beautiful, but her pale skin and slightly kinked nose and gauntness kept that beauty at bay. Henry thought she had the look of her mother, rather than her father.

She took the horse into a loose box and pulled the half-door closed behind her. Henry leaned in, watching as she sorted the horse out. She slipped the saddle and bridle off, balancing them across the top of the door, making Henry stand back. She allowed the horse to eat and drink as she started to groom him, firstly by picking out the feet, then grooming his body with a brush and curry comb, using long circular strokes which brought the coat up to a lustrous sheen. She knew what she was doing around horses, talking gently to the animal whilst working on him.

'It was a deliberate fire,' she said above the horse whispering. Her back was towards Henry.

'Eh?' He cocked his head to one side.

'It wasn't an electrical fault,' she spat, continuing brushing the horse. 'Some bastard burned it down and mutilated Chopin.'

'Any idea who?'

'Thought that was your job to find out?'

Henry pouted. 'I'm not sure if your mum wants me to anymore . . . anyway, how do you know the fire was deliberate?'

She turned on Henry, a sick look on her face. 'Take it from me, it was. Any idiot could smell petrol.'

'Who said it wasn't deliberate?'

'Fire Brigade. My dad's got a report. The insurance are paying up—'

Henry was about to say something when, from behind, the sound of the excavator stopped as the operator switched off. A lovely silence came to the stables. Birds could be heard tweeting, sheep baa-ing. But then there was the sound of footsteps approaching. Henry saw two men coming quickly towards him. One was John Lloyd Wickson, the other Jake Coulton.

'Hey you!' Wickson called out. He was pulling off a pair of heavy gloves and had industrial wellington boots on his feet, as did Coulton. Both men were wearing overalls. 'What are you doing? You can't just come on to my land and start talking to my daughter without my permission.' He was fuming.

Coulton loomed behind him. Before, Henry had not been able to place the head of security as he had only seen him from a distance. Now it clicked.

'Get the fuck off my land now,' Wickson boomed furiously.

Charlotte had stopped grooming the horse and had come to the stable door. 'Dad, it's all right.'

'No, it fucking isn't.'

'I think that'll do,' Henry said calmly, now getting his first proper close-up of the almost bankrupt multi-millionaire. He saw a rodent-like man, thin and nasty-looking. 'No need to swear, Mr Wickson.'

'Jake – get this fucker off my property. He's not even a real cop.' His security man stepped past and strode towards Henry.

'Come on, you.'

'You lay a finger on me, Jake, and I'll have your guts.'

A dawning of recognition plastered Coulton's face. Both men now knew each other. He stopped short. Coulton was a big, hard man, as tough as they came. He was also an ex-cop and Henry knew why he was 'ex'.

'Jake, escort him from the premises,' Wickson restated.

Henry held a finger up at Coulton, a small but significant warning. He was under no illusions that on a one-to-one Coulton would get the better of him. He was hoping it would not go that far.

'I'm here with permission,' Henry said. 'Mrs Wickson has asked me to look into why someone is mutilating your horses, see if I can find the person responsible.'

'Not now – permission withdrawn. Get him out of here, Jake.'

Coulton reached out with a big right hand.

'No need to touch me, Jake.' Henry knew when to withdraw.

'Walk him to his car.'

Henry's nostrils flared. He said, 'That's the last time I save your life, pal.' He looked at the silent figure of Charlotte and winked surreptitiously at her. He started to walk away, then stopped shoulder to shoulder with Wickson. 'You've got a lot of secrets, haven't you, Mr Wickson. Don't want people delving, do you?'

Wickson gave him a stone-cold deadly stare. Henry looked up and down at Wickson's protective attire. 'Been mending a tractor?'

'Go and don't return, or you'll suffer,' he whispered.

Henry set off back to the house. He saw the front door open and Tara Wickson run down the steps and jump into the Mercedes. With a scrunch of tyres, she accelerated away.

Jake Coulton caught up with Henry and gave him a push between the shoulder blades, sending Henry stumbling, almost making him lose his balance. Henry skidded and spun round.

'Come on, you fucker. Get off this property. Don't hang about.'

Henry stood his ground, chest expanding like a caveman.

'And don't even pretend you're a cop, Henry. You're suspended and soon you'll be a nobody, like they made me.'

'Difference being you were a criminal, Jake. You were an apple ridden with smelly worms. All I've done is make a mistake. And if you assault me, make no mistake, I'll get you and you'll lose this nice, cushy job because you'll be back in clink. So back off.'

They were standing about four feet apart from each other, both perilously close to invading each other's personal space. Any nearer and they would have had to grapple, such was the man-thing. The reek of testosterone filled the air. Henry knew he would have come off second best. Coulton's reputation had been as a hard cop, but his hardness deviated into intimidation, then into blackmail and then he went too far. A man he had arrested ended up with a broken jaw and the Discipline and Complaints department (now modernly renamed Professional Standards) used it as a platform to put surveillance on Coulton. He was caught on video visiting the man and threatening further violence if he pursued his complaint. Coulton was soon out of a job because he ended up with a criminal conviction and a three-month prison sentence. The only sad thing was that it had taken so long for the organization to get its act together and stuff him.

Henry edged away and made it unscathed to his car. He saw Charlotte and her father arguing back at the stables, could hear the sound of their raised voices. Then the excavator came back to life, drowning out anything more. Henry got into the Astra and set off, driving purposely slowly past the brooding figure of Jake Coulton, who watched him all the way down the drive.

He headed back to the main road, intending to drive home and think about future tactics when his mobile phone rang. He did not recognize the number displayed.

'Mr Christie, it's me, Tara.'

'I've just been escorted off your premises.'

'I'm not surprised.'

'Where are you?'

'On Garstang Road, near to St Mary's High School.'

'Can I see you? We need to talk.'

She hesitated. 'This is a bit close to home.'

'How about making your way up to Fleetwood? There's a café in the Floral Hall complex, overlooks the beach.'

'I know it. Fifteen minutes.'

Henry arrived first. He went into the café and ordered a bracing pot of tea and a couple of scones. He hadn't eaten since breakfast and was feeling dithery, particularly after his near fisticuffs with Jake Coulton. His blood-sugar levels needed a whacking big boost. He drank the tea sugarless, though, relying on the scone and jam to do the job.

He chose a table by the window, overlooking the beach, people-watching until Tara arrived. She looked flustered and breathless, but still very attractive with a pair of eyes that could have stopped any man in his tracks. Henry poured her a tea and pushed it to her with a scone.

'Do you still want me to help you, Tara?' Henry thought he would go for the direct route.

'Yes, but I don't know how.'

'It's unlikely that your husband and his gorilla will let me back at the house. He doesn't seem to want anyone nosing

178

around at all. Why is that? Surely it would be in his own interests.'

'Again – I don't know.'

'You don't know very much, do you?' He did not say it harshly.

She looked down at the scone, her eyes very unhappy. 'We pretty much lead separate lives. One of those things.' She shrugged her slim shoulders. 'Shit happens. It's never been a strong marriage.'

'Why marry in the first place then?'

She gave him a look which told him it wasn't his business. 'I'm just concerned about Charlotte. She's been a bit wayward recently . . . teenage-girl stuff . . . but the horse mutilation business has been really getting to her. I wanted to try to stop it for her. She needs a bit of steadiness right now.'

'Seems a bit more than just horse mutilation now, though, doesn't it? The fire, someone shooting at your husband?'

'The fire was accidental, an electrical fault.' Her eyes avoided Henry's. He reached out and tilted her chin. Her skin felt wonderfully soft.

'We both know different, don't we? And even if it was accidental, who mutilated the horse and why did that man take shots at your husband? And don't tell me it was a bloody poacher. He went on to kill two cops and a nurse. He's a professional killer and I got there just in time for your husband. Now there's a nationwide manhunt on for him.'

She raised her chin off the tips of his fingers.

'This stuff all comes right back at John Lloyd Wickson. What is he up to, Tara? Give me the answer to that, and I'll solve the horse problem.'

'Do you really think they're connected?'

'Is grass green? Is the Pope a Catholic? I didn't even begin to think you were that dim, Tara.'

Her slim body sagged. 'I'm just bothered about Charlotte. I haven't a clue what John is up to.'

'Then maybe you'd better start finding out, don't you think? One might just assist the other.'

Nine

Henry sat in his conservatory, slouched down in one of the comfortable wicker chairs, a stubby bottle of Stella Artois resting on his stomach, balanced there in the grip of his right hand. His mind churned through the day, trying to put things in order, to make sense of what he had learned. He shifted painfully, grimacing. The knife slash down his side was hurting, though it had not done so all day.

The visit to Manchester had been fruitless, if tantalizing. There was something not quite right about Jo Coniston's disappearance and nothing right at all about Sgt Al Major, her caring, sharing supervisor. Henry struggled to see a way forward with it, other than to do some desktop research into the news stories of the time and some of his own 'on the streets' research.

Next, his visit to the happy home of the Wickson family. It struck him that they were a deeply troubled trio of characters. John Lloyd Wickson was clearly up to no good in more ways than one. If she was to be believed, Tara did not know what he was up to, although even to Henry, some of his misdemeanours were blatantly obvious. Charlotte had her problems, too, probably caused by the relationship between her mum and dad. She was the only one of the three Henry felt anything like sorry for. The kids always get it, he thought bitterly. They may be amazingly adaptable, but it was always the parents who forced that adaptability on them.

He thought about Tara trying to do something to help her wayward daughter. Horses were obviously Charlotte's big love and someone was hurting them. Tara wanted her daughter's pain to stop. Henry wondered if that would ever be possible.

He sipped his reassuringly expensive drink. It was the

only one he was planning to have that evening because he had decided to go out and do some schmoozling, as he called it. A bit of dancing with wolves. Put himself in amongst the people who could help him, maybe. That was if he could get out. Tea time with Kate had been fraught, and when he hesitantly revealed his plans for the evening, frostiness descended like a winter's morning. She completely disapproved of his involvement in anything like this and it was straining her, despite his reassurances.

A deep sigh engulfed him. He adjusted his position on the chair. Looking round, he watched Leanne approach him from the dining room.

'Hi, kid,' he said, touching her arm. She kissed the top of his head and sat down on his knee. She wanted something. 'What is it, honey?'

'Dad,' she began, 'there's a disco on tonight down at the youth club in town and I'd like to go. It finishes at eleven. I've done my homework.'

Henry kind of shrugged his whole body. 'Yeah . . . and . . . ?'

'Mum says I can go, but I have to be back here and in bed for half-eleven.'

'And . . . ?' Henry waited for the punchline.

'Can you pick me up? Mum says she's too tired. Otherwise . . . otherwise I won't be able to go . . . and all me mates're going . . . Jackie, Lorraine, Kylie . . .' She started counting them off on her fingers. 'Louise . . . Charlotte . . . John . . . Debs . . .'

'OK, OK,' he said, defeated. 'I'll pick you up. But it's eleven on the dot . . . got that?' She nodded eagerly. 'Is that Charlotte Wickson, by the way?'

'Yeah . . . Ooh, Dad, you're an angel.' She kissed him.

'And who the hell is John?' His eyebrows rose.

Leanne stood up abruptly. Red embarrassment shot up her neck and attacked her face like nettle rash. 'Nobody,' she said petulantly.

'OK,' he backed off, holding out his hand. She slid hers into his and they squeezed each other's fingers. 'I'll pick you up, no probs. I'll take you, if your mum doesn't want to.'

'Thanks, Dad, that'd be brill. Love you.' She bounded off happily.

Henry settled back reflectively. In the distance he heard the front doorbell chime. Voices grew gradually louder until Kate appeared in front of Karl Donaldson, the big American from the FBI in London.

'Henry, Karl's come to see you,' she said coldly. She stepped aside and forced a smile on to her face. 'Tea, coffee, beer?' she asked Donaldson.

'Do you have water?'

'Flavoured? Fizzy? Still? Or from the tap?'

'Flavoured and still would be nice.'

'I'll get it.' She rounded the big man, glancing ever so quickly at her husband. The two men watched her go. Donaldson looked at Henry. 'Everything OK?'

Henry cleared his throat nervously. 'Yeah . . . Take a pew.' Donaldson sat on the two-seater sofa, almost filling it with his size, which was all muscle. He placed a black briefcase on his knees.

'I see,' said Donaldson.

'Yes, icy,' Henry confirmed.

Donaldson chuckled, but stopped abruptly and put his face straight when Kate reappeared with his tumbler of water, then went with a cob on.

'Anyway – how are you?'

'OK.' Henry winced to get some sympathy. 'Got a pain in the side, but it'll be reet,' he said, adopting a broad Lancashire accent. 'Am pissed off with you in some way for putting me into bat with FB, though.'

Donaldson looked contrite for a moment, then said, 'Business is business.'

'Yeah, I know. So why are you here?'

Donaldson flicked open the catches of his briefcase and lifted the lid. 'Got some information for you. Haven't told anyone else yet. Hot off the press.'

Henry almost said, 'Whoa, not a good idea,' but his natural inquisitiveness got in the way.

Donaldson extracted a brown manila file and opened it. There was nothing written on the front of it to indicate its content. 'Fast-track ballistics, remember?' He leafed through a few pages. 'Confirmed for sure that the STAR pistol the guy held to your head is the same weapon that killed Zeke and Marty Cragg. Also the weapon that killed my first undercover operative in Mendoza's gang. The same weapon was also used in four other killings across Europe. All four are individuals who either crossed or were rivals of Mendoza.'

'OK – same gun, but how do you know that Mendoza put the contracts out?'

'You know I've been working more or less full time on Mendoza ever since Zeke was murdered. I now have an informant quite high up Mendoza's chain of command who keeps feeding me tit-bits. I'm nurturing him slowly, but he may be of limited value because of his position. He only knows so much, even though he's quite an important player.'

'Why is he giving you stuff?'

'Ah-hah, good question. His motives are not yet clear to me and I don't trust the bastard . . . Anyway, no one else knows about him, got that Henry? I'm only telling you because I trust you.'

Henry nodded. It would go no further.

'That means Mendoza's hit man has taken out at least nine people?'

'More probably, but we just haven't made the links – yet.'

'And I had him – and he got away,' Henry said, punishing himself.

'Don't feel too bad, pal, we'll get him somehow . . . I've got some more information.' He fished out another sheet from the file, then looked at Henry. 'Your CSI's dusted your car, the car the hit man was using, and the weapons and anything else they thought this guy had touched and lifted some very useful fingerprints, together with some low-copy DNA samples, which I fed into our system.' He paused for a moment for effect. It worked. Henry sat bolt upright. 'We've identified the bastard.'

'Yes!' blurted Henry as though Blackpool FC had just won the FA cup.

'He has about fifty aliases but was born Paul Verner in 1960 in Nottingham, England.'

'Nottingham?'

'Yep. He had a string of juvenile cautions here, then his family moved to New York where his father was in engineering. But young Paul continued his wayward ways and fell into gangland pretty easily by all accounts. He got his first murder charge when he was seventeen. He was acquitted and never appeared at court since, but we know he went to work as a Mob-enforcer, graduating to full-scale hit man.'

'From bloody Nottingham?'

'Yep – full of outlaws, Nottingham.'

'Ah, Robin Hood, nice one. But Nottingham? I can't believe that.'

'He's been arrested several times on murder counts, but always walked before trial. Intimidated witnesses, usual story. He disappeared from view about three years ago, which pretty much ties in with the first dead body in Europe. France, actually.'

'Gone working for Mendoza?'

'On contract, to coin a phrase. We think things were getting too hot for him Stateside . . . he was under intense investigation following the murder of a loan shark in Brooklyn, then went to ground. Not been seen since – until this.'

'Interesting.'

'The family he worked for in the US have strong links with their Sicilian clan, who have strong trading links with Mendoza. We think his services were offered to Mendoza and being a Brit, with a British accent, he fitted in pretty well with the European scene.'

'The circle completes,' said Henry.

'And now he's here involved in some business for Mendoza and the American mob – and you interrupted him.'

'Yeah, it makes sense. Let me get this: Wickson gets involved in drug importation on behalf of the Yanks. He upsets them in some way. So Mendoza sends in Verner to do the business for his American criminal colleagues.'

'That could be it.'

Henry sank in his chair. 'He left a phone message for me.'

Donaldson's mouth opened. 'He what?'

Henry fetched the cordless house phone and replayed the

message for Donaldson's ears. The tanned American went pale as he handed the phone back to Henry. 'You need protection.'

Henry shook his head. 'I think he'll be too busy to be worried about me. I've just pissed him off, that's all. He'll get over me.'

Donaldson did not look convinced.

'Any photos of him?'

'A few.' He reached in the case and handed Henry a stack which he skimmed through. One was a police mugshot from years ago, the others mainly grainy black and white surveillance shots taken from a distance. A couple could have been used for press release, maybe.

His eyes narrowed. 'You said you haven't shown these to anyone else yet, or told anyone this info. Do you have your own agenda here?' Henry was thinking that the American might want to play his own game with this. It would not have surprised him. That was often how it worked, even within the same police force, never mind across other agencies which sometimes had conflicting objectives.

'No. I want the guy as much as your lot.'

'I take it you'll be immediately handing this stuff over to FB, then?' Henry smirked.

'All I'm saying is that I have no agenda that conflicts with your force. I want him brought to justice.'

Henry nodded acquiescence, knowing that the information would not be passed straight away to Lancashire officers, even though he did not know why not.

'So why tell me?'

'I wanted you to know what you've been up against. But, yeah, I'd appreciate it if you let me tell FB what he needs to know, when he needs to know it.'

Henry nodded and thought: Knowledge is power.

Leanne's youth club was located in a building in the centre of town, close to the Winter Gardens complex, which held unpleasant memories for Henry. He drove her in the firm's Astra, determined to get as much use from it as possible whilst his own was still being repaired. When she realized he intended to convey her in it as opposed to her mother's spic 'n' span Renault Clio, she threw a wobbler.

'I am not going in that heap of dirt.'

'It's the only way you'll get down to town, unless you want to go by public transport.'

'I will not be seen dead in it.'

'Have you got your bus fare?'

'In that case you must drop me off around the corner because I'll die of embarrassment if any of my friends see me climbing out of this.' Her face and screwed-up mouth said it all.

'Get in and stop whining.'

The car set off in a cloud of dark-blue smoke. Leanne shrank into her seat and hid her face behind her hands. 'Oh my God,' she said like one of the actors in *Friends*, 'this is so uncool.'

'It's a bloody car,' Henry said, enjoying himself perversely, 'and it almost works.'

He drove her into town and dropped her off as requested, around the corner from the youth club. As he pulled into the side of the road, and just before Leanne alighted, Henry checked his rear-view mirror and saw Tara Wickson's Mercedes. The car swished past with Tara at the wheel, giving Henry no sideways glance at all, not seeming to notice him.

Leanne leapt out of the offensive Astra, slammed the door and stalked away without a thank you. Henry could not believe how short her skirt was and how she dared show so much midriff. He almost dragged her back home to get her redressed in a sack, but said to himself, No, no, it's OK, don't get wound up . . . she's growing up. It's fine, but if that John lays a finger on her, he's dead meat.

He set off, slotting in a couple of cars behind Tara's Merc. To head to Poulton, she should have gone left at the next junction. She turned right.

Henry could do nothing else but follow her.

It was in his blood, the instinct of a cop.

Henry knew for a fact that the general public did not expect to be followed. People like himself, who had, for some part of their lives, led a clandestine existence, did expect to be tailed and knew what to look for. This is why he found it slightly

186

amusing on one hand and worrying on the other that Tara Wickson had no idea who was behind her. He could have attached his car to her rear bumper with a tow rope and she would have been none the wiser. The worrying thing was that he found out that someone was following him.

He had not been sure at first. He thought it was just coincidence, but his entrails tightened up when it went beyond coincidence and, as James Bond would say, into enemy action.

Which put him in a predicament.

He wanted to know where Tara was going, which meant he would lose her if he took action to shake his tail.

Unless the follower was after her and not him.

For the moment he decided to stick with Tara.

She drove across the one-way system near to the Winter Gardens and weaved through various roads down on to the promenade. Once on the seafront she turned right and headed north, moving quite quickly and racing through lights on amber. Henry managed to stay with her, as did the vehicle three cars behind him. He saw it was a plain Vauxhall Cavalier, grey coloured, the sort of car that blended into the background. There was one man in it, just a dark shape hunched at the wheel.

Henry held his breath and gritted his teeth.

Could this be Verner?

Tara carried on up to North Shore, then turned right into the car park of the Hilton Hotel, a red-brick monstrosity overlooking the promenade.

Henry, several cars behind, sailed past and glimpsed her screeching into a parking space and jumping out of the car. Henry drove on to the roundabout at Gynn Square and kept left to stay on the prom.

Three cars behind him was the Cavalier – staying with him.

He needed to be sure. He drove on, the tram tracks on his left running parallel with the road. The remnants of last year's illuminations were still strung from lamppost to lamppost. He was heading towards Bispham. So what better place in the world was there, he thought, to see if he really was being followed?

187

At the next set of traffic lights, he turned into Red Bank, Bispham's main shopping street. Further down the road was a Sainsbury's supermarket. He checked his mirror. The Cavalier had made it through the lights.

Henry swung a right into Sainsbury's car park. He hurtled round it and slotted into a space at the far side, jumping out of the car and running at a crouch, using other parked cars for cover, back towards the main road.

If his tail was of any standard, he would not come in behind him, but would find somewhere to hole up with a view of the exit and pick up the follow when Henry re-emerged on to the road.

Henry ducked low and watched the Cavalier glide slowly past down Red Bank. He kept hidden behind a Transit van. The driver of the Cavalier strained to look across the car park and Henry saw his face quite clearly. Some relief flooded into him. It was not Verner. That was reassuring, but nothing else was. He thought he recognized the driver, but was not sure. He wondered if it had anything to do with John Lloyd Wickson.

The Cavalier went out of sight. Henry stayed where he was, the Transit keeping him out of sight of the road.

A couple of minutes later, it reappeared, cruising slowly. It went past the car park and pulled in fifty metres up the road.

Henry wiped a nervous hand across his face.

Decision made.

He vaulted the low wall separating the supermarket car park from the footpath and walked smartly up Red Bank towards the prom.

Straight in, he thought. He did not have time to mess about.

Within seconds he was at the rear nearside of the Cavalier. Two more strides and he was at the passenger door. He tried the handle – locked – and contented himself by squatting down on his haunches and tapping on the window with his knuckles and giving the driver one of his best, nastiest smiles.

Henry could not have had a better reaction if he had cattle-prodded the occupant. He literally leapt in his seat, then pulled himself together and tried to brave it out. His face seemed familiar to Henry. He was sure he had seen the young man quite recently.

'Can I have a word?' Henry said through the glass.

The window descended electronically a couple of inches.

'What's up?'

'Why are you following me?'

'Whaddya mean?'

'I mean, why are you following me?'

The man bit his lip, his head flipped back and hit the head rest. 'Shit,' he said, cracking suddenly.

Henry then recognized him. He was the cop at the GMP surveillance unit who had let him in to see Al Major that morning.

'Bit off your patch, aren't you? And not that good at following people, either, not for a surveillance cop, that is.'

'If I'd wanted to follow you without being seen, I would've,' he defended himself proudly, realizing he had been well and truly blown out.

'Fine. Now tell me why you're following me and let's talk other than through a glass partition, shall we?'

The officer reached across and unlocked the door. Henry dropped in beside him.

'Is there just you?'

'Yeah.'

'Are you doing a favour for Al Major?'

'No, am I fuck!'

'What then? I'll tell you now, I don't like being followed. Makes me nervous and prone to rash acts of violence.'

'OK, OK.' He placed both hands on the wheel and gripped tightly. 'I needed to talk to you. I found out where you lived, waited for you and was trying to pick up courage, OK?'

Henry nodded. 'What's your name?'

'Ken Sloane.'

'OK, Ken Sloane, what's this all about?'

'You came to see Al Major this morning, yeah?'

'You let me in.'

'About Jo and Dale?' Henry said yeah again. 'I'm not proud of this, but I earwigged your conversation.'

'Ahh . . . and?'

'I'm not happy about it.'

'What, our conversation?'

'No.' He shook his head, bowed his chin on to his chest. 'The cover-up. I'm not happy about the cover-up. It's been nagging and gnawing away at me like a rat.' He sighed and raised his head. 'I was on duty the night they went missing.' He stopped, unsure how to continue.

Henry prompted him with a gesture.

'None of us should've gone out that night. Some of the team were off sick, others on leave, the motorcyclist crashed on the way out and the radios didn't fucking work.'

'I presume the investigation team have inquired about all these things?'

'Oh, yeah.'

'Where's the cover-up, then?'

'Al Major, the bastard.' Sloane scratched the back of his neck as though he was trying to get through to his brain. 'He told us to say nothing about the radios not working. He couldn't cover up the lack of numbers or the biker coming off his machine, but he covered up the radio bit. He threatened some of us and said we'd lose our jobs if that came to light. And you know what, like tarts we all went along with it. What a shower of shit we are. He's a shit sergeant now and harasses and slags off all the women who come on to the branch if they don't let him sleep with them. But there's others like him too, his mates on the branch. It's obscene. They all stuck together for him and no one got any blame for Jo and Dale. I'm not saying he had anything to do with 'em disappearing, but it wouldn't have happened if we'd had a full team and proper equipment.'

'Was he having an affair with Jo?'

'Yeah – but she saw through him quick style and dumped him. He couldn't let it go and had to keep on at her, the bastard.'

Henry looked at Ken, who was now allowing years of resentment to burst out.

'He sent us out poorly staffed and with no fucking radios to find one of the city's most dangerous crims.'

'Andy Turner.'

'Yeah – and Jo spotted him, trailed him, and then we lost contact, sort of.'

'Major says she lost him, then he told her to come back in.'

'I think she found him again. She didn't let go, that one. I'll bet she found him again, couldn't get through to us and I think Turner murdered them.'

'What makes you think that?'

'Turner went to ground, didn't he? Hasn't been seen for years, now, no intell, no info, nothing. I bet they stumbled on him and he whacked them. Has to be.'

'What if they didn't stumble on him? What if they decided to do a bunk together? Quit the rat race, go live on a beach somewhere? It has happened.'

'And leave everything behind? Their cars, their pads? Money in their bank accounts?' Sloane said in disbelief. 'No way. They were murdered, Turner did it and he did a runner after covering his tracks.'

'Interesting hypothesis,' said Henry. 'Never been proven, though. Even the police car they were using that night's never been found. Where the hell did that go?'

Sloane shrugged. 'You know as well as I do that it's easy to dispose of a car. It's either been crushed and recycled, or it's in a flooded quarry somewhere. But there is one thing I do know – Al Major should never have sent us out that night, knowing the radios weren't working. They're our lifeline.'

'The fact remains he did, though, Ken.'

'Well, I want something doing about it. I've sat on this for far too long and it's fucking me up.' He turned and looked pleadingly at Henry, his face distorted with distress. 'Help,' he said pitifully.

'Maybe the time's come to make a stand, Ken.'

'Jeez,' said Henry to himself, walking back to his car. 'Jeez,' he said again, trying to work out the implications, if any, of what Ken Sloane had told him. The same Ken Sloane who thought he was talking to an officer of a higher rank who wasn't suspended from duty. 'Jeez,' he said once more for good luck and got into the Astra.

191

He had sent Sloane off with the promise he would take the matter forward. The only way he knew that would happen would be for him to tell somebody in GMP, but Sloane did not want that to happen. He did not trust his organization. He wanted an outsider to look into it and at that time there was no one more on the outside than Henry. He was so far outside, he was out of bounds. But Sloane did not know that.

He drove back to the Hilton Hotel on North Promenade, glad to see that Tara Wickson's car was still there. She was probably killing time with friends in the bar, he guessed, until it was time to pick Charlotte up from the disco. Henry wondered if there was any value in hanging around to see her. He drove around the hotel car park and decided not to stay. He was going to go and do what he intended to do that evening, when Tara emerged from the front door of the Hilton, hand in hand with a man Henry did not recognize. He swerved into a parking bay and adjusted his rear-view mirror to watch the couple walk across to Tara's Mercedes.

Suddenly she broke away from the man.

They spoke a few words.

Seconds later they were in her car, kissing, silhouettes from Henry's viewpoint. Then her reversing lights came on and the Merc reversed quickly out of the bay. She drove north along the prom.

Henry followed. She went through Bispham, continuing north through Cleveleys and up into Fleetwood, working through the streets of the old fishing town before stopping outside the North Euston Hotel on the front. Tara and her man went arm in arm into the hotel and Henry let it go at that. He did not have the time or inclination to stay with her, as interesting as it was, though not, he thought, all that surprising. Tara had a lover. Whoopee-do, fancy that.

In a puff of black smoke he shot past the North Euston and headed back to his happy hunting ground of Blackpool and, in particular, to the drug-infested South Shore.

He felt comfortable here. It was like putting on an old pair of slippers. He had done much of his police work on the streets of South Shore. He had dealt with dozens of people around here, arrested lots of them, protected many of them. When he got out of his car it struck him he wasn't actually far from being one of them. As a cop he had been part of the fabric of life here, a denizen of the jungle.

The thought made his stomach churn. At least he was one of the predators, though.

It was 8.45 p.m. He had wasted an hour and a half already. He would have to leave the area by 10.45 p.m. at the latest to be in time to pick up Leanne from the youth club. Two hours. Not much time to mooch around, show his face, ask a few questions, ruffle a few feathers.

The evening had gone chilly. That good old Blackpool wind was starting to whip in from the Irish Sea as the tide came in; spats of rain were dripping in from a cloudy sky. He hunched down into his denim jacket, hands thrust deep into his chinos.

He started to wander.

The streets were as cold as the night, the dark skyline dominated by the structure that was the Big One on the Pleasure Beach, one of the world's most terrifying roller-coaster rides. A light at the top of the framework blinked its warning to planes wishing to land at nearby Blackpool airport: 'Don't hit me, it'll hurt.'

Henry sauntered along a few terraced streets. Much of the housing was now given over to customers of the DSS. There was a high level of unemployment in the area, which was one of the country's most deprived.

Near a corner shop, Henry paused in shadow. A group of teenage kids, some on mountain bikes, hung around outside the door, harassing customers who looked like easy targets, and generally behaving badly. Henry thanked his lucky stars his two girls hadn't gone down this route. He had been fortunate with his kids, despite his neglect of them over the years. Kate had done a fine job with them.

He watched the group. He would have liked to go and remonstrate with them, but it would have been useless and possibly dangerous. Good people had been killed making a point.

A scruffy-looking cop car – obviously from the same stable

as his borrowed Astra – crawled past, two officers on board. The youngsters stopped and watched and when it had gone, behaved even more outrageously than before, dancing around as though on the grave of law and order. Why hadn't the cops stopped and spoken to them? Henry wanted to know. His mouth turned down with distaste. Were they afraid?

Another pedal cyclist appeared from around the corner. This was an older youth, maybe eighteen or nineteen. He cycled towards the group by the shop. One member detached himself from them and met the newcomer.

It happened quickly. The handover. The payoff. A drug deal completed in less than the blink of an eye. Then the older boy – the street dealer – was away on his bike whilst the younger lad – the buyer – sauntered calmly back to the main gang, smirking as though he'd won the lottery.

Street life, Henry thought.

The dealer had disappeared from the scene. Henry knew who he was and maybe what he had witnessed would come in useful at some later date – if he ever got reinstated.

He did not know the name of the buyer, but watched as he now became a street dealer, handing out tiny packages to several outstretched hands. Henry doubted it would go any further than this. These guys would be the end users. The consumers of a product which could well have originated on the other side of the world. Passed through countless hands, making huge amounts of money along the way for the suppliers, middle men and deal makers. But not the users. These were the ones who ultimately provided the money on which the whole business was based. And where did that money come from, Henry thought cynically. High-volume crime: auto theft, burglary, street robbery. Crime that had spiralled out of control and there was nothing the police could do to stem its relentless progress.

Truth was, as Henry knew, that the government had missed the opportunity through a very short-sighted approach. Performance targets were easy in terms of crimes such as stealing from vehicles, and police forces had been bullied into dealing with this type of crime by the Home Office. The reality was that, on the whole, crimes like these were purely driven by one thing: drugs.

Now it had hit home that drug abuse was the actual cause of the problem, it was to late too do anything meaningful about it. The drug trade was so sophisticated that when a dealer or supplier was taken out, a replacement was operating in a matter of hours, or less.

Because the boat had been missed by not disrupting the trade twenty years ago, it was now impossible to claw anything back. Society was stuck with it.

Henry shrugged. Not his problem. He stepped out of the shadow and walked purposely through the cluster of youths outside the shop. They watched him with suspicion and their loud chatter ceased. They did not hassle him, stepped aside and let him pass.

He walked on and turned into the first pub he came to, the King's Cross. Not long ago a gangland killing had taken place here when three drug dealers lost their lives. The place had closed down for a short time after that, reopening with the fanfare of high expectation. Within weeks it had reverted to what it always had been: a hang-out for losers, druggies, prostitutes and gays.

Henry eased his way to the bar. Heavy-metal rock music pounded out from speakers hung from the ceiling. The smoke-filled atmosphere reeked of cannabis and human sweat. Henry had a bottle of Bud, ignoring the grubby glass proffered by the barman, choosing to sip from the bottle. It tasted sweet and light. He leaned on the bar. He recognized about a dozen people. Some he'd arrested. Others he'd dealt with under different circumstances.

Some eyeballed him.

He smiled at one man in particular, raising his bottle to him. The man single-fingered Henry and turned away in disgust. A cop in the place!

Henry didn't give a fuck. The guy he was actually looking for was not in. He necked the Bud and continued the trawl.

The next pub was smaller, but catered for a similar clientele. Except for gay people. It was a venue notorious for queer-bashing and some homosexuals had been severely beaten in the pub's car park. One had been raped by four heterosexual men. Nice folk, Henry thought as he recalled the incident. He had caught all the men responsible. Their prison sentences had been derisory.

There was just a smattering of people inside. A big screen had been pulled down and a live football match was being televised.

At the bar he had a Coke this time – again in the bottle. He distrusted the glasses in these places, liked to see bottle tops being removed if possible. This time he gravitated to a table in one corner from which he could see all entrances and exits. It was 9.30 p.m. He thought he could either sit tight and hope for the best, or continue on what could be a fruitless tour. Sitting and waiting now suited him. At least he could watch the football. This was a watering hole and sooner or later both predator and prey came to drink. If he was lucky, in the next hour or so, his prey would show and he would pounce.

He sipped the Coke. Finished it, got another, sat and sipped. He was reminded of a Rolling Stones' song, 'The Spider and the Fly': 'Sitting, thinking, sinking, drinking . . . Jump right ahead in my web.' It worried him slightly that he could relate many situations in which he found himself to the lyrics of songs.

'Come on, fly. I've got a daughter to pick up,' he mumbled.

9.50 p.m.

The door opened and a gaggle of half-drunk, half-stoned girls stumbled through. Short skirts, micro tops, tons of smeared make-up. His guts lurched. Did his eldest daughter Jenny do this sort of thing? They looked and behaved awfully.

Then a young man walked in, closely followed by another.

The first one interested Henry. He was dressed slickly. Designer gear, making Henry raise his eyebrows.

This was his prey. Troy Costain.

The man walked straight up to the girls. They were ecstatic to see him. Two of them draped themselves around his neck, kissing him as his hands felt them up without any complaint from them.

Henry smirked. 'You've come up in the world, Troy my laddie,' he said to himself.

Costain bought a round of drinks. The young man who had come in with him smooched with one of the girls. The drinks came. Alcopops.

One of the girls sidled up to the main man and whispered something in his ear. Her hand cupped his genitals, giving them a playful squeeze which almost made his eyes shoot out of their sockets.

Costain and the girl discussed something, then both turned and walked hand in hand towards the toilets. Costain touched his friend on the shoulder and mouthed a few words in his ear, causing him to leave the girl he had been getting intimate with to follow the couple out.

Henry waited a minute and then downed his Coke thinking, I'm going to end up in some grotty bogs again here. He followed the trio down towards the toilets.

Above the door marked 'Toilets' was also an exit sign. Henry knew that beyond the door was a corridor off which were male and female loos and at the end was the doorway out on to the car park.

He pushed the door open. The corridor was empty. The first on the right was the ladies. He entered without hesitation. Inside it smelled awful, a concoction of urine, shit, stale dope and cheap perfume. The walls were scrawled with obscene graffiti, the likes of which he had never seen in a men's toilet. His nose turned. He reluctantly stepped fully inside and did a quick recce. They were empty.

Back out and down the corridor, he twisted next right into the gents. It had all the smells of the female toilets minus the perfume, plus an overflowing toilet bowl which had flooded the tiled floor. Again it was empty.

They had gone out on to the car park to conduct whatever their business was.

Henry approached the exit door, which opened outward. He pushed and found it would not move. Slightly puzzled, he applied more pressure, but it still refused to open. He realized it had been wedged, a favourite trick of a dealer to prevent or at least telegraph unwanted interruptions.

Henry reared back and flat-footed the door. It gave an inch. He repeated the size 11 method of opening doors. It rocked open and he was through, out on to the concrete slope leading down to the car park, noticing the wooden wedge on the floor.

The two men and the girl were like rabbits caught in headlights.

The younger of the two men bristled and stood upright. The other two stepped back guiltily.

'Troy,' Henry called, 'need a word, pal.'

The younger man was obviously the minder. He glanced nervously over his shoulder, then back at Henry. 'What do you want me to do, Troy?'

'Knife the fucker,' came the response Henry did not really want to hear.

'Who is he?' the minder asked, not realizing that minders should ask questions later.

'A cop. Knife him, you cunt.'

There was the flash of a blade under fluorescent light. Henry saw it glint. A long, thin knife. Blood pounded in his ears. The side of his chest called out, reminding him how much a knife can hurt, even if it doesn't go right in.

'Put it down, son,' he said coolly, 'or I'll put you down.' Henry knew what sort of a character he was dealing with. This was no Verner. This was just a street kid. He took a step towards the knife-wielding minder, who, more scared than he was, stepped a pace back. 'Drop it, or you're fucked. I mean it.'

'Do him,' Troy called bravely from behind the girl. 'Fuckin' do him, Ashey.'

Henry opened his hands, exposing his unprotected torso.

'C'mon Ashey,' he dared him, 'come on lad. You either drop it or you go for me. No half measures, sonny. This is a big boy's game you're playing. Got the bottle?' he taunted.

'T . . . Troy?' he uttered nervously. The knife shook in his hands.

Behind him, the girl broke cover and did a runner. Henry did not care about her. It was Troy he wanted.

'Is this your first test, Ashey?' Henry asked him, taking another threatening step. 'Bottle? You need it, y'know?'

'You come any nearer me and I'll fuckin' gut you,' he warned Henry, taking a firmer grip on the knife.

'You sound like a fishwife.' Henry took that fateful step.

Ashey, minder to a major drug dealer, shrieked with fear. His hands flew up into the air, the knife disappeared into the darkness somewhere and never clattered down. Ashey turned tail and legged it.

'Ashey, you fuckin' twat, get back here, get back here!' Troy howled, but Ashey, his protection, had gone into the night. Troy looked nervously at Henry.

'Not much cop, was he?'

'Fuck you, Henry.'

'You gonna leg it too?'

'Might.'

'Go on then. I fancy chasing you.'

Troy took up the offer, spun quickly and went for it. Before he had gone five metres, Henry's big hands slapped down on his shoulders, followed by Henry's bulk. Troy staggered to his knees with Henry on top, forcing him face down into the tarmac which covered the car park. Henry placed his right knee at the mid-point between Troy's shoulder blades and dropped all his weight on to that point, almost crushing his lungs and heart. An agonized gasp escaped from Troy.

'You're hurting me.'

'Good,' said Henry. 'You're a little twat and I don't like you and now, to cap it all, you're dealing, Troy, and I don't like that very much.'

'Just a few Es is all,' he pleaded defensively.

'Oh, is that all?' Henry increased the pressure on his knee. 'That's OK then.'

'Aaargh!' The breath went out of Troy. 'Jesus!'

Henry eased off, stood up and dragged the doll-like figure up to his feet with both hands, frog-marched him to a car and deposited him face down on the bonnet. 'Now let's see. Empty your pockets.'

'I can't, not from here,' he whined, his cheek rammed down on the cold metal, his hands trapped underneath himself. He had a point, but Henry was unrelenting. His own face came down to within an inch of Troy's.

199

'Do your best,' he breathed into his nostrils. Henry did ease back slightly to allow him access to his pockets. 'Put it all on the car.' A selection of items slowly appeared.

'That's it,' Costain said. 'That's everything.'

Henry yanked him off the bonnet and drove him towards the high wall at the back of the car park and pinned him against it while he ran his hands over Troy's clothing, including a good root around the crotch area where good things often get concealed and cops are just too nicey-nice to search people properly. All Henry found was meat and two veg.

He spun Troy around and said, 'Let's have a look at you.'

Troy Costain was a member of the wide-ranging Costain clan that inhabited the Shoreside Estate in Blackpool, a notorious, run-down area, almost a no-go area for the cops, but not quite. The Costains pretty much ruled the roost by burglary, theft, cheat and general intimidation. They were feared by many people and often held at arms' length by the police. Troy, however, had fallen into Henry's grubby hands over ten years earlier when, as a spotty teenager, Henry had arrested him for some minor offence. Once in custody, thrown into a cell, Troy had crumbled. He was severely claustrophobic and had pleaded desperately with Henry for release and that he would do anything, admit anything, just to get out. Henry remembered smiling like a devil at Troy's pathetic whimpering. The upshot was that since then Troy had become one of Henry's best local informants ever. He had provided Henry with information which had tripled his arrest and conviction numbers. The pay-off was that Troy had been allowed to get away with some things he shouldn't, but that was the price of a good-class source.

Over the years Troy had become more reluctant to part with information and Henry had sometimes resorted to using brutal methods to obtain it. If necessary.

A return to the cells was probably long overdue, Henry thought.

'Well, well, well, my little informant, Troy Costain,' Henry beamed cruelly. His hand continued to search inside and under Troy's jacket. His fingers touched something cold tucked into his waistband. Their eyes met. Henry glared ferociously at him and extracted a two-inch-barrelled revolver. 'Troy, you carry a piece,' said Henry in disbelief, holding the offending weapon between finger and thumb.

Troy was caught and desperate. 'Just a frightener, Henry, I wouldn't fuckin' use it, you know that.'

'Is it loaded?'

Troy nodded.

'You stupid, stupid bastard.' Henry grabbed hold of Troy's shirt with his left hand and dragged him across the car park back to the car on which his possessions were displayed. 'What's here?' He kept hold of Troy whilst using the gun to sift through the items. A fat wallet, packed with money. 'How much in here?'

'Dunno . . . fifteen hundred?'

A bag of tablets. 'E?'

Troy nodded.

'How much do you make a week?'

'Two grand-ish . . . enough.'

Henry wanted to hit him very hard indeed. 'Got a motor nearby?'

'This one.' Troy nodded at the car he had been almost plastered all over. It was a BMW, white, tinted windows, alloys, spoilers, 'G' registered.

Henry chuckled despite himself. 'You fuckin' stereotype. Let's go for a little ride.'

'You are in very big trouble, Troy: carrying, dealing, fuck me. This is very big shit indeed. The way the courts are backing us up now, I'd say this is worth six to eight . . . years, that is.'

Troy was driving, keeping his face firmly forward. Henry saw Troy's Adam's apple rise and fall. He knew he was sitting next to a very frightened man.

The gun and the drugs were in the footwell at Henry's feet.

'Eight years in a cell . . . OK, let's be generous – five years for good behaviour and all that . . . five years being buggered daily whilst performing oral sex at the other end. That would be you, wouldn't it, because you'd have no clout at all in the nick. You'd be bottom of the ladder, pal. And your fear of confined spaces. Banged up every night in a cell with a couple of other guys, all of whom will fuck you in turns. Way to go, Troy!' Henry was remorseless. 'Why the hell are you carrying a gun, Troy? Why?'

'Protection.'

'Oh, good one. Always goes down well in court, that one. Not.'

'I'm in a dangerous business.'

'You're in an illegal business,' Henry corrected him. 'Pull in here and let's have a one-to-one, a bit of a cuddle.'

Henry had directed him up along the promenade and then on to the public car park next to the Blackpool central police station.

'Take a look at the nick, Troy. With this gun and those drugs you wouldn't walk out of there again. In fact, the next time you stepped out of a door would be when they release you from Wymott Prison in, say, 2010, give or take a year or two.'

Troy looked ill.

'I would ensure that all bail applications are refused,' said Henry, really rubbing it in. He smiled at Troy. 'So while you were waiting to go to court you'd be in custody all the way.'

'Bastard.'

'That's me. Love it to bits.'

'OK, you've made your point. What do I have to do? That's obviously what all this is about. You come looking for me, threaten me and I give you some gen . . . which is?'

'The deal is this: you do what I want to my complete and utter satisfaction and I'll consider giving you a verbal warning for the gun and the drugs. Obviously they'll have to be destroyed, but that's a small price to pay for getting some information to me and staying a free man, wouldn't you say?'

Troy shrugged like he could take it or leave it. The hard man.

'Ever heard of Andy Turner?' Troy nodded. 'I want to know where he is. I want to know within twenty-four hours.'

Troy shook his head sadly. 'That might be difficult.'

'Why, because he's legged it?'

'No – because he's dead.'

202

Henry fell silent as his brain chewed that over. 'Dead?'

'Word is he got whacked a couple of years back.'

'Who by?'

'No idea.'

'Find out.'

A guffaw shook Troy. 'Easier said than done.'

Henry pointed down between his knees. 'This is easier done than said. Eight years in the slammer. Very easy for me, love . . . Now find out the truth, OK? I also want a list of addresses for Turner and his friends and associates, business partners.'

'All in a day? You're nuts.'

Henry looked at his watch. 'Less than a day now.'

'Twat.'

'Am I! Let's drive back down south.'

'I don't know where to start, man,' Troy whined.

Henry knew the Costain family had a string of nefarious contacts right across Lancashire and down into Greater Manchester. He therefore knew Troy was lying.

'Fibber,' he said.

Ten

Armed with a revolver and a bag of drugs, Henry Christie felt very peculiar indeed. He had made Troy drop him off two streets away from where the Astra was parked, then watched his source drive away before trudging to his car, gun in one pocket, drugs in another. He hid the items in the hollow where the spare wheel should have been, hoping that Troy didn't have the brains to blob him in and call the cops anonymously. If Henry was found in possession of a gun and drugs, he'd have a hard time explaining it and could easily end up going down for it, rather as he had described to Troy, maybe for longer.

He drove back to town. It was 10.45 p.m.

As instructed, he parked around the corner from the youth club and sauntered back to stand across the road in a shop doorway where he could watch the club entrance. A few kids were hanging round the door. They were giggly and high spirited, but not in the same way as the youths he'd watched congregating around the shops in South Shore. These seemed much nicer, stepping out of the way for other pedestrians, and were polite too.

The youth club door opened. There was a blast of coloured lights and loud dance music from the disco inside. A couple of youngsters came out, one went back in and the door slammed shut.

Henry saw that one of the ones who came out was Charlotte Wickson. She was staggering about drunkenly, falling against the walls and the window of the charity shop next door. Henry's mouth went dry. Drunk? Drugged? She fell back against the window again and shouted an obscenity. The other kids laughed at her and suddenly the little gang seemed much darker and less friendly.

He started to wish that Leanne would come out, so he could take her back to the safety of home.

From around a corner a youth appeared on a mountain bike.

Henry gasped.

The same one who had dealt drugs to the gang down on South Shore. His name was Kevin Long and he had been dealing for a couple of years around Blackpool. Henry had never had any direct contact with him, but he knew Long well enough. His MO was to deal on the hoof from his bike and to evade capture by using his extensive knowledge of the backstreets and short cuts around town.

Long cruised up to the group outside the youth club door and stopped.

Charlotte Wickson pushed herself up from the wall and staggered up to him. He handed her a package and she shoved something in his fist. Then he was away around the corner.

Bursting with anger, Henry moved. He ran hard across the road.

Long saw him coming. He was always switched on for the surprise appearance of the cops. He clicked up a few gears, rose high on the pedals and tried to get some speed up.

Henry was almost on him.

Long pushed down – and his right foot slipped off the pedal. Before he could recover, Henry got him and drove him off the bike, smashing him bodily into the building line, against a clothes shop. He was easy meat, being all bone and no weight. Henry punched him hard in the lower gut. Long gasped and fell forwards, clutching his abdomen. Henry then swiped him hard across the face with the open palm of his right hand, sending the dealer spinning down to his knees. Henry flat-footed his ribcage and Long sprawled out, hurt and wheezing.

Henry, who found he had more strength than he could have imagined, dragged Long back up to his feet and put him face up to the wall again. He started going through his pockets, hoping like hell there wasn't a needle in one of them. Instead he found numerous wraps of drugs, a bundle of five pound notes and two pockets crammed with pound coins. Henry pulled these pockets inside out, scattering all the coins.

'Hey, man . . . fucker!' said Long.

Henry placed the palm of his hand against the back of Long's head and with a quick thrust, smashed his face into the wall with a very satisfying crunch.

'Jesus . . .'

Henry did it again for good measure, then he let go, as gurgling with the blood from his now shattered nose, Long sank to the floor. Henry went to a drain by the kerb and stuffed the drugs and money down it.

He crossed back to Long and placed a foot on his neck.

He was in a rage like he had never known. Blood pounded through him.

'If I ever catch you dealing around here again, I will kill you. Do I make myself clear? This is my patch and I don't want scum like you on it. Do you hear me?' Henry pushed his foot down hard. The way he felt now, he could easily have murdered him.

He raised his foot, stepped back.

'Go.'

Long scrambled to his feet, collected his bike and disappeared into the night.

Henry stood there for a good long time, controlling his breathing, wondering what he had become in that moment. A vigilante? Or just a father out to protect his daughter from the scum of the earth.

The moment was over. He had acted rashly, but now it was gone.

He decided there and then there would be no post-mortems on the incident. He took a deep breath and walked back around the corner to pick up Leanne.

The disco was over. The doors were open, the music finished, and the kids were disgorging untidily. Parents' cars were lined up outside, rather like school collection time. Henry stood near to the door, keeping his eyes peeled for Leanne, Charlotte and Tara Wickson.

Leanne emerged from a sea of sweaty kids, looking hyper and excited.

'Hi, kid,' he greeted her.

'Dad,' she said and gave him a hug.

'Good time?'

'Excellent.'

'Take any drugs?'

She came upright and looked at him, a deeply troubled expression on her pretty face. 'No. What was that supposed to be about?'

Henry was still uptight. He got a grip of himself and forced himself to come back down to planet earth. 'Sorry, nothing. You ready to roll?'

'Yeah.' Leanne hooked up to him. They walked arm in arm.

Behind them was the shriek of a girl.

Even before he turned, Henry knew it was Charlotte Wickson. She was being manhandled into the big fat Bentley by Jake Coulton, her father's security man. He had grabbed her bodily, his big arms wrapped around her in a bear hug. Her feet were lifted off the ground and she was kicking like mad, writhing and trying to break free.

'You get in the bloody car,' Coulton growled.

Her right heel kicked back and connected with his shin. He howled and threw her aside. She landed on her knees on the pavement.

All around, the other kids' parents simply stepped back and let it happen without interference.

That night Henry was not in the mood to be a watcher.

He pulled away from Leanne.

'Dad,' she said, warningly.

'It's OK.'

Coulton had got hold of one of Charlotte's arms and was dragging the unfortunate girl towards the big car.

Henry stepped up to him. 'Leave her,' he said. His anger was transparently evident, even from just those two words.

Coulton released her and stood upright, turning slowly to face the challenge that was Henry Christie.

'Back off, Henry.'

'Uh-uh.'

They stood face to face.

Behind them, Charlotte had rolled into a ball, sobbing uncontrollably.

'I'm here to collect her on Mrs Wickson's instructions. This is none of your business.'

'When you collect her like that,' Henry explained, 'I make it my business.'

Out of the corner of his eye, Henry saw a patrolling police van crawl in their direction. Coulton spotted it, too.

'She's a bit pissed and doesn't know what she's doing,' Coulton said. 'I've come to take her home – so get stuffed.'

The police van drew parallel with them. The driver wound his window down and leaned out. 'Gorra problem?'

Henry and Coulton looked at each other. Coulton tore his eyes away first and said, 'No, not at all.'

Henry said nothing.

'I'll just stay in the vicinity,' the PC said, sensing the tension.

He U-turned the van in the street and parked opposite.

Kids and parents who had been glued to the encounter started to drift away.

Henry bent down to Charlotte. She looked up at him with pleading, watery, drug-filled eyes. 'Come on, love,' he said. 'You need to get home. Come on, get into the car.'

'I don't want to go with that bastard,' she whispered.

'Come on, it'll be OK.'

'Yeah, come on you spoilt twat, get in the car,' Coulton said to her over Henry's shoulder. Charlotte howled.

'Shut it, Jake,' Henry warned him. 'Come on, come on love.'

'Please, please, you take me home.'

'I can't,' Henry said pathetically. 'Come on.'

All the fight drained out of her. Henry almost thought he saw it leave her, like a ghost. He helped her up and led her to the back door of the Bentley. Coulton opened the door and Henry guided her in. Instead of going on a seat, she prostrated herself in the space between the front and rear seats.

'She's a little cunt,' Coulton hissed into Henry's ear. 'Doesn't deserve fuck all.'

'If you lay a finger on her, Jake, I'll make it my personal responsibility to pay you a visit.'

Coulton laughed in his face, then got into the Bentley. He tore away from the kerb, two fingers raised in Henry's direction, then he was gone. Henry watched the tail lights fade. He looked over at the police van, nodded at the driver – a PC he did not know – then went to Leanne, who was waiting for him twenty metres down the road.

He gave her a hug. Arm in arm, they walked to the discreetly parked Astra.

'Sorry it's not a Bentley,' he apologized.

'She can keep her bloody Bentley. I'd rather have this – and you – any day,' Leanne said. It was the first time Henry had ever heard her swear.

'Do you have much to do with Charlotte?' he asked her.

'No – only met her at the stables. She goes to some posh private school out near Poulton somewhere.'

'Oh, I assumed she went to yours,' Henry said foolishly.

'Naah . . . I quite like her, though, in a funny sort of way,' Leanne said wistfully as she fitted her seatbelt. 'But she's not a happy kid,' she said, like a grown-up. 'Money doesn't make you happy, Daddy.'

'I don't think I'll ever find out on my wage.'

'It's love and family that make you happy. And laughs and fun.'

'Can't disagree with that.' Henry's heart felt like it was being twisted.

'We have a good family, don't we?'

'Yeah, we do.' God – he was starting to fill up.

'She doesn't.'

'Why not?'

'Her daddy isn't her real daddy.'

Henry almost swerved the Astra off the road.

Eleven

With his mind buzzing, Henry Christie was still awake at 2 a.m. He tried not to toss and turn so as not to disturb Kate, but lay there with his arms clasped at the back of his head, staring at the ceiling. He was reviewing his day, going round and round the block since Jane had called with the car at 8 a.m.

That seemed such a long, long time ago.

Since dropping her off and making her walk to the police station, Henry had not spoken to her.

Perhaps he should, he thought. But then again, perhaps not. She was far too tempting for him, even though he had promised himself not to get involved. There was still more than a spark between them, despite what she said, and under the right circumstances it could ignite into passion and danger. At least that is what his male ego led him to believe.

His mind drifted from incident to incident, like a butterfly on flowers, not really fathoming out anything from his sleepy analysis.

The biggest shock of the day had been Leanne's news about Charlotte and her parentage. Henry tried to speculate as to what significance that had on the family. Was the man Tara had her tryst with the real father, or just one of a series of lovers? Did it have any connection with the mutilation of horses? Did John Lloyd Wickson know he wasn't the father?

Bloody hell, he thought: a can of worms.

He peeled the duvet off him and rolled out of bed, grabbed his dressing gown and slid his feet into his Marks and Spencer slippers.

He needed a drink.

Without disturbing anyone, he hoped, he made his way

downstairs and to the fridge in which he kept a chilled bottle of Jack Daniel's. He poured a short measure and retired to the living room, spreading out on the settee. The ice-cold drink burned satisfyingly down his throat. Nice.

Fuck! He had a moment of anguished panic when he remembered that a gun and a bag of drugs were still stashed in the Astra parked in his driveway.

He had another drink to calm himself down.

When Troy Costain came up with the goods, he would lose the gun and destroy the drugs. If he could keep his nerve for the next day, that was.

He closed his eyes and thought about the drug dealer he had beaten up.

That had been a moment of pure rage, but one he did not regret. A kick for the common people, he thought triumphantly, and raised his glass.

Obviously if the little shit complained to the police about it, Henry would have to have it taken into consideration with the gun and drug possession.

He chuckled slightly manically.

The sour mash whiskey was making him feel mellow and sleepy, doing its job. He knew mind, body and spirit needed to rest. His body ached. His mind was warped. His spirit was battered.

He shuffled into a comfortable sleeping position, head laid back on the arm of the settee.

He drifted nicely.

Then the phone rang. It was Tara Wickson.

'Henry?' Her voice was dithery. 'Henry? Please come and help me, I don't know what to do.'

He struggled into an upright sitting position, not sure if he had been to sleep.

'What's the matter, Tara?' he asked blearily.

She was panting.

'What's the matter?'

'I'm standing here . . . in the kitchen . . . I've got a shotgun and I'm pointing it at Jake Coulton and I'm going to kill him . . . I'm going to kill the bastard . . . and then I'm going to kill that bastard of a husband of mine.'

211

Henry was suddenly very awake. 'Whoa . . . come on, cool it, calm down, Tara,' he said. 'Tell me what's going on . . . Keep calm . . . Keep rational . . .' As he was talking, he was racing upstairs, throwing his dressing gown off. He needed to get dressed and keep her on the phone, talking . . . because while she was talking, she wasn't pulling a trigger. He tried hard to recall some of the tips from his hostage negotiator's course, but his mind was pretty much a blank. He lurched into the bedroom and switched the main light on. Kate groaned, shielded her eyes from the glare and sat up, looking astonishingly annoyed and puzzled at the same time.

With the cordless phone to his ear, he shuffled himself into his discarded shirt.

'Now keep calm . . .' he was saying again as he tried single-handedly to get into his jeans. He could not be bothered with underpants. 'Tell me what's going on.'

Charlotte Wickson, wedged down behind the front seats of the Bentley, cried as she was driven away from the disco, feeling as though she had been abandoned by Henry and her mother, who had sent the dislikeable head of security to pick her up.

Jake Coulton threw the big, heavy car sharply around corners, braked hard, deliberately so as to make the ride as rough as possible for the recalcitrant teenager behind him. He heard her groan and gasp and felt good about it.

'You shoulda sat in the seat.'

'Fuck off,' she said.

He sneered and stopped at a set of traffic lights. He glanced over his left shoulder.

Something inside him moved.

She was wearing a very skimpy skirt, revealing her long thin legs, and a short, cut-off top that displayed her belly button. She wore little else. White knickers, high heeled shoes and make-up.

He dropped his left hand back between the seats. It came to rest on her side, in the gap between her top and skirt. Her skin was cold and goose-bumped.

His fingers slid upwards.

An electric-like jolt shot through her. She stiffened as

she realized what was happening and twisted away from him.

'Get off me, you sick bastard!' she yelled. She scrambled on to the back seat and huddled deep in a corner, as far away from Coulton as possible under the circumstances.

He laughed savagely.

The lights changed and the car surged through. Coulton grated his teeth, his nostrils flared and that something inside him grew even more. It was something he knew he had to respond to.

He drove out of Blackpool towards Poulton-le-Fylde, wondering how and when it could be. He reached up to the roof of the car and switched on the interior light. He could now turn his head round and leer at his passenger, who, with her legs drawn up defensively, was actually displaying more to him that she wanted to.

'Where's my mum?' she demanded. 'She should've picked me up, not you.'

'Who gives a fuck where she is, the slag? I'm here and that's all that matters.'

'I hate you,' Charlotte said through fingers that were covering her face.

'And I care?' he said, keeping one hand on the steering wheel and half an eye on the road. He threw himself back over the seat and grabbed Charlotte's arm.

She screamed and kicked out. The huge car swerved and he almost lost control of it as it veered across the road. But he kept going and also kept hold of Charlotte. He pulled her to the gap between the front seats and tried to drag her through it. She writhed and fought against him and broke free, scrambling to a position directly behind him, out of his reach. She tried to open the door. It was child-locked.

He cackled and put his foot down, now driving along the main road past Poulton. It was a long, straight stretch of road and the car's speed increased dramatically.

'You know your dad hates you, don't you?' he shouted.

'That's not true, that's not true!' she cried.

'Because you're not his. You're a little bastard.'

'I'm not. No, I'm not.' Her head was in her hands and she

sobbed pitifully. Her make-up, so carefully applied several hours before, was streaked around her face. She had hoped the drugs she'd bought would have taken her up on a higher plane. They'd had no discernible effect on her whatsoever, she thought.

'Your mum's a slag and you're a bastard,' Coulton almost chanted manically.

'No!' she screamed.

He laughed. 'No one cares about you, not even Mummy. But I do, Charlie, I care about you.'

She held her hands over her ears. She did not want to hear this.

'I'm all you've got.' The car slowed as they reached the outer limits of Poulton. 'And I'm going to show you how much I care, how much I love you.' He reached a set of traffic lights where he turned right into Lodge Lane towards the village of Singleton.

Charlotte sank further back in the plush leather seats. 'Where are you going? Where are you taking me?'

'Somewhere nice and quiet where we can chat.'

'Take me home,' she ordered him. 'Now.'

'You can't tell me what to do, Charlie. I'm in charge here.'

He turned off Lodge Lane into a dark side road.

'I'm going to blow his head off.'

'No! . . . no,' Henry said more quietly. 'Not till I get there at least,' he begged. 'Just wait, just wait for me, Tara . . . I'm coming to help . . . I'll be there soon.'

Kate had very quickly picked up that the situation was desperate and had helped Henry to get dressed, so that he was able to keep on the phone. She pulled his trainers on and fastened them.

The disturbance had also woken the girls and, slightly frightened and disorientated by what was going on, they stood sheepishly at the door of their parents' bedroom in their night attire.

'I've got to, I've got to . . . I'm going to do it . . . Fuck, I'm going to do it,' Tara said hysterically.

'Just take a breath, count to ten,' Henry instructed her with an authoritative voice. He could actually hear her inhaling, then starting to count. He put his hand on to the silent button on the phone so Tara would not hear him. 'When I hang up, will you call Jane Roscoe? Her number's in the phone book downstairs. Tell her I'm on my way to the Wicksons', OK?'

Kate nodded.

'. . . eight . . . nine . . . ten!'

'Well done,' Henry said, back with Tara. 'Now then, Tara, will you do something for me?' He stepped out of the bedroom, hurtled downstairs. 'Will you?'

'Do what?'

He dashed into the kitchen and unplugged his mobile phone from the charger and switched it on.

'Tara, I'm going to hang up very, very briefly and I want you to do the same.' He looked at the display on his mobile as it searched to register. It seemed to be doing it exceptionally slowly. He hated mobiles. 'Keep hold of your phone, because I'm going to call you back immediately from my mobile phone, OK?' Then he had a very fundamental thought. 'You are on your house phone, aren't you?'

'Yes.'

'Tell me the number,' he said. His mobile was still scanning the airwaves, getting nowhere. He had Tara's home number programmed into the phone, but he didn't want to lose her just because his phone would not pick up a signal. She recited the number for him. 'OK, right, got that . . .' At last his phone locked in. 'Right, after three, put the phone down and I'll ring back straight away, got that?'

'Yeah.'

'One . . . two . . . three.'

He waited for her to hang up before he did, handing the phone directly to Kate who was now downstairs with him. Leanne and Jenny – bedraggled, uncomprehending and beautiful, the pair of them – stood behind her.

As he dialled Tara's number he said quickly, 'As you can gather, she's got a shotgun and she's pointing it at somebody's head.'

His mobile rang out Tara's number. It sounded out for ever.

'Come on,' he said, searching for his car key. 'Come on.'
At last she picked it up.
'Tara – you OK?'
'Yes.'
'Is everybody else?'
'At the moment,' she replied ominously.
'Good – keep it that way. I'm just leaving the house now and I'll be with you as soon as I can. It might feel like a long time, but it will only be a short time, so c'mon, let's keep talking.'

It was violent, brutal and terrible.

Coulton was on her as soon as he stopped the car in the dark lane.

Charlotte struggled and kicked and scratched and bit and screamed, but she was no match for him. He was strong, agile and determined, driven by the inner demon which was unstoppable. She was, as the saying goes, only a slip of a girl; a girl who was drunk and drugged and was not functioning correctly.

She had no chance and Coulton gave no quarter.

He laughed as he forced himself into her, hurting her severely.

She could do nothing. The only good thing was that it did not last long, but afterwards he lay on top of her on the back seat, almost suffocating her, panting and moaning into her ear. She lay, trapped, sobbing.

When he pushed himself up, he looked down at her in disgust.

'What the fuck's up with you?' he sneered. 'It's only what your dad does to you, isn't it? Oh, sorry, but he isn't your dad, is he?'

He slid off her, got out of the car and walked round it, tucking himself in, readjusting everything. He bent in and looked at her. She was still crying, with body-rattling blubs. She had not moved, had not tried to cover herself up. 'By the way, you're a shit shag.'

He got back in behind the wheel.

'And by the way, too, if you tell anyone about this, you're

216

dead,' he threatened over his shoulder. 'You're dead and I'll
dispose of your body so you'll never be found.'

He laughed cruelly.

Charlotte curled up into a ball again and began sucking
her thumb.

'The dirty fucking bastard.'

The tone of Tara's voice had changed. As she related the
sequence of events that night to Henry, she became more
agitated, especially as she recounted the rape of her daughter
as it had been described to her.

'He's the one who's going to die, not my daughter.'

'Calm down, come on,' he soothed her, 'calm down.' He was
driving with one hand on the wheel, juggling the mobile phone
as best he could – as ever it was a motorist's nightmare that
new mobile phones were too tiny to wedge between shoulder
and ear. 'You're doing really well, Tara.' He hoped he did not
sound patronizing. 'He actually doesn't deserve to die—'

'Yes, he does.'

'No, no, listen,' Henry said quickly, trying to make his point.
'If he dies, he gets away with it. Don't you see? Killing is too
good for him. He won't suffer. It would just mean that you are
down at his level, can't you see that, Tara?'

She made no reply.

'So let's do it the proper way,' Henry cooed. 'Let's just
make sure that he gets to court and gets convicted and goes
to prison for a long, long time. Shame the bastard.'

'I want him dead.'

'No, come on, that's not the way to do it.' Henry realized
he wasn't getting through to her. He changed tack, deciding
it was better to give her no alternatives. 'Look, we need
to get him convicted, OK? That's what we're going to do,
Tara. Put him up in front of a court, expose him, show
him up for what a bastard he is and there's some things
you can do to help with that . . . First of all, is Charlotte
all right?'

'She's been raped. How can she be all right?'

'I think you know what I mean . . . is she there in the house
with you?'

'Yes . . . yes, upstairs . . . God, I want to pull this trigger . . . I want to see his face get blown to pieces.'

'I know you do,' Henry said. 'I understand that, but you phoned me for help, so whatever you do, Tara, wait until I get there. I have to talk to you, face to face, OK?'

No response.

'OK?' he pushed.

'Yes . . . yeah . . .'

'Right, what you've got to do is this,' he started. 'Make sure that Charlotte doesn't have a bath or a shower or a wash.'

'Why?'

'Evidence . . . I'll explain it when I get there. And make sure she keeps the clothing to one side she was wearing when she was attacked. We'll need that, too.'

'Right.'

'Hold on, I've got to put the phone down one moment.' Henry was approaching a roundabout and felt he needed both hands on the wheel, particularly at the speed he was travelling. He lay the phone on the passenger seat, negotiated the round-about and cursed when he saw the phone slide across the seat, away from him. He made a grab for it, missed, and it dropped down between the passenger seat and the door.

'I do not believe this,' he said with frustration.

Coulton drove Charlotte home in the Bentley. He made her sit in the seat alongside him. She complied numbly with the instruction, now beyond thinking or reacting in any way to him. She sat there in an almost catatonic state, staring blankly ahead whilst Coulton touched her legs and arms as he drove. His hand ran up her skirt, he tweaked her breasts, then grabbed her right hand, pulled her across and forced her to put it into his trousers.

She let it happen. She was doing something, but it meant nothing.

Even when he took hold of her head and forced it down to his lap. That meant nothing, either.

By stretching as far as his arms would go, Henry retrieved the phone, relieved there was still a connection.

'You still there, Tara?'

'Yes, yes . . . still here.' Her voice sounded feeble.

'I'll be coming up to see you later. I haven't finished with you. Once I get my energy back, I'll show you what sex really is,' Coulton told her as they stopped outside the house. He had noticed that Tara's Mercedes wasn't there, which meant he could do as he pleased. John Lloyd Wickson was home, but that wasn't a problem. He reached across Tara's lap, allowing his hands to slide over her thighs, and opened the door. 'Go on, fuck off. I'll be up when I've had a few drinks.'

Charlotte got out and ran to the house.

Tara Wickson lay quietly in the arms of the man she loved, snuggling up tight to him, feeling him taut and hard against her body. She reached down and held him. He breathed out, his hot breath in her face. She even loved the smell of his breath, always had done. He squeezed her bottom and slid a hand under her thigh, lifting her leg across him. He manoeuvred down the bed, squirmed, adjusted his position, enabling Tara to place his penis at the entrance to her sex, then to slide in.

Both gasped at the same time, looking deep into each other's eyes.

They made love slowly for the second time that night. Moving around each other's bodies with familiarity, respect, ease and excitement.

When it was finally over – it took them almost an hour – they lay coiled, arms and legs intertwined.

'That was amazing,' he whispered in her ear.

She shuddered at his words. 'Yes, it was. No one can make me feel like you do.' She kissed his chest.

They almost drifted to sleep.

His breathing began to regularize. She lay awake, staring at the ceiling in the hotel room. A tear rolled down her cheek.

For some reason he stirred with a jolt and woke up. He looked at Tara's profile in the dimly lit room, seeing the tear glisten. He moved up on to one elbow. 'What is it, darling?'

'Nothing, nothing . . . Honestly, just feeling a little sad.'

'Why?' He moved a wisp of her hair out of her face.

'Because we can never be together, because it will always be like this.'

He had no answer to that one. He laid a hand across her and cupped her breast. She did not react and this puzzled him.

'There's something else, isn't there? I can tell. I can read you like a book.'

'You're the only one who can. Yes, there is something,' she relented.

'Tell me,' he urged her gently, 'tell me.'

Her chest rose and fell. Her mouth twisted in thought. She looked at her lover. 'He knows about Charlotte.'

He flipped back on the bed and swore.

It was a cold drive home for Tara. She had felt guilty about not picking Charlotte up from the disco, phoning Jake Coulton to ask him to do it for her, but she had wanted to spend a little more precious time with her lover. They rarely saw each other these days and any time spent with him was treasured. In between seeing him she missed him dreadfully and would have loved to be with him always, but she knew it was not possible. Ever. Although things might change now, maybe.

She drove and enjoyed the car. It was a sturdy refuge for her these days, a barrier against the world.

Her thoughts were with the man she had left behind.

Maybe now something was possible.

She had tears in her eyes as she drove up the lane leading to the farmhouse. It was an effort to pull herself together, but she did.

The house was quiet. The Bentley was outside, so it meant Charlotte was back, which was good.

Her feet were leaden on the walk to the front door. She was so unhappy. It was only Charlotte that had kept her going these last few weeks.

There was a light on in the kitchen at the back of the house. With quiet steps she walked down the hallway and peeped in. Jake Coulton was sitting at the table, his back to her, shoulders hunched. He did not move. She guessed he had a drink in front of him, as usual. He slept in a room in what was affectionately known as the granny annexe, but Coulton

220

was far from a grandmother. Tara thought him more of a big bad wolf and did not like him much.

She moved away from the kitchen, back down the hall and up the stairs. On the landing she stood still. John was in the main bedroom. He would probably be asleep and Tara had no intention of joining him. They slept in separate rooms now. She moved along the wide landing and knocked softly on Charlotte's door before poking her head in. She expected her daughter to be well gone after her night at the disco. Instead she found her down in the corner of the room with a duvet pulled up around her, two terrified eyes watching the door.

Immediately Tara knew something bad had happened. 'Honey, it's me, Mummy. What's the matter?'

'Mummy,' Charlotte croaked hoarsely, 'oh, Mummy.'

Henry wasn't too far away now. He'd raced past two speed cameras, both of which had flashed at him and said triumphantly, 'Hah, gotcha!' He would be writing to the Chief Superintendent to try to get those rescinded, he thought, but knowing his luck he would end up six points richer and £120 poorer.

Tara was still talking. She had not pulled the trigger yet.

'Who's in the kitchen with you?'

'Jake Coulton and my husband.'

'Right, right,' said Henry, quickly running out of ways of keeping the dialogue going. 'How are you feeling now?'

'In control. In control of my life – at last.'

'Tell me about the shotgun. What sort is it?'

'Twelve-bore, single-barrel, pump-action, three cartridges in it and one in the breech with the safety off,' Tara reeled off.

'Put the safety on,' Henry ordered her.

'No way. It means I stay in control if it's off.'

Anger and bile rose in Tara Wickson like a monster breaking from the deep. She wanted to vomit when Charlotte recounted her tale of hell, and she began to seethe even more when Charlotte told her that Coulton had also tried to rape her in her own bedroom too, but could not get the necessary erection. Instead he had tried to go down

221

on her, but Charlotte had fought him off until he withdrew.

'Bastard,' she whispered. She held Charlotte close and reassured her. 'Wait here and don't move.'

The firearms cabinet was in the sixth bedroom, which had been converted to a study. It was hidden inside a cupboard and bolted to the wall to conform to stringent police regulations. All that was kept in there was the one shotgun, used for vermin control on the land. How appropriate, Tara thought, as she unlocked the cabinet and extracted the shotgun out of its clips. She often used the weapon for clay-pigeon shooting at a local club too, so she knew what she was doing with it, knew which end was which, knew the damage it could cause.

She sneaked back to the kitchen. The door was still slightly ajar. Coulton had not moved.

Tara sidestepped into the room, the shotgun held across her body.

She watched Coulton for a few seconds. He did not move, could have been asleep, sat there.

She tip-toed up behind him and rammed the barrel of the gun into the back of his neck.

'You raped my daughter.'

Coulton's eyes shot open. Indeed, he had been drifting into sleep, his head nodding. His eyes opened like those of a doll and he became as rigid as a statue. The cold muzzle of the shotgun nullified the alcohol in his system.

'Don't shoot,' he pleaded. He imagined his head being blown off. 'Please don't shoot. It's not what it seems.'

She jammed it harder into his neck. 'You deserve to die, you bastard.'

'It was a mistake . . .' he began.

John Lloyd Wickson appeared at the kitchen door in a dressing gown, shocked by the scene in front of him, bleary from alcohol intake. 'Tara?'

She looked at him, startled by his unexpected manifestation.

Coulton used the moment, contorted round and made a grab for the gun. Tara was quicker. She danced away from him and held the gun aimed at his middle. 'Get back and sit down.'

Coulton was half out of his seat. He smiled callously and continued to rise, his courage enlarged by the presence of Wickson.

'I said sit down.' Tara raised the gun. 'I'll use it. I will. You violated my daughter and no court in the land will convict me of murdering you.'

But he continued to rise and took a hazardous step towards her. One step was as far as he got. Tara pulled the trigger. The noise was incredible within the confines of the kitchen. The blast reverberated, pummelling eardrums with its aftershock. The shell blasted a hole in the cupboard door just inches to the side of Coulton's head. Smoke rose. Wadding settled to the floor and a horrified Coulton dropped back into the chair, covering his head with his hands.

Tara racked the gun with deliberation, her face a mask of hatred and resolve. 'Next time it's your head,' she said and promised, 'There will be a next time.' She spun to her husband. 'You join him.'

'What?'

'Do as I say.'

Meekly, John Lloyd Wickson complied.

'Now, you lousy bastards, what do you have to say for yourselves?'

'I've reached the track up to your house, Tara. If you hear a car coming, it's me. Don't worry.'

'OK, OK,' Tara said.

'I'm only a couple of minutes away.'

'He raped Charlotte,' Tara said to Wickson.

Wickson glanced sideways at his head of security, then back to Tara. 'And . . . ?' he said.

'What do you mean, "And?" He raped our daughter.'

Wickson shook his head. 'No, Tara, he raped your daughter, not mine. She isn't my daughter, she's yours. There is a difference.'

'Yes, she is yours, John, in everything but biology, she's yours – our – daughter.'

Wickson continued to shake his head and laughed. 'You

223

betrayed me. You let someone else impregnate you and then you claimed it was mine. You lied, you cheated. All to keep your way of life. She's not my daughter and I don't care. Now put the gun down and let's get this sorted, Tara, once and for all.'

'Sorted? In what way? You don't even care he raped Charlotte, do you?'

Wickson's face was emotionless. 'No.'

It was at that point Tara Wickson knew she was very capable of killing two people in cold blood. Part of her, the devil in her heart, urged this to happen. She wanted to see both men dead. She could see a future, without them, never mind the consequences. The other part of her, however, the reasonable person, knew this was very wrong and stupid.

Fortunately she recognized that the strongest part of her was the devil – which is why she picked up the cordless house phone from the wall by the Aga and called Henry Christie. He was the only person she could think of who could talk her down from this course of action: murdering two people.

Several lights burned at the big house. Henry stood by the Astra and surveyed the front of the building. He thought he saw movement at one of the upper windows. It could have been the breeze blowing the curtains. He shivered, once again feeling vulnerable. His mouth was dry from so much talking and from fear because he did not know exactly what he was going to come across. All he had to go on were Tara's verbals.

He glanced towards the stables. The JCB was still there next to the crusher. They stood like prehistoric monsters, darker than their background. Menacing.

'OK, Tara,' he said into his mobile, 'I'm walking up to the front door now.'

Twelve

A quarter of a mile away, another man shivered at the same time as Henry Christie. This man was laid out on the hillside overlooking the Wickson household. He was comfortable, but getting cold in spite of the layers of clothing on him. He had watched the arrival of Henry Christie with interest and, as Henry stood by his car, held him in the cross hairs of the powerful night sights on his rifle.

He adjusted the sights minutely and zeroed in on Henry's head, just to the temple by his left ear. The man had been testing the rifle the day before and knew it was perfectly sighted. The tip of his forefinger rested on the trigger. If he had pulled he would have blown a hole in Henry's head, probably taken the top half of it off.

Henry Christie would have been very dead indeed.

If only he knew he had been in the sights of a high-powered rifle.

But Henry was not his target.

The man lifted his cheek from the stock of the rifle, his keen sharp eyes watching as Henry said something into his mobile phone, then walked up to the house.

The man on the hillside wriggled his toes to keep the circulation going. He adjusted his position slightly and manoeuvred the plastic straw into the corner of his mouth to sip the high-energy drink next to him.

He was playing a waiting game, knowing that sooner or later his prey would appear. He was a patient man. Snipers had to be.

The front door was unlocked. Henry pushed the heavy oak-panelled piece of wood open and crossed the threshold.

225

'Tara, that's me coming into the house.'

She did not acknowledge.

There were no lights in the hallway. Henry let his eyes adjust. He saw something at the top of the stairs to his left. A dark shape. Charlotte sitting on the top step, knees drawn up under her chin, rocking back and forth.

'Are you OK for the moment?' Henry whispered just loud enough for her to hear.

She nodded.

'Good girl. Everything'll be fine.'

He gave her the thumbs up, then turned his attention to the hallway in front of him. He knew the last door on the right was the kitchen. He braced himself and said, 'I'm coming down the hallway and into the kitchen,' into his mobile phone. He ended the call, probably the longest he had ever made in his life – and dropped the phone into his jeans pocket.

It immediately started to ring, making him jump. He fished it back out and saw it was Jane Roscoe calling him. He knew he could not answer it. For the sake of Tara he had to keep things going, so he switched it off, put it back into his pocket, set off down the hall.

'It's me opening the door,' he called softly and pushed it open, clueless as to what he would find. That old song, 'Behind Closed Doors', came to mind. 'No one knows what goes on behind closed doors.' Back to song lyrics again, he thought. It was mad, the things that went through his head at times of crisis.

Had the sight that greeted him not been so horrendous, he would have giggled.

Jake Coulton sat white-faced at the kitchen table. Henry immediately saw the shotgun damage to the cupboard door above his head. No wonder he looked pale. He had almost lost his head. Henry could smell cordite.

Across from him was an equally pale John Lloyd Wickson in a dressing gown. His hands were palm down on the table and he looked very afraid.

Henry saw the relief in the faces of the two men as he came in.

Leaning against the cooker was Tara Wickson, holding the

226

single-barrelled shotgun in her hands, wavering it dangerously at a point midway between the men. The cordless phone was on a worktop. She'd obviously had it wedged between her shoulder and ear whilst talking to Henry because there was no way she could have held the gun in one hand and kept proper control of it.

She looked as sick and colourless as the men, but uptight, nervy and close to the edge.

'I'm here,' he said softly, 'here to help out.'

How, he had no idea.

The sniper on the hillside raised his eye from the telescopic sights and looked into the night-vision binoculars on the tripod next to his head. He had watched Henry Christie enter the house and close the door behind him, more curious than hell as to why the suspended detective should have appeared at such an hour.

It complicated matters.

He swept the binos across the front of the house to the stables and back again. He saw nothing untoward . . . but then he did and he froze tight. He looked across the field behind the house in the direction of the river, behind the dilapidated farm buildings.

Something had definitely moved.

There it was again.

He relaxed. A fox.

In their different ways, each of the three faces in front of him held expectation. To the men it was to save them from death; the woman wanted to be saved from herself.

Henry knew he had to take control.

'Right, Tara, first things first . . . I only know what you've said to me over the phone and it sounds like a hideous offence has taken place.' Henry paused, licked his lips, looked from face to face again, coming back to Tara. 'But even so, there is no cause for a shotgun, no reason to do anyone any harm, none whatsoever. Two wrongs do not make a right. So let me promise you this: this incident will be fully investigated and –' here Henry shot a shadowy look to Coulton – 'if this man has raped your daughter, he will go to prison for life.'

'What do you mean "if"? He has raped her, defiled her—'

'Yes, OK, OK,' Henry intercut in an effort to pacify her. He saw that Tara's fingers had taken a better grip on the shotgun, saw the forefinger on the trigger twitch portentously. He knew she was close to discharging it and that he needed to judge things supremely well here if there wasn't going to be a cold-blooded murder in front of his eyes. 'I believe you, Tara, but shooting him will not help you.'

'I'm not bothered about me anymore.'

'I know . . . That's OK . . . That's how you're feeling now, at this moment, but it won't be how you'll feel in the future, believe me. So come on, let's do away with the gun. Let's get the police here. Let's get them to deal with it properly. Let them make an arrest. Let them gather evidence. Let them get this brute sent to prison. Let them do the job they're paid to do. Like I said –' Henry looked at Coulton with contempt – 'killing is too good for him.'

'Fuck you, Henry,' Coulton spat malevolently.

Henry quickly took a further step into the room, judging distances, working out reaches, how far he would have to leap to grab the gun if necessary. The odds were pretty poor. He inched a little closer to Tara, surreptitiously, he hoped.

He ignored Coulton's little outburst. 'Tara, how are we going to do this?' He actually stepped towards her openly. She swung the gun in his direction. He stopped. 'Give me the gun. Just hand it over, then let's get the police here.'

Tara shook her head. 'This man has degraded my daughter. He has screwed her and made her suck his dick.' She stood upright. 'Before I hand this gun over, I want two things.'

Henry waited. The demands were coming. He only hoped they could be met.

'I want him degraded and I want him to admit what he's done.'

'How?' Henry did not like the way this was going.

'You talked about securing evidence? You talked about clothing, my daughter's clothing, how it needed to be kept?' Henry nodded. 'I want him to take his clothing off. I want him to stand there naked and ashamed and then I want him to confess his crime.'

This, Henry thought, is not progressing terribly well. Even though Tara had called him, had made a cry for help, she was still very close to a killing.

He shook his head. 'No, Tara,' he said softly. 'That is not a good idea—'

Before he could finish his rationale, Tara snarled, 'I don't give a fuck if it's a good idea or not. He does those things or he dies.'

She meant it. Henry swivelled to Coulton. 'It's your play, Jake.'

'No way.'

Henry chortled. 'Strip or die. I know what I'd rather do, because if you ask me, that's what I'd do in your position. Fact is that your clothes will be taken off you for forensic anyway.' Henry shrugged, glanced at Tara, then back at Coulton. He was trying to manage a situation that was almost out of his control, 'She's more than capable of blowing your head off and if this appeases her . . . ?' Henry looked at John Lloyd Wickson, the silent tycoon now, a man who had very little to say in the present circumstances. 'What do you say, John? Naked or dead?' Wickson remained schtum.

Coulton stood up slowly.

An expression of extreme satisfaction crossed Tara's face.

He began to unbutton his shirt. 'You do know that this will get the case kicked out of court, don't you, Henry?'

'I doubt it. And just at this moment in time, I wouldn't be too concerned about a court case, pal. I'd be more bothered about walking out of here still breathing.' Actually Henry agreed that this could compromise any legal proceedings, that the defence would use it very much to their advantage, but he wasn't going to admit this to Coulton or to Tara. All this was about was getting three people out of here alive. The worry about the court case could come after.

Coulton tugged his shirt out of his trousers, unfastened the cuffs and slid the garment off. He held it up between thumb and forefinger before letting it waft to the floor. 'That enough for you?' he said to Tara.

Once again she gripped the shotgun tighter and raised it to her shoulder, sighting Coulton down the barrel.

Henry saw him judder with fear.

'You strip naked, Jake.'

Coulton's jaw rotated. Henry could see him weighing up the distance between himself and Tara, knew what was going on inside his head: Can I do it? Can I get to her before she pulls the trigger? Is it too far?

He unbuttoned his trousers and unzipped the fly. His decision apparently had been that tackling her was too much of a risk. Live coward or dead bastard?

The trousers dropped. He kicked them to one side and stood there in boxers and socks. He had a very well-maintained body, Henry saw, though he did have some rather large, red and unsightly spots on his shoulders and back, which made Henry feel better.

'Socks and underpants,' Henry said.

The night air was cold, very cold. Cloud rolled in with a harsh wind. Rain began to fall, getting progressively heavier. It was turning into a horrible night.

The sniper did not notice the weather in as much as it affected him personally. He had lain in fields before, in far worse conditions than rain. Often lain for days on end when he was younger and did this sort of thing more regularly.

This was easy – and he was certain he would be there for this one night only.

Tonight his victim would die.

It was also a relief for Henry to see that Jake Coulton's penis was no great shakes. It was certainly not in proportion to the rest of his body, so shrivelled up and insignificant it seemed. Terror, though, Henry conceded, could have had some bearing on that. A display of his privates was not enhanced by the presence of a shotgun-wielding mad woman.

Coulton stood there, shoulders drooping, not covering himself.

'Now what?' he asked. The shape of his mouth was a mirror of his anger.

'Now, Jake, I want you to tell me what you've done.'

'Can he sit down?' Henry said.

Tara shook her head. 'No, I want him to stand there . . . actually, no I don't.' She changed her mind abruptly. 'What I want him to do is get down on his knees and I want him to admit what he's done and then I want him to beg for mercy.'

'Tara!' John Lloyd Wickson said. 'This has gone far enough. At least let him sit down, for God's sake.'

She spun on him and growled, 'Then it's your turn.'

'Tara,' said Henry. 'Come on, love, this is getting silly.'

'No, it's not,' she said, looking at Henry, but keeping the shotgun pointed at her husband. Henry knew straight away he had said the wrong thing. 'If the rape of my daughter is silly, then I've called the wrong person, haven't I, Henry?'

'You know what I mean,' he insisted.

The shotgun arced back to Jake Coulton, naked, pale, spotty and withered.

'All right, you can sit down,' Tara relented. 'Then admit what you did.'

He sat.

'Come on, then.'

Henry closed his eyes in hopelessness, feeling he had lost what little control he'd had; maybe he had never been in control and maybe the cops were right about him. Maybe he was guilty of what he was accused of, maybe he was a man who misjudged things and, worst of all, maybe he didn't deserve to be a cop.

'Tara, don't do this,' he tried. 'It will weaken the case against him.'

She gave him a withering look and he knew she did not care now. He could see it in her eyes that she was going to kill him now – whatever he said. Her primal instincts had been broken open and she was reacting in a very extreme way to protect her child.

'Speak,' she said to Coulton.

She crossed the kitchen and lifted Coulton's chin with the muzzle of the shotgun, then pushed the gun into his throat.

'For fuck's sake, Tara,' Henry protested. 'I've come to get you out of this and you're not listening to me.'

It was as if she hadn't heard a word he said.

'Speak,' she repeated. She raised his chin even higher so he could look at her along the barrel, eye to eye.

He swallowed a big dollop of fear.

'Did you rape my daughter?'

'I . . . I . . .' he stammered.

'Not good enough.'

'Yes, I did.'

'What did you do?'

'I raped her.'

'Tell me more . . . admit it all, you bastard.'

'I . . . picked her up from the disco like you asked me to do . . . and I drove her home.' In spite of his nakedness, he was sweating. Rivulets poured down the back of his neck, down his face, under his nose. One drop of sweat rolled on to the barrel of the gun.

'Tara, that's enough,' Henry said.

'No, actually, it's not, because I want him to tell me everything, every last detail.'

'There is no victory in this, Tara.' Henry was desperate. 'Can't you see?'

'It's not about victory, Henry, it's about truth and justice . . . So, go on, Jake, tell me about how you raped a fourteen-year-old girl.'

'I did it on the back seat of the Bentley,' he said shakily. 'I forced her down and forced myself on to her.'

'Did she resist?'

He nodded as much as the barrel of the gun would allow.

'And yet you still did it?'

'Yeah,' he gasped.

'Did she enjoy it?'

'No.'

'Did you enjoy it?'

Coulton did not reply.

'Did you? Did it give you a feeling of great power?'

Coulton closed his eyes. 'Please, take the gun away.'

Henry watched the scene, feeling powerless to intervene. The well-built, strong figure of Jake Coulton seemed to be shrinking with each second. He had become small, insignificant and pathetic. Whilst part of Henry's mind liked this, another bigger part hated what he was witnessing. He hoped it would end soon. Without bloodshed.

'Now you know what it's like to be degraded, don't you Jake?'

Tears streamed down his face. 'Yes.'

'To be powerless, to have all your dignity stripped away.'

'Yes,' he squeaked.

'Why did you do it? What gave you the right to think you could do this to my daughter?' commanded Tara.

Coulton's tear-filled, frightened eyes looked across at his boss, John Lloyd Wickson.

'Because he said he didn't care if she got raped because she wasn't his daughter, not his flesh and blood.'

Silence hit the room with the speed of a lightning strike.

Henry felt a chilly draught from the kitchen door as though someone had come in through the front door and let the night in.

Please cops, get here soon, he prayed.

No one moved. Jake sat there, chin resting on the barrel of the gun, stricken by fear into immobility, having realized he had said the wrong thing, in the wrong situation, as Tara's head revolved slowly to look directly at her husband.

Henry knew in that instant just how John Lloyd Wickson must have felt. It was that single occasion when something dark is revealed, some inner secret outed, when your stomach churns over and a frozen prickle runs over your body, and every square millimetre of skin contracts tighter than cat-gut strung across a tennis racket.

Wickson shook his head. 'I didn't,' he croaked, wilting under Tara's eyes. 'It's not true,' he back-pedalled, sensing the imminent danger to himself.

'You are as much a bastard as him,' she said. Her chest rose and fell as she struggled to maintain control. Henry recognized the moment: she had lost it.

Everything then slowed down. Every infinitesimal detail of what took place in the following seconds was seen and analysed microscopically in Henry's head and, he had no doubt, in the heads of the people fortunate enough to stay alive.

He was watching the shotgun and Tara's fingers on it.

The forefinger that was wrapped around the trigger.

The trigger being pulled back at the same time as the muzzle was pushed harder into the soft skin underneath Coulton's chin, the shotgun angled upwards.

Henry heard himself roar: '*Nooooo!*'

He flung himself towards the gun, like a goalkeeper diving for the low, hard-struck penalty. Both feet left the ground. His hands were outstretched, but he knew he could not stop it happening.

The trigger went back.

There was a massive blast.

There was recoil.

And Henry would never forget what happened to Jake Coulton's head.

The blast went in below the chin, diagonally up and through his head.

Henry's ears pounded with the shock wave.

He was still in mid-air.

The cartridge blasted a hole in Coulton's chin no bigger than the diameter of the muzzle.

The shot burst through his skin up through the 'V' in his jaw, expanding and widening all the time as it travelled, destroying bone, tissue, skin and organs, until it emerged, ten times bigger than it had entered, from the roof of his head, completely removing the top third of Coulton's skull, taking with it brain, blood and membrane, covering the wall and cupboards. At the same time, Couton's body was lifted completely from his chair and thrown back against the wall with a thud.

Tara recoiled, controlling the shotgun, racking another shell into the breech like an expert. She twisted away from Coulton, knowing she had done the job she set out to do, with the intention of carrying out another job, one that had just come along: to murder her husband.

Henry knew intuitively what she intended.

Tara turned the weapon on Wickson. He threw his arms up. Some defence!

But Henry was on her now, grappling for the gun, forcing his weight on to her. She attempted to push him away and in so doing discharged the weapon again, the shot this time blasting into the ceiling.

Henry tore it out of her hands. She turned on him with the look of a tigress blazing in her eyes. For safety he threw the shotgun across the kitchen, skimming it across the floor before turning back to Tara. She powered into him, beating his chest with her fists, hitting his recent wound, hurting him. He wrapped his arms tightly round her and held on for dear life as she squirmed, fought, wriggled. All the while he spoke hypnotically to her, did not raise his voice.

'Tara, Tara, hold it, come on down, it's over, just hold it,' he said. She managed to free an arm and punched him on the jaw, cricking his head back with a snap. That hurt too. But he trapped her arm again and held on, never easing his grip, until the fight dissipated out of her and she became a floppy mess in his arms, could no longer stand up. She sank to her knees. Henry let her down and she began to sob dreadfully.

Henry looked over at John Lloyd Wickson. He sat there wide-eyed, stunned and speechless. Henry panted, gathered himself and turned to Jake Coulton.

He was sitting against the wall, having slithered down like a ragdoll, his head lolling forwards on to his chest, exposing the massive, gaping wound on the crown, which was disgusting. A mass of blood smeared the wall. His right foot twitched as though he was keeping time with music.

'Jesus,' Henry hissed.

John Lloyd Wickson moaned, turned on his chair and dropped to the floor, retching.

Henry swallowed back his own revulsion. He had seen such death before, seen people shot to death, but had never watched someone have their head blown off with a shotgun. He had always turned up post-event at shotgun deaths. He knew he was deeply shocked by the spectacle and wondered what he had got himself into – not for the first time. Involved with a family cut through with abuse, adultery, mistrust and criminality. It was like many of the families he dealt with on council estates, but of a much greater proportion. Everything with this family seemed to be magnified and he put that down to one thing: money.

Wickson coughed up vomit.

Tara wept at his feet on the floor.

Jake Coulton sat there, horribly murdered.

Upstairs, a young girl shivered after being raped.

Henry blew out his cheeks, his eyes and mind not believing the tableau around him. His hands rested on his hips. He prayed even harder for the arrival of the cops because he just wanted to hand it all over.

The kitchen door creaked and opened slightly.

'Charlotte, love, don't come in,' Henry called. 'Please stay out there.'

The door continued to open. And it wasn't Charlotte who was standing in the hallway.

Henry stiffened up; his jaw, though, fell slack.

'Hope you don't mind me coming in?'

Not as if there was any choice in the matter. Verner pushed the door open, and stepped into the kitchen, as confident as he could be, a smile of victory on his face and a pistol in his right hand. He placed his foot on the shotgun which Henry had thrown across the floor. 'Goodness, what a mess. Still,' he said, looking at Henry with a big smile, 'saved me a job.'

Thirteen

The mobile-phone gun was one of several toys that Verner liked to have at his disposal. Always useful in case of emergencies, such as being arrested. He would never have used such a weapon for an actual contract killing because they were unreliable and apt to explode in the hand, which would never do when face to face with someone you have been contracted to assassinate. On those occasions a proper weapon would always be used as unreliability was not an option. But as a standby, to have a mobile-phone gun or a cigarette-packet gun or even a belt-buckle gun was very reassuring. They came in handy if you didn't want to be in police custody.

Verner knew that on the continent of Europe, the police were very aware of disguised weapons, but that British cops, being the smug island race they were, still thought they were the stuff of fiction and did not expect to find them pointed in their face in the same way, say, French cops did.

That was how Verner had been able to get underneath the guard of the two armed officers who had been escorting him at the hospital.

By playing on the British sense of fair play, which still existed within the police, he had been able to persuade the officers to let him make a phone call on the understanding they could record the number dialled and then listen in to the conversation. Except their sense of fair play had ended up with them dead. He had then been able to coerce the petrified X-ray nurse to get the handcuff key from one of the dead cops and release him.

It had seemed almost surreal to him to be pointing a mobile phone at someone and threatening them with death.

When free, he had of course been obliged to kill her too.

Verner did not like leaving witnesses, even innocent ones. He had actually felt a tinge of remorse for that, for a few minutes, but having to apply his mind to escaping had flushed that idiotic emotion right out of him.

Getting away had been a breeze.

Within an hour he had been in Manchester, dressed in clothing stripped from a poor soul unfortunate enough to be about his size and build. He had left the guy stripped naked and trussed up like a turkey in an empty room. He hadn't even seen Verner hit him, which is why he was allowed to live. He had stolen a Ford Focus from the staff car park and tootled unchallenged away from the hospital.

He dumped the car on a side street near Manchester city centre and made his way to the Radisson Hotel on Deansgate, booking in for a couple of nights under an assumed name. Using a credit card, also in a false name, which had been taped to his inner thigh, together with £150 in ten pound notes – Verner rarely left anything to chance – he visited Marks and Spencer and was reclothed, fed, re-moneyed through cashback and a cash machine and feeling good within an hour. He also visited Boots the Chemist for some ointment for the dog bites on his arms.

His next port of call was the bed in his hotel room where, after taking some aspirin, he lay down and slept for a few hours.

He woke at 5 p.m. that day, feeling stiff and sore, but rejoicing in his freedom. It had been a close run thing for him, probably the nearest he had come to being incarcerated in a dozen years.

He showered and shaved and dressed himself in his new M&S gear, smart, casual and practical. He left the hotel and walked across to the Arndale Shopping Centre and bought a pay-as-you-go mobile phone (a real one this time) and a couple of SIM cards from the Carphone Warehouse.

Manchester actually felt quite warm. He strolled up Deansgate and called his controller.

'Things went slightly awry for me,' he admitted to the man. 'I did the job, conveyed the message, but I got caught by the police. I got away, though.'

'I know. It's all over the news.'

'Have I been named?'

'Not yet . . . Do you think you will be?'

Verner thought about the question. 'It's possible . . . I usually leave no traces, but I didn't have time to clean up behind myself this time.' His teeth were grinding as he remembered how things had panned out for him. His job had been simply to frighten the life out of John Lloyd Wickson. Wickson, he knew, had become involved with the importation of drugs for the Mafia and was now trying to extricate himself from any obligation to them. But the Mob did not allow such things. Once they got their hooks into you, they did not let go until the funeral was over. All Verner had been tasked to do was bring Wickson, and his hard-arsed sidekick, Jake Coulton, back into line. It would have all gone OK if not for the interfering of Henry Christie, a man Verner now had a grudging respect for.

'It's possible then, you may be of no further use to us,' Verner's controller said. 'One of your attributes was your ability to remain undetected. If the police get to know who you are . . .'

The words chilled Verner's spine. 'It's true I may need to move back to mainland Europe, but I will still be of great value to you. I offer a service that is second to none.'

There was a beat of silence over the phone which again had a physical effect on Verner.

'Yes, you are good,' the man conceded, 'still . . . we would like you to carry out one more task for us, then withdraw to Spain where your role will be reassessed.'

Verner did not like the sound of that. His enthusiasm waned. 'What is it?'

'We feel that the target has stretched our patience too far for his own good. He has made contact and made threats. We would like to terminate our correspondence with him, and that of his head of security. Is this something you could achieve with a business deal?'

'Yes,' he said firmly.

'Ensure he knows what he has done wrong prior to terminating the contract, please.'

'Leave it with me.'

*   *   *

239

Verner did not care why his employers suddenly wanted Wickson out of the picture. All he was concerned about was doing the job well, getting paid for it and then doing a runner. He had banked over half a million dollars and that would keep him going until he decided he could reappear and resume work. He even knew where he would hide out: India was very cheap.

He ate in a pizza place on Deansgate whilst he worked out his plan. The first necessity was to rearm himself. It would be far too difficult to source a reliable rifle, so it would have to be a handgun. He actually liked close-quarter work best anyway. It was far more satisfying than looking down telescopic sights and seeing somebody fall over. The problem with a handgun, though, because of the distance involved was that it was easier to leave physical evidence behind: DNA, fingerprints, eyewitnesses. All these things were a possibility being near to the victim, but they were not insurmountable by any means.

After he had found himself a gun, he would find the correct clothing.

The last slice of pizza marinara slid into his mouth, complemented by the last swig of the one glass of red wine he allowed himself. He paid cash and left the restaurant, emerging back into the mid-evening streets of Manchester.

It was time to mix business with pleasure.

He found his pleasure in a basement club on the edge of Chinatown. It was an expensive place, populated by business types and classy-looking hookers drinking pricey cocktails at the bar.

The one he hit on was in her mid-twenties.

He watched her for a while before making his move. She looked drug clean, which was always a factor for him, and seemed pretty much in control of herself, although he knew both things were unlikely.

'Can I buy you a drink?' Verner asked her, sliding in next to her.

She was sipping a brightly coloured concoction through a twirly straw. She removed her lips from the top of the straw and smiled at him. 'You can. A Long-Hard Screw, please,' she said, naming the chosen cocktail and, less than subtly, providing Verner with her job description.

Verner almost choked, but ordered one and a beer for himself. Cost: £15.

He watched the money disappear into a till.

Lifting his glass, he said, 'Cheap at half the price. Cheers.'

'Cheers to you.' Her red-lipsticked lips surrounded the top of the straw of her new drink and she drew some into her mouth. 'Nice,' she said, eyeing him suggestively. 'You want some action?'

Verner nodded. 'Just a fuck.'

'I'm sure I can accommodate that.'

'How much?'

'Two-fifty.' He did not even blink. 'Half up front.'

'What's your percentage?'

'None of your business.'

'OK at my hotel – the Radisson?'

'Fine by me.'

When it was over, Verner lay spread-eagled and naked on the double bed in his hotel room. Aggie, as she told him she was called, started to get dressed. The whole sex act had taken just over four minutes, from the second she got hold of him, slid a ribbed condom on to his highly sensitive prick, to entry, to ejaculation. Short and sweet, but Verner did not care. It satisfied his needs. She had moaned and writhed in all the right places, told him she loved him, and that was OK with him. He loved her for about six seconds.

She pulled on her tiny knickers, not much more than a thong. Her eyes looked at his body. 'You really needed that, didn't you?'

'Yeah.'

'I could stay the night, you know? You could recover and we could have a long fuck, a really good session. Only cost one-fifty more.'

'No, thanks.'

'OK.' She hooked her skimpy bra on, her eyes still on his

241

wiry body. 'Got a lot of bruises on you.' She bent down and placed a finger on a large bruise on his thigh. He winced. 'Been beaten up?'

'Something like that.'

'And your arms – they look a mess, too.'

She got no response and could tell he did not want to do small talk. That was fine with her. She could go any way the client wanted: chatter or silence, brains or dumb. She was out to make money, offer a service and then leave.

'You don't do drugs,' he said. He had been watching her all the time for the giveaway signs. There were none.

She shook her head. 'Did once, don't now. Got a three-year-old kid to bring up. Clean as a whistle now. It fucks you up.'

'Good for you.'

'But I can get you something if you want.' She turned to him and curled her fingers around his penis, now limp and damp, and quite small. He removed her hand.

'No thanks.'

'Whatever,' she shrugged.

Verner sat up, watching her complete her dressing. 'Is he waiting down in reception for you?'

'Who?'

'Your pimp.'

'Not your business. I fuck, that's all you need to know.'

'But he knows you're up here, doesn't he?'

'Look, don't start getting all weird on me.' She eyed him suspiciously. 'You've been a good client, OK. Time for me to go.' She eased herself finally into her tight, short, body-gripping dress, picked up her shoulder bag and trotted to the door.

As it closed behind her, Verner quickly scurried around the room, dressing fast. Then he was out, down the corridor, running down the stairs towards the reception area, easily beating the lift down which he knew Aggie would be using. He was on the ground floor twenty seconds before the lift doors opened. Aggie stepped regally out as though she owned the place.

Verner hid behind a wide pillar and watched her teeter on

her high heels towards the revolving doors of the hotel. She stopped to light a cigarette, then picked her mobile phone out of her bag and made a quick call. Instead of leaving the hotel, she dropped into a leather sofa by the door, crossing her long legs, displaying her stocking tops, and bouncing her feet angrily. It would seem she had been told to wait.

Verner sat down too, out of her sight.

A few minutes later a smooth-looking black guy shouldered his way into the foyer.

Aggie stood to meet him. She handed over the wad of notes that Verner had given her. The black man counted them carefully there and then, not bothering about who might have been watching him. He smiled, nodded and gave Aggie a hard kiss on the lips, steering her out of the door – probably en route to her next assignation. On a poor night, Verner reckoned she would be earning her pimp at least two grand and taking less than ten per cent of it for herself. Slave labour.

Verner moved swiftly across the foyer. As Aggie and her pimp stepped on to the pavement outside the hotel, he was only feet behind them. An old, but beautifully maintained Ford Granada was parked on the kerb on the double yellows, a driver ready and waiting. Aggie opened the back door and glided in. The pimp went to the passenger door.

Verner was behind him.

'I want to talk business,' he said to the man's back.

The black man rose slowly to his full height – six-three – and rotated slowly, his eyes wide at the gall of someone approaching him like this.

'I don't do business.' He had a deep, booming voice with a Manchester accent, which even when spoken normally had the power to intimidate. He had a cut across the upper part of his left cheek that had been stitched badly. He was not a stranger to blades.

Verner held up his hands and stepped back. 'I need something and I'm willing to pay for it. I'm a stranger in town and I need help.'

The black man towered over Verner. As well as being tall, he was wide and looked dangerous. In spite of that, Verner was not awed. He knew he could have taken him down within a second.

'What is it you want, stranger?'

'A gun.'

'Fuck off,' he laughed loudly.

The pimp turned away and reached for the door handle.

'I'll be in the Printer's Arms,' Verner said, giving him the name of a pub he'd seen on a dark side street off Deansgate. 'I'll be in the bar until eleven. I mean what I say. I'm not a cop or anything. I'll pay good cash for the right one – a handgun, preferably a pistol. Five hundred for the right one.'

The pimp regarded him unsmiling. He blinked and got into the Granada. The car swished away into the night. Aggie craned her neck to look round through the back window. Verner waved. He knew he was in business.

As the name suggested, the Printer's Arms had once been the haunt of members of that profession, particularly in the days when Deansgate housed the massive regional offices of newspapers like the *Daily Mail*. It had been frequented by typesetters and journalists alike and was not unlike the pubs that once used to be found off Fleet Street during its heyday. It was small, crowded, noisy and friendly and still retained that atmosphere, although the clientele now frequenting it consisted mainly of the middle-aged denizens of Manchester who knew a good pub when they tasted one. Its media history was just that – history.

Verner struggled hard to find a place at the bar.

He ordered a pint of Guinness, very cold, very black and wonderful. He sipped it as he leaned on the bar.

The sex with Aggie had been a good relief for him. It was just what he had needed: quick and straight to the point.

Now what he needed was a gun. He wanted that to be quick and straight to the point, too. He knew Manchester's underworld was flooded with illegal firearms and that getting hold of one was easy, if you knew who to ask. Verner did not, but guessed that a pimp would know or would, in fact, be able to supply one. It had been a risk, but calculated.

A small man with a round, pock-marked face squirmed into

244

the bar alongside him and ordered a short. He was mid to late thirties and Verner knew he was it.

He waited for the approach, sipping the Guinness, not taking any notice of the man. He had an urge to sink the drink in one, but held back. He had to have full control of his faculties and even one pint of the black stuff could be a deciding factor in business like this.

The small man sniffed his whisky. Without looking at Verner, his nose hovering over the rim of the glass, he said, 'I hear you're looking.'

'Depends what for,' Verner answered, knowing that the conversation would be in code, just in case they were being listened to by the cops.

'What do you need?'

'Something small, light, compact, reliable.' He could have been describing a condom. 'And never used.'

'Could be difficult. Secondhand is usual.'

'I have the right amount.'

'I might be able to find what you need.' He tossed his drink down the back of his throat and shivered as it hit the spot. He slammed his glass on the bar. 'One for the road,' he told the barman. For the first time he looked at Verner, who saw that the guy's complexion was atrocious. He quickly drank the second whisky. 'I'll be outside the door. Give me five minutes . . . Oh,' he checked himself, as though this was an afterthought, 'show me the colour of it.'

Verner placed his pint down, opened his jacket and let the small man see the contents of his inside pocket.

'Good enough,' he said and then was gone.

A moment later, Verner quit the bar too.

By the time he stepped outside, the gun dealer was nowhere to be seen, having vanished like a rat into the darkness. Yeah, vermin, Verner thought with a mental sneer. He disliked having to deal with such people, but necessity was driving him here. He dashed across Deansgate, dodging the traffic, and backed into the shadow of a shop doorway from where he could see the main door of the Printer's Arms.

A few legitimate customers came and went.

Fifty metres down Deansgate, a car stopped and the pock-marked man who had just been in the bar got out. He leaned back into the car and conversed with the driver before slamming the door shut. The car set off, then turned down by the Printer's Arms, disappearing up the poorly lit side street. It was being driven by Aggie's pimp.

The small man walked to the door of the pub.

Verner walked back across the road, coming up behind the small man, who was no wiser that he had been across the road, watching.

'This way.' He indicated to Verner that he should follow him down the side street.

'Can I trust you?'

The small man sniggered, but said nothing.

Verner followed. Within metres, the brightness of Deansgate had been replaced by the dark of the narrow street, the sound of vehicular and pedestrian traffic just a background murmur.

He led Verner to a small car park at the rear of what could have been an office building. There was one car on it, the one Verner had seen drop the small man off a few minutes earlier, the one driven by Aggie's pimp. Verner's senses were acute. He could sniff the danger in the air and was ready for anything, supremely confident of his abilities, no matter what might come his way.

'Stop here,' the small man said. He took a small torch out of his pocket and flashed it a couple of times, then said, 'Come on.' He walked towards three huge metallic dustbins on wheels on the car park, pushed right up to the building. They were due to be emptied soon. The smell said that.

As they approached the bins, the black pimp, together with another man, a white one, stepped out and revealed themselves.

Verner took stock of the situation.

'I thought you might be able to help me,' he said to the pimp.

The black man's wide smile flashed in the darkness and Verner almost giggled at the stereotype.

'What have you got?'

'Come over here, back here.' The black man took a pace

246

backwards and to one side. He also had a torch in his hand, which he flashed down to the ground. There was a large piece of oily rag spread out, once part of a blanket, with two pistols on it and four magazines. Verner recognized the makes and models immediately.

One was a mass-produced Eastern Bloc monstrosity, the other a reasonable-looking Glock.

'How clean are they?'

'Does it really matter?'

'To me it does. How reliable are they?'

'Sold as seen,' said the black man.

Verner felt the presence of the other two men who had quietly moved round to be behind him.

'Ammunition?'

'Two spare magazines with each. Forty-five rounds in total.'

'How much?'

'The Glock is five hundred; the other is two.'

'Not cheap.'

'I guess a man like you needs a gun,' said the pimp, 'and would be prepared to pay whatever the cost.'

Verner nodded, knowing full well he would not be paying a penny for either gun. Had it been a straightforward, trustworthy transaction, he would have bartered and gladly paid, but he instinctively knew this was going to turn sour. 'But you're wrong, actually, the gun isn't for me. I need to make a call to my boss, just for the nod.' He already had his mobile phone in his hand, one bullet left in it.

'I don't think that'll be necessary,' the pimp said. He nodded to his compatriots.

Suddenly Verner's arms were pinned to his side by one of the men behind him. Not the small guy, because he came around the front and yanked open Verner's jacket.

Verner let it happen, still holding the mobile phone in his hand.

'Just chill, pal,' he was told by the small man with the complexion like the face of the moon, 'and it'll soon be over.' His hand went into the inside pocket which Verner had shown him contained the money. Except now there was a bar

247

of soap in it with razor blades stuck into it. The small man's hand grasped what he thought was going to be a wad of cash. He screamed and pulled his hand away, blood dripping.

Verner stamped his heel down the shin of the man holding him and finished the movement by smashing his heel down hard on the man's toes. He dug his right elbow back into his ribs, then his hand shot up and he stabbed the antenna of the mobile hard into the man's eye. He shook the man off, who staggered backwards, holding his injured face.

'Jesus, Jesus,' the small man yelped, nursing his lacerated hand between his knees, just in the exact position Verner needed him. He grabbed the back of his head and pounded his face down on to an upcoming knee, bursting his nose beautifully.

Verner pushed him aside, spun quickly on the man who had been holding him – who was tending his injured eye. Verner leapt at him and head butted him hard and accurately on the bridge of his nose.

Broken nose number two.

Like a cat, he turned low, back to the pimp, who had watched Verner's sudden and unexpected display of violence with shock. But he was a man of the street and was recovering fast. His hand went inside his well-cut jacket.

Verner pointed the mobile phone at him. Just one left. It had to count because the pimp was pulling out a handgun.

There were perhaps four metres between the men. Verner knew that phone guns were pretty inaccurate even over close ranges, so he had to get close enough to ensure it was effective.

He took a step forward, decreased the gap.

The handgun in the black man's hand was almost out.

Verner aimed the mobile-phone gun at the man's chest. Go for the large body mass. It might not be fatal, but whatever happened, the man had to be put down. He pressed the button on the keypad. There was a crack and a kick and the bullet fired into the pimp's wide chest, knocking him down on to his arse. He rolled over and came back up, his own gun now out and in his hand. Verner powered in and kicked the gun out of his hand, then, twisting so he was side on, kicked him flat-footed in the face, sending him rolling across the car park.

Broken nose number three. A record for one night.

This time the pimp did not get up.

Verner picked up the gun, which had skittered away a few feet, then went to stand over him.

He thought about ending the life of all three men there and then.

The black man clutched his chest, trying to stem the blood gushing out from the bullet hole just above his heart.

Verner weighed it up quickly. If he killed them, the cops would dig the bullet out of the pimp's chest and soon make the link to the ones they had pulled out of two dead cops and a nurse in Preston. But if the pimp and his little gang stayed alive, there would probably be little chance of them going to the cops to report the incident. The problem would be if the pimp died anyway.

'That'll teach you a lesson, amateur,' Verner said. He pointed the gun at him, almost pulled the trigger, decided not to.

He scooped up the Glock and the spare magazines, pocketed them and threw the pimp's gun into one of the rubbish bins.

He returned briefly to the Radisson, collected his belongings and left. It would have been more than foolhardy to stay there, so he walked down the street and got a room at the Travel Lodge, paid cash, locked himself in, dropped on to the wide double bed, aching and sore.

Time for some recuperation.

He slept for ten hours.

Next morning he walked to Piccadilly Railway Station, grabbing an Egg McMuffin on the way for breakfast. He was in luck – and smiled at the thought of luck – when he gazed up at the departures board. A train for Blackpool was soon to be leaving, calling in at all manner of romantic-sounding places on the way. He noticed that the last-but-one stop was Poulton-le-Fylde. He knew he would not be getting off there. He bought a one-way ticket and found himself a seat in a sparsely populated carriage towards the front of the train.

He enjoyed train travel, liked the perspective it gave on places. He settled comfortably for the journey.

It passed uneventfully and, sooner than he thought, he was alighting in Blackpool. As he emerged, the chill wind of the coast slapped him in the face. He had never quite known anything like it. Bracing, he thought.

He strolled slowly into town and found a nice-looking guest house near to the centre which would be a useful base for a few days. He did not expect to be staying for long. He intended to get his job done quickly and get away. He spent the rest of that day browsing, shopping, and being a tourist.

He even walked past several foot-patrol coppers, but not one gave him a second glance.

Fourteen

'Sit.'
Verner waved the pistol, indicating Henry should do as he was told. Nervously he moved across to the kitchen table and sat next to John Lloyd Wickson. Tara remained slumped on the floor, whimpering into her hands covering her tear-stained face.

'Shut it,' Verner said to her, getting annoyed by her snivelling.

Unlike Henry, she took no notice. Her world had crumbled, was destroyed, and nothing Verner could say or do would make anything worse for her.

'Henry, shut her up, will you?'

'It'll mean me getting up again and going across to her.'

'Do it, then – but don't do anything stupid. I know you too well. You're a bit of a hero, aren't you?'

Henry stood up slowly, went and bent down next to Tara. He took her shoulders and shook her gently. 'Tara, you need to be quiet . . . please . . . this man will do something stupid if you don't.' She did not respond. He could tell his words had not penetrated at all. He shook his head at Verner, who, he saw, had picked up the shotgun in his left hand, the pistol now tucked into his waistband.

'Get back to your chair,' he told Henry. When Henry was seated, Verner inspected the shotgun. 'Nice weapon. Devastating at short range.' He glanced at Coulton and laughed. 'But you already know that, don't you?' He began to empty the shotgun. The cartridges dropped out of the weapon on to the work surface he was next to.

Henry saw a chance. Verner was holding an empty gun and he had the pistol in his waistband.

251

'Don't,' Verner said, anticipating the possible move. 'You'd be dead before your ass even left the chair.'

Henry settled down, obviously having telegraphed his move.

Verner reloaded the shotgun: three cartridges, racking one into the breech, then letting the gun hover at a point equidistant between Henry and Wickson. He kept it aimed there, covering the both of them, and moved across to Tara.

'I told you to be quiet,' he said. With one lightning, stunning and expertly executed blow, he hit Tara with the stock of the shotgun across the side of her head.

Tara toppled over, unconscious and bleeding.

Both Henry and Wickson rose from their chairs, but Verner was already covering them again, a look of dare on his face.

'There was no need for that,' Henry said.

'I make the rules, Henry.'

Both men sat back down, horribly aware of Tara bleeding heavily from the deep wound inflicted by Verner's blow.

Verner circled away from them to the opposite side of the table.

Coulton had stopped moving now. There was no more twitching and dancing.

'Good shot, eh?' Verner commented. He pulled a chair out, spun it round and sat on it, resting the shotgun across the back of it.

'Cops'll be here soon,' Henry said.

'And that's supposed to give me the frighteners, is it?'

Henry shrugged. 'Just stating a fact.'

'Thanks.' Verner turned his attention to Wickson, who was probably having the quietest, most withdrawn period of his life. He was terrified and it showed. 'Now then, Mr Wickson. You have deeply upset the people who employ me. I don't know much about it, to be honest, not my business, but I do know they helped you out of some financial difficulties and now you want to turn your back on them.' Verner cleared his throat. 'Not acceptable. You owe them and you want to welch on payment.'

'I owe them nothing,' Wickson whispered.

'Tell him, Henry. He doesn't seem to have grasped the concept.'

Henry tried to play it dumb, wanting to string this out for as long as possible. 'I assume that the people who employ you are the Mafia?' Verner nodded. 'In that case, John,' Henry said to Wickson, 'once you're in debt to them, they don't let go.'

'Exactly.' He winked at Henry. 'You know your stuff, don't you?' To Verner, he said, 'All they want to do is share in your business. Only a small percentage.'

'Fuck 'em,' Wickson said.

'No. Nobody ever fucks with us. Look, all they want is a few measly per cent of your legitimate business, which, as we know, has great expectations.'

'What're those?' Henry said, latching on with interest.

'The future of Blackpool,' Verner said. 'The Las Vegas of Europe. Big plans for this place . . . and Mr Wickson, as we know, will be very much involved in the demolition and reclamation of buildings and land when all the new casinos go up along the sea front. He'll make about fifty million, rough estimate – won't you?'

Wickson stayed immobile and said nothing.

'But he would never have been in a position to do that had my employer not assisted him to remain solvent in the first place, isn't that the case?'

'I helped you out once, paid my debt to you and found other ways of keeping my business afloat until the Blackpool dream comes true.'

Verner laughed uproariously. He turned to Coulton. 'Did you hear that, Jake? The Blackpool dream!' The dead man did not respond.

'It doesn't work like that, John,' Henry said. 'I presume you mean the fuel laundering out back?'

Wickson nodded glumly.

'No doubt they want a piece of that, too,' Henry said. He was looking at a desperate man, someone who had steered his business into deep trouble and in an effort to save it had turned to the wrong people, people who would never let go. They had saved him from bankruptcy and then he had found a new, illegal way of keeping going – by laundering fuel. It all fell into place for Henry now. The dilapidated farm buildings at the back, the articulated fuel tanker Henry had dodged the other day.

Wickson had obviously seen fuel laundering as a way to make quick money. Henry knew the profits from it could be immense. It was a relatively new type of illegal activity in the UK, becoming more and more prevalent. It involved the conversion of red diesel into a fuel which appeared to be normal diesel. The excise duty rate of just over three pence per litre on red diesel (which contains a red chemical dye) contrasts with a rate of almost fifty pence levied on ordinary diesel fuel. This equates to a profit somewhere in the region of £14,000 per tanker of fuel. Good money by anyone's standards. 'How many tankers a week leave here?' Henry asked.

'Four.'

'Bloody hell,' said Henry, doing a quick add-up in his head. Over £50,000 a week. 'You know that they'd never let you give that up, don't you? Even when you're making legitimate money from the Blackpool dream, they won't even allow you to stop laundering fuel. You naïve arsehole.' Henry shook his head.

Wickson's face screwed up as though he was about to vomit again. He started to retch, then hurled up on to the kitchen floor, which was covered with a variety of substances which it had never thought it would have on it. His head went down between his knees, then came back up. He wiped his mouth on the sleeve of his dressing gown.

'Well – cosy chat over,' Verner announced brightly. 'I'll let you into a secret,' he went on conspiratorially, tapping his nose. 'I don't always kill people with bullets. I like to vary things if I get the opportunity – like tonight, Henry and John. That's why we are now going for a short stroll. I have an excellent idea for the both of you, which in terms of evidence left behind, will be nil. Up and out of the kitchen door.' Verner waved the shotgun. 'Don't do anything foolish or I'll revert to type and blow you both to . . . heaven . . . or, in your case Henry, hell. It's not too late for your souls to catch up with Mr Coulton's here. Wonder which way he went? Up or down?'

'You're mad,' Wickson said.

'Oh, yes.'

'Come on, John,' Henry told Wickson. He stood up on very shaky legs, but Wickson could hardly move. Henry assisted him to his feet and Verner directed them outside the house. The door opened on to a patio. 'We're going to the stables, which, incidentally, I burned down. But I bet you already knew that.'

'And mutilated a horse?' Henry stated questioningly.

'And that,' he confirmed. 'Shoulda seen his eye pop. Go on, get walking. Keep together and keep your hands on the top of your heads.'

Henry and Wickson walked ahead of him.

'Why are we going this way?' Wickson asked.

'You'll see, you'll see.'

They emerged from the back of the house and went down the short lane to the stables. The rain had stopped but the ground was wet.

Henry looked ahead and said, 'Jesus,' under his breath. He realized why Verner was taking them this way. 'Jesus,' he said again.

'OK, you two, stop here.' They had only walked a few feet. 'Step apart, now . . . bit more . . . say five feet apart . . . that's it, good . . . now, whilst we are going to walk to the stables, we are going to do it three in a line, shoulder to shoulder. I'll be in the middle. Henry, you'll be on my left, John you're my right-hand man.' The two captives looked puzzled. 'Just good practice,' Verner said. Henry understood. He was covering himself. If he had walked behind them, he would have been exposed, but by walking between them it gave him a degree of safety. Henry also understood why he had been chosen to walk on Verner's left. Verner did not see Wickson as a threat. He was just a blubbering idiot, whereas Henry was a danger. Keeping Henry to the left meant that, being right-handed, Verner could keep the shotgun pointed at him naturally as they walked. 'Right you guys, by the left . . .'

Henry needed to know some things before he died, just for peace of mind in the afterworld.

'Did you kill the undercover FBI agent and Marty Cragg?'

Verner cackled with laughter. 'You think I'm going to confess all my sins to you, Henry?' They walked on in silence for a few yards, then Verner said, 'Course I did.'

Ahead of them at the end of the path was the excavator and the crusher.

Charlotte Wickson had lain terrified at the top of the stairs, straining to listen to the confrontation taking place in the kitchen: the harsh words, the threats, the blast of the shotgun; then the arrival of Henry Christie, then more shouts, then the front door opening again and a man she did not know entering the house with a gun in his hand. She remained in the shadows on the landing, hidden from view.

The man closed the door behind him and stood there, head cocked to one side.

On the landing, not twenty feet away from him, tears streamed down the young girl's cheeks and she shook as she endeavoured to keep her crying silent, to hold back from uttering something which would have revealed her position. The man actually looked up the stairs. She was sure she would be spotted. If he had turned the light on, he would have seen her.

Then came more voices from the kitchen, raised higher, more desperate, then another shotgun blast, screams, the sound of a scuffle. The man who had just entered the house slid down the hallway out of sight.

Charlotte almost collapsed with tension.

Things went quiet. She could not even begin to imagine what was going on, had no conception of what might have happened.

After all, she was merely a teenager.

One who had recently discovered that the man she thought was her father, wasn't. Wickson had taken the revelation badly, and so had she. But even worse, he had reacted in such a way that had sent Charlotte spiralling out of control. He hated her. He had told her as much. Hated the fact she was not his flesh and blood, despised her, wanted to disown her, rejected her desire to be loved unconditionally by him, pushed her away and called her horrible names which were more applicable to a prostitute on the streets.

As if it was her fault.

She had been hurt, confused and upset by the revelation. She had known her parents' marriage was not good, had not been for years, that they increasingly led separate lives. Yet, like all kids, she believed they would stay together.

Her mother had tried to keep things going, and for some reason, although she blamed her mother for the situation, she could not bring it in her heart to hate her.

It screwed her mind. Chewed her up, spat her out.

The drugs had saved her, or so she thought. They were an escape. So was the alcohol. So was her horse . . . her poor horse. Now he had been hurt too.

And then she had been raped.

And now this. What was going on in the kitchen?

It all went quiet.

She came silently down the stairs, knowing exactly where to tread, which steps creaked, which were safe. At the foot of the stairs, she stayed still, listening. Nothing. She walked down the hall to the kitchen door, which she pushed slowly open.

She saw the legs first. Her mother's legs.

She opened the door wide, ran in and slid down next to Tara, whose face was covered in thick red blood pouring out of a deep, nasty cut on her temple.

'Mum,' she cried. 'Oh, Mum.' She believed Tara was dead. Then she groaned and moved, spreading relief through Charlotte.

Just then, the young girl glanced quickly round and her eyes fixed on Jake Coulton's lifeless body.

At first it took a few moments for her juvenile brain to register what it was seeing.

Then she screamed.

The three men heard the scream, even from where they were, almost 200 metres away from the house. All three heads turned to look.

'My daughter,' Wickson gasped.

Henry gave him a stare laced with ice, but said nothing.

They had reached the point where the excavator and the crusher were parked up for the night. They looked at the machines, immense pieces of equipment. The crusher was designed to be fed bricks, stone, rubble, boulders or whatever, which it literally crushed to a specified size and then spewed out via a conveyor belt either into a pile, or into another machine called a screener which further sorted the stone.

Henry had often seen them on building sites which were being prepared and cleared of debris prior to building actually taking place. The use of the crusher meant that nothing was wasted. He knew very little about the machines, but could easily imagine the power that the jaw-like crushers would need to exert to break up stones and rocks. He had never before stood next to such a machine. It was huge.

What they might do to a man unfortunate enough to fall into the jaws was unthinkable.

'OK, John,' Verner said brightly, 'climb up on to the machine.'

'Why?'

Henry almost tutted. Wickson had not got it.

'Just climb up there and stand next to the jaws.'

Then it dawned on him.

'No.' He shook his head. 'No.'

Verner stepped back and swung the shotgun round to point directly at Wickson's face. 'Just remember what this did to Mr Coulton.'

Wickson looked at Henry, who could do or say nothing to help. Whatever happened here, death was inevitable. How it happened was the issue.

Reluctantly, Wickson clambered up the ladder on the side of the crusher and stood gaping down into its huge metal jaws.

Verner pressed a button on the side of the machine. The engine of the crusher coughed horribly and its powerful diesel engine came to life. He pressed another button on the control panel and the crushers started to move, to grind nonexistent substances.

'Jump in,' Verner shouted. He raised the shotgun.

Wickson shook his head.

'Do as you're told.'

Wickson's eyes were drawn inexorably to the powerful jaws. He had been working with crushers in the building trade for

258

many years and had stood in this position many times. He knew exactly what the jaws could do.

He turned away, horrified by the thought.

'Fuck it,' Verner said. 'I knew this would happen.' He fired the shotgun. The blast punched Wickson in the stomach, as though he had been hit by a fist. He staggered backwards and dropped into the mouth of the crusher, into the jaws which immediately began to devour him, churning him into an unrecognizable mush, swallowing him into its belly. He was passed underneath a powerful magnet designed to sort out any metallic objects from the rubble, then he was disgorged on to the conveyor belt, as though it was serving up a meal.

The magnet had lifted his Rolex watch up.

There was nothing left of Wickson that was discernibly recognizable as human. What remains existed were deposited on the pile of shale that had once been bricks and rock.

'My god, you fucking brutal bastard,' Henry said, deeply shocked.

'Name of the game . . . Now it's your turn, Henry,' he shouted over the engine noise. 'They'll never be able to tell you apart when you both get slopped together in a bucket. Now get up there and jump in, or I'll shoot you and carry you up there myself. I'm good at the fireman's lift.'

Verner backed away from Henry, cautious, keeping him covered all the while. Henry reached out to the crusher and placed a toe on to the ladder on its side.

The sniper had seen the three males emerge from the rear of the house and walk towards the stables. Looking down the telescopic sight of the AW sniper rifle, he recognized Henry and John Lloyd Wickson and then – unbelievably – Verner.

He swore.

He had not seen Verner enter the house. How good was that? Hell, he must have been dozing or something. How had he got in without being seen? The sniper was sure he had been looking hard and concentrating, but sometimes you can try too hard and then miss very simple things. Maybe that's what he had been doing. Alternatively Verner could have got in through the back of the house somehow.

The sniper smirked as he watched the three men progress towards the stables, Verner taking up a position between them, shotgun in hands, pointing loosely at Henry.

A good move by Verner. It gave him just enough protection.

The sniper's mind raced: what the hell had gone on inside the house? Where was the wife, the daughter?

On reaching the site machinery at the stables, the men disappeared out of his sight completely behind the crusher.

Next thing, Wickson was standing on the platform on top of it and the crusher fired up moments later.

Why?

Then Wickson seemed to jump backwards and fell into the machine, which ate him up and then spat him out.

The sniper's stomach churned at the horror. It was more than horror, it was revulsion, complete disbelief. But he only had a matter of moments to take in what had happened to the millionaire, because Verner suddenly came into view, stepping out from behind the cover of the crusher, brandishing the shotgun, presumably at Henry Christie.

The sniper had to settle quickly, get over what he had just witnessed, concentrate. Regulate the breathing, keep steady.

And fire.

At first Henry did not realize what had happened, and nor did Verner – but it was the latter who caught on first. It seemed like magic as the shotgun was somehow driven from his grasp by an invisible force and dumped on the floor.

Verner and Henry, for the most fleeting of moments, looked each other in the eyes, their brows furrowed, and then, just a fraction of a second before Henry, Verner put two and two together and computed the answer: he was being shot at.

Verner dived to the ground, wresting his pistol out of his waistband.

Henry saw his chance. He scrambled up the side of the crusher and jumped on to the platform on top, hoping to hell that whoever was shooting had not been sent to kill him, or that he would not be mistaken for Verner.

He ran across the width of the crusher, trying not to look

down at the gnashing jaws which seemed to want more food, and dropped down the other side, literally leaping down the dozen or so feet to the floor. He landed hard, stumbled a few steps and raced towards the stable block that had survived the fire.

Verner rolled under the protection of the crusher, an expression of annoyance creasing his face.

His first thoughts were that someone had been sent to eliminate him because he was of no further use, now that the cops knew who he was. They would always be on the lookout for him and that was not good for a hit man, a profession that required a high degree of anonymity and blandness. His face would be plastered all over the country and maybe Europe and therefore his use was now limited. It was often the way with professional killers who had passed their sell-by dates. They knew too much and if they did get arrested they might talk and broker deals, so they had to be disposed of to make way for the next kid on the block. It made professional sense. That's what his controller had hinted at when he'd made his phone call.

He laughed and hoped that the gun in his hand, the one he had acquired from a backstreet car park, worked.

Henry slammed against the wall of a loose box, panting heavily, options coursing through his mind.

Who the hell was up there – probably in the same spot Verner had occupied only days before?

It looked like Verner's time had come.

But Henry was under no illusions that his own time might have come too. Whoever was up there, sniping away, was probably just as likely to pot him, he suspected . . . although he hadn't done so yet.

Henry knew he had to do two things: get himself out of here and try to get Tara and Charlotte out of the way as well.

There was no quick and easy way back to the house – in cover, that was.

The direct route was out. That was just too open. The only way would be to skirt around the outside of the stables, head across the field to the old farm buildings behind the house, and use them as cover to get to the rear of the house itself.

He moved. There was no time to waste.

*   *   *

The sniper on the hillside seethed with frustration at himself. He could not believe he had missed Verner. The cross hairs on the sights had been bang on Verner's head, but as he squeezed the trigger, something somewhere went ever so slightly wrong. Maybe he pulled the rifle, moved a fraction . . . maybe, maybe, maybe. The fact was he had missed but at least he had managed to knock the shotgun out of Verner's hands.

Sharp shootin' at its very best, he thought cynically.

Next thing, Verner had rolled out of sight before he could send another bullet screaming at him and Henry Christie had cleared the crusher like some sort of athlete, although his very dicey landing was not graceful at all.

The sniper could easily have taken Henry as he ran to the stables, but he allowed him to reach his destination unscathed.

Verner was his target. He was the man he had been sent to kill, wanted to kill, was determined to kill.

Verner scrambled away from the crusher, keeping the machine between him and the sniper, and dropped into the drainage channel which ran parallel to the path all the way back to the house. It was cold and very wet in the bottom of the ditch, smelly too, reeking of rotting vegetation. Keeping low, Verner started to creep back in the direction of the house, but moving as quickly as his elbows would take him in the slush and mud, and keeping his gun out of it.

Henry pitched himself headlong into the field, using a low hedge for cover, not once daring to raise his head. The sobering thought that he might get it blasted off was good motivation to remain hunkered down. He stumbled on the uneven ground, falling forwards on to outstretched hands, which sank with a slurp into the soft, wet earth. He made it unscathed to the point where the field met the concreted yard by the dilapidated farm buildings where Wickson carried on his illicit trade in fuel laundering.

Keeping to the shadows, he rose wet and dirty from the field and ran to the gable end of the nearest building, then scuttled his way around the back of it. His intention was to skirt all the way around and re-emerge near to the back of the main house, where he knew he would be on open ground when he ran to the kitchen door. A risk he would have to take.

Charlotte Wickson had been transfixed by the spectacle of the dead man in the kitchen. It took her a long time to look away from him and back to her injured mother. Tara's eyes opened. They were vague, bloodshot, distant. They closed again.

'Mum . . . oh, please, Mum,' Charlotte begged.

As if by magic Tara's eyes flipped open again. This time they were clearer, more focused. 'Charlie,' she wheezed.

'Mum, we've got to get out of here.'

Tara put a hand on her wound. 'I know . . . Help me up.'

Charlotte supported Tara to get to her feet.

Henry had never been a particularly fast runner. He had been a rugby player in his younger years, but had succeeded in that through sheer bloody-mindedness, guts and willpower rather than through anything such as speed and agility. As he pinned himself against the old farm building, he could see that the kitchen door was at least a hundred metres away, across a wide expanse of manicured lawn and concrete patio – and that there was no other way to get to the house. He had to sprint like hell, out in the open, to get there.

He wondered where Verner had got to.

The crusher was still gnashing away near to the stable block. Presumably there was still a sniper up on the hillside. Verner was not to be seen as Henry cautiously peered out from behind the safety of the stone building.

Where was he? Still pinned down behind the crusher?

Henry doubted it. He was too resourceful to let that happen to him – which is why Henry wanted to get to the house and get the females out of there somewhere safe and sound. He knew that Verner would see Tara as unfinished business as she was a witness against him, one who needed to be eliminated, even though Henry believed that nothing she had seen would have registered with her. Verner did not leave people alive.

Henry counted to five, then launched himself out of the shadows and into the open.

263

The back of the house seemed to be a very long, long way away. More than his estimation. Felt like half a mile.

He felt very naked and vulnerable, exposing himself like this.

His arms pumped, fists clenched, expecting something very bad to happen to him.

He hit the back wall of the house running, breathless, heart and ears pounding with blood.

He twisted through the kitchen door, sliding the bolt across to lock it. He found the room empty with one exception: Jake Coulton was where he had been left, sitting up raggedly against the wall, his massive head wound exposed dreadfully.

Repulsion at the sight made Henry queasy for a moment.

'Unlucky, pal,' he said and crossed the kitchen to the inner door which led to the hallway, picking up his mobile phone from the table as he passed.

The sniper used a combination of uncorrected vision – his eyes – his telescopic sights and his night binoculars to comb the area below him for Verner. He scanned from the house, along the path to the stables, and back towards the old farm buildings. He had watched Henry Christie make his way across the field and then disappear around the back of the barns, but his main concern was the whereabouts of Verner. He had lost him completely.

A little bit of panic set in.

Verner could not be allowed to get away.

He searched desperately for a glimpse of his target, kicking himself for not having blown his head off when he'd had the chance. That was what lack of practice did – made you stale.

Verner lay deep in the ditch, having inched the full length of it, so that he was at the point where it ended close to the house. He was perhaps twenty metres away from the gravel-covered parking area at the front of the house. The fact he had made it so far reassured him. It meant that the gunman on the hill could not see him and did not know where he was – but he was under no illusion that as soon as he emerged from the mud, there was a good chance of him being picked off.

He was deeply curious as to who had been hired to take him out of the picture.

Ramirez was good. He was a Spaniard who had worked around the world for various organizations, but he was expensive, probably too costly to be doing a job like this. And last Verner had heard, Ramirez was somewhere in Latin America.

It could be Orlando, an Hispanic hit man working out of Florida. He was good at long range, but if it had been him, Verner knew he would have been dead by now.

So it had to be a second-rater, or someone out to make his spurs. Verner plumped on who it was. Jackson, the British ex-Army guy who had, recently, had a slightly suspect record of achievement. He had missed the last two hits, despite bragging he was a long-range specialist.

That thought made him feel better.

He took a chance and raised his head slightly. Four cars were parked on the gravel: Wickson's Bentley was nearest to him, then parked next to that was the heap of crap Henry Christie had arrived in, then Tara's Mercedes and then a small black sports car belonging to the late, great Jake Coulton.

Two down, Verner thought. Wickson and Coulton. If I get the chance to take Henry Christie and Tara Wickson, I'll be pleased enough. Firstly because they were both witnesses and secondly because he wanted to kill Henry anyway. If I can do that, he thought, I'm sure I'll be able to outwit the sniper on the hill. But I'm going to have to be quick about it.

They were in the hall. Charlotte was trying to drag, cajole, push her injured mother towards the front door.

Henry came into the hall, dishevelled, dirty and desperate in appearance. Charlotte saw him. She opened her mouth to scream.

'It's me, Henry,' he said, holding up his hands. 'I'm a bit of a mess.'

She stifled the scream by clamping both fists over her open mouth.

Henry knelt down by Tara, who had slithered down the wall into a heap. He inspected her head. Verner had hit her very hard, causing a deep, wide gash. Henry could see the grey of her skull in the split on her scalp. It needed to be treated quickly. Lots of blood was being lost through it. Henry switched on his mobile, but the battery died with a pathetic bleep. He looked around and saw a house phone on the wall, rose and grabbed it, holding it to his ears. Nothing. It was dead. Had Verner cut the wires before entering the house?

'I've got my mobile phone upstairs,' Charlotte volunteered.

'Go get it . . . go on, go,' he shooed her.

The youngster dashed upstairs, leaving Henry with Tara. He pondered whether or not to get her to her feet, but decided against it.

He went to the front door, a big, solid oak thing with one small pane of glass in it, distorting any view outside. He turned the handle and opened the door a fraction, peering out with one eye. The crusher was still churning away hungrily. He looked towards the hill in the distance, but saw nothing. Who the hell was up there? And where was Verner? Had he been driven away? Henry doubted it.

Immediately outside the house were the cars, parked in a variety of different ways. The black sports car and Tara's Mercedes faced the house; his Astra and the Bentley, parked almost side by side about ten feet apart, were backed up to the house, so they faced down the driveway.

He was weighing up whether it was worth trying to get the females out into his car and to get them the hell away from the house, or to do a runner with them into the fields and get them to lie low and wait for the arrival of the cops . . . and where were they? he wondered. Would they ever feel the need to turn up? Henry was thinking like a disgruntled member of the public again.

Quite simply he did not know what to do for the best.

A thought struck him like a bolt of lightning.

Charlotte came flying down the stairs and handed him her mobile phone. He pushed it back into her hand. 'Call the police – 999.' She looked shocked at being asked to do such a task, and dropped to her knees beside Tara. Henry squatted down beside them and said urgently, 'I need to get to my car . . .

No, it's OK,' he said, halting Charlotte's intended interruption. 'I'll be straight back, then we're going to lock up the house, sit tight and wait for the cops, OK?' He nodded enthusiastically. Charlotte nodded back, less enthusiastically. 'OK, you get the police on the line while I go to the car. I'll only be gone for seconds.'

He stood up, knees, as ever, cracking, and went to the door. His car was perhaps fifteen feet away. On the left was the Bentley, which would give him some cover from the hillside if necessary. It would take just seconds, he reiterated to comfort himself. In his mind he process-mapped his task, step by step, visualizing it. He crouched down and pulled the door open. Then he had another thought. What if it all went wrong when he got to the car? Over his shoulder he called, 'Charlotte, come here, love.'

Reluctantly she crawled across to him, not wanting to leave Tara.

'When I go out,' he said in as plain English as he could manage so he would not be misunderstood, 'you close the door behind me. But stay by the door – don't go back to your mum, OK? Stay by the door and let me back in when I come running, OK?'

She nodded.

'Make sure you let me in,' he said, just to make sure she had got it.

'Right.'

'Good lass.'

He edged out of the door, then sprinted to the back of the Astra.

Verner found a foothold on a rock from which he could propel himself towards the parked cars. He repositioned slightly until he was in exactly the right position and would not slip. He braced himself, counted down, his muscles coiled. Then he exploded like a greyhound out of the traps.

The sniper was fractionally late picking him up. He fired three shots – crack, crack, crack – all three bullets marginally behind the running figure of Verner, who flung himself out of sight behind the Bentley. Frustrated, the sniper put another couple of shells into the body of the Bentley.

Henry had the hatchback of the Astra open. He was crouching down behind the car, delving into the recess where the spare wheel should have been. He heard a noise behind him, went very cold, spun round slowly, keeping his right hand behind his back.

Knelt down by the back nearside corner of the Bentley was Verner.

'Boo!'

Verner was in a combat kneel – one knee on the ground, the other drawn up – and had his pistol pointed directly at Henry's heart.

'Changing the wheel?' Verner said.

'Something like that,' said Henry, his lips hardly moving.

'Got ya.'

Henry gave a gracious nod and sniffed something in the air: petrol.

'Looks like you're a target too, though.'

Verner mirrored Henry's nod. 'So it seems.' He relaxed with the gun, letting it waver slightly. 'I'll be OK . . . the guy's not a very good shot.'

Henry's right hand came from behind his back, clutching the handgun he had confiscated from Troy Costain. He had no idea if the thing would work, whether it was loaded with blanks, or what. He simply prayed as he leapt to one side and, as he rolled, loosed off two shots at Verner, whom, once again, he had surprised.

Verner took one in the right shoulder, flinging him back on to the gravel. The other one buried itself in the wall of the house.

Henry rolled twice, came back on all fours and scuttled behind Tara's Mercedes.

Verner struggled back on to his knees, managing to keep hold of the pistol. Intense pain seared through his shoulder, upper chest and neck.

He looked down at the wound and touched it with his free hand, the tips of his fingers coming away covered in blood.

Shock rippled through him. He caught his breath, feeling light-headed and disorientated.

He slumped against the Bentley in an effort to keep upright as he scoured around for Henry.

'You bastard,' he cried.

Henry was prone on the gravel, looking underneath the Mercedes, trying to work out Verner's position, aiming his gun along the ground. He could not be sure where he was, was not even sure he had hit him.

Verner could not think straight. He had never been shot before, but had always thought it would be a piece of cake to be wounded. Yet it hurt so much. He touched the wound again, wondering hazily why it was so bad. It was only his shoulder, for God's sake. His fingers moved over the joint and then, even to his slightly befuddled mind, it was clear why it was so awful: the exit wound. The bullet had blown out the whole of the back of his shoulder and shoulder blade. Now he had no feeling down his arm. It was as though it was no longer there. He tried to keep hold of the gun, but his fingers did not work. It dropped with a 'clink' on to the ground.

He hauled himself up to his feet by using the back wing of the Bentley, smearing blood across the shiny bodywork. His head was spinning and the smell of petrol invaded his nostrils as he staggered around the back of the car, clutching at the smooth body to try to stay on his feet, but finding no purchase for his fingertips. He stumbled, not knowing where he was now, his brain seeming to have lost all sense of place, yet he could still smell petrol. He fell to his knees again and with a surge of clarity realized he had fallen into a puddle of petrol which was gushing out of a hole in the side of the car, like beer out of a punctured barrel. He gagged on the fumes which rose around him.

Verner slumped down on to his hands, so he was on all fours. The brief moment of clarity disappeared from his mind as he fought the intense pain in his wounded shoulder. He remained in that position for a few seconds, then his right arm folded under his him, unable to support his weight. He sank face down in the petrol.

'Need . . . to . . . move,' he said to himself.

With a massive force of willpower he pushed himself up to his knees with his left hand and tried to get to his feet by pulling himself up on the side of the Bentley, heaving himself up by using the door handle.

The next bullet from the sniper was right on target, slamming into Verner's back, just below his left shoulder blade. It hit him with such force, it pinned him against the car. The next bullet struck him in the lower back. The next one missed completely and hit the centre of the rear wheel, ricocheting off with a ping and producing a tiny spark which ignited the rising petrol vapour with a whoosh. The flames clawed up Verner's petrol-doused trousers, rising and engulfing him.

Henry ran to the front door of the house, screaming for Charlotte to open up. Good kid, she responded and Henry threw himself through the gap into the hall. Charlotte slammed the door behind him and locked it. He returned to the door and put his face to the mottled glass pane, trying to see what was happening, even though he knew that he was asking for trouble by doing this.

His countenance morphed into horror as he saw, though the distorted glass, the burning figure of Verner stomping around next to the Bentley, silent, no screams coming from him, as the flames ate him.

Henry watched open mouthed, but riveted.

Then, in a flash, it was all over for Verner.

The sniper put another bullet into him. This time it went into the side of his head, destroying the brain cortex, and killing him instantly. Verner jumped sideways in a grotesque way, hit the side of the Bentley and dropped to the ground, where he lay unmoving, apart from the flames rising up from his torso.

A procession of police cars turned into the driveway leading to the house, their blue lights flashing dramatically.

At last, Henry thought sourly, help had arrived.

Fifteen

H enry knew what he had to do, but it was a finely balanced thing. He needed to keep control, to hold people back, and it was damned hard because of one simple fact: he had no power as a cop and no one was obliged to listen to him if they did not wish to do so.

He insisted that Tara was taken to hospital immediately, accompanied by Charlotte. That, at least, got them off the scene and out of the way of any police questioning, which is what he wanted. He needed to get all the attention on himself so he could keep a grip on proceedings.

He faced a barrage of questions from Jane Roscoe and a detective superintendent from the SIO team by the name of Anger . . . by name and nature, Henry thought. Henry did not know Anger, but learned he had recently been appointed on transfer from Merseyside Police.

Henry kept it all as simple as he could, straight to the point, telling them the story he wanted them to hear. When he had had enough of their pressure, he told them he wished to make a statement that he would write himself in his own time.

That did not go down particularly well. The investigators wanted to take his account of the night, to question and clarify, to dig, as they went along, but he told them to sod off. 'I've been a cop long enough to be able to do my own, thanks,' he said. 'OK,' he shrugged, 'you've got three dead people here, but they aren't going anywhere. Concentrate on the scene and see if you can find the person who whacked Verner.'

Anger stared at him hard. 'Don't tell me how to do my job,' he said.

Henry looked back at him through half-closed lids.

There was a stand-off.

'OK,' Anger relented, 'but you do your statement here and now, no matter how long it takes.'

'Fine,' Henry said, also giving way, knowing he would not be allowed to go anywhere without giving the police at least something. A PC gave him a few blank witness statement forms and Henry went to sit in John Lloyd Wickson's study, noticing, as he sat at the desk, the open firearms cabinet on the wall. He considered it through squinted eyes, then quickly began writing. It took about ninety minutes for him to get a draft of the basics which would suffice for the moment. He would flesh it out later, as appropriate.

He handed it to Jane Roscoe.

'No trace of the marksman, sniper, whatever you want to call him.'

'Didn't think there would be.'

Jane glanced through the statement, her brow furrowed as she read. 'It's a bit . . . thin, don't you think?'

'It'll do for now,' he said. 'It's been a tough night and I need some sleep. Unless I'm a suspect, I'm off.'

She gave him a very suspicious look. 'Don't leave town.'

'Some hope.'

He jumped into the Astra and drove quickly away, not even daring to look back at the crime scenes: one with a charred, bullet-ridden body, the other with no body at all, just some mush, the other with a virtually headless man.

He had to get somewhere very quickly.

Although he had a very pressing task of his own to complete, Henry drove quickly to Blackpool Victoria Hospital and abandoned the Astra near the entrance to the A & E department. He made certain to lock the car and strode into the hospital and was relieved to find someone he knew working behind the reception desk. He was less relieved to see a few uniformed cops hovering around the waiting area, guessing they were here in connection with Tara Wickson. He hoped it would not come to a blagging contest with them.

'Hello, Henry,' smiled the receptionist. Then she looked at him properly and saw what a state he was in: muddy face, clothes and shoes. Her eyebrows lifted, but to her credit she did not say anything.

'Hi, Jackie.' He leaned on the counter and smiled back at her, hoping to recreate his usual air of laid-backness when on business at the hospital, which he often was. 'How's it going? Busy?'

'As always.'

'I'm dealing with a job out at Poulton. One of the witnesses was brought in here a couple of hours ago by the name of Tara Wickson?'

Jackie tapped her computer, pointed at the screen with her finger. 'Let's see . . . yes, that's right.'

'Could do with seeing her for a quick chat. It's pretty urgent.'

'Ooh, is it a murder?' Jackie asked enthusiastically.

'A most brutal one,' Henry said without a word of a lie. 'Hence the appearance.' He stood back and showed himself.

'Let's see now . . . She's been seen . . . head wound . . . X-rayed . . . and admitted. It's Dr Caunce dealing if you want a word with her.'

Henry knew Caunce. He knew most of the A & E doctors because so much police business came through the hospital doors and the relationship between cops and doctors was usually pretty good.

'Where can I find her?'

Jackie was about to pick up a phone when she glanced up past Henry and said, 'There! Doctor Caunce,' she called.

Henry turned as the good doctor came towards him. She was stereotypical of the harassed doctors of the casualty wards the country over: young, tired, world weary, good-looking, stethoscope hanging around the neck, clipboard in hand.

'Hi, Henry, what can I do for you? God, you look a mess!'

'Yeah, yeah, I know,' he said. 'Tara Wickson?'

'Ahh . . . in deep shock . . . bad wound to the head. I've admitted her for observation on one of the general wards, but I have some concerns over her mental health at the moment. What exactly happened to her? I haven't been able to get a straight tale from anyone.'

'She witnessed a murder.'

273

'Ahh,' Caunce said again. 'That explains a lot.'

'Can I see her? Which ward is she on?'

'Not actually been taken to the ward yet. She's still in a cubicle down there.' The doctor pointed. 'She's sedated, not with it at all. Traumatized.'

'Is her daughter with her?'

'Yes.'

'I do really need to talk to her.'

'Fine,' said Caunce, 'but it won't be easy.'

Henry nodded and peeled away down the corridor.

'Henry,' Caunce called after him before he had gone two steps.

'Yep?' He turned.

'You still damned-well married?'

His face looked pained. He and Caunce had, in the past, done a lot of serious flirting which had never gone anywhere, but which had a lot of potential.

'As good as,' he admitted.

'Well, just so you know – I'm between relationships as we speak.'

'Good to know. I'll bear it in mind.'

They were in a curtained cubicle. Charlotte was sitting beside the bed, holding her mother's hand, her head resting on the edge of the bed. Henry slid in through the curtain and observed the scene for a few moments. Tara's eyes were closed, with deep, recessed black marks around them, reminding Henry of a panda. Her skin was pale, almost translucent. She looked nothing like the glamorous woman he knew she was. The bandage wrapped around her head did not help, either. Henry winced, knowing that to treat the wound, they would have had to shave part of her hair off.

Charlotte raised her head and looked at Henry. She was an exhausted mess, hardly able to keep her eyes from shutting down. It did not help, Henry thought, that she had been taking drugs earlier and had then been raped. The night would have been bad enough without those added bonuses. He wondered who would be available to give her some immediate care. Obviously she could not go home.

274

'Hi,' she croaked weakly.

'Hi.' He stepped over to her and took her hand. 'How's your mum?'

'Totally out of it. I've never seen anyone like this before. She's really, really ill, I think.'

'She's been through a lot.'

'Henry, what happened? What was it all about? Where's my dad?'

She didn't know and Henry found himself at a loss. 'Look,' he said, not wanting to duck out of the responsibility of telling her, but believing it was the better course of action at this moment in time. 'I'm not completely sure myself. Don't worry your head about anything at the moment, other than looking after your mum, eh? She needs you right now.' Charlotte looked devastated and unable to cope with that. He lifted her chin. 'How are you?' he asked tenderly.

She raised her chin off his fingertips and then stared at the floor, making no reply.

'Your mum's going to get looked after in here, but you need to be looked after too, Charlotte, at least for a few hours.'

'I'm staying here,' she bristled. 'I'm staying with my mum.' Her eyes watered. 'Is Dad dead?'

Henry nodded. 'Sorry.'

She took that initial blow well, looking more puzzled than anything. He knew that sooner or later, no matter how bad the situation had been at home, Wickson's death would hit her hard. No matter which way it was looked at, he had been her father all her life, even though he wasn't biologically. She would be unable to think of him differently, ever, Henry guessed.

'Your mum's going to get transferred on to a ward shortly and all she'll be doing is sleeping all day. There is nothing you can do to help her here. You really can't stay. They've nowhere to put you.'

'I want to,' she protested.

'You need to get some sleep yourself. You need somewhere to crash out, because when your mum wakes up, she'll need you to be strong and if you're a wreck, you won't be strong, will you?'

Even through her bewildered thinking, Charlotte could see the logic of this. 'I don't want to go home, though . . . I saw Jake,' she said. The expression on her young face made Henry want to get hold of her, hug her and reassure her that it would be all right, that the memory of the horror would fade in time.

He hoped he did not live to regret his next offer. He hoped also that it did not sound perverted. 'Would you come to my house? You could crash out on Leanne's bed. She wouldn't mind. My wife's there. You'd have a good sleep, some food and then get back here refreshed. That's what your mum will need.'

'Please . . .' Charlotte started to crumble. 'That would be nice.'

Henry led her out of the hospital via Dr Caunce. Henry gave her his home and mobile numbers and told her to instruct staff not to let the police interview Tara before Henry had had a chance to speak to her.

Caunce gave him a strange look, wondering what was going on. 'But you're a cop, aren't you?'

Henry winked. 'Don't worry about it.'

'I won't,' said the doctor, 'because I now have your mobile phone number.'

There was no natural-looking way of disposing of a gun and a bag of drugs, Henry realized. He had driven out past Poulton-le-Fylde and over Shard Bridge, which spanned the River Wyre, which flows into the Irish Sea at Fleetwood. He was relieved to see that the tide was in and the river, consequently, was high. Just what he needed. He parked the Astra on Old Bridge Lane, just on the northern side of the river, and strolled back along the bridge with a plastic bag in his hand containing the said illegal items.

He walked as casually as he could, trying to give the impression he was out on a morning stroll. He could not get rid of the feeling that everyone who drove past him was looking at him and knew he was a villain.

There were no other pedestrians on the bridge.

He stopped half-way across, leaned on the parapet and gazed down the river toward the meandering right-hand curve on which the Blackpool and Fylde Yacht Club was situated. He then stared directly down at the water below him. It was a muddy brown colour, as ever. He had passed over the Wyre hundreds of times during his life and never seen the water any different colour. He would not have liked to swim in it. It was not the least inviting.

From the direction of the flow, he could tell it was on the ebb.

Several cars drove past. Then there was a gap in the traffic. He scanned around furtively. No one in sight. No cars, no people.

He acted quickly, opening the bag and tipping out the contents into the river.

The gun dropped into the water with a splash and sank immediately.

The bag of drugs fell on to the surface and kind of settled there, floated away like a tiny boat towards the sea. He watched it sail away, then sink.

A big sigh of relief made his body shudder.

'She's still asleep,' Kate whispered to Henry on his return home. 'She had a shower then went straight to bed. She's exhausted, poor soul. Just what has been going on, Henry?'

'Don't really know where to start,' he said, 'other than I would really like a massive hug.'

There was no need for a second request. She needed one as well. Kate fell into his arms and they both squeezed tight.

It felt very, very good.

Henry needed his bed too, so following a long, hot power shower, he fell on to the kingsize, closed his eyes and was instantly asleep. He was deep out of it for about four hours but when he woke to visit the loo he could not get back. He tossed and turned for an hour, thoughts and plans tumbling through his brain, some jumbled, some very clear.

In the end he gave up and got up.

Kate was downstairs, pacing the house on pins. 'She's still asleep,' she answered Henry's question. She gave him another hug and then held him out at arms' length. 'Now are you going to tell me what's happened? It's all over the TV news. It sounds horrible.'

'It is, was,' he confirmed. 'I'll tell you over a brew.'

They sat in the conservatory and he told her what she needed to know, stunning her with the violence of the night. Her mouth regularly drooped open as he recounted the grim details.

When he had told her enough, she asked, 'And how are you, love?'

He thought about it for a long time, then nodded. 'I'm OK, actually,' he said, surprising himself. He knew that not long ago he would have been very deeply affected by the night's events, that they could have sent him over the edge, but now he was a much stronger man. He looked into Kate's eyes and knew why. He felt like he could face anything with her behind him. She was his rock and it had taken him a long time to realize it. Kate and the children. They were all he needed.

'I love you,' he said simply.

'And I love you.'

They leaned forwards and kissed each other, pulling apart when a noise from the dining room make them look up. It was the pathetic figure of Charlotte, wearing Leanne's dressing gown.

They were back at the hospital at 5 p.m., wending their way through endless corridors to the ward on to which Tara had been transferred. It was not official visiting time, but they were allowed in. She had been placed in a side room and Henry stiffened when he saw a uniformed cop on the door. A barrier because Henry knew him and he knew Henry. But did he know that Henry was suspended? He braved it, nodded at the officer and ushered Charlotte in ahead of him. 'It's her daughter,' he whispered into the officer's ear as he went past.

'OK,' he whispered back.

Tara was propped up in bed, awake, tired, but looking much better than she had done. The big wrap-around bandage had been removed from her head and replaced by a more practical-looking dressing. Most of the left side of her head had been shaved and Henry could see how swollen it was.

She was overjoyed to see Charlotte, who rushed into her arms.

'My baby,' Tara cried, hugging her closely.

Henry hovered in the background, shuffling, letting them have their moment. Finally they parted and looked at him.

'Thanks for looking after her,' Tara said.

'She was almost well behaved,' he laughed. 'How are you?'

'Better . . . sore . . . still a bit dazed.' She breathed in deeply. 'Ready to face the music, I think.'

'Have you been seen by the police yet?'

'Briefly. They're coming back to see me later this evening.'

Henry scratched his head whilst he thought things through, something that required him to make a decision that went totally against the grain of his career as a police officer.

'Charlotte, would you give me and your mother a few minutes alone?'

Tara and Charlotte exchanged glances. It was apparent Charlotte did not want to leave, but Tara squeezed her hand. 'Please, love.'

She left the room and sat in the corridor outside.

'Do you feel up to talking?'

'Think so.'

'Do you remember everything that happened last night?'

'Up to a point. The point where I shot Jake and tried to shoot John. Everything after that is a mess.'

'Do you feel strong enough to be told?'

Tara swallowed, nodded. Henry gave her the facts very succinctly, not glossing over anything, but not going into great detail. There was silence at the end whilst Tara digested the information. She sighed and tears formed on the edges of her eyes.

'John's dead?'

'Yes.'

'What does Charlotte know?'

'Only that he is dead, not how he died. Someone'll have to fill in the gaps for her at some stage,' Henry said.

'Yes. So now I've got to be questioned about Jake Coulton's death.'

'You'll be questioned about the whole night. The police are going to need a lot of answers.'

'I'll get charged with murder, won't I? Then I'll lose Charlie for good. I'm only just clinging on to her as it is.' A note of panic crept into her voice.

'Well,' Henry said hesitantly, going down his chosen road at last, 'that remains to be seen.'

Tara's eyes flicked open. Henry took a deep breath and said again, 'That remains to be seen.'

Next morning Henry sat in an interview room at Blackpool Central Police Station. He was on one side of the table and on the other was Jane Roscoe and Detective Superintendent Anger. Both had frustrated faces of stone and were not particularly impressed by Henry. Henry had spent some of the time looking at Jane, assessing how he felt about her, puzzled by the conclusion he came to.

They had worked their way through Henry's statement fairly superficially to start with and were now going through it with a detective's toothcomb. Anger was asking the questions. Jane was looking as hard as she could. Hard cop, hard cop, Henry thought. Good combination.

'So you arrive at the Wickson house, having had this frantic phone call?'

'Yep.'

'Tara Wickson saying that she thought there was a prowler around the house and stables?'

'Yep.'

'Why didn't she call the police?'

'As I've already explained, I was looking into some shenanigans at the stables involving the mutilation of some of her horses. She thought the prowler, if there was one, might be connected with this. Jane knows all about my connection with the Wicksons, don't you, love?'

Her face did not change.

'You arrive there and make your way to the kitchen . . . What did you see?'

'A man called Verner, the guy who took potshots at John Wickson earlier this week, then killed two of our officers and

280

a nurse. He was holding a shotgun, pointing it at Jake Coulton, John Wickson and Tara.

'I stepped into the scenario from hell, suddenly found myself being covered by a shotgun too.'

'What happened then?'

'Verner stuck the gun under Coulton's chin and blasted his head off.'

The interviewing officers did not say anything for a few moments.

'Pretty bad, eh?' said Anger.

'Understatement.'

Under further questioning he told them that Verner smashed Tara on the head with the butt of the shotgun because she was making so much noise after seeing Coulton murdered. She had been hysterical. Henry went on to describe the way that he and Wickson had been marched out to the crusher and then Wickson's messy death. There was nothing fabricated in that, nor the fact that someone then started shooting at Verner from the hillside.

The next fabrication came when Henry was questioned about the moment he and Verner faced each other next to the Bentley.

'You see, Henry, the post-mortem showed that Verner had been shot in the shoulder by a completely different type of round to the ones fired by the sniper. The bullets from the sniper have been identified as 7.62 NATO calibre, but the one in the shoulder is more likely to be a .38 calibre, snub-nose, fired from a revolver or a pistol.' Again, it was Anger explaining this.

Henry shrugged. 'Your point is?'

'Are you saying that when he appeared at the Bentley, he was already wounded in the shoulder?'

'I would say so. Look, it was dark, it was very stressful, lots of very nasty things had happened. I'm pretty sure that when he came round the back of the car and surprised me, he was already wounded, OK?'

'What were you doing at your car?' That was Jane. 'You left the two women in the house while you went to the car for something. What?'

It was a doozy of a question and almost floored Henry, who knew that he could not hesitate in his reply. 'I went to get the wheel brace, actually, so that I could use it as a weapon to defend us while the police arrived, if necessary. Problem was, though, there wasn't one there, just like there wasn't a spare tyre, because you gave me a shit car to use to do a shit job.'

'How do you explain Verner's shoulder wound?' Anger insisted.

Henry snickered. 'I can't explain it . . . I haven't got any explanation for it . . . perhaps someone else was out there after him with a gun . . . perhaps the guy on the hill did it . . . perhaps, perhaps, perhaps.' A lyric for every situation, Henry thought.

'Impossible,' said Anger. 'We found the sniper's exact position, where he'd been laid up. He was too far away to have shot him with a pistol or a revolver.'

'Are you saying I shot him?'

'It's something we need to clear up, Henry,' Jane said. 'A loose end.'

She stared at him. He felt the hairs tingle on the back of his neck. She knew he was lying.

'I am not impressed with you, Henry,' Anger said.

'Have you caught the sniper yet?' Henry asked.

Neither detective answered.

'No, didn't think so.' He smiled winningly. 'Not impressed with you. You've got the guy who killed two police officers, and many, many more people. I doubt you'll ever find the sniper, but that's the way it goes. All right, Verner's dead and burned, but why don't you look upon it as a glass that's half full as opposed to half empty? There's no need for a long drawn-out trial, just a few inquests . . . think of the money that'll be saved.'

Anger stood up and stalked out of the room, leaving Henry and Jane sitting across the table from each other. There was a sub-zero silence between them which seemed to go on forever.

'Is that it, then? Have I done my public duty? Come in voluntarily, answered your intrusive and very uncomfortable questions, when it was me who went through hell. And you have the audacity to disbelieve me.'

'Yeah, that's it,' Jane said, 'and I'll let you know something, Henry – it stinks. I have a very bad feeling about this whole thing. My intuition tells me this statement is a pack of lies. When Kate called me she said Tara was the one pointing a shotgun.'

Henry swallowed and fended the accusation by saying, 'Did you see Tara Wickson? Did she say anything different?'

Jane bit her lip. 'No.'

'Well in that case, Jane, I'll be off.' He got to his feet and walked to the door.

'Henry,' Jane blurted. She turned to him, tears forming in her eyes. 'Is there any hope for us?'

His shoulders dropped. He shook his head. 'No, no there isn't,' he said softly.

Epilogue

'I should've been a bloody cop.' Troy Costain took a mouthful of lager, swallowed it, wiped his mouth and said, 'Should've.'

Henry looked sardonically at him. 'Sure you should.'

'Well . . . I'm as bent as a nine-bob note, whatever a nine-bob note is – before my time – so that's one ability; and I can get information out of people.'

'Yeah, all the competence you need to be a cop,' Henry agreed.

'Yep . . . I tell lies, I nick things, I hit folk who aren't bigger than me and I get people to open up to me.'

'A natural charmer.'

'Exactly. It's my Romany background.'

'My arse!' said Henry. He ordered himself and Costain another pint. They were in a little pub in the village of Singleton near to Poulton-le-Fylde where it was unlikely that their tryst would be witnessed by anyone of significance to either of them. Even so, Henry was wary. It was often the meets like this in out-of-the-way places that went belly up. Sometimes it was better to do it right in the middle of town, to hide in a crowd.

They wandered out to the beer garden and sat at a table. It was just about warm enough to be outside.

'What sort of bullets are in that gun of yours?' Henry asked him.

'Eh? Fuckin' hell, that's a bit of a heavy opening question, isn't it?'

'Well . . . ?'

'Dunno,' he shrugged. 'I bought the whole kit and caboodle from a guy from the smoke who was up here selling stuff. Didn't ask. Just bullets – why?'

'No reason,' Henry said, remembering how he had blasted a huge hole in Verner's shoulder that had almost removed the top right-hand quarter of his torso. He leaned back. 'What have you got for me, master detective?'

'Listen, I know you nicked my gun off me, an' all, but I want you to know I been through a lot of pain to get this gen, talked to a lot of heavy dudes who were very suspicious of me, so before I tell you, I want some guaranteed dosh. A ton'll do.'

Henry almost choked on his Stella.

'You are in no position to bargain, Troy. That gun and those tabs are enough to send you down, lad, so don't fuck with me.'

'OK, just thought I'd give it a go,' he admitted through his misshapen teeth.

'Twat,' sighed Henry, though not surprised. 'Come on, speak.'

Costain looked up to the sky, amassing his thoughts and putting them in order. 'Andy Turner disappeared just over two years ago, hasn't been seen since.'

'I know that.'

'On the day he disappeared he half-killed a dealer called Goldy who was trespassing on his patch. The only other thing I could find out was that on that same day he had a meet with a guy to discuss a deal.'

'What guy?'

'He was a Spaniard, apparently some big shot on the international scene. Supposedly Turner had big plans to expand.'

'Who was the guy?' Henry persisted.

'Henry, I haven't got a fuckin' clue, OK, other than he might've been called Lopez? But that's all any fucker knows. All I know for certain is that Turner really hurt this dealer in Crumpsall – check your records, I'm sure you'll find out who and when – and then he got dropped off at some Indian restaurant in Rusholme . . . then was never seen again.'

'You've been a big help,' Henry said sarcastically. 'You spoke to heavy dudes to get this information, did you?'

'Yeah, I did actually,' snarled Costain. 'Now I've done my bit . . . what about my merchandise?'

'The gun and the drugs?' Costain stayed tight-lipped. 'Got rid of them for you. Nasty, nasty things.'

'You got rid of 'em? You mean you haven't got 'em any more?' Henry shook his head. 'I might as well have not told you anything,' Costain protested. 'I got all that information thinking I was being blackmailed and you'd already dumped the gear?'

'Cruel world, innit, Troy?'

Costain was glad to get out of Henry's company and head back to his seedy haunts in Blackpool. Henry was happy to see him go, leaving him alone in the pub to mull over what had been said. The big question in his mind was: how many Spaniards were operating in Britain? Henry knew there were a few, but they were pretty rare commodities. So who was the Spaniard that Andy Turner had met on that night, two years earlier by the name of Lopez?

What Costain's meagre information did do was confirm to Henry that Jo Coniston and her partner had latched on to Turner in Rusholme and that their disappearance was definitely connected to this.

He walked back into the pub and ordered an espresso. He was feeling cold and needed a shot of something hot and black. He took the drink outside, shivering slightly. Using his mobile – a new one, with a new battery – he called Karl Donaldson on his mobile down in London.

'Henry – how are you?'

'I guess you have a pretty good idea how I am if you're still in contact with the cops up here.'

'Yeah, true. You had a rough time again.'

'Goes with the territory. Karl, can I be cheeky?'

'Cheeky? Why yes, pal. Why change the habit of a life-time?'

'I need a favour.'

It was just before seven o'clock the following evening in Henry's home. He and Kate were sitting at the dining table, all the dinner things between them, each fingering the stem of a wine glass. They had just eaten with both daughters, a rare

287

but pleasant occurrence, who had both vamoosed to leave the washing-up to their parents. Thank heavens for the dishwasher, Henry thought.

'That was good, the whole family,' Henry observed. He had made the meal and they had all said how much they enjoyed it.

'We should do it more often.'

'We'd have to chain the girls down.' They smiled at each other. 'I love you, y'know,' he told her, then shook his head as he thought bitterly of the bad times he had put her through over the years. And yet, here they were, still together. Nothing short of a miracle, he thought. She had stayed with him through thick 'n' thin, all his idiotic times, and though she had wavered once or twice (only to be expected), she'd clung on and been there for him, even through the divorce.

Henry opened his mouth to ask something very important, but the sound of the doorbell kept him silent.

'I'll go.' Wearily he got to his feet.

He was surprised to see Tara Wickson there. She looked almost back to normal, though on close inspection her eyes were tired and drawn underneath the make-up. She was wearing a hat, cocked at an angle, covering her shaved head.

'Could I speak to you?'

Henry looked beyond her. A Jaguar was parked up on the road. Charlotte was in the back seat. Behind the wheel was the man Henry had seen Tara meet at the Hilton Hotel. Her lover.

'Yes, do you want to come in? What about . . . ?' He pointed to the car.

'They'll wait.'

'OK.'

Henry led her into the house and introduced her to Kate, who greeted her warmly.

'I'm sorry, Mrs Christie, but could I just have Henry's ear for a few minutes?'

'Be my guest. Can I get you anything?'

Tara refused politely. Henry took her into the conservatory, pulling the patio door closed behind them. She sat on the settee, Henry opposite on a chair.

'First of all I want to say I'm sorry for dragging you into this whole, sorry mess. I should never have asked you.'

'What's done is done. You weren't to know how it would escalate.'

She inspected her nails. Henry could tell she was far from recovered and that she was still close to the edge – a position he knew well, but one he had decided to avoid in future. 'I suppose it's only right that you know all the ins and outs of things, as far as I know them.'

'I am curious. That's the detective in me, but you don't have to tell me anything you'd rather I did not know. I probably know more than you think, anyway.'

'I think it's only right and proper – after all, you nearly got killed twice,' she said and took a deep, thoughtful breath. 'Mmm,' she said, 'a potted history: John and I married young, too young, both of us pretty immature, even though we believed different.'

'I can relate to that.'

'Anyway,' she shrugged sadly, 'he was just starting out in business and I wanted to be a homemaker. He spent all his waking hours dedicated to being a success. I was neglected day in, day out, or so it seemed. I fell into an affair with a man who made me feel good about myself, something John could never do. Unfortunately I got pregnant to him. I convinced John it was his, although how he fell for that I really don't know. The marriage continued. Charlotte's birth brought us closer together for a time, but then business took over again. I decided to make the best of a bad job . . . We had money, cars, houses, so I lived a material life and brought Charlotte up pretty much single-handed.'

Tara sniffed back some tears, pulled herself together.

'Can I get you anything?' Henry asked.

'No, I'm fine.' Her voice was frail. 'He never knew Charlotte wasn't his. It was a well-kept secret.'

'Until recently.'

Tara nodded. 'Our relationship was increasingly bad. I knew things weren't right with the business, but I never took much notice of that side of things. What he did to make money didn't actually interest me, that's why I didn't know what he was up to. I just knew that he was at his limit financially and he was desperate and now I know he resorted to desperate measures to get back on line. I still don't know the details, only that some very iffy-looking characters started turning up to see him.'

'He was involved with the Mafia,' Henry blurted, regretting it immediately.

Tara's face dropped. 'My God,' she uttered. 'They bailed him out?'

'Yeah – and then they had him by the short and curlies. He tried to break free, but they wouldn't let him go. He was far too useful for them. His engineering import business was ideal for drugs trafficking – importing crushers, then building them here. Lots of places to secrete drugs in the crates. His fuel laundering gave big profits that they wanted a percentage of – and, above all, he was on the periphery of the regeneration of Blackpool. If it came to fruition, he could have made over fifty million. They wanted a piece of that, too.'

'My God,' she said again. 'Anyway, it was obvious the whole thing was getting to him and to me and we argued and argued until, one day, during a ferocious row, I blurted it out about Charlotte . . .' Her voice trailed off. 'Trouble was, she was listening in at the time.'

'Ah,' Henry said knowingly. Kids and ears and doors.

'I've spent the last few months trying to keep her on the straight and narrow.'

'Hence the horses?'

'She's always been into them, but she started drifting . . . started doing rebellious teenage stuff, times two. The horses kept her normal, that's why we started going for lessons again. It gave her focus. That's how she met Leanne, who she adores by the way, and that's how I met you.'

'And then the horses started being mutilated?'

'I even thought it could have been Charlotte doing it.' Tara closed her eyes painfully and winced.

'How's the head?' Henry asked.

'Very, very sore. My brain's still a bit woozy,' she said. 'On the night they burned down, I caught her coming back from the stables. She said she was just checking on Chopin. I'm still not sure if I believe her. Was she mutilating the horses in response to what was happening to her?' Tara looked desperate for an answer.

'No,' said Henry firmly, remembering Verner's boastful admission. 'She wouldn't hurt a horse. I saw her with one the day that Coulton threw me off your property. What it was,' he said, 'was the Mob putting pressure on John. You've read *The Godfather*, seen the film? They like hurting horses. Did John like horses?'

'He was passionate about them. It was the only thing he cared about outside work. I wish he'd been half as passionate about me,' Tara said wistfully.

'They probably knew that. They hit people where it hurts them.'

'And it was destroying Charlotte, too, finding horses mutilated. That and the discovery that the man she thought was her father wasn't sent her into orbit. I feel like I've failed her very badly.'

'I don't think you have. You love her, she knows that and she'll be fine,' Henry said reassuringly. 'Children are very resilient.'

'Only because we adults oblige them to be.'

It was a sentence spoken with passion and Henry had to agree. It was the actions of adults that dragged kids along in their wake. He should know. His stupidity in the past must have had deep and long-lasting effects on his two girls. He was intelligent enough to know that, even though they appeared to be straight-down-the-line kids now, there would be scars there somewhere.

'But I do think we'll be OK,' Tara said resolutely. 'I'll make damn sure we will be.'

'Good,' Henry said.

Tara chewed on her bottom lip, held Henry's gaze and said, 'Why did you lie for me, Henry?'

He shifted. His neck reddened and his bottom tightened. 'I'm not a hundred per cent sure myself.'

'You didn't have to. I would have faced what I did, answered to the law.'

'I know . . . and my instincts as a police officer told me you should be punished for what you did, but I thought you'd suffered enough. Justice, to me, is a peculiar creature. It's not black, it's not white, it's just a murky grey, and as far as I'm concerned, justice is done . . . and it's something I'll have to deal with, so don't press me on it.' He paused. 'Not a particularly good explanation, I'm afraid.'

'I won't push you, then.' She leaned forward and touched his cheek with her fingertips. 'Thank you, Henry Christie. I believe you saved my life.'

'I'd love to say it was a pleasure.'

They both laughed and the moment lightened.

'Immediate plans?'

'Getting away from it all, just for a couple of weeks. I know we'll have to come back to it, but I think we need a break. My friend has a villa on Lanzarote. We'll chill out and burn brown, I reckon.'

'Sounds good.' He hesitated. 'Is that guy in the car Charlotte's father?' Tara nodded. 'Does she know?'

'One thing at a time, Henry. If ever. At the moment he's just a friend, OK?'

At the door Henry waved them away. Charlotte looked back, waving madly at him until the Jaguar turned out of sight. As Henry closed the door, the house phone started to ring. It was answered by Kate.

'For you,' she said, holding the receiver out, a disapproving look on her face.

'Henry? It's me, your Chief Constable,' FB's voice machine-gunned down the line. 'Seven a.m. – my office – headquarters – tomorrow morning, please.'

'Seven . . . ?'

'Yes – I start that early to keep the bastards on their toes. Be there.' He hung up.

Henry slowly replaced the phone on the hook with a feeling of horror. 'Shithead,' he said.

At 6.50 a.m. next morning Headquarters was quiet, it being a place where, generally, nobody started work before eight. He had no trouble parking Kate's car at the front of the building, having been allowed access on to the campus through the security barriers with no fuss whatsoever, which surprised him somewhat. That had felt rather good, like old times. He looked across the playing fields to the new major-crime unit building – known as the Pavilion as it had been constructed on the site of the old cricket pavilion – behind which was the block that housed the SIO team. Henry's heart juddered as he thought he would dearly have liked to have a job in either of the buildings. Fat chance of that, he thought.

He went into HQ, was given a visitor's badge to pin on, and made his way up to the Chief Constable's office on the quiet middle floor. He knocked on the outer door and entered the secretary's office, as it was impossible walk straight into the Chief's office from the corridor these days. In times gone by, not very long ago, each chief officer had their secretary and that was it. Now there were desks for an assorted bunch of people as the police service desperately tried to modernize. The Chief now had a secretary, a staff officer, an assistant to the staff officer and an assortment of administrative staff. A clan of people ministering to his every whim.

The Chief's staff officer, a chief inspector called Ray Collier, who Henry knew reasonably well, was already at his desk, obviously already cute to the new bosses' working arrangements. He looked up when Henry came in and gave him a pleasant nod. 'Go straight in, Henry,' he said brightly.

'Cheers, Ray.' How could anyone who worked directly for FB seem so happy? Henry wondered.

Henry bore left to the Chief's office, finding the door propped open and FB inside behind his desk. He knocked and stood on the threshold.

FB did not look up from his paperwork. 'Come in, shut the door, grab a coffee and siddown.'

Not surprised by this manner, Henry did as bid, taking a seat opposite the wide, leather-topped desk, more suited to a Victorian industrialist than a 21st-century police chief. He had poured himself a coffee from the filter machine, no milk. He sipped it, his hand shaking ever so slightly, either from nerves or the alcohol he had imbibed the night before. He could not be sure.

FB continued to read some important document or other and

Henry almost chuckled. FB's psychological games continue, he thought.

Git.

Finally he looked up as though Henry's presence was a surprise.

'Good news or bad news?' he said.

'Er . . .' Henry hesitated.

'I'll start with the good news,' FB decided for him. 'As from Monday you're officially reinstated and disciplinary proceedings have been dispensed with.'

Henry was gobsmacked. He quickly put the coffee down on FB's desk before he spilled it.

'Pick that up,' FB said, glaring. 'It'll mark the wood.'

'S . . . sorry,' Henry was bewildered. He picked up the mug and held it with both hands. 'How?'

'I've spent the last two days, pretty much, reviewing the case as I promised and got to the bottom of it. I've spoken to several people at length, not least Detective Chief Superintendent Bernie flaming Fleming, who I put the screws on.' He gave a short laugh. 'Basically he stitched you up to save his own sorry hide, didn't he?'

'I would say that – but I'm biased.'

'And so would I, actually, having looked at the balance of probabilities. I weedled it out of the miserable little toad that you had requested a full-blown firearms operation and he turned it down. That's why you did what you did, isn't it?'

Henry nodded, but kept quiet. He was not one to look a gift horse in the gob.

'Anyway, big sods, little sods, you're back on Monday and he's decided to retire.' FB gave him a leerful smile.

'So he really is going to suffer?' Henry could not help but blurt sarcastically, thinking that a chief super's pension was worth about twenty-five grand a year with a lump sum of about £150,000.

'Just be thankful I'm batting for you, Henry. You just don't appreciate me, do you? Anyway – but – and it is a big BUT, I don't have any sway at all in the trial and inquest that're coming up, so expect a very rough ride there, Henry. You were suspended because you disobeyed a lawful order and your judgement was called to account, so don't expect any defence lawyers to give you an easy time.'

'I won't.'

'My history with you, a very long and tiresome one, means I supported you, but don't expect that your return to work will be heralded with flags and celebrations. A lot of people in this force are putting a very big question mark over your head. You will have your work cut out to regain any credibility whatsoever.'

'I know,' Henry said glumly. 'Thanks. But what's the bad news? PACE inspector at Burnley? Best Value Inspector?'

'Worse than that.'

'Go on.' Henry's heart sank.

'When you come back you'll be working directly for me. You'll be retaining your temporary rank of Chief Inspector.' That same leering smile was on his face again. 'I have a job for you. When you've finished it, then you might go to Burnley on shifts.'

By 7.15 a.m. Henry was back in his car, too dithery to start the engine, elated but wary of FB's motives. The future sounded slightly menacing. He tried a few deep-breathing exercises to bring him down from the roof.

'Calm . . . keep calm . . . Phone Kate, tell her the news . . . Don't gabble.'

He reached for the mobile which he'd left on the top of the dashboard. As soon as he picked it up, it rang, making him jump. He could not really get used to the little sods.

'Henry, it's me, Karl.'

'Early bird.'

'Been up working all night. Called you at home, but Kate said you were seeing FB at HQ. Everything all right? Anything to tell me?'

'No, everything's OK and I've nothing to tell you.' He wanted Kate to be first to hear his news.

'I have news for you, but I'll be brief. You asked me to make some checks with my source in Spain?'

'Yeah.' Henry had asked Donaldson if he could speak to his informant in Mendoza's organization to check to see whether

295

he knew anything about the Spaniard who had been operating in the north of England two years ago, who had met Andy Turner on the night he and two surveillance cops disappeared. Henry hadn't held out much hope of any result. 'Is this OK for a cellular line, Karl?'

'I'll keep it mysterious. The person you enquired about is actually my source. He says that he was working for the big man –' Henry knew Donaldson was referring to Mendoza here – 'at the time referred to. He was seeking new business for him and he had to deal harshly with your local criminal for stepping out of line, making threats.'

'Harshly?'

'He put our dead friend on to him.' Henry knew that was a reference to Verner. 'He dealt with the local man, but also with two officers of the law who stumbled across him in the act.'

'Jesus,' Henry said. 'They found him doing the deed?'

'Affirmative. He was forced to deal with them in the only way he could. All three are buried . . . somewhere . . . source doesn't quite know where. He helped our friend to dispose of their car to a scrap dealer, as well as getting rid of our friend's car, which was extremely wet.'

'Wet', Henry knew, referred to blood. He was slightly annoyed at Donaldson for talking about Verner as a friend. Henry was stunned by the news. It meant that Jo Coniston and her partner had been killed and buried by Verner. Henry thought about Jo's mother, the distraught woman he had met in the White Café. Hard though it would be, there might be some possibility of closure for her now. Depending on how Donaldson allowed the information to be used, it could be that Greater Manchester Police would be able to re-open the investigation into the disappearance of their two officers properly. At least that is where Henry's thoughts took him in those moments. When he was reinstated, he would push it, he decided, no matter what Donaldson said. The problem was that it could possibly compromise the source and Henry would have to think about the greater good. Was it more important to bring down Mendoza, or to bring to an end the suffering and agony of a mother? Discuss.

Henry laughed shortly. Donaldson had described his informant in Mendoza's organization as being quite high up but of
limited value, if Henry's memory served him correctly. From
the information Donaldson had just passed, that was nowhere
near true. The source had his finger on the pulse of Mendoza's
organization if he could come up with stuff like that, and also
if he had the authority to order hits on people. That meant he
was very high up in the pecking order, one of the players.

Henry had a sudden, very dark thought. Could this informant, so high up in Mendoza's firm, have also ordered the hit
on Verner? Or did he at least know who had carried it out?
Presumably he knew where and when Verner intended to waste
John Lloyd Wickson.

'Your source is very good,' Henry commented. 'Better than
you let on.'

'And getting better. He might put the big man on a plate
for us yet.'

'Maybe he could nail the guy who disposed of our friend?'

Donaldson went quiet. 'No, I believe not. I've asked him
and he says he doesn't know. Can't say it's something I'm
going to push. Our pal was a guy who needed to be dealt with.
Justice was done. He's dead and won't be killing any more of
our people.'

'I'll lay odds he knows, though,' Henry commented, but
didn't press further. Just for his information he asked if the
informant had a code name.

'Yes, he does. I call him Stingray.'

'I won't ask why,' said Henry. 'He wouldn't be called
Lopez, by any chance, would he?'

Donaldson chose not to reply to that.

Donaldson hung up his phone at the end of the conversation
with Henry, feeling as though he had been rumbled. Henry
was a suspicious son of a bitch and made the American feel
just a teeny bit nervous.

He stood up, crossed to the window and stared blankly down
at Grosvenor Square, wondering if he could ever confide in
his friend. He knew he could not. Apart from the fact that
Henry was far too straight-down-the-line to allow anyone

to get away with anything, no matter what their crime, he would also have some very disparaging things to say about Donaldson's marksmanship. It was very, very rusty. He sniffed a laugh and returned to his desk. He logged on to his computer for the first time that day. It was 7.30 a.m., British time. That meant just after midnight on the eastern seaboard of the US. He knew that the Director of the FBI would still be at his desk. He never left until 1 a.m. at the earliest, always arrived no later than 6.30 a.m. Donaldson brought up his e-mail facility and typed a short note to the Director.

It read: 'Carried out instruction as requested.'

He sent it direct and encrypted for the Director's eyes only, a man Donaldson trusted with his life.

He looked at the blank screen for a moment before going into his 'Sent Items' folder and deleting the message, then going into 'Deleted Items' and finally and irrevocably scrubbing the message. Then he locked his workstation.

On the floor next to him was the padded case which contained the Accuracy International Police Sniper Rifle. He reached down, picked it up and carried the 6.2kg weapon down to the post room. He handed it over, together with the letter of authorization which would ensure it was sent in that day's diplomatic bag back to the armoury at Quantico. Donaldson was given a receipt and watched the weapon disappear. Once it got to the other end of its journey, the weapon would be destroyed.

All he could think of was how out of practice he was.

In days gone by he could have picked off somebody from almost any distance, through almost any weather conditions, with one shot. In fact, he had once done so. The fact that it took him so many shots to bring down Verner annoyed him, niggled constantly. I need to get more practice, he thought. I'm getting very rusty indeed.